JANET PYWELL

Someone Else's Truth

"A story of misunderstanding, kindness and reconciliation."

For everyone struggling with their own perception of truth...

Foreword

"Never be afraid to raise your voice for honesty and truth and compassion against injustice and lying and greed. If people all over the world...would do this, it would change the earth."

William Faulkner

January

Jane

Jane's perspiring heavily and her feet hurt. She's tired and she's had enough. She also wants to punch Rachael's smug face.

'Left, two, three, clap, right, four, five, six, jump. Try and stay in step, Jane.' Rachael claps her hands in time to the dance music from the tinny box on the floor of the community centre. 'Forward, walk, one two three, back, two three, side — and clap. Jane! Forward, quickly, well done.' Rachael smiles.

Jane frowns. She turns, trips and bumps into Femi who steadies her with a quick squeeze of her hand.

'Easy, Tiger,' Rachael calls.

In the row behind her Marion is keeping pace, turning with precision and clapping in perfect timing. On her left, Amber keeps up effortlessly with the class, as does Frances who is jumping around eagerly and with far more energy than anyone else. Jane is convinced Frances is out of step but Rachael isn't picking on the local vicar. It's not fair.

Jane claps along with the group.

'Breathe, two, three. Walk!' Rachael lifts her knees and

marches on the spot like a toy soldier and the class mimic her.

Jane's throat is dry and her heart is thumping.

With her back turned, Rachael leads them forward in a march. Amber grins and winks and Jane breaks into a nervous giggling fit.

'Concentrate, Jane!' Rachael spies her in the mirror along the far wall. 'It's no wonder you're out of sync. That's not good is it, for a clock-maker? I thought your timing would be much better. I hope your watches keep better time.'

Behind her Marion snorts a quick laugh.

If Jane weren't sweating her face would have coloured in embarrassment so she concentrates on the floor, counting the beat of the music and watching her feet. She hates this song anyway. Rita Ora might never let her down but everyone else does.

'And...slow,' Rachael calls and the groups footsteps grow softer. 'Breathe... easy, two, three, and shake your arms, your wrists...'

Jane copies everyone else. Some of them are smiling at each other proud of their Monday exercise dance class. But Jane can't smile. Her face is set in a grimace as pain spreads down her spine and into the back of her thighs.

'Thank you everyone. See you next week,' Rachael calls and the group breaks into a spontaneous round of applause. 'Jane,' she calls loudly. 'Try practising this week, learn to take smaller steps and place your feet gently on the floor.'

Jane's breathing slows but her blood pressure is rising, until she feels Amber's hand on her arm.

'Come on,' she whispers. 'Let's get out of here.'

Jane doesn't need more encouragement. Her leggings are sticking to her hot thighs, and she throws an orange puffer jacket over her damp t-shirt.

'Drink?' suggests Amber as they head out into the cold. 'I haven't seen you over Christmas.'

'It's not my favourite time of year.'

Amber stares. 'I didn't know that.'

Jane shrugs. How would you, she wants to ask but instead she says, 'Better get off home, now. I'm really trying to stick to my diet.'

'How's it going?'

'It's only week one.' Jane shakes her head. 'I hate January.' Then under her breath she adds, 'but not as much as Christmas.'

'Call in for coffee tomorrow, Jane. Karl's on holiday so I'll be in the café.'

'How's Ben?'

'He's busy coming up with new ideas for the business,' Amber says. 'He wants us to take on a kiosk in the harbour this summer.'

'That's a good idea.'

Amber tilts her head in the dark. 'Why don't you think about it too? Your jewellery would go down a treat.'

'It's the cost of everything, Amber. I doubt I've made enough profit in the last few years to be able to invest in another premises.'

'It's only rent - for a few months. Let Ben investigate it all and then we can look at it together?'

'Great, thanks, Amber.'

A light comes from inside the community centre as the door flies open.

'Night, ladies,' Femi calls and waves over her shoulder. Frances follows her outside and pauses for a minute at their side.

'Are you alright, Jane?' Frances asks.

'Fine.'

'Rachael wasn't kind to you tonight so I had a word with her.'

'You didn't have to do that,' Jane protests, feeling another surge of embarrassment.

'Oh, I did. She can't speak to you, or anyone, like that. It's not appropriate to be unkind.'

The door bangs and Marion and Rachael come outside together, their warm breath leaving vapour trails in the darkness. 'Anyone coming to The Ship?' calls Marion.

Amber, Jane and Frances shake their heads.

'So, it's just you and me then, Rach.' Marion links her arm through the dance teacher's. 'God, it's so cold you could freeze your ti—'

'Night, everyone,' Frances calls quickly, and her car door clicks open.

Marion and Rachael's footsteps recede into the darkness as they head toward Harbour Street and Amber squeezes Jane's arm. 'Don't take it to heart.'

'Why is she such a bitch?' Jane asks.

Amber shrugs. 'Rachael was never this mean. She's got worse since she's been hanging around with Marion.'

Jane replies, 'I thought after you'd got rid of JJ and Marion's boutique closed that both of them were gone - for good.'

Amber grins. Apart from Ben, she had never told anyone what had happened between her and JJ, and how as a result, JJ, the previous owner of The Ship, had left Westbay in a hurry.

'There's a decent group of shop owners in Harbour Street and we can all support each other - in spite of Marion. She closed for a month but she's now determined to keep the boutique open.'

'Well, I guess she has to make money too.'

Amber pulls her coat across her chest. 'See you tomorrow for coffee.'

'Thanks, Amber.'

As she turns in the direction of her home she calls over her shoulder 'Give some thought to the kiosk.'

Jane turns towards home where the neat rows of old fishermen's cottages are small and pretty. She glances into the windows. Lights are coming on. Some people haven't yet drawn their curtains or shutters to keep out the cold night. A girl is curled up on the sofa reading and a young boy is watching TV. In another, a couple are preparing supper, and although Jane likes to see what others are doing, she feels increasingly lonely. She doesn't know how to shake off this feeling of utter desolation.

* * *

An hour later, Jane is sitting on the floor, wearing her denim dungarees packing golden Christmas baubles into a worn red box. She has done this since she was a child. They had always kept the decorations up until twelfth night and, like every year, she thinks the old tissue paper could be replaced but, like every year, she packs them quickly, rhythmically and methodically away. Four years since Dad died and it doesn't get any easier.

She sighs and rocks back on her heels. 'Well, I'm not spending another Christmas alone,' she says aloud. 'I swear to God. I'll do whatever it takes but I'm not spending another Christmas like this. It's bloody miserable.'

She stares at the naked Christmas tree that she will pack in the box and store away until next year and then pulls angrily at the silver tinsel lying on the windowsill and along the brick chimney mantelpiece before rolling it in a ball and tossing it on the floor. She takes the burnt candle stubs and hurls them in the bin. 'I'll go mad', she continues her solitary monologue. 'I've got to sort myself out. I don't want to be alone.'

Holding a box in her arms she pauses in the hallway and gazes into the mirror at her sad reflection - her grey streaked hair that used to be blond, brown eyes that once shone with happiness and her mouth that was always turned up in a permanent smile.

'Look at you! You're pathetic. Overweight. Pale. Bags under your eyes. Ugly.'

In the kitchen her iPhone pings. Distracted she puts the box on the table and picks it up.

Hey gorgeous, wanna meet up?

She gazes at the photo staring back at her. A prematurely grey-haired man that you'd see in a Saga advert smiles back at her. She knows he doesn't really look like this in real life. He's either photo-shopped it or stolen it from another profile, but she doesn't care. He lives five miles away and she's lonely.

At forty-seven she needs to know that her life isn't over and that there is still a chance she might meet Mr Right. Besides, this is the beginning of a new year so she takes a deep breath and is filled with resolve. She has the same opportunity as everyone else to make the most of her life. It was too late for a family and children but it wasn't too late for love.

She texts quickly back with practiced ease. *Thursday?*

* * *

The pub is in the city centre. It has low beams, cosy nooks and a fireplace at the far end. The decorations are still up but instead of it having an air of festivity, the pub feels forlorn as if the party was over a long time ago and everyone has gone home.

Jane didn't want to meet him in Westbay in case anyone saw them together. She also didn't want him to know where she lived or that she had a successful business in Harbour Street, one of the prettiest roads in Westbay.

She stands in the doorway and pulls her red scarf from her neck and a few heads turn in her direction. She scans the room quickly. There's no one who looks like Saga-Man. She sighs and checks her watch. Bang on seven. He's late and she can't bear tardiness but she waits at the counter to be served.

'Gin and tonic,' she orders, 'with lime. Make it a double, please.' Once she has her drink, she finds a corner table and waits. She checks her phone. Ten minutes later the door opens and an overweight man with balding hair in his fifties approaches her table.

'Jane?'

'Gordon?'

He smiles and shrugs off his coat. 'Nice to meet you. I see you have a drink. I'll be back in a sec.'

She watches him, wondering if he's arrived deliberately late so that he didn't have to buy her a drink. He's broad and stocky and he walks like a sailor on an uneven ship, rolling from side to side with his hands in his pockets. He pulls out change and counts it carefully and places it on the bar before his pint is served.

Jane wonders how he knows the exact cost of a pint.

A few minutes later, with his drink in his hand, he slides

onto the bar stool opposite her. 'Cheers.' The froth leaves a cream moustache on his upper lip and he wipes it with the back of his hand. 'Nice to meet you.'

Jane smiles back.

'What do you do then, Jane?'

She sighs. He's straight in there with the question she hates most. She feels he's assessing her, working out what job she has and how much she earns. 'I'm a receptionist,' she lies.

He nods thoughtfully as if it's a profound and interesting subject.

'What about you?'

'I was a contractor, built houses — privately, you know the sort of thing.' Jane nods although she doesn't and he continues, 'Big houses in Richmond and Chiswick, then when business was booming, I bought a place in Alicante, so I go backwards and forwards to Spain now.' He goes on to explain how much he's earned and invested in property over the past thirty years and how hard he's worked.

'Is business still booming?'

He shakes his head. 'Everything's changed since Brexit.'

There's a white patch of skin where his wedding ring used to be.

'And what about family?'

He picks up his pint and takes a long gulp. 'Wife left me. Took the kids — and the dog, which I miss more.' He laughs. 'She's gone back to Leeds to be near her mum.'

'How old are the kids?'

He waves his hand. 'Twenties, they don't talk to me now.'

'That's sad.'

'That's life.'

'And your wife?'

'She didn't understand the stress I was under, you know, making lots of money for her to sit on the beach all day and go to the salon and get her nails painted and her hair done.' He finishes his pint and smacks his lips. 'Another drink?'

Jane nods. 'It's a double,' she says as he heads to the bar.

Gordon rocks on his heels at the bar, waiting. When the barmaid comes over, he takes his time ordering. He's chatting to her for a while. The barmaid glances over to where Jane is sitting and she's suddenly self-conscious.

'Have you been in this pub before?' Jane asks when he returns with their drinks.

'No, but she's very friendly. She's a smasher.' He nods at the barmaid and tries to catch her eye again with a smile, but she's busy and doesn't look at him.

'So, where were we?' he asks.

'You were telling me about your kids.' The gin hits the back of her throat.

'There's nothing to tell. You know kids, they're protective of their mother.'

'And has there been anyone else since?'

He scratches his head and wiggles on his chair. 'A couple of dates. Nothing serious. I thought I didn't want to get involved — I didn't want to get *hurt again*.' He stares into her eyes. His green eyes have brown rings around his large irises and his voice softens. 'What about you, Jean?'

'Jane. It's Jane.'

'Yes, of course, sorry.' He places his hand over hers and she's comforted by the touch of his skin and his thick fingers. 'It's been a long day.'

Jane stares at him conscious that he's moved his stool closer and their faces are inches apart.

'What's your story,' he whispers. 'Husband, kids?'

Jane shakes her head. 'I think I've always picked the wrong guys. You know, the bad boys.'

He nods wisely and sips his pint then rests his hand on her knee.

She says, 'You see, my dad was a lovely man. There is no one who could ever measure up to him. He was kind and sensitive and...' her voice trails off, as she's jolted by a memory of her father bent over his work top, showing her how to repair the winder on a Cartier. 'He knew things. He knew everything; he was very wise.'

Gordon shifts uncomfortably. 'Any boyfriends?'

'I was with Trevor on and off for years - that was before I moved here - but he was married.'

Gordon raises his eyebrows.

'I knew that. I didn't want to move in with him or for him to leave his wife. It just suited us at the time. But then it all stopped.'

'Stopped?'

Jane nods. She doesn't tell Gordon about the evening she went out to celebrate her Dad's birthday and that she saw Trevor in a restaurant with a younger and more attractive woman. They were holding hands.

'Then I met Dave. He was wild. He just wanted to party, but he took drugs and was sometimes off his face in the middle of the day.'

Gordon's eyes widen and his finger traces circles across her knee.

'Then I met Ritchie. He was a banker. He told me he was divorced, but he wasn't.'

'How long did that last?'

'A few months.'

'Anything more recent?'

'Not since I moved here four years ago.'

'One-night stands?' Gordon smiles.

Jane shakes her head. 'Not my scene.'

'Threesomes?' Gordon traces the inside of her thigh.

Jane giggles. 'Never say never.' She downs her gin and by coincidence Gordon's glass is also empty. 'My round. I'll give you the money if you get it?'

Gordon smiles and takes the notes she offers him. She watches him at the bar. He's confident. He's flirtatious with the barmaid who must be young enough to be his granddaughter and Jane wishes she'd eaten dinner before she came out. She thought they'd only be an hour but the time is passing quickly and she's quite enjoying the attention of Gordon's hand on her leg.

'Here you go, Princess.' He slides the glass onto the table. His hands brush the inside of her thigh and Jane is pleased she wore a skirt.

'What are you looking for?' she asks.

'I think I'm looking for you.' He leans forward and kisses her gently on the lips.

Jane scans the pub quickly. She hasn't been kissed in public for years and she's suddenly wary, she pulls her leg away from him.

Gordon smiles. 'I think you like a good time.'

Jane nods. 'I also like walks by the sea, jigsaw puzzles and jewellery.'

'Jewellery?' Gordon glances down at her hands and notices the assortment of unusual rings on most of her fingers. He glances at his watch.

'That's a Skagen watch,' Jane says.

He nods.

'Jewellery is my speciality.'

'That's an expensive hobby.' Gordon swings his legs aside and away from Jane.

'Did your wife like nice jewellery?'

He nods. 'All women like bling,' he says. 'It's a costly process. You go for a drink and the next thing the woman wants an engagement ring.'

Jane laughs. 'And what do you want?'

'Well, it's important to have a bit of fun, you know, see if you get on and you're well matched.'

'How many dates do you go on a week?' Jane's question seems to take him by surprise.

'Maybe two or three.'

This time Jane is surprised. 'You look nothing like your picture.'

'I know.' He laughs. 'One of my mates changed it for a laugh.'

'But you didn't change it back.'

'Nah, no point. It's only a bit of fun.'

'You don't sound serious about dating. You said on your profile that you wanted a serious relationship.'

'I do, but you've got to try everything first.'

'Everything?'

'Well, you know, make sure you like the same things. It's pointless tying yourself up with some old woman who's frigid, isn't it?'

Jane's mouth opens.

'It's true,' he continues, 'Women lead you on and then complain when you get horny. I mean, it's no joke when the woman gives you all the vibes and encouragement, then turns into Mother Theresa at the end of the night.' He gulps his beer then places his hand on Jane's knee. 'I think I'm pretty good at reading women. I've had lots of experience, and with Spanish women too. You're basically all the same. You want to look good, have great sex and then sit at home without makeup and not make any effort—'

'Wait a second.' Jane holds up her hand. 'Are you serious?'

'Of course, although you can't say any of this any more as it's not PC, is it? It's not politically correct. Everyone's gone mad. The world is crazy now. You can't speak your mind and say what you think — it's all woke! But it's the truth.'

'But equally, your opinion of women is outdated—'

'Babe, I'm sixty-two, what do you expect?'

'You said on your profile you're fifty-three.'

'Ah, profiles. It's all rubbish. It's just a man and a woman wanting to meet for sex.'

'Is that what you think?'

'Isn't that why you're here?'

'No.'

'You didn't mind me stroking your leg, did you?'

'That's not the point. I thought we had a connection.'

'Connection? You're pissed and I'm not far behind you. Look, we can either go back to mine, I only live around the corner or...' He looks over his shoulder and lowers his voice. 'We could go into the toilet here.'

Jane blinks.

'Come on. Don't look so shocked. It's not as if you're a virgin, is it?'

'That's not the point.' Jane picks up her iPhone.

'What are you doing?'

'Calling a taxi.'

Gordon let's out a heavy sigh. 'Oh, FFS.'

* * *

Gordon was right. Jane is very drunk. She gets the taxi to drop her at the small supermarket on the corner near her home. She has no bread to make a sandwich and she needs something to soak up the alcohol. She also buys a bottle of vodka.

Walking home, Harbour Street is quiet. The Christmas lights have been taken down, there's a calm softness to the evening and her footsteps seem to whisper on the pavement.

'What a dick,' she whispers. 'What an absolute waste of time.'

The old clock tower strikes nine o'clock and Jane clutches her purchases as she cuts down the alleyway. It's cold and she shivers, thinking of random snatches of conversation with Gordon.

'It's what women want, he says. Sex.' She snorts, thinking of the way she had given him money for a round and he hadn't given her back any change. She'd picked up her coat and left the pub without saying goodbye. He didn't deserve it. 'It was no wonder his wife had left and his kids don't speak to him. He was hitting on the barmaid, for God's sake!'

'Who was hitting on the barmaid?'

Jane stops, suddenly conscious of someone beside her. She frowns and squints in the lamplight, recognising a familiar face.

'Oh, hello Ozan.'

He smiles. 'It's Yusef.'

She giggles. 'Of course, sorry, I can never tell you guys

apart.'

'I'm the better looking one.' Yusef laughs, throwing back his head. His long dark hair is lush and thick under the streetlamp. 'Have you been out, Jane?'

'I went to a pub in town.'

'Ah, good night, was it? Here let me take that for you. You don't want to drop that bottle. Oops.' It slips from her grasp and he catches it. 'Saved.' He grins and follows her along the narrow pavement. 'I didn't know you lived here,' he says, as she produces a key from her pocket.

'How would you? You only own the barbers opposite my shop,' she replies pushing open the door and switching on the hall light. She leaves the door open so he follows her inside.

He whistles. 'This is lovely. Very cosy.'

Jane reaches for a glass. 'Drink?'

'Why not?'

She pours neat vodka and pushes his glass across the kitchen counter. 'Cheers.'

'Cheers!' Yusef smiles.

'All men are shit,' she says, after downing her glass and pouring another one.

'Women are just as bad,' Yusef replies. He's never seen this side of Jane before. Normally she works in her jewellery shop, day and night, barely going out, and when she does she wears trendy dungarees, Doc Marten boots and mismatching scarves and hats. Tonight, she's wearing a colourful dress, black tights and a low-cut top that reveals bigger breasts than he'd expected.

'Men only want one thing.'

'That's what Naomi said.'

'Naomi?'

'My ex.' Yusef shakes his head. 'All women are shit,' he says. 'Did you buy the bread for a sandwich?'

'Do you want one?'

'I'll make it.' Yusef makes himself at home. He pulls out an assortment of cheeses from the fridge wrapped in decorative paper, clearly leftover from Christmas, and smells them before cutting neat squares and laying them on the bread.

Jane perches on the stool at the kitchen counter watching his long, quick fingers.

'You like hairdressing?' she asks.

'I love it.' He looks up and smiles.

'You and Ozan are always smiling. Why are you so happy?'

'Because we get to do what we enjoy doing, every single day.'

'I enjoy making jewellery but I'm not happy.'

'Why not?' Yusef cuts the sandwich in half and pushes a plate in front of Jane, then pours them both another glass of vodka.

'I guess it's an age thing,' she mumbles.

'Why do you say that?'

Jane laughs aloud. 'Look at you, you're only twenty.'

'You don't look much older.'

She ignores his compliment. 'You have your life ahead of you, Yusef. Everything is possible. All your dreams can still come true. You have your own business and your life is perfect.'

Yousef nods. She wasn't entirely wrong, *The Grooming Room – Esquires of Westbay,* was his dream and with his brother, they have a very successful business.

'You have time,' she wails. 'My hourglass is emptying. The

sand is falling between my fingers and I can't catch it. I'm not as fit or as fast or as driven as I used to be.'

'I think you're pretty fit.' Yusef downs his vodka.

'You're just saying that because you feel sorry for me. You see an old woman who shuts herself away in a shop, who never goes out, who never speaks to anyone. A woman who doesn't have a life.'

'No, I don't.'

'You must.' Jane finishes her sandwich and dabs her lips with a square of kitchen roll.

'I'll tell you what I see.' He leans across the counter. 'I see a strong woman in our community who helps those around her. You're a good friend to Amber and you supported her to get rid of JJ so the old travel agency wasn't turned into an amusement arcade. You're friends with Ian and Derek. You're popular. The vicar is a good friend —'

'But that's not what it's all about, is it?'

Yusef frowns. 'To have respect and friends in the community is very important.'

'But that's not about me, is it?'

Yusef pours more vodka, but Jane puts a hand over her glass and shakes her head. 'That doesn't stop me from being on my own, does it?' she whispers.

Yusef leans closer. 'You're lonely?'

'Of course I'm bloody lonely. Then I go into town to meet someone and he wants to shag me in the toilet.'

Yusef bursts out laughing. He can't stop and that's when Jane starts to laugh too. He's wiping his eyes and his tummy begins to ache. How can this shy jeweller who works cross the street, who is old enough to be his mother, make him laugh so much?

She giggles. 'His profile picture was like a man on a Saga holiday: greying hair, debonair and confident but in real life he was an overweight builder who is probably addicted to Viagra.'

Yusef laughs louder.

'I'm destined to meet awful men,' she adds. 'It's in the stars.'

Jane likes the way Yusef laughs. He's not at all self-conscious. He's confident and attractive and without a shirt his body would be all muscle. When Yusef stops laughing Jane says, 'He was over sixty and he asked me if I'd be up for a threesome in the pub toilet with the barmaid.'

Yusef explodes with laughter. He doesn't know if Jane is telling the truth but it's very funny and he imagines her with her skirt pulled up over her waist and he imagines the feel of her skin against his body.

Jane laughs but loses her balance on the stool and Yusef catches her in his arms. It seems the most natural thing in the world for them to kiss. Their lips meet and overwhelmed with passion, delight and surprise Jane opens her mouth to Yusef's probing tongue.

Jane feels the firmness of Yusef's chest and she rips his shirt from the waistband of his trousers and marvels at the softness of his hairless, strong body. She bends and kisses his nipples and that's when he lifts her face to his.

'Are you sure, Jane?'

'I have never wanted anything more,' she replies, laughing, and she takes him by the hand and leads him upstairs.

* * *

After they've made love, Jane props up the pillows and sits up in the bed. She pulls the duvet over her breasts. Beside her, Yusef lies with his hands over his head snoring softly his legs spread wide across the sheets.

'That's sobered me up,' she whispers. 'What an earth am I doing?'

'You're living,' Yusef replies quietly with his eyes still closed. 'It's time for you to find some excitement.'

'Not like this.'

He rolls onto his side and leans his head on his hand and gazes at her. 'Why not?' He has a flower tattoo over the left side of his shoulder, over his chest and down to his waist. It's incredibly beautiful and it suits his lean, muscular body.

'How old are you?'

'Twenty-four.'

'I'm forty-seven.'

'Cougar,' he roars softly and turns his hand into a claw.

'It's not funny.'

'What are you looking for?'

Jane considers his question. It's easier to talk in the half-light of the dark January night and Jane answers quietly, 'I'm looking to share my life with someone special.'

'Is that why you use dating sites?'

'How did you know?'

'I guess that's how you met Mr Saga-Man aka Mr Viagra - which just for the record, I want to add, I do not use or need.'

Jane places a hand on his chest. 'I can tell.'

Yusef clutches her hand. 'You're a very sexy lady.'

'You make me feel that way.'

'Good.'

'What about you? Do you have a girlfriend now?'

'Not now...' his voice trails off. 'Not any more.'

'What happened?'

'Nothing' He pulls his hand away and turns to lie on his back staring at the ceiling.

'I've told you about my Saga-man,' she prompts.

'It's complicated,' he replies, and Jane can see he is struggling with emotion.

'She must be very special.'

'She is.'

'Can you be together?'

'Not now.'

'Why not?'

'Because it's not me she wants.'

'How could she not want you?'

Yusef smiles sadly. 'That's what I asked.'

'Maybe you should talk to her.'

'It won't make any difference.'

'Why not?'

'Her mind is made up.'

'So, change it.'

'I can't.'

'Why not?'

He refuses to speak, so Jane asks, 'Can I speak to her for you?'

He wipes a tear from his eye with the back of his arm so Jane snuggles down beside him and cuddles into his long, naked body.

'You really like her, don't you?'

'Yes.'

'Life is short, go and get her.'

'I can't.'

'Tell me why?' she asks softly.

'Because it would kill the one person I love most in the world.'

'Ozan?'

'Yes. He's in love with her too.'

* * *

Jane makes tea and toast for them both and then insists he leaves her home before it's light and the neighbours wake up.

'Will I see you again?' he asks.

'You work across the road from me, so I should think so.'

Yusef spreads Marmite on his toast. 'No, I mean, like this.'

'I don't think it's a good idea.'

'Why not?'

'Well, aside from our obvious age difference, I think people would laugh.'

'But what do *you* want?'

'Yusef, you're lovely. You're kind and gentle and easy to talk to, it's just that I'm looking for someone—'

'Older?'

'Yes.'

'Why?'

'Because in the longer term you and I want different things. You like to go out clubbing and meeting people and I want to stay at home and do jigsaws and get cosy beside the fire.'

'We can do both.'

'I'd get very jealous if I saw young, attractive, girls flirting with you all the time.'

Yusef smiles. 'Naomi told me that I can't help myself.'

Jane finishes her toast. 'You need someone your own age too, Yusef. Someone who shares your taste in music, computer games or hobbies. We're from different generations.'

'It didn't seem like that last night.'

Jane's cheeks redden. She looks away and then turns deliberately to face him. 'Please, promise me you won't tell anyone?'

Yusef looks at her. 'Why?'

'I don't want to be another conquest.'

'You're not.'

'Good.'

'But, I promise I won't tell anyone.' He frowns seriously.

'Thank you.'

'But, just for the record, I would like to see you again.'

'We can have coffee sometime.'

'Really?' His face brightens.

'We can bump into each other.'

'Can I come here again?'

'I don't think that's a good idea.'

He scratches his head. 'But we both enjoyed ourselves and we really get on. You're so easy to talk to.'

'It won't do either of us any good.'

He grins. 'I think it will.'

Jane reaches for his jacket and throws it playfully in his arms. 'It's time for you to go.'

He leans forward and kisses her briefly on the cheeks. 'Thank you.'

'I don't think you should thank me.'

He stares at her and then says. 'When I bumped into you last night, I was very upset but explaining everything to you, made me see things better.'

'Do you mean about Naomi and Ozan?'

'I shall now bow out gracefully and be a gentleman. I will

give them my blessing.'

'That sounds like a good plan and besides, I do think that you will meet the right person for you.'

They walk down the hallway together and he pauses at the front door with his hand on the lock. 'How is it that you believe I will meet the right person, but you won't?'

'Perhaps I will.'

'Perhaps the stars will realign this year and the right man for you will come along.'

'Maybe.'

He opens the door and before he steps outside and closes it behind him, he whispers, 'And if not, I am here for you, Jane.'

* * *

Jane opens the shop with the same regularity each morning. She lifts the blinds, checks the window displays, makes coffee and then sits at her workbench behind the counter until customers arrive. She has some repair jobs that she has put off until after Christmas, plus there was an order for a special handmade pair of earrings for a 21st birthday due the middle of January.

After the Christmas rush of shoppers, January is notoriously quiet. Sometimes people want to return a gift, but it is all usual, normal and predictable. That's what Jane likes, predictability. She hated to admit it but she likes routine, monotony and a timetable. It's what keeps her organised but more importantly, she feels safe.

At eleven o'clock she puts a note on the door to say she'll be back in ten minutes. She walks slowly enjoying the cold wind on her face and that Harbour Street is quiet. Outside her hangover eases. On the right, leading to the harbour, a large van is negotiating the narrow route between the stone legs of Colossus, the clock tower, while to her left a van is parked on the kerb, delivering boxes to *From the Heart Gift Shop*. Jane calls out a brisk hello and Kit looks up and waves.

Jane can't see Eva in the flower shop or Ben in the art gallery but Ian is serving a customer in the grocers and Tracey, from Step Ahead beauty salon, comes out into the street. They meet at the café door.

'Hello Jane,' she says, pulling her scarf closer. 'It's bitterly cold today and I'm desperate for a coffee.'

'Hi Tracey, how's business?'

'Slow.' Inside Tracey calls out, 'Morning Amber. Hello, Faisal. No Karl today?'

Faisal grins at her while cleaning a table. 'Karl and Molly have gone to the Canary Islands for a week.'

'Lucky!'

Amber turns from the coffee machine. 'Morning ladies'

'I'll have a latte,' says Tracey. 'I haven't got long as my next appointment is due.'

'I'll make it quickly.' Amber turns away again.

'I think it's just the boys who are busy,' Tracey says. 'There's always a queue outside the barbers, isn't there?'

'I hadn't noticed,' Jane replies, feeling her cheeks colouring.

'What? And you're right opposite them. Goodness, I'd be glued to the window staring at them the whole time. Those boys are proper eye-candy, don't you think?'

Amber smiles and presses a lid on the cup. 'Too young for me,' she says.

Tracy nods. 'Yeah, I suppose so, I forget. Goodness, Jane, it hadn't crossed my mind but you could probably be their mother. Thanks for the coffee, Amber. See you both later.'

'Later,' Amber calls out and she laughs as Tracey closes the door. 'She's not the most tactful but her heart's in the right place. I think it's taken her a while to get her confidence back after Dan dumped her.'

'She seems alright to me.' Jane wishes her tone didn't sound so brusque, but Amber doesn't seem to notice.

'I've got some information here on the kiosk. Have a read of it, Jane, while I get your coffee ready,' she says pushing a small booklet toward her. Jane scan reads the information doubtfully, it's only January and she isn't sure she wants to tie herself into anything just yet.

'It's a big step.'

'It's only from April to September,' Amber says. 'It would be perfect.'

'But I couldn't employ anyone,' Jane replies. 'It all becomes far too complicated.'

'Look, let's take a walk down there. Have you time on Sunday and we can have a look together?'

Jane agrees. Not because she wants to rent a kiosk in the summer but because she's desperate for company, especially at the weekend when time drags.

The café door opens and it's suddenly busy.

'I'll text you,' Amber calls as she turns to make another coffee.

Outside in Harbour Street, Jane glances toward the art gallery across the road where Amber's partner Ben works. She's thinking of Yusef and wonders how other shopkeepers would react if they knew the truth. 'They must never find out,' she whispers.

* * *

On Sunday morning the rain pauses at mid-day and Jane is pleased to receive a text from Amber.

Meet us in the harbour - 30 mins?

She pulls on her multi-coloured Doc Martens and throws a coat over her olive green and black dungarees. Jane knows that Amber and Ben live on the far side of the harbour and that Ben inherited his family home. Jane has been invited there a few times in the past two years since Amber took over the café and although Jane hadn't been part of the political scene when Amber first moved to Westbay, she now takes a keen interest.

When she moved to Westbay, Jane's initial focus was on her business and making ends meet. There had been a time when she hadn't managed to keep up with the rent on the shop but eventually she'd negotiated a deal with bank and the owners to buy the property. She'd remortgaged her cottage as collateral and she's happy that she's safeguarded her financial future. When Covid came along, unlike many other small businesses, Jane had found a way to survive. She'd spent all her time creating an online business. She hooked up with online shopping sites and was now shipping her jewellery all over the world. The only problem was that she needed help. She needed someone who could help her manage the online business while she focused on the design and making of the jewellery. One thing she had learnt was that she couldn't afford to be cheap.

Jane's Jewellery was getting a name as an expensive but reputable brand, and she needed help — someone who knew about staff. Jane didn't know anything about having employees.

Amber and Ben are standing at the deserted Artisan market; coloured beach hut-styled kiosks are set back from the water's edge and fishing boats line the harbour wall.

Amber is wearing a multi-coloured woollen coat and flat cap which look cool and trendy, while Ben wears a leather bomber jacket and jeans. They look perfect together, tall, good-looking, smiling and successful.

This is the partnership Jane wants. The perfect Yin and Yang. Like sun and moon or wind and rain — a happy balance. She didn't want someone too like her or anyone too handsome or too young. She wanted someone who would complement her and she would do the same for him. She would be the perfect partner for the right man — a man who was happy in his own shoes. A man who is confident and intelligent but not cocky or smart, a down-to-earth man who loves normal things like a jigsaw. A man she would snuggle up with and watch a film, and be happy watching sport or football with. She wanted a man who would smile and tell her everything would be alright, a man who would think things through with her and give his honest opinion without bias and without gain — a man like Ben.

Was that too much to ask?

'Did you see how busy it was here last summer?' Ben asks.

'Sometimes.'

'Then you'll know that anything goes. There's food from Thailand, prints and pictures, photographs, handmade jewellery, craft shops, clothes...' He waves his arms. 'Just about everything.'

'So, what will you do?' Jane asks.

'We can either offer breakfast with coffee, donuts and

sandwiches or we could aim for the lunchtime trade and offer oysters, fish, chips — simple things —and maybe even picnic baskets for the beach.'

Amber screws up her eyes and looks around at the fishing boats bobbing on the tide in the harbour as if weighing up their options.

'It will all depend,' Ben explains, 'if we want to use the Bistro or the café side of our business. We've been keeping them separate because of the accounts but we have to make the decision soon because these kiosks are popular and they will soon go.'

'I think my jewellery will be too expensive.' Jane frowns.

Amber digs her hands into her coat pocket. 'So, why not do a cheaper brand? That way, you can appeal to two different markets.'

'It might take away my exclusivity,' Jane replies. 'Although, it would be a good idea and I could certainly use some of the jewellery I sell online. That's not nearly as expensive as the stuff I put in the shop.'

'It would be good to expand your business,' Ben agrees standing beside her.

'What about staff?' Jane is encouraged by their enthusiasm. 'You guys are always so optimistic.' She laughs. 'You could talk me into anything.'

Amber holds up her hand. 'No. Please take your time and think what suits you best, Jane. I just thought it must be so hard trying to make all the business decisions. Sometimes you just need ideas and someone you can talk things through with—'

'I used to talk to Dad a lot. I wish you'd known him. He was happy just fixing and repairing things but it was me who ran the business side of things. I stocked the shop, managed the customers and the orders. But you're right, Amber. Since losing Dad, I haven't been able to speak to anyone — apart from the bank when I remortgaged my home.'

'But you're doing alright, Jane.' Ben smiles, but then he's distracted and turns away. 'I think that's Tommy over there.' He raises his hand and strides off towards the stranger near the fishing boats.

'So, what about staff?' Jane asks.

Amber shrugs. 'We haven't got that far yet.'

'Doesn't Ben work with a lot of young people in London?'

'He does, but they're often homeless and although he's formed a charity and helps them with woodwork and things, not all of them are interested in the hospitality industry. I'm lucky I have Karl and Faisal but there are often lots of students around in the summer looking for work.'

'It sounds like another headache.' Jane watches Ben saunter over to a man leaning over the railing watching the boats.

'Maybe you're right. Come on. Let's get a coffee. It looks like Tommy has been out here for ages. He looks freezing too.'

'Tommy?'

'He's a friend of Ben's. You must have seen him walking around town with his wife — a beautiful Iranian woman?'

Jane shakes her head.

'He used to be a fisherman but he had a heart attack last year. Bless him. He still spends all his time down here in the harbour. It's his home.'

Amber insists on buying takeaways from a small coffee shop and they take them over to where the men are chatting together.

'I bought you a latte, Tommy.' Amber hands him a cup and

he appears surprised.

'That's very welcome.' He smiles. 'Thank you.'

After introductions, they chat for a while and Jane regards Tommy while blowing on her coffee. He has deep-set serious eyes and a worried frown.

'Hey Jane! Amber! Hi you gorgeous people!'

Jane's body stiffens. She recognises the cheerful voice behind her and she's frightened to turn around.

'Hi Yusef, where are you going looking so smart?' Ben claps him on the shoulder and Yusef pulls him into a man-hug.

'Hi.' Yusef is looking directly at her.

'Hi.' Jane looks out to sea.

'Hey, Tommy, my main man, how are you?' They shake hands. 'You all having a good time?' Yusef's tone is cheerful and upbeat. He doesn't wait for an answer. 'My cousin's birthday lunch today.' He pulls on his suit jacket. 'Thought I'd dress up, proper-like.'

'You look gorgeous, doesn't he, Jane?' Amber smiles.

'Do you think?' Yusef stands taller and moves closer to Jane. 'You like?'

Jane steps back, blinks and nods her head. 'Yeah, it's great.'

Amber laughs. 'See, we all love you, Yusef.'

'Yeah?' He looks at Jane who will not look at him.

Ben throws his arm over Yusef's shoulder. 'Don't be so needy, mate.'

Yusef laughs. 'Gotta hone my skills, you know? Well, guys, have a good day.'

To Jane's relief, Yusef steps away and after he's gone, she breathes a small sigh. Could anyone guess? Did they know? He'd been too friendly with her and she suddenly feels very self-conscious and uncomfortable.

'I'm really sorry, I have to go. I've got to get back. Yusef just reminded me, I have to call my aunt. It's her birthday too,' she lies. She smiles, and still clutching her coffee tightly she walks quickly through the harbour, under the Colossus clock tower to the safety and security of her lonely home.

* * *

Once she's at home, she begins to work. Jane sits at the dining table with the radio on in the background, sorting through her tools, wires, bits of gold and silver. She picks up her pad and begins designing earrings and matching necklaces; small, delicate sea creatures; sea horses, starfish, dolphins and seals. Then suddenly she hurls the sketchpad across the room where it hits the wall and crumples to the floor.

She puts her face in her hands and warm tears fall down her cheeks. 'You stupid, stupid woman! The whole town knows. They must do. That bloody, Yusef. How could I be so stupid?'

February

Tommy

The floor is hard and uncomfortable and Tommy stares up at the ceiling. There's a smell of damp from the carpet and a draught coming in from the window. Or was it from under the door? Either way, for a man used to being out in all weather, he wasn't comfortable or happy. The man lying on the floor beside him is about to fall into a deep sleep, his breathing growing deeper, and on his other side, a strange woman is within touching distance.

Tommy wiggles his feet and then remembers he's not supposed to move. He's supposed to be in some trance-like state, emptying his mind. But how is that possible? How can anyone just switch off like that? How can you go from a busy head to an empty head by changing focus — or position — or just stretching?

Yoga.

The doctor said it would be good for him.

It wasn't.

Tommy didn't feel good at all.

Relax, the doctor had said. Well it wasn't relaxing at all.

If his wife was here, Sunita, she'd be lying beside him trying to make him laugh and he would have to snuffle a hearty giggle. But he has no one to make him laugh now and this isn't at all funny.

He glances at his watch and he takes a quick look around. They're all ages. The young ones are wearing black leotards and skimpy tops stretching over their toned bodies. Then the ones like him are wearing baggy track pants and oversized t-shirts. He rests his head back and stares up at the ceiling trying to remember all the positions; downward dog, cat something or other and even a warrior. The last person Tommy felt like was a warrior. He was, in fact, the opposite. It's funny how appearances can be so deceptive. A fisherman stereotype is burly with a thick grey beard and Tommy wasn't like that at all. He really looked after himself. He was slim, well-toned, average height and he still had his own hair and teeth. Who would have thought he'd have a heart attack? The thought of that alone was likely to give him another one. He wasn't overweight. It wasn't diet or drink or stress — well, he didn't think it was. The surgeons fixed him with two stents and sent him back home to the real world and he still hadn't felt like a warrior or even a fisherman — worse still — he had felt sorry for himself.

Before the heart attack he was always busy; working, helping friends in their gardens and time seemed to fly past. He filled his days easily but now what? Now he can't work and he's supposed to take it easy. What's the point of that? What's the point of living?

The man beside him suddenly snorts awake and twitches.

This is so boring. Tommy closes his eyes.

Is this what death is like? Does it smell damp?

He's a fisherman. He's been around water for most of his life yet the dampness now seeping into his nose and through his joints irritates him. How can he relax?

If he was with Sunita and they were sunbathing on a luxury sun lounger by the Indian Ocean, then he would drink a cocktail and snooze and swim — that was relaxing, none of this forced tranquillity, and the music — it's a mixture of tinkling and droning. If Sunita were here, she'd say it would make her want to pee.

He giggles.

What would happen if he just stood up? Just got up right now while they're all meditating and stepped over their bodies, saying excuse me, excuse me, as if he were in the cinema. What would happen?

He sighs.

Fishing. He loved it. He missed the excitement of the early mornings, the squawk of the gulls following the boat home, the banter of the men, the thrill of the catch, the worry of the tides or the touch of fear when the weather unexpectedly turned.

The yoga teacher's melodious voice tells him the class is over and he listens to everyone getting up but he doesn't move. Tommy lies as still as a boat in a dry dock; rigid, eyes closed, arms stretched out beside his body as they move around him. Someone smothers a giggle but still Tommy doesn't move.

Has he died? Could he move if he wanted to?

What would happen if he were to lie here forever?

'Tommy?'

He opens his eyes.

'Tommy? Are you alright?'

He blinks. The overhead fluorescent tube is dazzling and he

covers his eyes with his arm.

'The class is over.'

'Ah. Thank you, Simon.'

He stands back as Tommy gets to his feet.

'Did you enjoy that?' Simon asks.

'Er, yes. Good.'

'It's your first time, isn't it?'

'Yes.'

'Don't worry that you found it difficult or that you couldn't get the right pose or keep your balance very well. These things take time.'

'They do?'

Simon smiles. 'I've been doing it for ten years.'

Tommy claps him on the shoulder. 'That's what keeps you looking so young.'

Simon nods. 'It keeps me healthy.'

'Are you a vegetarian?' Tommy asks.

Simon smiles. 'How did you know?'

'Just a guess.' Tommy ambles toward to exit.

'See you next week?' Simon calls.

Tommy waves over his shoulder and mutters, 'Not bloody likely.'

* * *

They bought the Victorian house just off the square, near the church at the top end of town, twenty years ago but Tommy walks deliberately past the turning and heads down towards the harbour.

As a thirty-year-old young fisherman he'd been shocked and surprised to meet a pretty girl who made him laugh.

They'd met in the city department store café. She was writing in her diary and his hands were full with coffee and a bacon sandwich. He had nowhere to sit. All the tables were busy so he'd coughed. When she looked up he'd asked if he could share her table. Her smile was radiant and they began talking immediately. She'd just moved to the city and she was working as science teacher at a local school. She told him how her parents had fled persecution in Iran. Tommy said he'd never met an Iranian and Sunita said she'd never met a fisherman. They were equally fascinated with each other.

To this day, Tommy would swear that it was love at first sight but Sunita insisted that it was the second time — a Sunday morning when they proudly walked down Harbour Street arm in arm. Sunita loved it. She loved the sea and the harbour and, as she grew to know him, she loved his boss, Matt, and the camaraderie of his fellow fishermen.

Tommy pauses to look at the flowers in the shop beside the art gallery. He often used to buy them for Sunita. Eva always has the best flowers and plants, especially at Christmas.

Tommy smells garlic, cumin and curry and he looks across the road toward the Indian takeaway. Sanjay was his friend and he missed him. He'd gone back to India after his father died and his cousins were now managing the business. Tommy hadn't been in there for some time.

Sunita loved Indian food.

Tommy proposed a year after they met and although they hadn't been blessed with children, they were happy. As a teacher Sunita had children at school and then Tommy's sister was having a baby. Although Elsie lived in Yorkshire, Tommy thought they could enjoy their niece or nephew without all the responsibility.

It didn't quite work out how they planned.

Elsie's husband, Frank, didn't like Sunita. He was upset that Tommy hadn't married a local girl and he thought that marrying into a different culture would cause all sorts of problems in the future. It was for this reason that Elsie also stopped speaking to Tommy. They didn't even come to the wedding.

Tommy was upset. Sunita asked if he wanted to call the whole thing off, but he refused. He wasn't going to be tied to their small-mindedness. Although he was bitterly upset and disappointed by Elsie, he was angrier with Frank. They'd grown up together and they went to the same school. Frank was opinionated and too uncouth for his sister, but Tommy hadn't said anything at the time. He'd gone to their wedding and he'd been pleasant and polite. Later, when they were expecting their baby, he'd congratulated them and he'd been happy for them both.

Tommy walks under the clock tower and the moon shines high in the dark sky. There's a cold February breeze from the north coming across the sea and he inhales the salty sea air. He walks past the old lobster pots and fishing lines to the colourful kiosks of the Artisan market and leans against the rails. The boats are low in the water. He knows the tides by heart. It would be a late start tomorrow for Matt and the gang.

He'd never shown Elsie the harbour. They'd never come to Westbay.

Sunita had tried to be a kind and loving sister-in-law. At first, she'd bought cards and gifts for the baby — Michelle. Elsie had sent photos back. She'd been a pretty little girl but then Frank had wanted less and less contact and, over the years, they'd lost touch completely. Tommy hadn't bothered.

He'd been busy. He was happy with Sunita. They had lovely holidays, but they never went to Yorkshire. Then, five years ago, Elsie contacted him to say that Frank had left. He'd found someone else and moved out. Tommy was pleased to hear from her but the distance between them was so great that they had nothing in common. Conversation on the phone was stilted. Hundreds of words that could have been said have been eroded with time. Time that never comes back and truth that remains unsaid. Sunita might have made an effort had Tommy asked her, but they had both felt rejected and hurt. Time passed and nothing had healed. They all moved on.

Tommy digs his hands into the pockets of his duffel coat and walks back to Harbour Street. A couple, arm in arm, leave Harbour Bistro.

'That was the best steak,' he says.

'It's my favourite restaurant in the world,' she replies.

Tommy pauses to look in through the window. There are red balloons and hearts hanging from the ceiling and candles on the tables. He slaps his forehead with his hand and hastening his step, he whispers, 'Oh no, Valentine's Day. I'd completely forgotten.'

* * *

The phone is ringing as he walks through the front door. He struggles out of his coat and tosses it onto a kitchen chair, pulling his mobile from his pocket. 'Hello?'

'Tommy? It's Elsie.'

'I've just been thinking of you.'

'Have you?' She sounds pleased, and surprised. 'How are you?'

'Fine.'

'Are you out of breath?'

'I've just walked in the door.'

'You're not overdoing it, are you?'

'Don't start. I'm fine.' He pauses, wondering why she's calling. The last time he spoke to her was after his operation two months ago. She'd been concerned but she hadn't bothered to ask him if she could come down and look after him.

'Are you alright?' he asks.

'It's Valentine's Day.'

'I know.'

'This is the day Frank left me.'

'I'm sorry.' Tommy rubs his head and goes into the kitchen with the phone tucked under his chin. He clumsily fills the kettle.

'What are you doing?' she asks.

'Nothing,' he lies. 'Why have you called, to remind me he left you?'

'No. I need your help.'

Tommy pauses with the kettle in his hand. 'My help?'

'Yes. I'd like Shelley to come and stay with you for a few months.'

'Shelley?'

'She's your niece.'

'I know who she is, but I've never even met her.'

'You met her once, in London. Don't you remember?'

Tommy frowns. He had a vague memory. Elsie had been to London to visit a friend and he had travelled up and spent a few hours with them. 'I don't remember her.'

'Well, you can get to know her.'

'She can't come here.'

'Why not.'

'Because, well, because, what would she do all day?'

'She'd amuse herself.'

'Well, I can't look after her.'

'You won't need to. She's twenty years old. She can look after herself.'

'Didn't you say she was going to University?'

'She did, but she's dropped out. She hated it.'

'Well she can't come here.' Tommy pulls a mug from the cupboard.

'She has to,' Elsie insists, 'She has nowhere else to go.'

'Doesn't she have any friends?'

'They're all at uni.'

'What about Frank?'

'Frank is useless and he's busy with his new family.'

'New family?'

'He has twins now. Don't you remember?'

He didn't. Tommy rubs his head. 'Well, why can't she go to you?'

'Because, it will do her good to be away from me and be somewhere different. Besides, she doesn't want to come home. She couldn't wait to leave here.'

Tommy sighs. 'This really isn't my problem, Elsie.'

'She will be company for you.'

'I don't want company.'

The phone goes silent then Elsie says slowly, 'Look, I'm sorry about what happened to Sunita but it's been four years. I know how hard it must be for you but you've had a heart attack and Shelley will be with you. There will be someone in the house again. There will be life there.'

Tommy looks down the hallway. He'd walked in without

a light. He knew the way to the kitchen, but the rest of the house still lay in darkness.

'What do you do with yourself, every day?' Elsie asks.

'Lots of things.'

'Like what?'

'I keep busy.'

'Doing what?'

'I went to Yoga tonight.'

Elsie laughs. 'I know you Tommy, that is not something you'd enjoy.'

Tommy grins. 'You're right about that.'

'Please, Tommy, help me out? Just for a couple of weeks. See how you get on. You might even like each other.'

Tommy scratches his chin. 'I suppose she could come for a week.'

'Great. You'll hardly notice she's there.'

'Really?'

'Promise. I'll let you know the day she's arriving. Oh, and by the way, she's a pescatarian vegan.'

* * *

It takes Tommy a week to sort out the spare room. He knew that if Sunita were here it would be all neat and tidy with her woman's touch, but over the past few years, he's used it as a dumping ground for his clothes and just about anything else in the house he didn't know what to do with.

By the time he's finished the bedroom it looks sparse but comfortable; a double bed, a lamp either side of the bed, a table and a chair because, if she's anything like the kids that Matt and the gang have, they spend all their time in their bedrooms on the computer.

He wanders into his bedroom where he's left a biscuit tin that's now full of old photographs. He sits on the end of the bed and lifts the lid very slowly as if the memories will burst out and surprise him. There are pictures of him as a boy, with Elsie, and with his parents. He wonders where the time went. Some images are black and white, especially the ones of his grandparents. He remembers their home, a pet hamster, and a cat called Crumpet. But sometimes there are gaps in time. What happened in the intervening years between the photos? His memories are boxed around the photographs. Although Tommy isn't one to dwell on the past, he pauses at the pictures of Sunita. She certainly was a beautiful girl. A wonderful woman who had brought light and joy to his life. She was uncomplicated and calm. He liked that about her. She was happy just to be in his company. They would listen to music, read, do a jigsaw or the crossword and then they would have their own interests. He would watch football and she would sew. She made the most incredible garments; dresses, skirts, blouses and what he loved about her most, was that she made it all seem easy. Nothing was too much effort and she sewed as if she had all the time in the world. She never hurried. She was neat and precise. She was a perfectionist. She had made curtains, tablecloths, napkins and, the first year they'd met, she'd made a special table set for Valentine's Day. Tommy had been so pleased and excited that he'd gone out and bought a special candle, which they lit and put on the dining table between them as they ate. Since then, it was their tradition. Each year he bought a candle and put it on the special tablecloth with red and gold hearts. Even though she was no longer here, he had kept the tradition. This year was the first time that he had forgotten.

* * *

A week later, Tommy is wandering along Harbour Street with his hands in his pockets. It's Elsie's birthday next week and he wants to send her a gift. They've spoken briefly a few times since he agreed that Shelley could come and stay and he's pleased at the bond they're forming again. It's easier now. Without their partners there are no barriers — even though Sunita would have welcomed Elsie, it was Frank who always blocked their contact.

He'd lost twenty years of his sister and now he wanted to make up for it.

Sunita had never been one for grand gifts or gestures. Laughingly she'd always said, 'So long as we have a holiday each year, that'll be my present.' But sometimes, Tommy had taken her away more than once each year. They travelled all around America and then Canada, but his favourite place was Africa, on safari, under a black sky studded with millions of stars shining like diamonds. These had been precious moments.

Now, he felt woefully inadequate to purchase a gift for his sister. He pauses to look in the window of the boutique. The mannequin is stylishly dressed in a woollen silver coat and olive-green beret. It takes him by surprise as Sunita had worn something very similar many years ago after a holiday to the south of France. She had always been ahead of the game with fashion ideas and he smiles at the memory of him laughing, saying he'd buy her some onions and a bicycle.

'It's pretty, isn't it?'

He turns at the sound of the voice by his elbow.

'I'm just opening up. Do you want to come inside?'

'Er no, I was just looking.'

'That's a beautiful coat. Is it for a present?'

'Well...'

'Come on in. Don't be shy.' She laughs and in one quick motion she unlocks the door, switches on the light and beckons him inside. He's rooted to the spot but she stands holding the door open and he has to step forward.

'Let me take my coat off and I'll help you. Don't worry, it's what I do. I get loads of guys like you in here.'

'You do?'

'Yes, of course.' She shrugs off her coat and hangs it up in a room at the back. He sees her checking her reflection in the mirror. She pulls down her short skirt, smiles, and rubs lipstick from her front tooth with her finger, then turns to face him. Her eyebrows raise and her smile widens when she realises he's watching her. She says, 'Do you see anything you like?'

He blinks and digging his hands deeper into his pockets, staring at the floor, he shakes his head.

'No? Then let me see what I can do about that.' She pulls a blouse from the rack. 'Let's start with this. You tell me if it would look too young on her, or too old or too frumpy. Could you see her wearing this?'

Tommy frowns then clears his throat. 'I don't know.'

'Gosh.' She replaces it quickly on the rack. 'We need to think about this then, don't we? Look, why don't I put the kettle on and we can have a coffee and chat about her?'

Tommy looks at the door.

'Come on, I won't bite you and I've seen you lots of times

walking around town. You hang out with Matt down at the harbour, don't you?'

Tommy nods.

'Fisherman?'

He nods.

'Thought so.'

'Why?'

'I can always tell. My name's Marion, what's yours?'

'Tommy.'

She walks into the back room and he hears her filling the kettle and rattling mugs. He scratches his head. He wasn't the stereotypical fisherman. He raises his shoulder to smell his coat and he sniffs.

'Don't worry,' she calls from the kitchen, 'I won't hold it against you... unless you want me to.' Her laugh tinkles into the shop and he can't decide if he's uncomfortable with her obvious flirting or if he enjoys it.

She returns a few minutes later and gives him a mug with a picture of a vivid red poppy.

'I guessed you like it strong and no sugar?'

'Thank you.' He takes it from her.

'So, who is this gift for? Lover, wife, ex-wife?'

'No, no, my sister.'

'Ah, well, that's a relief.'

'Why.'

'I can't bear it when married men come in and buy a present for their lovers. It doesn't sit right with me. I have high standards and I'm very principled.' She pulls her shoulders back and stares at him. 'Why doesn't your wife help you buy something?'

Tommy sips his coffee. 'She's passed.'

'Oh, I'm sorry.' He feels the touch of her fingers on his arm. 'Long ago?'

Tommy hates direct questions especially about Sunita from a stranger, but he can't move, and he doesn't answer. Four years, but for him it could have been yesterday.

'Well, I'm here now. Let's have a look.' She moves to a rail of dresses and smiles at him. 'I'm surprised we haven't chatted before. I've often noticed you in The Ship.'

'I haven't been in there for a while.'

'I know. I've missed you.'

Tommy isn't sure but it sounds like her voice has turned husky, perhaps she's going down with a cold.

* * *

A few days later, Tommy is at the station waiting for Shelley's train. He's busy looking at the picture Elsie sent him on his phone and he reads the message again.

Of course, you'll recognise her, you daft bugger.

'Hello.'

Tommy looks up into the brown eyes of a pretty red-head. Not a natural red head. It's electric red, the colour of fire, or the sun when you squint your eyes. It's brilliant.

'Are you Uncle Tommy?'

'Hello. Shelley?' He doesn't know if he should hug or kiss her but she takes charge and thrusts her shoulder bag at him.

'If you take that, it's bloody heavy, I'll take these.'

'*Two* suitcases?'

'What do you expect? Where's your car?'

'We're walking.'

'Walking?'

'Yes.'

'How far is it?'

'Ten minutes.'

'Let's get a cab.' She points at a waiting taxi.

'It's quicker to walk and it's only down there.' He'd never got a taxi in his life from the station. That's why he has legs. Besides, the doctor told him to exercise. 'Follow me,' he calls over his shoulder.

It's gone seven o'clock and although it's been raining, it's stopped and now there are large, black puddles everywhere. Occasionally she lets out a scream or a yuk!

He grins to himself and walks on wondering if she'll be like Elsie when she was younger. He opens the front door and drops her bag in the hallway and then helps her lift the two cases inside.

'This is a lot of luggage for a week.'

'A week?' She walks past him and into the kitchen. 'This is cool. Homely.' She runs her hand along the sea-green coloured granite worktop. 'Someone has taste.'

'Sunita — your aunt. She did it all.'

'Do you miss her?'

He moves past her to fill the kettle. 'Tea? Coffee?'

'Have you got any beer?'

'I think there's some.' He knows there's beer in the fridge but he's surprised. He wanted a child but he's got an adult.

She opens the door and reads the labels. 'Westbay lager? Is this any good?'

'I like it.'

She tosses him a bottle and waggles hers in the air. 'Have you got a thingy or shall I use my teeth to open it?'

'Wait. I have one here.'

She giggles.

He opens her bottle first and she seems genuinely amused. 'What a gentleman.'

'Of course.'

'Mum said you were old school.'

'What does that mean?'

She shrugs. 'I guess it was a compliment — and certainly better than my dad.'

Tommy takes off his coat and offers to hang up her puffer jacket. She's wearing dungarees printed with an assortment of dinosaurs and a blue T-shirt.

'Are you hungry?'

'I got a burger at the station.'

He nods.

'Did you eat already?' she sips her beer.

'I'll make something later.' He had waited deliberately thinking that he might cook them pasta and they could chat over dinner but she has already wandered off.

'Do you mind if I look around?' she calls from the living room.

'Go ahead. I'll show you your bedroom.'

She walks on ahead of him as he indicates his bedroom at the back, hers at the front, and the bathroom in the middle.

'I have an en suite, so you get the main bathroom to yourself. There's a box room there.' He indicates with a nod. 'It's a junk room, no need to go inside.' But he needn't have worried. Shelley heads to her room and without kicking off her boots she throws herself, beer in hand, on the bed. Froth from the beer bottle bubbles up and spills down her clothes and she laughs. 'I hope you have a washing machine?'

Tommy pulls the last of the bags into the room and watches

his niece lying on the bed looking appreciatively around the room. Then her eyes fix on him, and she stares.

'Well?' she asks.

He shifts uncomfortably. It's the second time this week that he's felt intimidate by a woman. First Marion, and now Shelley. By the time he had walked out with a gift for Elsie, he had grown to like Marion. Now he hopes it might be the same with Shelley but perhaps it might take a little longer.

'I'll be downstairs, if you need anything.'

* * *

Tommy feels a creeping sense of disappointment as he tosses the minced beef into the frying garlic and onions. He'd thought meeting his niece would be a joyful occasion, but after all this time, she'd managed to make him feel like Jeeves the butler. He is a stranger in his own home and now he can hear her clattering about upstairs, opening cupboards and drawers and banging the wardrobe. He wasn't used to it. No one had stayed with him and now he realised, clearly too late, that he liked his own company. He liked peace. He liked solitude.

He opens a second beer for himself and then finds an open bottle of red wine and splashes a healthy dose into the pan. The pasta is almost cooked. He opens a tin of chopped tomatoes and stirs it all carefully together.

He's serving his dinner into a bowl when Shelley appears. She's changed into her pyjamas, thick warm ones with rein-deers, and she's also wearing fluffy red bed socks. Distracted by a shopping bag on the corner of the worktop, she peers inside.

'What's this?' she pulls a bright purple sweater from the

bag.

'It's a present.'

'I hope you don't like whoever you bought it for.'

'It's from a very expensive boutique in town.'

'Take it back. Trust me. If there's anyone you know who would wear this, then they shouldn't be a friend. No one could have such bad taste.'

Tommy is unable to tell her the truth. He'd bought it for her mother.

'Have you got the Wifi code?'

He nods at the router on the windowsill. 'It's on that.' Then he sits at the table and eats slowly.

'I didn't know you were cooking pasta.'

'I asked if you were hungry.'

'I am now.' She stares at her phone, scrolls, types a few messages and when she's finished she looks up. Tommy pauses with his fork half way to his mouth. 'Help yourself.'

She finds a bowl, serves a good helping then sits at the table opposite him.

'Didn't you eat at the station?' he asks.

'I'm always hungry.' She glances at her phone on the table and it pings.

'I don't have many rules in the house but the first one is, no phones at the dining table.'

'You've just made that up.'

'Maybe, but it's a rule now. It's rude.'

She shrugs and turns her phone over so she can't see the screen.

He says, 'Your mum told me you're a vegan.'

She looks at him and then burst out laughing. 'She can never get anything right.' She shakes her head. 'Bless her, it's impossible.'

'What is?'

'Well, for a start. Pescatarians eat lots of vegetables, grains, beans and legumes like tofu. They also eat fruit and dairy products. So, on that basis, it's impossible for a vegan to be pescatarian because a vegan won't eat fish or dairy or any animal products.'

'Oh.'

'She always gets muddled up.'

'So, what do you eat?'

'Everything.' Her phone pings and she looks at it but decides to ignore it.

'Fish and meat?' He frowns.

She nods. 'I was a vegan for a while but that's because Daniel wouldn't have meat in the house.'

'Daniel?'

'My boyfriend.'

'Oh.'

'Well, my ex. We broke up.'

'Are you upset?'

She splutters dramatically. 'Are you joking? He was a control freak.'

Tommy eats as she explains her failed three-month relationship with a boy from Uni. He's only half listening and not really interested. He's more keen on trying to see the similarities in Elsie at this age. They have the same cheeky smile and dimples, and that way of looking over your shoulder into the distance, before settling their eyes back on you once they've decided on the right sentence. They both search for the right word with intensity and thought.

'Well, who wants to put up with that?' she asks.

Tommy stands up. 'There's yogurt for dessert.'

'That spag bol was good and I like yogurt. What would you have made if I was a vegan pescatarian?' She smiles.

'Mushrooms on toast.'

'So, how do you see this working out between us, Uncle Tommy?'

'Just call me Tommy,' he growls, putting a selection of yogurts on the table.

'Don't think that I'm going to be some sort of hausfrau. I'm not a cook or a cleaner and I'm certainly not a carer so don't get any ideas that I'll be running around after you. I'm going to get a job.'

'A job?' He sits down.

'Yes.'

'For a week?'

She smiles but this time she looks unsure. 'Mum told you, didn't she?'

'Told me what?'

'That I'm here for the summer?'

Tommy stares at her, thinking of the suitcases and trying frantically to remember the conversation with Elsie. He'd said a week. He may even have said a few weeks but certainly not the whole summer. 'She said you dropped out of uni.'

'I hated it. It was awful. Media Studies. Who wants to do that?'

'Then why did you choose it?'

'Dad said he wasn't paying for anything unless I went to uni.'

'So, he's stopped paying now?'

'Yes, that's why I need a job.'

'You could have done that in the first place.'

'I was looking after mum.' She frowns at him. 'Didn't she tell you?'

'No.'

'Oh, she can be a bit forgetful sometimes.'

Tommy wonders if Elsie has been deliberately forgetful or just manipulative, taking advantage of him.

Shelley reaches for a yogurt. 'I think she feels sorry that she hasn't seen you in all these years.'

'You do?'

'Yes. Dad's a real plank. Mum's better off without him.'

'Don't you get on with him?'

'I won't be babysitting anytime soon.'

Tommy laughs loudly and Shelley grins.

'What was Sunita like?' she asks quietly.

'She was very special. Very gentle, calm, quiet and thought-ful.'

'The opposite of me then.' She laughs.

He nods thoughtfully, wondering how the dynamics would be if Sunita was still here.

'I think mum regrets not getting to know her, you know, not giving you guys the opportunity.'

'Opportunity?'

'Yeah, to be friends. All this time has gone. All my life. And you guys have barely seen each other. She regrets it now. But it's a bit late. I think that's why she wanted me to come here. It's like she wants to share me, with you. I mean, you and Sunita never had kids so with me around it will be like you've, you know, suddenly got one.'

Tommy scratches his chin. This is complicated. 'How can you just inherit a twenty-year-old?'

Shelley shrugs.

Tommy shakes his head. 'I think she didn't know what to do with you.'

'She told you that?' Shelley pulls on her bottom lip. 'I was wondering what she told you. If she'd been honest.'

Tommy shrugs and scrapes the bottom of his empty yogurt pot.

'She's dying,' she says softly.

Tommy looks up, his spoon in the air. 'What?'

'She had cancer a few years ago and it's come back. I don't think she wants me around.'

Tommy says quietly, 'She never told me.'

'She was diagnosed a few days before Sunita died. She didn't want to burden you.'

* * *

Tommy lies in bed staring up at the ceiling. He's conscious that there's someone else in his home and that his niece is asleep in the spare room. He lies on his back thinking of Elsie and about all the possibilities — living or dying. Then his mind turns to Sunita, then to Shelley — this magnificent force of power and life and youth all bursting into his home — wrecking his peace.

There are so many coincidences going through his head. Elsie's first diagnosis with Sunita's passing, then Tommy's heart attack six months ago with Elsie's second cancer diagnosis. Shelley insisted that her mother had pushed her to go to uni and that she wanted her gone while she was going through another gruelling round of chemotherapy. Shelley told him her mother didn't want her daughter to be her carer.

'You have your life to live,' she'd told Shelley, and Tommy

could imagine Elsie saying that.

Elsie had been like that as a child. She was never the victim. She was always brave, positive and strong, and yet somehow the world, or fate, or whatever it was just kept hurling more crap at her.

Tommy remembers her as a young girl with hopes and dreams. They'd shared plans for their futures, but then they had grown apart. Time changes you. You evolve and you can only hope that you continue to like each other and want to be together.

There were lots of families that weren't close. How many times had one of Matt's gang complained about spending time with the in-laws, especially at Christmas. Families weren't all happy. It doesn't matter how rich or famous you are, there would always be jealousies, different versions of the truth, quarrels and disagreements. Sunita taught him that there was no shame in being wrong and that there didn't have to be a score card of good and bad. All it took was a recognition of being wrong, an apology, a kiss and then a line drawn under it. Move on.

And now Tommy can only describe this as catastrophic. His only sister, his nearest relative, is dying. Talk about running out of time. He rubs his face with his hand and he's surprised his cheeks are wet.

Where has the time gone?

After Shelley had told him the news his instinct had been to pick up the phone and talk to Elsie, but Shelley had stopped him.

'Let's find out why she's done this,' she suggested gently. 'You'll never find out the real reason if you ask her directly. She will lie and tell you what she thinks you ought to know.'

'So how do we find out?'

'Let's play for time and feed her what she wants to hear.'

'Like what?'

'Well, I will say I'm settling in nicely and that everything is great. Then you can tell her how wonderful and helpful I am in the house, and how lonely you were—'

'I wasn't.'

'She doesn't know that. I think she's sent me here so that if anything happens to her, we have each other. So, let her think it's worked so she has one less thing to worry about.'

'But she's on her own,' he cries.

'Margaret, her lovely friend and neighbour, always takes her on hospital visits and she'll look after her.'

Tommy sighs.

'Look, trust me. Let's see how it goes with us but in the meantime, tell her it's perfect and how great we're getting along and I can stay for the summer. That will stop her from worrying.'

Tommy had nodded slowly and agreed to give it more thought. But now he's in bed alone nothing seems to make sense. His only sister is running out of time and, if tonight was anything to go by, it was going to be a very long and exhausting summer with Shelley.

* * *

The next day Tommy heads into Harbour Street with the shopping bag tucked neatly under his arm. His stride is long and his determination resolute. Marion did tell him to bring it back if he wanted to. She had cast her hand around the shop. 'You could buy something different every day and then bring it back and exchange it. Just so long as it hasn't been worn, obviously.' She'd smiled. 'This could be a great way for us to get to know each other, Tommy.'

The thought of now seeing her bright red lips made him feel both nervous and excited. There are a group of women in the shop so he walks past it. He'd assumed it would be empty. He goes into Harbour Café and is pleased there's no queue and that Amber is behind the counter.

'Hi, Tommy. It's good to see you.'

He returns her smile. 'Hello, Amber. I'll have a white coffee, please.' He's conscious she might notice the name on the bag under his arm.

'Sitting in or heading to the harbour?'

'I'll go to the harbour.' He decides quickly, paying for the coffee.

'You might see Ben down there. He's looking at the kiosks.'

'I'll look out for him.' Tommy gives her a quick salute with his finger and picks up the coffee. It would be good to see Ben. He's sensible. He'd know what to do. Outside, Tommy weaves in and out of the crowds but then he catches a sign hanging in a shop window.

Jewellery isn't just for Valentine's Day.

He had said that once. It was Easter, their last together, although neither of them knew it at the time. He'd seen a pretty pair of pearl earrings that reminded him of the depths of the ocean and his deep love for Sunita. She had been surprised and delighted and he'd said that jewellery isn't just for Valentine's Day. Now he smiles at the memory.

Inside the shop someone waves at him. He can't see properly because of the sunlight, and he leans forward so his nose is touching the glass. He recognises the woman who had been with Ben and Amber a few weeks ago in the harbour. Although she'd been muffled up in the cold, he knew those brown dancing eyes. He turns to look over his shoulder to see if she's waving at someone else but she's smiling at him. He raises his hand. Then he looks down at the display cases and there's a pretty pair of silver seahorse earrings. He's always loved the sea and he's naturally drawn to the animals of the ocean, so he pushes open the door and steps inside.

'Hello,' she says. 'I thought I recognised you.'

She's wearing a lime green jump suit and a beige jumper. Her hair is tied up in a scrunchie, making her look young and vulnerable.

'I'm Tommy.'

'Yes, I'm Jane. Jane's Jewellery.' Her laugh is nervous and he wonders why. 'But of course, you must know that because that's why I'm in here. You know, on this side of the counter and...' her voice trails off and her smile wavers.

He points at the window. 'I like the sea horses.'

'Me too. Would you believe, I've only just put them in the window?' Her voice is excited and she speaks quickly, 'Would you like to see them? I only made them a few days ago and I wasn't sure if they were detailed enough. You never know if this sort of thing is going to sell, do you?' As she's talking she's already taking the earrings from the window and she lays them on the glass counter.

'They look very pretty.'

'Would you like to put your package here and have a proper look at them?' She points to a chair in the corner, and he wonders why anyone would sit and wait here. He puts down the package and picks up the earrings.

'They're very fine,' he says. 'And you made them?'

'I make most things in here.'

He looks around the shop for the first time. It's upmarket and exclusive. The displays are carefully designed to draw your eyes to matching sets; necklaces, bracelets, broaches and rings. He nods approvingly. He lifts them up to the light.

'The detail is amazing. How do you manage to make everything so small?'

'A magnifying glass helps.' She laughs. 'A big one.'

He grins. 'Of course.'

'You look like you have an eye for this sort of thing.'

'I just know what I like,' he replies honestly.

'That's a very lucky talent. I have lots of people in here who can never make up their minds. Sometimes they even ask my opinion as if they're my best friend or I'm going to know what their wife or husband or sister would like.'

'Really?'

'Yes, some people can be quite strange.'

'And others can't make a decision,' he adds.

'Exactly.'

'I'll take them,' he says.

'I haven't told you how much they are. In fact, I haven't even put a price tag on them yet. I was just about to do that when you came in.'

'That will save you a job then.'

'You may not like the price.'

'It doesn't matter.' He returns her smile and feels confident that she won't rip him off.

'Whoever they're for – she must be very special.'

'She is.'

'I'll gift wrap them for you.'

'Thank you.'

He watches her quietly as she takes out a piece of paper wrapping and a small red bow, then rings up the till. He's surprised at how reasonable they are. Half the price of the sweater in the bag.

'Are you going to the harbour?' she asks as he places the small box in his pocket.

'Yes.'

'It's a beautiful day.'

'Amber said that Ben is down there, so I hope to catch him.'

'I won't hold you up then. Have a good day.'

'Thank you.'

She calls out as he reaches the door. 'Tommy?'

He turns.

'You forgot your bag.'

He stares at it on the chair. He doesn't want to carry it around the harbour and now he doesn't want to take it back to the shop. He frowns and scratches his head.

'Is it a gift?' she asks. 'From the Très Chic Boutique?'

'It was but...'

'Is it to go back to the shop?'

'Yes.'

'I can take it for you.'

'Really?'

'Yes, I'll ask for a credit note.'

'Will she do that?'

'Marion? I'm sure she will.'

'That would be very kind.'

'I'll pop down later, so call in next time you're passing and I'll give it to you.'

'I'd be very grateful.'

'It's no bother.'

March

Jane

There is something special about March that Jane loves. Spring shakes away the winter, the nights become shorter and brighter, and there's a promise of warmer and happier days ahead.

With Christmas and New Year firmly over, Jane is keeping busy, making jewellery and selling online. She barely has time to look up let alone have any more dates. In fact, since that last disaster with Gordon in the city, and meeting Yusef on the way home, Jane has abstained from even thinking about men. She doesn't want a relationship. She's even stayed off the dating sites.

It's time to focus on her business. There is no way that she's going to let her reputation slip. She didn't want people to talk about her like they did about Marion who virtually lives in The Ship and flirts with any man she sees. The locals, and especially other shop owners in Harbour Street, know what she's like and Jane is determined not to be associated with her.

It's almost five o'clock when Jane steps into the boutique.

Their greeting is polite but wary. Jane opens the package.

Marion looks confused. 'I don't recognise it,' she says, pushing the sweater back at Jane. 'It's not from here.'

Jane pulls out the receipt. 'Tommy asked me to drop it back for him.'

Marion is clearly annoyed. 'It will have to be a gift receipt.'

'That's fine. Thank you.'

'That's strange you bringing it back. Do you know Tommy well?' Marion asks, taking the receipt.

'Not really.'

'He's a fine catch, for a fisherman.' Marion laughs at her own joke.

Jane smiles briefly. She's in a hurry and she doesn't have time for Marion's smutty comments. She knows Marion is flirtatious and doesn't care if men are married. Marion just wants a good time and once she's had a drink or three, then any man was fair game. It was no wonder Tommy hadn't wanted to come back to the shop.

'You're not married, are you Jane?'

Jane hates it when certain women make a point of stating the obvious so she turns away pretending not to have heard. She pulls out a pretty dress with a floral design. It isn't her style and nothing in the shop would match her baggy, colourful dungarees. Besides, the price was more than Jane takes home a month.

'Jane?'

'Um?'

'You haven't come back to the dance classes?'

'I've been busy.'

'Dating?'

'Working.'

'At night?' Marion raises her eyebrows suggestively.

'I'm selling lots of jewellery online and I catch up with my orders when I get home.'

'Lucky you! I didn't make any money when Covid was happening and I had to shut the boutique. I was almost bankrupt.'

'The government helped though?'

'Well, to be honest, I was going to close before Covid, but I've managed to keep going. I suppose not going to the pub for months on end saved me a fortune, although the supermarket did well out of me.' She laughs. 'Every little helps.'

Jane takes the gift voucher.

'Why don't you come out one night? Rachael and I go to the pub after class. You could meet up with us. Rachael's a right laugh and I think you'd like her if you got to know her.'

'Thanks.'

'Look, Jane, us single women have to stick together. You know the song.' She begins singing a Rihanna song, wiggling her hips and raising her hands in the air. 'I'm a single lady, I'm a single lady. Put your hands up.' She bursts out laughing. 'We have great fun. Ronnie and his band sing every Thursday in The Ship and they have a new group starting on Wednesday. Did you know that Wednesday night is the new Friday night? So many people are working from home and they go out more often because they're not commuting and can stay in bed longer the next day. And did you know that over half the people who work from home, work in their pyjamas? I mean, when they go online they put a bit of makeup on, but you know, it's all a bit more free and easy. To be honest, I think I was born in the wrong era.'

Jane considers this for a minute and then replies, 'I don't

think kids drink very much now. In fact, I read that most of them haven't had or don't even have sex, not like in the sixties.'

'Ooh, you are a dark horse, Jane. Who would have thought you knew stuff like that? I bet you're on those dating apps. I must look up your profile. Perhaps I can help you find someone. I'll check you out on Tinder and let you know.'

Jane shakes her head. 'I'm not on dating sites.'

'Then you should be. I can set you up a profile, if you like?'

'No. Thanks. It's not necessary.'

Marion stares at her. 'Oh, I get it. The proverbial penny has just dropped. Are you gay? Is that why you hang about with Amber?'

'Amber?'

'Well, you must know she moved here with her girlfriend, Cassie? Didn't you meet her? She was a really lovely girl — we got on really well — she wasn't at all like Amber. I think Amber's tough and it's no wonder she ended up with Ben. Are you like that? Do you swing both ways?'

'No.'

'Maybe you like younger men, do you? Have you seen that Ozan and Yusef? I can never work out which one I fancy more.'

'They're children.' Jane's tone is acid and she turns to go.

'Well, lucky you, having that eye candy opposite you. If I were you, I'd be staring at the barbers watching those boys all day. I wouldn't get any work done. They're so sexy!'

'Marion, please.' Jane holds up her hand.

Marion steps back and looks offended. 'I thought you were one of the girls.'

'I am, but I don't like referring to men, even boys, as if they're cattle at a market any more than I would like it if they did it to us.'

'Take my word for it. They do it all the time, baby.'

Behind Jane, the doorbell tinkles, and it's Jane's excuse to leave but she pauses in her stride as a tall, leggy girl with electric red hair pushes past.

'Is the manager here?' she asks.

Marion looks up at her. 'I'm the owner. Does that count?'

'Depends. Do you have any jobs?'

'For you?'

'Yeah.'

Marion eyes her up and down. 'Well, I like your dinosaur dungarees; the only other person brave enough to wear anything around here, like that, is her.' She nods at Jane and the girl turns to look her up and down. 'And she's old enough to be your mother.'

* * *

It's Tuesday evening when Amber persuades Jane to go for a drink in The Ship.

'It's the best night to come here,' says Amber. 'They have live music most nights and it's packed.'

Jane spots Marion and Rachael on the far side of the bar with a group of men and she turns quickly away.

'Hello, ladies.' Paul, the manager, smiles. 'Good to see you both.'

'Is Ricky working tonight? Amber asks.

'No, he's studying but Faisal is in the kitchen picking up some extra pay.'

Amber smiles.

'How do you know all these people?' Jane asks as Paul

prepares their drinks.

'You must have met Faisal. He works in the café with me and sometimes in the Bistro. He's a refugee and he's doing really well. He's friends with Ricky and Ahmed, Femi's two boys.'

'The lovely Femi,' Jane says. 'She's perfectly matched with Lawrence.'

'Femi helped us, last year, to get all the paperwork and training to be foster parents.'

They head to a table beside the fire.

'It must make a change for you to be served drinks?' Jane says.

'I won't lie. It's great to have an evening off. There's no point opening the Bistro every night in the winter but it will be all go again from April.'

'And you definitely want to manage a kiosk too?' Jane sips her drink.

Amber grins. 'It does seem a crazy idea, but you never know until you try.'

They're distracted by a group of lads coming into the bar, laughing and joking and teasing each other. Amber waves and Jane looks away but then she feels a hand on her shoulder.

'Hello, gorgeous ladies. What are two beautiful women doing out in a pub unescorted?'

Amber laughs. 'Hello Yusef. Are you all celebrating?'

'It's our cousin's birthday and we are obliged to take him out.' He places his hand on his heart and bows but his left hand rests on the back of Jane's chair. He touches her hair and she leans away.

'Another cousin?' she says.

'We have hundreds.' He laughs.

'It's a week night,' Amber says. 'You'll feel rotten tomorrow.'

He nods seriously. 'The last time I drank too much I met a very beautiful woman who invited me back to her house and we made love all night.'

Amber laughs. 'Too much information.'

Jane's face flushes. 'Don't let us keep you.' She stares icily at him.

He smiles back at her. 'Time with you, is never wasted.' He places his hand on her shoulder and she shrugs him off.

'I think your friends are looking for you at the bar.' Amber nods to where Ozan is waving and beckoning for Yusef to join them.

'Then I shall bid you beautiful ladies, goodnight.' He blows a kiss to each of them and Amber pretends to catch it. After he's gone, Jane stares into her glass.

Amber asks. 'Did he upset you?'

'He's drunk.'

'Yeah, but he's young. Didn't we all do it when we were his age? I know I did.' Amber puts her glass to her lips and regards the boys. 'They're harmless and Ozan and Yusef work really hard. It's good to see them enjoying themselves.'

The pub door opens and Tommy strides in with a red-headed girl in tow. They stand at the bar and Jane recognises the girl who asked Marion for a job. She's wearing a pink puffer jacket and skinny ripped jeans. She has long, false, purple nails that she taps on the bar while in deep conversation with Tommy.

'That must be Tommy's niece,' Amber says. 'He said she was coming to stay.'

'She's a pretty girl.'

Amber grins. 'I think the boys approve.'

The boys are checking out the girl but after a few minutes they turn away. Some are on their phones as if they're sharing photos, showing their screens to each other and laughing.

'How did we ever manage before mobiles?' Jane asks, wondering how soon she could leave. Yusef had touched her hair with such familiarity that it had both shocked and excited her and now she watched him drinking shots.

'So, about the kiosk.' Amber leans across the table so her back is to the bar. 'I think I might give it a go. I think you should too, Jane. Ben seemed optimistic that we can share staff and we can help each other out.'

'Really?'

'We have a foster boy with us now—'

'How's it going?'

Amber replies, 'We passed all the training and we've had all the checks. Noah has only been with us a few days. He's sixteen but he's very shy. He barely speaks so it might be good for him to help out. We can all keep an eye on things between us...'

'You think it will work?'

Amber nods enthusiastically. 'I've chosen our kiosk. Perhaps you'll take one one too? That's why I thought we'd celebrate with a drink.' Amber lifts her empty glass.

Jane's heart sinks. She knows it's her round. She has to go to the bar. She moves slowly, pulling her jacket over her waist and slides up to the far side of the bar, away from the boys and Tommy and his niece.

While she's waiting, Tommy raises his hand. She smiles back and then remembers that she has his refund in the shop. She doesn't want him to think she's kept it so, once she has the drinks, she walks back to the table via Tommy and whispers.

'Call into the shop, I have your refund.'

His eyes light up. 'Thanks, Jane.'

She looks at the girl, checking out Shelley's silver-cubed earrings.

'They weren't for her.' He grins. 'They were for someone else. This is Shelley.'

Jane smiles. 'Hello Shelley, I saw you in the boutique.'

'Yeah?' Shelley looks at her and then grins. 'Oh, yes, the dungaree lady.'

Over Shelley's shoulder Yusef is staring at her. It's a powerful and dangerous gaze then he's distracted. He whispers something to the boys and they look over to where Jane is standing and they burst out laughing.

Suddenly embarrassed and with her cheeks flaming red, Jane excuses herself and strides back to the table where Amber is messaging on her phone, completely oblivious to the incident at the bar.

She slides the drinks onto the table and from the corner of her eye, she sees Yusef on his phone and that's when Jane's iPhone pings in her pocket.

She pulls it out.

I have to see you again — urgently. Yx.

* * *

Marion is shrieking with laugher at the bar. Distracted, Amber and Jane turn toward the commotion where Yusef has his arms around Marion's waist. She has wrapped her arm across his shoulder and is gazing adoringly into his eyes.

Jane's heart sinks.

'Gosh, it's all go tonight.' Amber grins.' I thought we'd have the place to ourselves. If Yusef's not careful, Marion will eat him alive.'

Jane watches the show. Marion is clearly entertaining the boys and they're laughing. She swings around Yusef's neck, clearly worse for wear. Her skirt rises up and she plants a kiss on Yusef's cheek.

'Should we do something?' Jane asks.

'Marion's a cougar. The younger the better.'

Jane feels a stab of envy and fear. What if Yusef went off with her tonight? Sickness rises in her throat.

'Do you want to go?' Amber asks.

Jane can't stop watching them. The drunken show is punishing and agonising. Marion pulls away from Yusef, slapping his bottom before heading for Tommy. She pushes her arm through Shelley's and grins flirtatiously, while pushing her breasts towards Tommy.

'There's nothing worse than a drunk woman.' Jane continues angrily, 'I think they're worse than men.' Her cheeks sting at the hypocrisy of her angry tone. Only last month she had been like Marion. She had pulled Yusef off the street and into her home. Now she feels guilty and ashamed. Who is she to judge?

'You can't put every drunk woman in the same category as Marion,' Amber says evenly.

Tommy roars with laughter.

Jane shakes her head feeling suddenly very angry. 'Let's go.'

* * *

At home, in the quiet sanctuary of her bedroom, Jane undresses quickly. Her ears are still ringing from the raucous laughter. They were having so much fun while she slid out the side door with Amber.

She relishes the comfort of her soft pyjamas, but then her iPhone pings.

I'm outside. X

She types back immediately.

Go home.

I have to talk to you. XX

You're drunk.

I want to tell you something. 2 minutes. Please. XXX

Jane pauses before replying.

I'll talk to you tomorrow.

Now. This can't wait. I'll tell you through the letterbox. Come downstairs? XXXX

Jane tiptoes downstairs without putting on a light. Yusef's body is outlined against the glass. He must sense her presence because he pushes open the letter box and whispers.

'Jane? Are you there?'

She giggles. 'Of course, I am. It's not a bloody seance.'

His body collapses with helpless laughter and he slumps on her step.

'You have to go home, Yusef. You're drunk and you have to work in the morning.'

He slurs, 'I think I love you.'

'No, you don't.'

'Why do you say that?'

'Because you've told everyone about us. I can't trust you.'

'You can,' he says angrily. 'I didn't tell anyone.'

'You all turned and laughed at me.'

'I told them I thought you were the most beautiful woman in the pub.'

'That's not funny. It's embarrassing.'

'It's the truth.'

Jane sighs. 'Go home, Yusef.'

'Will you come out with me one night? We could have dinner?'

'No.'

'Please.'

'Yusef, I'm tired and I need to sleep.'

'Can I talk to you tomorrow?'

'Maybe.'

'Maybe?' He sits up a little straighter. 'Can I bring you coffee and we can chat?'

'Only if you promise to go home now.'

She sees his outline stumble against the wall as he rises to his feet. 'Tomorrow?'

'Yes, goodnight.'

'I love you, Jane.'

'Go home.'

'Only because I love you.'

'Goodnight.'

'Goodnight, beautiful angel.'

Jane grins and walks back upstairs. He's got that wrong. That's one thing that Jane isn't — an angel.

* * *

Jane has served two customers and finished soldering a bracelet when she looks up to see Tommy in the doorway. She pulls off her magnifying goggles, stands up from her desk and meets him at the counter.

'Morning, it's a fresh one out there,' he says, rubbing his hands.

'I thought you'd be used to all weathers.'

'I think I've grown soft.' He grins. 'There was a time when a force 9 gale wouldn't have taken it out of me, but I guess as we grow older we get more vulnerable.'

'You're not old, Tommy.'

He smiles. 'I don't feel old but my body has betrayed me. It was a shock having a heart attack. It's the sort of thing that happens to other people, not me.'

'But you've made a full recovery?'

'I think so, but my days at sea are over and when a chapter closes—'

'Another one opens,' she adds.

He laughs.

'I've got your gift voucher here.' She reaches for the envelope under the counter and slides it across to him.

'I don't suppose I'll use it.'

Jane smiles. 'Is Shelley going to work there?'

Tommy shrugs. 'Marion can't decide. She thinks she might need some help at Easter but who knows...?'

'Everywhere gets busy from Easter. Shelley is bound to pick up work if she wants it.'

'She needs a job now. It's not good for a young girl to be sitting around on her phone every day, is it?'

Jane shakes her head then to her utter dismay she sees Yusef walking past the window with a take-out coffee and before she's had time to think he's opened the door and he's standing right in front of them.

'Here you go, my angel.' He places the coffee on the counter and slaps Tommy on the shoulder and laughs. 'Hey, Tommy, my man, long time no see. How you doing?' They fist bump.

'How's your head?' Tommy grins back at him. 'You were well on your way last night.'

'I was the first to leave.'

'Aye, you were.'

'That's because....' In a loud stage whisper he says, 'I'm in love.'

Tommy laughs. 'I hope you didn't go and see her in that state.'

'I did, you know, Tommy, I did.' He winks at him and then smiles at Jane. 'What do you think?'

Jane answers slowly, 'I think you should be very careful.'

'Why?' He smiles.

'She might appreciate discretion.' Jane stares hard at him.

'Ah, well in that case, I'd best be off. Enjoy your coffee, my-beautiful-neighbour-in-the-jewellery-shop-across-the-road.'

'What do I owe you,' Jane calls to his retreating back.

He pauses at the door and turns before he waves. 'I'll think of something.'

After he's gone Tommy looks thoughtfully at the coffee on the counter as if it's a chess piece and he's not quite sure what to do with it.

'That was kind of him,' Jane says, to break his train of thought. 'Would you like to share it with me, I can pour half into a mug?'

Tommy holds up his hand. 'No, thank you. I..., I didn't know that everyone was so friendly in Harbour Street and that they bring coffee to you. I'll know for next time.'

Jane smiles. 'You're always welcome here, Tommy — with

or without coffee.' Then with a sudden stab of realisation that she's flirting and sounding like Marion, she adds quickly. 'And please do bring your wife one day, I'd like to meet her.'

He stares at her and in a very quiet voice he says, 'Sunita died.'

* * *

The embarrassment of Yusef bringing Jane coffee and flirting with her is nothing compared to the sick feeling when Tommy tells her that his wife is dead.

She stares at him in shock.

The shop is still and peaceful but suddenly a cuckoo calls the hour and jumps from the clock on the wall. Jane's startled. The universe is playing a very sick joke.

Tommy looks at the wall with bewilderment as if realising where he is.

'I'm so, so, sorry, I had no idea.' She stumbles over her words. 'Sodding clock! I'm so sorry.'

Tommy holds up his hand. 'Please don't be, Jane. It was four years ago.'

Jane disappears and returns a moment later with an empty mug. She pours half of her coffee into it and nods at the chair.

'Please, I'm not busy.'

He takes the coffee and sits down seeming grateful for the warm drink.

Jane is overcome with a sense of protection. 'When I met you in the harbour,' she says, 'Amber insisted that I must have seen you walking around town with your wife — she said she was a beautiful Iranian lady — and I just assumed she was... alive.'

He shakes his head. 'It's an easy mistake and you're not the first.'

'Death is so final,' Jane says. 'I lost my dad a few years ago and it's like my whole world crumbled. But you must have been through hell.'

Tommy stares at her. 'It's life, isn't it? We just have to get on with things.'

Jane nods. 'Life is never the same after you lose someone special.'

'Too much time on your hands.'

'Tell me about it.' Jane laughs and points around the shop. 'Far too much time.'

He speaks slowly, 'You see, the thing is, when you're living in the moment everything is taken for granted. I see it with Shelley. She's not grateful for what she has. She's not worried about life or death, or anything really. She lives in real time. In the moment. She's not fretting about the past or the future, about dropping out of uni or getting a job or anything. I was always like that but then suddenly — bang! Life throws you a curved ball and your whole life is in smithereens.' He shakes his head. 'I used to believe in God. When I was a fisherman, I'd say my prayers and God answered me. I could hear his voice on the wind. I could feel him lifting me over the waves and I could feel his hand on my back guiding me back to shore. But then...' he pauses. Jane waits, sipping her coffee slowly. 'Then, well, Sunita who was pure goodness, kindness personified, hits a sheet of black ice and the car hits a tree. She dies instantly. There's no time for goodbyes or I love yous. It's all just... over. One minute she's there and the next minute the house is empty, as if she's flown away and taken my soul with her.' Tommy rubs a hand over his face. 'Sorry, I'm not sure where all that came from.'

'That's okay. I understand.'

The shop door opens and Jane recognises a client who has come to collect a watch. She wants to shout that she's closed, she's not working. She wants to push the customer outside but she can't.

Tommy stands up quickly.

She watches helplessly as he places his mug on the counter, and without a word, walks out into the street.

'I've come for my Cartier,' the woman says, beaming proudly, 'I hope you've managed to fix it?'

* * *

Jane spends the next few weeks working harder than ever. She's had a big order from Seattle and by the time she's made everything, and boxed it all up and sent it off, she's exhausted. She's also emotionally drained.

Listening to Tommy talking about Sunita has reminded her of the loss of her father and she finds a jigsaw that she'd once done with him. It's a very old one: Trooping the Colour with Queen Elizabeth II on horseback and hundreds of Lifeguards. It's painstaking because they all wear the same red uniform, bearskin hats and white plumes. The only thing to tell them apart is the shade and the sunshine.

Jane leans over the kitchen table. Her back is sore and her eyes are tired but she knows it's a good way to occupy her mind. With her father she had always started with the square edges then they had each taken a different part of the photo, either sky or horses, or the sandy coloured floor of Horse Guards Parade.

When she met Dave, he did jigsaws differently. He would hold up the picture on the box then pick up each jigsaw, piece by piece, and try and match the colours with the picture on the box before laying them on the table in the approximate place he thought matched the picture. When they first met, she was delighted and fascinated, but by the end of their relationship it irritated her and she wanted to throw the whole lot at him.

She wouldn't be feeling so much angst and so confused if she hadn't gone to the supermarket earlier this evening. It had seemed like a good idea to pop out and buy some eggs to make an omelette for supper, but as she walked home she happened to glance in the window of Harbour Bistro. She'd slowed her pace thinking she'd see Amber or Ben, but the only person she saw was Tommy.

He was sitting in rapt conversation with a woman who was leaning provocatively across the table showing off her deep cleavage and biting her red lips playfully and in a seductive manner.

As Jane searches for the piece of the puzzle with the face of the Queen's horse, she's wondering about the sea horse earrings. If Tommy's wife has passed away and they were not for Shelley, then who were they for?

* * *

Jane closes the shop at lunchtime and Yusef waves at her from the barbers. She raises her hand but doesn't stop. She heads toward the harbour, passing under the Harbour Street clock and past the rows of fishermen selling cockles, mussels, shrimps, crabs and lobsters. There's a short queue at the fish and chip shop and Jane navigates her way past the coffee shop and through the small Artisan market.

She pauses at the quayside. The tide is high and there are a few fishing boats moored in the harbour. It's too early in the year for the pleasure crafts that take tours along the coast and even the yacht club in the small marina is closed. At the weekend, Jane likes to sit on the beach and watch the regattas — small dinghies and catamarans — race around orange buoys. But today, it's still March and very quiet.

She leans on the railing for a while. This is where she first saw Tommy and she's determined to find him. It's been a week since their conversation about his wife and she's worried. She's also been looking out for Shelley, but she hasn't seen either of them.

Gulls squawk overhead and Jane looks up. The sun appears from behind a cloud and she sighs. She's worked so hard she's forgotten what daylight is like. She closes her eyes enjoying the warmth on her face.

'Doesn't it feel good?'

'Yes.' She doesn't open her eyes.

'I thought I saw you walking in this direction.'

Jane doesn't reply.

'I'd like to finish our conversation.'

'Now?'

'Yes.'

'Here?'

'Well, I would prefer to take you home to bed but—'

Jane's eyes fly open and she steps away. 'Shush, Yusef. Anyone might hear you.'

'No, they won't. Look, this place is deserted.'

'That's not the point. I don't want you talking to me like that. Anytime. Anywhere.'

'Okay, calm down, baby-cheeks.'

'I'm not your baby-cheeks.'

'You're prickly today.'

'Yusef, you must stop! Please. This is becoming tiresome. You're a really nice guy and I'm really sorry about what happened—'

'You are?'

'Yes, of course.'

'But you enjoyed it.'

'That's not the point. It should never have happened. It was wrong.'

'How could something so wrong, feel so right?'

'You've nicked that line from a song.' Jane laughs.

Yusef grins. 'You guessed.'

Jane sighs. 'Can we please just be friends again, like we were?'

'No fringe benefits?'

'No benefits of any kind. Just normal shopkeepers, working in harmony—'

'Who love each other.'

'Who *respect* each other.'

Yusef turns and leans against the rails. 'So, you're definitely not interested?'

'Definitely.'

'Don't say I didn't offer.'

'I won't.'

Yusef nods. 'Alright. I'm sorry, Jane. But you really are a very special lady and I hope you meet someone nice one day.'

'Thank you.'

'Right, I'll head back to work now. I'll see you around.'

'Yes, thank you, Yusef.'

'Just one thing, I do suggest that you change your Tinder profile, even I know it's you.' He grins.

'Get out of here.' Jane punches his shoulder playfully and she watches him walk away with his cocky gait, smiling and whistling without a care in the world. She laughs, her heart suddenly much lighter, feeling free.

'I think he's got a crush on you.'

Jane turns around and she's staring right into Tommy's smiling eyes.

* * *

The sunlight catches his eyes, and he looks relaxed and pleased to see her. 'I'm glad I found you. I've been wanting to catch up with you since—'

'Me too.' Jane replies.

'Is that why you're here?'

'One of the reasons, but I'm actually enjoying the sunshine.'

'Come on, let's sit on the beach for a while. Do you have time?'

Jane checks her watch. 'I have twenty minutes until I have to open the shop again.'

Tommy nods and takes her arm, guiding her along the harbour. It seems a natural thing for him to do, but she can't help but wonder if he did the same with Marion. Did he take her home? Did they sleep together? And if they did, is it any concern of hers?

Tommy looks out at sea. 'I like coming to the harbour, but it does make me feel redundant.'

'So, you're retired now?'

'I suppose I am.'

'But you will have to do something, won't you?'

He frowns as he indicates a bench for them to sit. 'Will I?'

'Aren't you bored? What do you do each day?'

'Well, that's what I want to talk to you about I need some advice.'

Jane stares at him wondering what possible advice he could be seeking from her.

'The thing is, it's very strange having a twenty-year-old in the house. And, she's a woman.'

Jane smiles. 'What's the problem?'

'Well, in the beginning, she was in her bedroom most of the time on her phone. You know what kids are like. I'd ask her to eat dinner with me, which she did at first. Then she wasn't hungry, or she'd eaten a burger or something else out, and now I hardly see her.'

'Where does she go?'

Tommy shrugs. 'I don't know. How can you ask a young woman what she's doing? I'm her uncle and I barely know her.'

Jane looks out to sea and watches a plane overhead leave a vapour trail.

'How long is she staying?'

'Probably for the summer.'

'Gosh!' Jane grins. 'You'll have to sort something out then.'

'I know.' Tommy shakes his head and leans forward with his arms resting on his knees. 'If Sunita were here, she would know about stuff like this but, well, now she's not here, I don't know who else to ask.'

'Have you asked Amber?'

'Amber and Ben are so busy. I did mention summer work for Shelley and Amber said to speak to her later, but I'm worried about now — today, this week.'

'Well, you need to communicate with her. Does she have any hobbies?'

'I don't know. I've hardly spoken to her.'

'I saw you in the pub and you were talking a lot.'

'She'd had a message from a boyfriend. He missed her and he was bothering her. She said that if she didn't get out of the house, she would go mad and that she didn't want to go into a pub on her own.'

'Well, that's a start but what did you talk about?'

Tommy sighs. 'Her mum — my sister, Elsie.'

'Oh.'

'She has cancer and Shelley is worried she might not pull through.'

'That's awful.'

'Yes.'

'What can you do?'

'Well,' he pauses, thinks and he seems to make a decision. 'Elsie and her husband — Shelley's father — didn't approve of Sunita because she was a foreigner, so we had no contact for almost twenty years. I saw Shelley once when she was about six or eight, and that was it, so we're not close. But then after Shelley's father left them Elsie got cancer the first time. It was when Sunita died. She didn't want to tell me, but now she's asked me to look after Shelley. What do you think that tells me?'

'It's not good.' Jane says, taking all this information on board and trying to assess the information without being overly emotional. 'But, you clearly need to talk to Shelley and be open and honest.'

'I think it might be easier if there's a third person, you know, to help us navigate the conversation. She might make more of an effort, you know, if there's another woman there.'

'Oh.' Jane is wondering about Marion. Is that what he wants Marion to do? To help him form a bond with Shelley? Is that why they went out for dinner?

'Would you come for dinner?'

'Me?'

He laughs. 'Yes, you.'

'Why me?'

'I think she would like you and you both wear dungarees.'

Jane looks at her watch and stands up, she wasn't sure what she was hoping for, but it certainly wasn't this.

'I was thinking we could all go for a burger?' His eyes widen hopefully.

Jane stares at him and she doesn't quite know what to say. She gets a burger and Shelley, while Marion gets the Harbour Bistro and a bottle of expensive French wine.

* * *

The following evening they go to the burger bar in the square opposite the church. Jane had hoped that they might even upgrade their dining options to the Italian, but Shelley is insistent and, like a lot of her generation, Jane believes she is completely lacking in introspection. There's a sense of entitlement, arrogance and a hint of rudeness. Shelley ignores the waiter and pushes past him to the table beside the window. Without looking at anyone, she pulls her phone out of her pocket and starts scrolling.

'You know the rules,' Tommy says. 'Put it away, please.'

'But we haven't ordered yet,' she replies.

'It doesn't matter. This is our time, when we get to chat to each other.'

Shelley scowls at him and puts her mobile in her back pocket. They spend a few minutes discussing the menu and after the waiter has taken their order Jane sits back to regard Tommy's interaction with his niece. She's still not quite sure what he wants her to do. It's not as if she has experience with children either.

'Shelley's staying with me for a few months,' Tommy explains to Jane unnecessarily but she takes the cue.

'This is a great opportunity for you,' she says smiling at Shelley.

'Why?' Shelley seems genuinely puzzled.

'Well, it's a long holiday beside the sea, in a lovely place.'

Shelley looks out of the window. 'It is a pretty place.'

'You like it?'

Shelley nods.

'Do you swim in the summer or do any sport?'

'Not really. I like swimming if it's warm enough. I usually go away with dad and his family to Greece for a few weeks — that's nice.'

They take about holiday destinations for a while and Tommy warms to the subject telling them the places he and Sunita travelled to and he tells a story of how their suitcase went missing and Sunita made him go swimming in his boxer shorts.

Shelley stares at him and Jane smiles politely. Fortunately, the waiter arrives with their burgers. They're not Jane's favourite and as the others pick up the food in their hands and eat chips with their fingers, she does the same. The conversation naturally falls silent as they eat, murmuring her appreciation, Jane is pleasantly surprised. She hadn't realised she was so hungry.

'I've never eaten here before,' she admits.

Tommy raises his eyebrows. 'Best food in town.'

'Don't let Amber hear you say that,' Jane replies, and when Tommy's face darkens, she quickly looks at Shelley. 'Do you like to cook?'

'I make a good roast chicken.'

Tommy seems impressed. 'I'll make a note of that.'

'What other hobbies do you have?' Jane's enthusiasm for making conversation is diminishing as fast as her burger and when Shelley shrugs, Jane stares out of the window.

'Perhaps if you could meet some young people your age, that would help,' she says.

Shelley looks at her with interest.

'There's Femi's boy, Ricky, who works in the pub and his friend Faisal who works for Amber. They must be about your age.'

'Ricky has a girlfriend now,' Tommy says. 'He's only about seventeen but there's always Karl from the café and Molly.'

'Karl is older, I think.' Jane frowns. 'It's hard to keep up with them all.'

'I like Karl's style, he's a cool Rastafarian.' Shelley nods. 'I met him in the café.'

'Have you done any bar work or waitressing?'

Shelley shakes her head. 'Dad always gave me an allowance.'

'What about craftwork? There are lots of craft stalls, art-work and galleries, would any of that interest you?

Shelley shakes her head. Her phone pings in her pocket and she jumps up. 'I need the bathroom.'

After she's left the table, Tommy shakes his head. 'She's

hard work, isn't she?'

Jane smiles. 'It's an age thing.'

'Do you think it will get better?'

Jane laughs. 'I think you're asking the wrong person.'

'You're doing really well, at least she's responding to you.' Tommy orders the bill, and while he pays Jane looks out of the window, wondering how she would feel if Shelley were her daughter. What would she do?'

Shelley returns to the table and Jane says to her, 'I like your rings. They're interesting.'

Shelley holds up her hands, she has a ring on each finger, bronze, silver, iron, some are flowers and there's even a skull on her thumb. Jane spends a while looking at them. They are cheaply made, costume jewellery that's sold in accessories shops popular with young people.

'I make jewellery,' Jane says.

'Do you?' Shelley looks interested.

'I have a shop in town and I sell jewellery.'

'Do you like this?' Shelley pulls put a silver necklace from her t-shirt with half a heart. There's an inscription on the back but Jane can't read it.

'It's very pretty.' Jane knows it's cheap but it must mean a lot to Shelley. 'Who has the other half of the heart?'

'Well, that's the thing. I have it.'

Jane smiles. 'Did you buy them both?'

'Yeah, you see, what happens is, you wear it and then when you find the one you love, then you give him the other half. That's how you know you've met, *the one.*'

'That's an interesting concept. What's on the back?'

Shelley turns it over but half of the words are missing. 'When the two halves are together it says, *Together forever, never to be separated.*

'How beautiful.'

'Isn't it a neat idea?'

'It's very clever.'

Tommy leans across the table. 'So, you both end up wearing half a heart?'

'Yes, and when we are together we will be a whole heart.'

'That's very romantic. Do you have anyone in mind that you would like to give it to?' Jane asks.

Shelley shakes her head decisively. 'I thought I did, but you can't trust anyone. Everyone lets you down in the end so I'm going to be really careful next time.'

Jane nods. 'That's sensible.'

'Perhaps you should make these in your shop. I think you'd do really well and you'll probably make a fortune.'

'You could be right.'

'I could help, if you like?'

Jane looks at Shelley's big earnest eyes, and sees more enthusiasm than she's seen all evening. Across the table, Tommy is smiling and nodding enthusiastically. Jane thinks quickly. She didn't sign up for an assistant. This isn't why she's here and she feels cornered into a situation that she can't wiggle out of. 'If you want to come by the shop sometime, I could show you the things I make—'

Shelley's phone pings. Distracted, she stands up. 'Are we going Tommy? Have you paid? I'll meet you outside.' Then she disappears into the darkness of the street, leaving Tommy with his mouth turned down and his hands upturned on the table.

'What do you think?' he asks. 'It's gone well, hasn't it?'

Jane looks at him. It wasn't quite the evening she had

planned but she smiles brightly. 'Let's see what happens next.'

* * *

It's Easter in Harbour Street. Jane knows it will be a busy weekend. She's changing the window displays, swapping rings for necklaces and bracelets and she pauses to look outside. Secretly, Jane is congratulating herself on what her dad would have called her business acumen. It's a sixth sense and Jane often looks at the other shops in the street thinking about the business models for their business.

She's always surprised that at the top end of Harbour Street, Kingdom Pet Shop and Mobile2Go phone shop, survive. They never seem to be that busy and she knows, from experience, that the rent in this street is astronomical.

Yesterday she saw Shelley in Marion's Très Chic Boutique. Jane only caught a quick glance. She couldn't stand and stare, but she was sure she saw Shelley behind the counter. It looks like she's working for Marion now. That's another business model where stock appeals to locals and tourists alike. It's expensive, but Marion does very well all year round.

Ian the grocer stocks a wide variety of seasonal produce but Derek the butcher doesn't have to worry as much - probably BBQ food in the summer and turkeys at Christmas so that's pretty simple. Then Eva, in Darling Buds & Blooms, also does well all year round. She has developed a great reputation and supplies bars, restaurants and hotels with regular fresh flowers. Eva, originally from Poland, works hard. Jane knows that she's divorced and for a while Jane thought that she was dating Sanjay, the handsome film-star looking owner of the

Indian takeaway, but after his father died at Christmas he went back to India and his cousins now run the business.

Jane wonders if Eva is lonely. Occasionally, she sees her twins in town when they come home from University. Perhaps they would be good friends for Shelley. Amber had suggested they may work in the kiosks in the summer.

She glances across the road to The Grooming Room where Yusef and Ozan are both busy. They don't look in her direction. Beside her shop, Kit and Jenna, the owners of From The Heart Gift Shop, are hard-working, juggling their two children with a busy business. This morning, Kit is hanging colourful bunting outside in anticipation of a warm Easter and the promise of summer to come.

Shelley appears and stops in front of the window. She waves and instinctively Jane beckons her inside.

'Hi, stranger,' Jane says, closing the doors to the window displays and giving Shelley her full attention.

'Hi.' Shelley looks tired and there are dark circles around her eyes. 'Yeah, sorry I didn't come past earlier.' She looks at the floor.

'Everything, alright, Shelley?'

'Yeah, not bad.'

'What have you been doing?'

'I'm thinking about joining a gym.'

Jane nods. 'That would be good for you.'

Shelley nods and looks vaguely into the distance.

'Can I help in any way?'

Shelley sighs. 'I'm bored.'

'Did I see you in the boutique with Marion?'

'She wants me to work with her, so does Tommy, but it's so boring. It's awful. It's for old women. I'll die in there.'

Jane laughs. 'That's very dramatic.' She heads to the back of the shop and the counter where she has a few brochures on her products that she wants to show Shelley.

The door opens. 'Hello, you gorgeous, beautiful people. Two stunning girls together.'

Jane's head jerks up and Shelley spins around.

Yusef is smiling at Shelley. 'I don't think we've met officially? I'm Yusef.' He places his hand on his heart. 'But I did see you in the pub a few weeks ago.'

Shelley smiles. 'Shelley.'

'Weren't you with Tommy?'

'He's my Uncle.'

'Tommy's a top guy. He's my main man, my man-crush.'

Shelley laughs and Jane feels her neck tightening.

'So how long are you here for... Shelley.' Yusef moves closer to her and Jane can sense that this is not good but she can't move.

'Yusef, did you want something?' she asks.

He looks at her as if he's forgotten he was in her shop.

'I was going to show Shelley a few things.' She points to the back of the shop but Shelley looks reluctant now as if she'd far prefer to talk to Yusef.

'I was wondering, are you at home later?' he says.

Jane shakes her head, her eyes begging him to stop but he continues smiling and talking.

'I know you like jigsaws and I've got a great one for you. It's a Mike Jupp jigsaw — *I Love London*. It's really different and I think you'd really like it.'

Jane stares at him. 'You could drop it here in the morning.'

He nods then turns his attention to Shelley. 'Will you be here in the morning?'

Shelley shakes her head, laughing, her eyes are radiant.

'That's a shame. I love to see beautiful ladies. All I have to do is look out of my window and feast my eyes on you two beauties.'

Shelley looks out of the window. 'Esquires?'

'I am one half; my uglier and less charming brother is the other half.'

Shelley laughs but Jane's heard it all before.

'Well, I'm sure Ozan is missing you, Yusef. Don't let us hold you up. And please don't go to any trouble about the jigsaw.'

'It's no trouble,' he replies mildly. 'I picked it up in a second-hand shop.' Then he grins at Shelley. 'I love your hair and if you ever want it shaved you know where we are.'

On his way out, he winks at Jane and it's only after he's closed the door that Jane realises she's been holding her breath. Her body is tense and she cannot move.

'Oh-My-God. He is absolutely gorgeous.' Shelley has gone to the window and is watching him cross the road. 'Yusef. Wow. Now things might start picking up — at last.' She turns to grin at Jane. 'I think you might have just saved my whole summer. Have you got a job? I could look out of this window all day.'

April

Tommy

The conservatory, at the back of the house, overlooks the garden. Tommy finishes his cereal watching the blue tits on the bird feeder and remembering how much pleasure Sunita got from sitting in this garden room, sewing.

'Are you going out today?' Shelley's voice comes from behind him, and he turns around in surprise. He thought she'd already left for work. He looks at his watch. It's almost eleven.

'I thought you'd gone to the boutique.'

'Not today.'

'Didn't Marion want you to work every day?'

She shrugs, slides into the armchair opposite him, curls up her legs and looks at her phone. 'Are you going out?'

'Why?' He puts the bowl on the table and picks up his coffee.

She raises her eyes to the ceiling. 'Can you never just answer a question?'

'Can't you?'

'You can be very irritating.'

'You're in my house, I'm allowed to be whatever I like.'

She stares at him. 'You don't have to keep reminding me I'm a guest and that I'm indebted to you.'

'I didn't say that,' he replies with mild amusement. 'Besides, emotional blackmail doesn't impress me.'

'It's not blackmail. It's about being kind.'

He laughs. 'You're lecturing me on kindness?'

She becomes engrossed in her phone and ignores him so he looks out of the window and they sit in silence for a while. He watches her from the corner of his eye, scrolling, reading, concentrating, then she types something and her phone pings.

'Right.' She stands up. 'I'm going out.'

'What are your plans today?'

'Dunno.'

'Where are you going?'

'What are you, my keeper?'

'No, I'm your interested uncle.'

'Yeah.'

'Have you heard from your mum?'

'I texted her yesterday – she's fine.'

He nods. 'I spoke to her.'

'How come?' Shelley seems surprised.

'I try and talk to her a couple of times a week, you know, give her a bit of moral support, tell her how you're getting on—'

'Me?'

'Of course, she still worries about you.'

'Did you tell her about my job?'

'I said you'd started in the boutique a couple of weeks ago and that you're out a lot and that you seem to be making friends.'

She stares at him and he's surprised by her direct gaze. She's a pretty girl and so like his sister at that age.

'She liked the earrings I sent her,' he adds.

'I'd like to work in Jane's shop. Can you speak to her for me?'

'I don't know if she has a job.'

'I asked her, but she couldn't wait to get me out of there. It's like she didn't want me around. But she likes you. You could persuade her.'

'I don't think she likes me any more than—'

'But you took her on a date.'

'I didn't.'

'Well, she came with us to the burger bar. I thought you fancied her. You can't live on your own forever.'

Tommy stares at his niece. He'd asked Jane to help him with Shelley, not out on a date.

'Or do you prefer Marion?' Shelley laughs. 'She's always talking about you and that wonderful meal you had in the Bistro. She says you're the most engaging man she's met in years. She loved her date with you. I think she'd be up for it.'

'Up for what?' Tommy frowns.

'You don't need me to explain *that*! Besides, when you take a woman on a date to a restaurant like that they obviously think you're into them, yet you haven't taken her out since. Why?'

'Marion asked me to go with her. She invited me. She'd been given a voucher for Christmas for the restaurant and she had no one else to go with.'

'Okay, so now you have to invite her back. You have to take her somewhere.'

'Do I?'

'Of course, or she will feel that it wasn't a good investment and that you're a user.'

'I hadn't thought of it like that.'

'You don't get anything in this life for nothing. Even you must know that. Right, see you later, don't wait up!'

* * *

Tommy is unsettled and after a late afternoon pint in The Ship and a quick chat with Paul, he wanders through Harbour Street. He's planning on going to the harbour to suggest a game of snooker with Matt or one of the gang. It's Friday and he knows there's a pretty good chance that one of them will be up for a game.

He's walking past Marion's boutique just as she's locking up and she blocks the pavement.

'Hi, Tommy, haven't seen you for ages.'

He hasn't seen her since the night they had dinner a few weeks ago.

'Hello, Marion, I've been busy and with Shelley starting work I didn't want to interfere.'

Marion frowns at him. 'You couldn't interfere if you tried, Tommy.'

She places the key to the shop in her pocket. 'Where are you off to?'

'I'm heading for a game of snooker with the boys.'

'I was going to The Ship, but I could tag along with you, if you like?' She slips her arm through his and pulls him along the street. 'It would be good to catch up with you and have a proper chat.'

'That's going to be a bit difficult with the boys around.'

'Well, you know what to do then?'

'What?'

'Take me out for dinner.' She smiles but her step doesn't falter.

'Tonight?'

'Why not?'

'Well, I was going to see if the boys fancy a game of snooker.'

'So, you haven't actually arranged anything?'

'Er, no, not really but they always go on a Fri—'

'Then that's settled.' She stops walking and faces him. 'I fancy Italian, what about you. Do you like Italian?'

'Erm, yes.'

'Well, come on then. We can have a couple of drinks in The Ship afterwards.' She turns him around and still with her arm hooked through his, she marches back up Harbour Street and toward the Italian in the square, smiling. 'This is turning out to be a great Friday.'

Tommy is silent. He can't help thinking about how they turned around outside *The Grooming Salon*, but when he looked across the road he'd seen Jane staring out of her shop window.

Jane had seen Marion's arm hooked firmly through his and her face was one of shock — but there was also another expression that he can't quite figure out.

* * *

Tommy isn't hungry but he orders a pizza and beer, and Marion orders king prawn pasta and a large glass of Chardonnay.

'This is a wonderful surprise, Tommy. How thoughtful of you.'

Tommy tries to smile but his mouth doesn't work so instead he takes a sip of beer.

'I haven't seen you for so long, I thought you were avoiding me.' She touches her bottom lip.

'I've explained that,' he says seriously.

'So, what have you been up to?'

Tommy shakes his head trying to remember how he fills his days. He gets up a little later, he takes more time with his breakfast, he wanders down to the harbour where the time flies and he waits to see if Shelley contacts him or if she's coming home for dinner. Some nights he meets the boys for a drink, but more recently he's been at home watching TV or doing a jigsaw.

Marion doesn't wait for an answer.

'You know, in all this time we've been friends I've never been to your house. How is that possible? I remember Sunita asking me round but we never seemed to manage to get a day sorted out.'

'You knew Sunita?' This was news to Tommy. Marion never mentioned it when they last went out for dinner.

'She'd come in the shop sometimes.'

'But she used to make all her own clothes.'

'Ah yes, but where do you think she got her ideas?'

Tommy shrugs. 'I guess in her head.'

'She often used to pop in, but what would you know, Tommy? You were at sea most of the time, weren't you?'

'Well, I worked, yes, but I'm sure she would have told me.'

'You must have forgotten.' She reaches across the table and lays a hand over his. 'It must have been so hard for you after the accident.'

'Hello, Tommy, hello Marion.' They both turn to see Frances, the vicar, standing by their table. 'How are you both?'

Tommy notices the way Frances' gaze lingers on Marion's hand over his and he pulls quickly away, but not before the person standing beside Frances has seen everything.

'Hello Jane,' Marion says, beaming happily. 'Hello Frances. You caught us.'

'Caught you?' Frances smiles but there's a question in her eyes.

Marion leans toward her and says loudly. 'It's our second date.'

Tommy wants to shake his head but he can't look at any of the women. Instead he keeps his head firmly bent, gazing at his half-eaten pizza.

'Well, we won't interrupt you, then.' Frances straightens her shoulders. 'Have a wonderful evening and I'll see you tomorrow, Tommy.'

'Erm, yes, thank you, Frances.' Tommy watches Jane and Frances disappear to the far side of the restaurant. He can't see them at their table and he breathes a sigh of relief. 'Why did you say that?' he asks. 'Why did you say we're on a second date?'

'Why not? It's true.'

'It's not a date, Marion. It's dinner.'

'That's the same thing, isn't it?'

'Look, you invited me and now I've invited you back and—'

'I know. We're just getting to know each other and it's early days yet, Tommy.'

'But—'

'Shush. Let's not complicate things further by justifying ourselves to anyone. Our relationship is our own and it's no one else's business'

'It's not a relationship.'

'Look, I know how hard it's been for you since Sunita. But what I'm saying is, you don't need to be on your own. I'm here for you. As a friend, of course. I care about you, Tommy. There, I've said it. I'm very fond of you and I have... feelings for you.'

Tommy clears his throat.

'I don't expect you to say anything back. Let's simply relax and see what life brings. As we both know it's very short and it's not a dress rehearsal.' She laughs. 'We're too long in the tooth to play games. Life is for the living.'

Tommy watches her, wondering if she could possibly slip in any more clichés and in a sudden mood of determination to change the subject, he says.

'So, tell me, how's Shelley getting on?'

'Shelley?'

'Yes, in the shop.'

Marion lifts her empty glass and indicates to the waiter to bring another one before she answers and when she does she says, 'I wish I could answer that.'

'What do you mean?'

'She didn't tell you?'

'Stop playing games, Marion.' Tommy raises his voice. He grips his beer bottle, getting a little bit fed up at being played along. 'Tell me what?'

'She only lasted three days.'

'You mean she wasn't there today?'

'Not this week at all. She came in on Monday, left early on Tuesday, didn't come back on Wednesday. Did half a day on Thursday last week and then said she'd had enough. She asked me for her pay and said she was quitting. Didn't you know?'

Tommy looks into the distance, staring at a spot on the floor. 'Then where has she been going and what has she been doing?'

Marion shrugs. 'Maybe you should ask Femi.'

'Why Femi?'

'Because I think Shelley is hanging out with Ahmed and Faisal.'

* * *

Tommy has been to the vicarage many times in the past few years. He was never a particularly religious man, although he did always thank God for the right wind, tides and weather. He admired all of nature and he believed that if God created Heaven and Earth then of course, that included all the beautiful life in the sea.

Now, he sits in the lounge on a comfortable sofa and when Frances brings in a tray with tea cups and shortbread biscuits, his face lights up.

'You remembered.' He laughs.

'Eat as many as you like.'

Tommy watches as Frances pours the tea into china cups. That was something he'd thought was so kind, from the day of his first visit. She didn't assume that he was a rough-necked fisherman in his thick woollen sweater and boots. She'd treated him as she would her own husband, with warmth, understanding and respect. He had been in the church. He'd lit a candle for Sunita and tears had streamed down his cheeks. He couldn't stop them, and she'd insisted he come back to the vicarage for tea. It was one of those life changing moments. It had renewed his faith in the world. After Sunita's car crash and his heart attack Tommy still welcomed their monthly chats and he marked them religiously in his diary. He had never missed one.

'So, how's everything?'

Tommy sits back with the tea cup and saucer balanced on his knee. 'Where do I start?'

Frances laughs. 'I see you're getting on with Marion.'

His head jerks up. 'Not in the way it looked last night.'

'Oh, okay. But it's none of my business anyway.'

Tommy sips his tea. 'I don't seem to be able to say the right thing to anyone. Sometimes I feel tongue-tied and manipulated and even though I know it's happening, I feel helpless to stop it.'

'That can happen to us all.'

'I can't imagine it happening to you, Frances.'

'Oh, but it does. People tell me what they want me to hear and not the real reason or the truth. I have to try and see through things.'

'Really?'

'For example, take some of our regular churchgoers, if they miss a Sunday service they expect the wrath of God and I have to remind them that ours is a gentle, forgiving and kind God. Sometimes their excuses are so elaborate that even I can see through their web of intricate details. I think if people tell you too much, it's overkill and very often the next time you see them, they've even forgotten their own lie.'

Tommy nods. 'I wish that were true with Shelley.'

'How are you getting on with her?'

Tommy had told Frances on his last visit about Elsie's cancer and about Shelley's visit, and although they hadn't yet met, Tommy was sure that Frances would get on with her. Frances liked everyone.

'It turns out that I thought she was working in Marion's boutique, but she quit and never told me.'

'Why do you think that is?'

Tommy rubs his cheek. 'I have no idea. Sunita was so upfront and straight forward. I always knew where I stood but now with these women, I'm all adrift—'

'Which women?'

He ticks them off on his finger. 'Well, Marion thinks we're dating. Shelley treats me like I'm the lodger in my own home and Jane, well Jane I'm not sure what she thinks.'

Frances grins. 'Goodness, Tommy, you've had a busy month.'

He laughs and takes another shortbread. 'Well, if God works in mysterious ways, like this, she must be a woman or, to be more woke, I'd have to say They.' He laughs again and Frances smiles.

'I think Shelley is obviously having an effect on you.'

'She's not working at the boutique and Marion tells me she's friends with Femi's boys, Ricky, Ahmed and Faisal.'

'Have you spoken to Femi?'

'I'll go and see her afterwards.'

'You might be as well to ask Shelley directly too.'

'She didn't come home last night.'

'Well, you need to set the ground rules with her. Out of respect she must let you know what's happening and what she's doing.'

'I've texted her, but she hasn't answered me.'

'You'll have to tell her that you need to know she's safe and that you're worried about her, on top of the worry you have with your sister's heath. You must be careful with your own health too, Tommy. You can't go through all this stress. It could make you ill.'

Tommy finishes his tea and places it on the tray. He leans forward and clasps his hands. 'Did Jane say anything last night about me being with Marion?'

'No.'

'Good.'

'Why? Is that important?'

'Well, I don't want her to get the wrong idea. I was hoping that she might take Shelley under her wing, you know, and offer her a job in the kiosk for the summer. But Jane's not very forthcoming.'

'Maybe you should speak to her.'

'I don't want anyone to get the wrong idea. I mean, Marion took me to the Bistro for dinner and I asked her for a job for Shelley, but it didn't work out. I don't want her to do the same thing with Jane.'

Frances laughs. 'You can't keep taking women out for dinner and asking them for a job for Shelley. She's twenty. She has to stand on her own feet. It's time she sorted herself out.'

'Elsie's spoilt her because Frank left, and she feels guilty because she's going through chemo treatment again.'

Frances nods in understanding and Tommy checks his watch. 'Right, I'm going to leave you in peace, Frances. I've got a plan now. I'll speak to Shelley and I'll speak to Femi and find out what's going on.'

'Good idea.' Frances stands up too.

He kisses her on the cheek, pulls on his jacket and after saying goodbye he heads into the church. He walks softly and quietly to the front. He picks up a candle, strikes a match and places it in the holder. He sits halfway down the aisle in the same seat where Frances found him three years ago. It was a year after Sunita died and he had come to the church to light a candle but he had been overwhelmed with grief. It hadn't helped that a family of tourists had entered with two toddlers, who began running up and down the aisle until the mother told them off in a stern, loud whisper. It didn't stem his tears. In fact, it made him realise how far removed from real life he had come. He thought about the circle of life, and how they had been unable to have children, and he had wept. Tears of regret, hurt, loss, pain — it had been all consuming and long after the noisy family left, he had sat there alone.

He'd thought he was alone. It was only after he stood up and he saw Frances in the pew at the back of the church that his step faltered, and for some reason he had collapsed in her arms and cried on her shoulder like a baby.

* * *

By coincidence, it's Femi who finds Tommy. After leaving the church he is walking across the square when he hears his name.

'I thought it was you, Tommy. How are you doing?' Femi smiles at him, genuinely pleased to see him. She hugs him tightly. 'You look good.'

Femi is wearing a purple coat and red trilby over her black, curly hair. She's a striking Caribbean-woman with a strong sense of purpose. His only regret is that Femi never met Sunita. He was sure they would have become firm friends, but their paths in Westbay had never crossed.

It was Femi who, as a volunteer for the RNLI, saved his life last year resuscitating him on the fishing boat and keeping him alive until the ambulance could take him to hospital. She'd never looked for any reward and always played down her actions, saying it hadn't been that serious. But the doctors in the hospital had told a different story. She had saved his life.

'You look amazing too. I think Lawrence is good for you.' Tommy laughs when she blushes.

He'd met Lawrence on a few occasions with Ben. Shortly after he came out of hospital he'd wandered into Ben's art gallery, curious about the paintings on display. There had been several paintings of birds; a green woodpecker and a toucan that he'd almost bought for Sunita. But then he'd realised that Sunita was no longer here, and he'd left in a hurry. After that, if he was walking past, Ben would call him inside on the pretext of showing him something different - a wooden carving made by one of his students in London or on one occasion a bird box that Lawrence had designed. Tommy recalls spending a pleasant half an hour with the men talking about nature and the sea.

Femi links her arm through Tommy's and brings him back to the present. 'You should come over for dinner sometime or go out with Lawrence on one of his field trips. He saw a flock of curlews last week and he hasn't stopped talking about it. Look, I'm just going to work, but I wanted to have a quick chat with you about Shelley.'

Tommy stops suddenly and faces her. 'I'm very worried. She didn't come home last night. I think she's seeing Ricky.'

Femi shakes her head. 'It's not Ricky. He still has his girlfriend but she's befriended my other son, Ahmed's, friend. Faisal. is the refugee we're all helping and he's working with Amber in the café. Sometimes he does shifts in the pub. He's just getting on his feet and he lives in Amber's caravan. Shelley told him that she wasn't happy staying with you, but that she had nowhere else to go, and because Faisal was a refugee from

Syria and he's been in that situation with nowhere to go, he feels sorry for her. But he doesn't want her there with him. He's in a relationship.'

'It's not fair on Faisal.'

'No, and it's not fair on you. I know you're doing everything you can for Shelley, but she needs to sort her game out.'

'Thanks, Femi. I'll speak to her. I was worried—'

'No harm's been done, but she's led a different life to my boys and I—'

Tommy holds up his hand. 'You're the best foster mum. Thanks for telling me. Now I know what's going on and what I have to do.'

Femi kisses him on the cheek. 'I'm going to be late for work, Tommy. Let me know how you get on or if you need me to have a word.'

'She's my responsibility,' he says. 'I'll sort it.'

Tommy watches Femi walk away. He digs his hands into his pockets and walks up the hill toward his house.

Shelley needs to get a job. It will keep her out of trouble and give her an aim and a sense of purpose. She must start taking life seriously. She needs to fill her day doing something worthwhile.

* * *

When he gets home, Tommy checks Shelley's room. He hasn't been in there since he sorted it all out before she arrived and when he opens the door, he looks around in disgust. The beautiful room that he had been so proud of is now a complete tip. There are clothes lying all over the floor, on the bed and over the chair. The table he'd assumed she might use to work on, is littered with make-up and discarded food boxes, dirty plates, cups and glasses. There's even a takeaway bag with the remnants of Indian food and the room reeks of curry and the sweet smell of weed. He closes the door.

He texts Shelley.

I don't care where you are or what you're doing. Come home immediately. Tommy.

He sits and waits but he's impatient and angry and he knows that he mustn't get upset. He makes tea, sits in the conservatory and regards his garden with detachment. All of this used to be fun with Sunita; the house, the garden, life. Now everything is a challenge. The good days all seem such a long time ago and they belonged to a different person. Tommy knows he's changed. He's not happy. He's not content and he certainly has no purpose.

The front door bangs and he hears her footsteps before he sees her.

'What's up?' Shelley stands in the doorway. She's wearing a mini skirt and her red hair is a mess.

'Please sit down.'

She flops onto the other chair and swings a leg over its arm. Her phone is in her hand. 'I got your message.'

'Please put your phone down.'

She stares at him but he looks right back at her and so she lays it on the arm of the chair.

'When your Mum phoned me, I can't say I was enamoured with the idea of having a twenty-year-old in my home. But having been estranged from my family for so long, I was desperate to build bridges. No one can live in the past, holding grudges and building resentment and, as angry as I was with Elsie for letting Frank separate us, I knew I had to be the better person. I wanted Elsie to see the man I am; kind, thoughtful and forgiving.' He leans forward, clasping his hands. Shelley watches him with big eyes. She looks tired and wary but she doesn't move. 'I began to look forward to meeting you. You'd been a pretty little eight-year-old with pigtails and a crooked smile when I last saw you and, to be honest, when you came off the train, I couldn't believe what a fantastic job your mum had done. You are pretty and you seemed smart, talkative and interesting.' He pauses and clears his throat. 'I wasn't prepared for you to move into my home and treat me as if I'm the hired help.'

Shelley opens her mouth but Tommy shakes his head and holds up his hand.

'I haven't finished. I prepared your room with love and anticipation, and tonight when I went in there, I saw that you live like a pig. It's disgusting. It stinks. There's uneaten food and it reeks of weed. Secondly, I wanted you to come and go in this house with freedom, but also with respect. Sadly, you have shown me no respect at all. You have no manners, no kindness and no thoughtfulness for anyone other than yourself. Thirdly, you seem to think it's perfectly acceptable to also sully my name in my town. I don't appreciate that you have said to people that you're not comfortable here. It insinuates that I am not caring for you. I also don't like the fact that you're taking advantage of vulnerable people, a refugee like Faisal who is working hard to support himself and find a new life. You cannot sponge off him or introduce him to drugs. He needs stability and security—'

'I—'

'This is not a discussion, so please listen, Shelley. You have pushed me too far and I will not be humiliated. I have taken great pains to talk to Marion to get you a job, which you haven't even had the grace to tell me you quit after less than week. I feel that you have taken from me and given nothing back. Life doesn't work that way. So, I'm giving you two days — and I mean two days. You can turn this situation around now by going upstairs, cleaning your room, changing your sheets and living like a decent human being. I've shown you where the washing machine is and where the clean sheets are. I don't expect you to work in the boutique, but I do expect you to go and apologise to Marion. And then I expect you to offer Faisal an apology. He has not complained about you because he wouldn't, but Femi is concerned. She's taken him under her wing, as she has done with all her foster boys. Finally, I expect you to look for another job, help in the house, and be here to have dinner with me at least once a week so that we can build a friendship and get to know each other.'

Shelley blinks and bites the inside of her mouth.

'If you think you can turn this situation around then you're welcome to stay. If not, I suggest you go upstairs and pack your bags.' Tommy stands up. 'I'm going out now. I have bought food for dinner for us tonight. I'll leave you to make up your mind but think carefully, Shelley. Your time is running out. You have two days.'

Tommy walks down the hallway and pulls on his coat. He's conscious that Shelley hasn't moved. He'd expected an argument or some comment but she's said nothing. He doesn't know whether to feel relieved or very sad.

* * *

Tommy walks down to the harbour and when he sees Matt

coming in on the fishing boat he walks away. It's punishment watching them all arrive back in their boats. Some days it's just too hard. He wants to be a part of it but he can't. Those days are over. Everything changes and time moves on. He wanders along the promenade by the beach huts, thinking how pretty they are and when he sees Lawrence he waves but doesn't stop.

Tommy doesn't want to talk to anyone. He feels the April wind in his short hair and the cool breeze on his cheeks. Spring will soon turn into summer and what will he have to show for it? His great intention of helping his niece — a project that he thought would keep him busy and give him purpose — has failed.

It's getting dark when he walks back to the house and he's already resigned to the fact that Shelley will have phoned her mother, complained bitterly about her treatment, and will have packed to go home. Failing that, she will have called Frank who will take great pleasure in coming to Westbay to remove his daughter from Tommy's house. They had never been close at school; they had a different set of friends, but it had never sat well with Frank that his girlfriend at school dumped him and then went out with Tommy. He was a guy who could never forgive.

The lights are on and he can hear Shelley in the kitchen. She has music playing.

'Hello,' she calls cheerfully.

He removes his coat and is surprised to see the kitchen table laid for two. She's also frying the mince.

'I'm making cottage pie.'

Tommy takes a beer from the fridge and sits at the table. 'Thank you.'

He watches her at the stove. She's adding herbs, garlic and onions and then she turns to say, 'I cleaned my room.'

Tommy nods. 'Thank you.'

He watches as she puts the meat into a serving dish and adds the mashed potato. She places it in the oven, rubs her hands together and turns to smile at him. 'Done.'

Her phone is on the counter. She doesn't look at it but it's the source of music in the home. He doesn't know the tune but it's a pretty song – better than half of the thumping beat music she has been playing recently.

'Look, I'm going to do better,' she says. 'I've given some thought to what you said and I'll find a job — one that I like.' She grins. 'I'll speak to Marion tomorrow and I've texted Faisal already to apologise and he's cool about everything.'

Tommy sips his beer.

'And, I've been thinking about what you said. It's not healthy to not have a job, is it? It's like you've got no purpose. Nothing to do. So you fill your time up with stupid ideas in your head and make bad decisions, and quite honestly, you can have too much time, can't you?'

Tommy nods.

Shelley leans forward across the table. 'When there's too much time in the day, and you've nothing to do, time goes on and on and on. It stretches into the distance, into infinity and beyond.' She grins. 'Infinity and beyond like in the film *Toy Story*.'

Tommy nods and smiles. He remembers Buzz Lightyear.

'There's no purpose to life. There's no point in anything, is there?'

Tommy clears his throat. 'So where will you look for a job?'

'I don't think Jane likes me but I'll ask Amber. Faisal says she's really nice. Ricky says there might be work in the summer in The Ship but I don't want bar work.'

Tommy raises his eyebrows.

'I hate working in the evenings,' she says. 'I prefer to get up and do something, so I'll ask around.'

'Good.'

'There's one other thing, Tommy.' She looks meaningfully at him. 'I think you should also look for something to do as well. I don't mean a job as such: I know you were a fisherman, but I don't think it does you any good sitting around all day. It's not healthy and, like me, you need a purpose.'

Tommy stands up. 'I'm going to watch the news before dinner.'

Shelley stands in front of him.

'I mean it, Tommy. You're an intelligent man. You may not be able to fish any more but you've a lot of talent and there's a lot that a man like you can still do.'

Tommy turns on his heels and walks out of the room. 'It's not over yet. You've got two days.'

* * *

It's pouring with rain the following afternoon, and Tommy sits at the kitchen table with a jigsaw he found in the cupboard. He needs a sense of purpose, even if it is just completing a jigsaw and seeing the whole picture. This picture is of a farmyard; there are so many colours and shades and different animals and it takes up all of Tommy's concentration. It stops his head from getting too busy. The time passes quickly, and he's surprised when just after five o'clock the front door opens.

'Hello?' Shelley calls from the hallway.

'I'm in here.' He doesn't turn around. He's intent on finding a difficult piece and he's irritated to be interrupted.

'I've got something for you.'

'What's that?'

'Look.'

Tommy turns around and his mouth falls open. 'What the f—'

Shelley is holding a tiny Siamese kitten. It has a white body, black paws and black ears. 'It's a present — for giving me a second chance.'

'I don't want a present.' Tommy stands up. 'And I don't want a cat.'

'It's a kitten. It was abandoned.'

'Well, it can't stay here.'

'Why not?'

'Because I don't want a cat.'

It miaows and Shelley pushes it into his hands and he's forced to take it. He's surprised at how light and tiny it feels. It's all bones and white skin and big blue eyes. It wiggles from his grasp and he has to catch it before it falls. He holds it tightly to his chest and feels it's tiny beating heart.

Meanwhile, Shelley pulls off her jacket, throws it over the chair and pulls out a few tins of cat food and a bag of cat litter from her bag. 'See? I've come prepared. I'll train her to poop in the tray.'

'She's not staying.'

Then with a flourish Shelley pulls a bottle of wine from her bag. 'We're celebrating.'

'We? I'm not keeping her.'

'I got a job today.'

Tommy almost drops the kitten. It's wriggling in his hands and it wants to get down. 'Where?' he asks.

'Pop her on the floor and let her explore. Lucas in the Pet Shop said I can work there. I start tomorrow.'

'Really?'

'Put her down and let her explore, Tommy. Come on, let's think of a name for her. What's for dinner?'

'I made chicken stew.'

'Great. I'll get some glasses.'

'She'll have to go.' He hasn't put the kitten down.

'Where to?'

'Where did you get her?'

'I found her near the harbour. She was all alone and starving, wandering around lost and she made a beeline for me. I couldn't leave her behind, the poor thing. She could get eaten by foxes or seagulls.'

'Well, she can't stay here.'

Shelley produces a tin of cat food. 'She's probably hungry.' She pulls a saucer from the cupboard and begins to spoon the cat food into the dish.

At the smell of tinned chicken, the kitten miaows louder and when Shelley pushes the saucer across the floor, Tommy sets her down and she begins to eat.

'See! She's starving.'

'You can take her to the pet shop in the morning.'

'I took her there already. That's how I got the job. I thought they might take her. Lucas was very impressed with me — and her.'

'Do they have pets in there? I don't remember seeing any.'

'No, but we chatted about animals and I've had hamsters, guinea pigs, mice and three rabbits. He was dead impressed and the boy who normally works there is going on holiday, so I get a few days working with him, showing me what to do — you know, training — then I can work in the shop.' Shelley smiles. 'Look, isn't she beautiful? What shall we call her?'

Tommy scratches his head while he watches the tiny creature eating.

'She might have escaped. She must belong to someone,' he says.

'I've checked with the vet and she's not microchipped.'

'You've been to the vet?'

'Of course, it's the first thing I did. She's healthy enough, a bit malnourished but she'll be fine. She's like us.'

'She's not like us.'

Shelley grins. 'She needs some TLC.'

'Isn't there a website or a Facebook page or something that you can post a picture and see if anyone has lost her?'

'I'll do that later. Let's eat. That stew smells good.'

While Tommy ladles the stew into dishes, the kitten miaows and begins to sniff around the kitchen.

'She can stay one night,' he says.

'You won't even know she's here. She can sleep in my room. She won't disturb you, I promise. Have you never had a pet before?'

'We never had time. Sunita was at school and I was working, then in the holidays we'd go away.'

'Then this will be a new experience for you. You'll fall in love with her. I know you will. I already love her.'

'Love doesn't happen that easily.'

Shelley laughs. 'She needs a name.' She miaows louder. 'I know pussykins, you need a name. What shall we call you?'

'She's not getting a name.'

'Grumpy!'

Tommy looks at Shelley, unsure if she's talking to him or naming the kitten.

'So,' Shelley says brightly. 'That's my end of the bargain. I kept my side of it, and I still have a day in hand. What about you? Have you got a job yet?'

Tommy places the stew in front of her.

'What about Marion?' he asks.

'Oh, I forgot. I'll speak to her tomorrow.'

'Don't forget.'

'I won't, but what about you? Have you thought about it?' she insists. 'What have you done all day?'

'I'm doing a jigsaw.'

Shelley laughs. 'Well, I guess that's a step in the right direction. It's better than wandering around town on your own all day, looking lost.'

* * *

The following morning before Shelley leaves for work, she gives Tommy firm instructions.

'I've changed her litter tray and she's had breakfast. I'll pop back at lunchtime but spend time with her. She's very playful and she'll love company.'

'Will you find her a home?'

'Of course.'

'Go on those Facebook sites?'

'Yes.'

'Don't forget. She can't stay here.'

'Look at that rain outside. You're not going to throw her out on the street.'

The kitchen window is being hammered by wind and rain and Tommy looks down at the kitten sniffing by his feet. 'Just make sure you sort this out today.'

'Yes, sir.' Shelley laughs and leans down to give him a peck on the cheek. 'You'll fall in love with her.'

'I won't.'

'By the way, her name is Almond Blossom.'

'Almond Blossom? You can't call her that.'

'She's that colour. It suits her.'

By the time Shelley leaves, Tommy is processing just how much they know about kittens. Shelley certainly seems confident and in control and she's taken responsibility. The kitten purrs and rubs against Tommy's leg, miaowing appreciatively and he scoops her up.

'You're a noisy one, aren't you?'

She miaows again, and Tommy puts her on his lap where she kneads his trousers with her claws.

'Ouch.' He laughs. 'You need a manicure, Almond.'

By lunchtime, Tommy is absorbed in his jigsaw and Almond is curled up on the chair beside him sleeping peacefully. The front door bangs and Shelley calls out, 'Hello.'

'I'm in here.'

'Where's Almond Blossom?' The kitten has already woken and seeing Shelley, she arches her back and miaows. 'I did some research and Siamese cats are notoriously vocal.'

'Tell me about it.'

Shelley leans over his shoulder. 'Great jigsaw. It looks fun. What's this?' She points to an empty cotton reel attached to some wool. 'Have you made this?'

'She didn't have a toy and I remembered some of Sunita's sewing stuff upstairs.'

Shelley laughs, and rolls the cotton reel along the floor watching Almond Blossom jumping. 'Isn't she delightful?'

'Have you found her a home yet?'

'I'm working on it.'

'Nothing on Facebook?'

'Not so far.'

Tommy looks at Shelley who won't meet his gaze and he wonders just how hard she's been trying to relocate the kitten.

'How was your morning?' he asks.

'I love it and Mario and Luke are so lovely. They got married at Christmas a few years ago and Frances did their blessing in the church. They said she's amazing.'

Tommy nods. He likes anyone who likes Frances.

'Marion saw me in the pet shop.'

'Did you speak to her?'

'I ran out after her and I apologised.'

'What did she say?'

'She said that she's disappointed that she hasn't seen you and that you really get on well together. She said that you can't keep holding onto the past and that it's time to move on.'

'Did she?'

'She also said that she wants to see you again, so I suggested she call you. I told her you were shy.'

'I'm not shy.'

'Then ask her out.'

'I don't want to.'

'She's right, Tommy. I know you loved Sunita but imagine if it was the other way round and you had died. Would you want Sunita to sit in the past, drowning in self-pity, and not going out with anyone or sharing her life and having fun?'

Tommy thinks about it. 'I wouldn't want her with just anyone.'

'I know.' Shelley adds softly, 'But if you don't start looking, how will you ever know if you've met the right one? It's time, Tommy. This is your time now.'

*　*　*

Tommy makes sure that Almond Blossom has fresh water and the litter tray is clean and the cotton ball is where she can find it, then he pulls on his jacket. The rain has stopped and the sun has come out and he imagines a giant rainbow in the sky. He needs some fresh air.

Almond is very vocal as he pulls on his boots. 'It's alright. I'll be back soon. We've been playing but now you must sleep. You're still a baby and please don't claw the sofas.'

He closes the front door and heads down towards the town, through the square and into Harbour Street. It's mid-afternoon and it's busy, but he deliberately crosses the road to avoid the pet shop in case Shelley comes running out, accusing him of neglect. He steps out of the path of an angry mother pushing a buggy while shouting into her mobile and side-steps a lady with a walking stick. When he gets to Jane's shop, he's surprised to find the door locked. He cups his hand against the glass and looks inside but it's empty.

'Hey, Tommy my man. How are you doin' bro?' Yusef darts across the road. 'You stalking the lady?' He laughs. 'Or buying a ring for someone special?'

They fist bump and Tommy smiles. He's used to Yusef's banter but he's unnerved that he can't see Jane without Yusef knowing. He's like a dog protecting his master or in this case, protecting Jane. Yusef doesn't wait for an answer. 'She's in the harbour mate, you know, she's opening up one of them Artisan stalls.'

Tommy nods and they fist bump again. 'Thanks mate.'

Tommy makes his way to the harbour. Today the tide is high and all the boats are in. The fish have been sorted, weighed and sold and Matt and the crew have all gone home. Tommy wanders towards the Artisan market and he's pleased to see Jane, wrapped in a lime green woollen coat, measuring the table.

'Hi.'

'Tommy, hi.' She continues measuring and ignores him as she writes down a few figures on a pad.

'The coffee kiosk is open, do you fancy a latte?' he asks.

Jane looks surprise and nods. 'Thanks.'

Tommy spends a few minutes in conversation with a young boy and it dawns on him that this is Amber's stall; Harbour Café, the one selling picnic baskets. 'Are you working here all summer?' he asks. 'Are you Faisal?'

The boy nods and smiles.

'I'm Tommy, Shelley's uncle.'

His smile freezes.

'Did she apologise to you?' Tommy hands over the cash.

Faisal nods.

'Good. That's good because I didn't want her taking advantage of you.'

He shakes his head. 'It's fine.' He hands Tommy his change.

'I've heard you're a hard-working boy and I wish you all the best.' Tommy reaches out and shakes the boy's hand. 'Looks like good coffee, thank you.'

When he returns Jane is watching him with interest.

Tommy hands her a coffee. 'He seems a good boy.'

'Faisal is lovely. I think he'll be here for most of the summer.'

'Who's going to run your stall?'

Jane shrugs. 'Amber is confident she knows someone.'

Tommy sips his coffee and stares into the distance. 'Look, I've been thinking, and I don't want you to get the wrong idea, but I just wanted you to know that me and Marion...well...'

'That's fine, Tommy. You don't have to explain yourself to me.'

'No, I mean, what you saw in the Italian, it wasn't like that. I mean, it isn't like that. We're not... I'm not...attracted to her.'

Jane stares at him. 'It's fine, Tommy. You don't owe me an explanation.'

'I do. I want you to know because you know what Marion is like and I've gone along with it because I don't want to offend her, but it's not what I want.'

'I know it's not a kind thing to say but I think anyone you choose would be better than Marion. She's a player.'

'I can tell.' He grins.

Jane laughs. 'So, what will you do?'

'I'll tell her. I mean, I have told her already but she's not taking no for an answer.'

Jane sips her coffee thoughtfully.

He continues, 'I'm beginning to realise that women just do what they want. Shelley is the same. She came home with a kitten last night.'

Jane laughs and Tommy watches how her eyes light up. They shine as if she's lit up on the inside.

'Do you know anyone who's lost a kitten?'

Still laughing, Jane shakes her head.

'Shelley's got a job in the pet shop. I read her the riot act and told her to sort herself out and I think it might have worked.'

'All kids push boundaries.'

Tommy stands straighter. 'Well, let's hope we've turned a corner. She seems much happier.'

'Maybe you'd like to come to dinner?'

'Can you cook?' he teases.

'I make a mean moussaka.'

'My favourite.' Tommy is smiling. He hadn't expected to be invited to Jane's for dinner and he feels a quiver of excitement at the thought of spending an evening with her. 'What time?'

'How about seven?'

'Perfect.'

Jane smiles. 'That will give Shelley time to get home and sort the cat out before you both come over.'

Tommy nods, he can feel his smile fading. He hadn't anticipated taking Shelley with him.

May

Jane

It's been a week since Jane invited Tommy and Shelley over to her house for moussaka. But as it turned out, they didn't come. When Tommy got home the kitten wasn't well, so he drove Shelley and the kitten to an emergency vet in the city. Tommy texted Jane and they decided on a rain check.

Only now, it's May. Jane is working ridiculous hours and barely has time to look up, let alone cook dinner for anyone. Although the days are long, Jane is filling the time more than she ever thought possible. The shop is doing well but it means that she must create more products to sell for the stall and also online. She spends most evenings creating costume jewellery that's easier to make, cheaper and fast selling.

One evening, she's hunched over her kitchen table working when there's a knock at the door. She answers it and is surprised to see Amber.

'Come in,' she cries. 'I'd welcome a break. I think I've even got a bottle of wine somewhere.'

Amber spends a few minutes admiring Jane's craftsmanship, then they head outside to the small terraced garden where the air is still warm.

'Are you coping with all the work?' Amber asks.

'It's tougher than I thought it was going to be.'

'I was hoping Eva's two children might have come home from uni - but they've gone travelling. Ben and I are working flat out.'

'Doesn't he run a charity?'

'Yes, in London, and now we have Noah with us. This kid's only sixteen and he's in a pretty bad way. We're trying to feed him up at bit. He's very quiet. He hardly speaks, and when he does, he's monosyllabic. It might do him good but we'll have to see.'

'How long is he here for?'

'Ben is working with the social workers to find him some-where more permanent.'

Jane nods.

Amber continues, 'He's really talented. He makes the most incredible things out of wood; birds — parrots, woodpeckers, owls but he also makes things like ferris wheels, carousels and pretty ornaments — some are even musical.' Amber pulls out her phone and she spends a few minutes scrolling though some pictures and videos.

'This is just an idea, but if you're having trouble filling the stall, then you could share it with him. He could work on the stall during the day. We've been rotating with our staff from the café and the restaurant, but we might run out of reliable help with all the shift work at the Bistro.'

'I thought there would be lots of teenagers or kids back from uni?'

'There would be normally but I think that after Covid, when all the borders were locked down, many of them now want to go abroad. So, we have a bit of a shortage. Noah is very reliable and working in the kiosk might help his confidence.'

'How are you so kind, Amber? I don't know how you and Ben do it.'

'We have so much, Jane. It's good to share.'

'I know, but you make it seem so effortless.'

'It's all down to Ben. He has the ideas. He's seen where these kids come from and he understands what they've experienced. He's also frightened about where they could end up. I think he wants to save the world.' Amber laughs. 'Anyway, it's just a thought and it might be a temporary solution for you - and Noah.'

* * *

Jane works in the shop until ten o'clock before heading to the Artisan market in the harbour where she lifts away the wooden shutters and lays out her goods. She chats to one or two of the other stall holders: crafts, candles, soaps, local photographs all framed in different sizes, and there are a few new food stalls too; burgers, ice creams and hot dogs, including Amber and Ben's summer picnic boxes.

Jane's busy until Amber arrives with Noah. He's pulling a trailer, a mini wheelbarrow, that Jane recognises from Ben's art gallery and it's full of wood carvings.

'Noah, this is Jane.'

He has a mop of curly hair and he looks at her with big brown eyes.

'Hi, Noah. Gosh, did you make these? Your craftwork is incredible. You're so talented. I wish I could make things like this.'

He nods seriously as she picks up an old-fashioned ship.

'Is this the Cutty Sark?'

Noah nods.

'Did you go down to the Thames where it's moored?'

Noah nods again and that's when Tommy appears, sauntering along in a short-sleeved navy shirt and beige chinos.

Amber waves at him. He comes over and she introduces Tommy to Noah.

Tommy can't help but admire the ship. 'The detail is incredible,' he says picking it up and rotating it in his hand. 'How old are you?' Tommy asks and Noah looks at Amber.

It's Amber who replies, 'Noah is sixteen, and he's staying with us for a little while until a long-term foster family is available. We're very lucky to have him.' She smiles.

'Do you think you could make one of those?' Tommy points to the fishing boat in the harbour. 'They're all a bit different but if you do one of the red ones, I'll buy it from you.'

Noah's face lights up as he smiles and nods.

'Look, I have to go back to the shop,' Jane says quickly, checking her watch. I'll pop back at lunchtime.'

Amber replies, 'Don't worry, I'll be here. I'll help Noah set up and see how we get on. Faisal is nearby, so unless we get very busy there won't be a problem and it's not really that crowded at the moment.'

Tommy walks with Jane towards town. She says, 'I'm a bit worried about Noah, he's not saying much.'

'He might be a bit shy.'

They walk quickly under the clock tower and into Harbour Street.

'Look, I'm sorry our dinner got cancelled,' he says.

'Me too.'

'The weather is so lovely, perhaps we could get some fish and chips and take them to the beach one evening?'

'I'd like that. How's Shelley?'

'She's happier, she's working in the pet shop and she seems to be getting along fine.'

'That's a relief.'

'Well, I did have a chat with her and it seems to have worked.'

'I knew you would sort it out. How's your sister?'

'Elsie's having the treatment now. She said she's no fun to be around as she's not feeling great and at least this way she can sleep or do what she wants without worrying about Shelley. I think they chat or certainly message each other every day. They're very close.'

'I think you're a lovely uncle.'

Tommy smiles. 'Oh, and did I tell you we have a new addition?'

They arrive at the shop and Jane pauses with the key in the lock and she turns to look at him.

'A kitten. Shelley found her last week and brought her home.'

'Goodness. How is that working out?'

'She's a sweet little thing, quite vocal, always miaowing. Last night, I was in the garden miaowing back to her and when I went to check, it was Shelley in the kitchen miaowing thinking Almond Blossom was in the garden. We were miaowing at each other and the kitten was in the lounge fast asleep.'

Jane laughs. 'Almond Blossom?' She pushes open the shop door. 'That's a pretty name. I think you're becoming quite attached to her, Tommy.'

'Don't tell, Shelley,' he replies. 'I've already told her she has to take the cat with her when she leaves.'

* * *

The following morning, Tommy arrives at the shop early carrying two hot coffees. 'I thought you might need some sustenance.' He takes a jam doughnut from the bag. 'The rest are for Noah,' he explains.

'Noah?'

'I spent some time with him yesterday afternoon as Amber had to rush off to the café. He likes doughnuts.'

'That's kind of you, Tommy.'

'Well, I won't keep you. How about fish and chips on the beach?'

'Friday night?'

'Perfect.'

He leaves the shop and Jane's drinking her coffee when the door opens and Rachael walks in.

'Hi, Jane.'

'Hello, Rachael.' Jane is thinking quickly. She hasn't seen Rachael since she stopped the dance class in January. She hasn't brought anything in to be repaired and she doesn't look like she is about to buy anything either. Jane feels her body tense.

'I haven't seen you for months.' Rachael smiles.

'I've been really busy.'

'I hope I didn't offend you at the exercise class.'

'That was such a long time ago, back in the winter. I've forgotten all about it.' Jane meets Rachael's stare, and she smiles.

'You didn't come back.' Rachael tilts her head in a challenge.

'As I said, running this business and the stall in the harbour, as well as all my online work is exhausting. Never enough hours in the day.'

Rachael nods. 'We thought we hadn't seen you out much in The Ship or around town.'

Jane moves to stand behind the counter as if she's busy. 'Can I help you with anything?'

'I was going to buy something for Marion. It's her birthday.'

'Okay. Just have a look around and if there's anything you like the look of just ask.'

'I'm going to have a small get-together, just a few close friends, as a surprise on Friday, are you free?'

'No, sorry.'

Rachael arches her eyebrows. 'Have you got a date.'

'Now that would be telling.'

'Well, I'll let you know the details when I get organised. Just in case your date falls through. I've still got your number from the dance group.'

Jane nods. She's annoyed she'd given her phone number so freely.

'Anyway, I won't get Marion's present just now. I'll pop back later in the week.'

Jane nods. 'Bye Rachael.'

Rachael flicks her fingers. 'Oh, by the way, do you know where I can find Tommy? That's who I really want to invite. He and Marion are really close and she won't have told him about her birthday as she wouldn't want him buying anything really expensive.'

Jane shakes her head.

'Don't you see him?'

'Sometimes he pops in.'

'In here?'

Jane smiles. 'This is a shop, Rachael. I know it's not Tesco's but I do have customers.'

Rachael smiles but it doesn't reach her eyes. 'See you later, then.'

After she's let herself out of the shop, Jane breathes a sigh of relief. She's unpacking a new batch of Nordgreen men's slim watches when the door opens.

Yusef grins. 'Hello, gorgeous.'

'Hi, Yusef.'

'You okay?'

'I'm fine, thank you.'

He comes to the counter and they face each other. 'Are you missing me?'

'Nope.'

He smiles. 'Not even a little bit?'

'Nope.'

'Do you want to know how I am?'

'How are you, Yusef?'

'Naomi and Ozan are dating and they're serious.'

'Are you upset?'

'Yes, I was but then, no. I don't know. It's tough.'

'Lesson learned. If you meet a nice girl, then you have to treat her right.'

'It's too late now.'

'Maybe Naomi wasn't the right girl for you,' Jane suggests.

'Maybe. Nice watches.'

'Aren't they lovely.' She hands him one to hold and he places it on his wrist.

'Can I have this?'

'No.' She laughs, taking it from him and he grins back. 'Unless you pay for it.'

'You've the loveliest smile.'

'You say that to all the girls, I've heard you.'

Yusef laughs. 'I've been caught out.'

'Yes.' She smiles at him.

'I think Tommy likes you.'

'Um.' She places the watch back in the box.

'Have you slept with him?'

Jane's head shoots up then she looks over his shoulder. 'I think there are people outside your shop, queuing.'

'Just putting it out there, in case you hadn't noticed him.'

'Thank you, Yusef. But please concentrate on your own relationships.'

He smiles. 'I'll always be here for you.'

'Get out of here.' She laughs. 'Go and do an honest day's work.' She comes around the counter and pushes him in the middle of his back and out of the shop.

He says, 'Careful. This is physical, I could get to like this, Jane.'

* * *

On Thursday afternoon, Jane shuts the shop and heads to the harbour. It's very busy; couples, families, babies in buggies, children eating ice creams, families eating fish and chips, couples at tables filled with cockles, mussels, crab and whelks. It reminds Jane that she hasn't eaten and her stomach rumbles. She wants to get to the market stall before it closes.

When Jane arrives some of the stalls are closing for the evening, some have already shut, but some of the food ones are still open. She can see her market stall has closed and she stops in her tracks. She would have to wait until tomorrow to speak to Amber or she could go past the café or the Bistro.

She's about to turn away through the crowds of people when she sees Tommy leaning on the railing looking out to sea.

He's wearing long navy shorts, a white t-shirt and casual loafers. He's chatting away to the person beside him, pointing out the fishing boats, the harbour entrance and the small marina that houses the more expensive pleasure boats and yachts. He's smiling, animated and so completely engrossed in his conversation that he doesn't see her. At his side, Noah, who is a head shorter, is looking down into the sea, his head moving in every direction that Tommy is pointing. He doesn't seem to be speaking but he's taking everything in. Every now and again, Tommy leans down and says something and Noah nods. It's engaging to watch them together and Jane wonders what Tommy might have been like as a father. He's certainly doing well with Shelley by all accounts, and he seems to be much happier.

Jane turns back in the direction of Harbour Street and goes in search of Amber in the Bistro.

After the heat of the sunshine the restaurant is pleasantly cool and Jane finds Amber outside the back on the small patio. It's enchanting, with olive trees decorated with fairy lights, small intimate tables, candles and soft music.

'Jane? Is everything alright?' Amber says looking up from folding napkins.

'I think so, you tell me?' Jane laughs.

Amber nods. 'I think so.'

'This sounds like a good business. We both *think* everything is alright.'

Amber laughs. 'Tommy says it's all good.'

'Tommy?'

'Yes, didn't he tell you? He's been helping out. He gets on

really well with Noah. I was there yesterday but I had to rush back for a delivery. Ben was in London and Karl was busy. I didn't want to leave Noah alone but Tommy was in the harbour and he offered to step in. When I got back the two of them were as happy as anything. Then he said he'd go down all day today so that I could get on with my work here.'

'Tommy is working on the stall?' Jane says slowly. 'I just came from there and they were looking out to sea and Tommy was chatting away to Noah.'

Amber laughs. 'Noah told me last night he likes him, so…' She shrugs. 'I said that you'd be happy to pay Tommy but he wouldn't hear of it. He said it gives him purpose and he was looking for something to do.'

'Really?' Jane frowns.

'He said it was volunteer work and that we could count on him as long as we needed him.'

Jane smiles. 'Wow!'

'Come on, we don't open for another half an hour. It's nice and quiet. I'll pour you a glass of wine. You look like you could use one.'

Amber walks Jane to the bar where she pours her a glass of chilled Pinot Grigio and a water for herself.

'To be honest, I think this is doing Tommy good,' Amber says. 'Tommy has needed to do something for a while, and I was talking to Ben about it.'

'You guys can't help anyone else. Look at everything you've taken on, including Noah.'

'Well, once we had all the foster papers and completed the training, there was no excuse. Ben has been wanting to help for ages. Our home is only a temporary stop for him until the authorities find a more permanent place, but I must say, it's great having Tommy to support him on the stall.'

Jane sips her chilled wine.

Amber continues, 'Have you been invited to Marion's birthday party?'

Jane nods. 'Rachael messaged me. It's in the Italian tomorrow night.'

'They wanted it here, but fortunately, we're full.'

Jane laughs. 'I thought after JJ left, that Marion might be more subdued but she's found an ally in Rachael.'

'So, you're going?'

'No, I— I...'

Amber smiles. 'You're looking very secretive. Are you seeing someone?'

Jane shakes her head. 'It's nothing.'

'Nothing?' This time it's Amber's turn to laugh. 'You're blushing over nothing.'

'I'm not blushing.' Jane touches her cheeks.

'I was a lawyer. I can spot a lie across the road.'

Jane laughs. 'It's not a secret. Fish and chips on the beach hardly constitutes a date.'

'I think that's one of the most romantic things to do. Take a bottle of wine. Watch the sunset. Ummm...'

'Stop umming.'

'Well, who with? Or do I have to trawl the beach looking for you?'

'You're too busy.'

'True.'

'Tommy,' Jane says quietly. 'But it isn't a date.'

'Tommy. Wow! Lovely. He's a good guy.'

'I know but—'

'It's early days yet.' Amber finishes for her.

'There's nothing in it. You know, we're friends and I think we get on and we chat a lot.'

'He needs to get out and about and move on with his life. As wild as Shelley is, I think she's been good for him. She's got him taking an interest in life.'

'Did you say Shelley is wild?'

Amber regards Jane and nods. 'She was a bit full on with Faisal but she's backed off now. Femi was worried as she didn't want him getting into smoking weed and stuff.'

'Is he still friends with Ahmed?' Jane asks referring to Femi's other foster child.

'Yes, they get on really well. When they get any spare time, they are at the Syrian refugee centre helping others out. They're really good guys.'

'So, I wonder who Shelley is hanging out with now?'

'She's helping Mario and Lucas in the pet shop. They're happy with her so maybe she's settled down a little now.'

'Let's hope so, for Tommy's sake.' Jane drains her glass. 'Thanks for that Amber. I must get back, I have two online orders that I need to finish and send off tonight.'

'Night, Jane.'

'I'll have a chat with Tommy tomorrow and make sure that he's okay helping Noah.'

'Okay, but please do me a favour?'

Jane pauses and waits.

Amber says, 'Forget about everyone else. Just have a lovely, fun evening and enjoy the magic of a warm, romantic sunset.'

* * *

On Friday evening, it's still hot, and the whole town is busy with locals and tourists heading to the pubs and the beach.

Jane and Tommy carry their fish and chips away from the town centre, along the promenade, beyond the harbour where it's quieter, but the sunset is just as beautiful.

'I've brought a bottle of chilled wine.' Tommy puts the bag on the beach and pulls out a big soft rug and lays it on the pebbles. Then he pulls out two plastic flutes and pours the liquid carefully.

Jane opens a sachet of mayonnaise. They face the dying sunset. There's a welcome cool breeze and the gentle rhythm of the receding tide as it scrapes back over the stones.

'Cheers!'

They tap glasses and sip the chilled Pinot Grigio.

'This is the life,' Jane says.

'You can't beat the sea.' Tommy begins to unwrap his food, then, using the small sachets, he adds vinegar, salt and ketchup.

They eat in silence, enjoying the peace, relaxing in each other's company.

'I thought you were going to cancel on me,' Tommy says.

'Why?'

'It's Marion's birthday party.'

'I thought you might be going.' Jane grins, pleased that he's with her and not at the party. It's a small victory but it's an important one for Jane.

Tommy smiles. 'I can honestly say that there is no place I'd rather be than here.'

Content to eat slowly and watch the families and people around them, they chat easily and with genuine friendship.

'You get on well with Noah,' she says.

'Poor lad, he hardly says a word but I know he likes me

talking to him. So, I explain lots of things and tell him stories. I ask him first though. I say, Noah, is this something that you would like to know more about? And he nods — he's never yet said no.' Tommy laughs.

'What do you talk about?'

'Different things, the harbour, the boats and fishing of course. Then I tell him how I did woodwork at school and what a disaster I was—'

Jane laughs.

Tommy smiles. 'I tell him how it's changed here. How it was when I first moved here twenty years ago and how the town has changed. I talk to him about Amber and Ben and how they have made such a difference to the community and I tell him how small things are important, and that small acts of kindness change many people's lives.'

'That's lovely.'

'It's important for him to know. I've told him it's alright for him to enjoy his time here, that he has his whole life ahead of him and one day he might make a difference to someone else's life and that he can go on to do great things.'

'Jesus was a carpenter.'

'Indeed. Although we haven't talked religion, yet.'

Jane smiles. 'Well, it's only been a few days. You've the whole summer ahead of you.'

Tommy grins. 'He doesn't say much but when people ask how much things are, he points to the labels. I try and let him be autonomous and independent, and he counts the change. Today he sorted the tippy-tappy thingy for the credit card. In another few weeks he might start chatting and maybe he can be left alone.'

After they've eaten, Jane gathers their empty food parcels

and walks over to put them in the bin, secure from the seagulls. When she returns the sun has set lower.

Tommy pours another glass of wine and they lean back on their elbows watching the horizon turn crimson, purple and orange until the sun slowly fades.

'You must have done this a thousand times,' Tommy says to her. Their faces are close to each other, close enough for him to see the tiny crow's feet at the corner of her eyes.

She shakes her head. 'Not often enough. You forget. I forget.'

'Forget what?'

'What it's like to have someone to share it with.'

'But you haven't always been alone, have you?'

'I've had several bad relationships, bad choices on my behalf. A shrink would say, low self-esteem and she doesn't value herself...'

'What would you say?'

'I would say... I would say.' She squints at the sky. 'Probably, that I was a daddy's girl and that when mum died of pneumonia, I was twenty and I didn't want to leave him. They were older parents. Mum was forty when she had me, and dad was ten years older. She had heart problems and health issues for years.'

'I'm sorry.' Tommy reaches out for her hand and Jane is surprised by his warmth.

'Dad was heartbroken. I felt selfish about going off to university, so I stayed. He had a shop and he taught me everything about watches and clocks. It was alright but I never really had much of a social life.'

'Have you used dating apps.'

'Once or twice. But they've always been a disaster.'

Tommy nods. 'That's always been my fear, although to be honest I haven't been ready— oh look!' He waves to someone in the distance and Jane sits up conscious that the sun is no longer keeping her warm and there's a sudden chill from the breeze coming across the sea. She shivers and puts her arms around her knees, scanning the promenade to see who Tommy is waving at.

'There's Shelley,' he says. He calls out, 'Shelley, over here.'

Jane follows his gaze. Shelley is wearing tiny pink shorts and has long brown legs. Her t-shirt doesn't cover her midriff, yet she holds a pink shawl over her shoulder. Her face lights up and she smiles and waves back but that isn't before she's dropped the hand of the man who is walking beside her. Shelley bounces across the stones genuinely pleased to see her uncle and she appears excited and happy.

'Tommy,' she cries. 'What are you guys doing here?'

She smiles at Jane. Her eyes are big and her makeup is perfect. She looks stunningly beautiful. Westbay suits her. She's no longer the stroppy young adult. She seems to have morphed into a beautiful young woman in the space of a few months. Her hair is no longer electric red, it's a soft pink.

She turns her attention to the young man who has followed Shelley across the stones. Jane opens her mouth but her words are stuck. Her throat constricts and she can't swallow.

'Tommy, my main-man and the lovely jeweller. Hello, Jane.'

Yusef is bare-chested. He carries his t-shirt at his side and Jane stares at the flower tattoo over his shoulder, down his back to his hip. She remembers trailing her hand over his body in her bed and how they had made love with passion, uninhibited due to the alcohol they had both consumed.

'Yusef.' Tommy stands up and clasps him his chest as if they are the best of friends. He doesn't seem to have noticed that his niece was holding his hand or if he does, Tommy doesn't care. 'How great to see you guys.'

Shelley smiles. 'We're just heading into town for a drink.'

Tommy grins. 'So are we, aren't we, Jane? It's getting a bit cold now the sun has gone down. Look at you, Jane, you're shaking.'

Tommy bends down to pick up the rug and very gallantly places it around her. He squeezes her shoulders and Jane sees a flicker of something in Yusef's eyes.

'We can all have a drink together if you like, can't we, Yus?' Shelley says slipping her arm through his and she pats his flat, muscled stomach. 'But you'll have to put a shirt on or everyone will fancy you, won't they, Jane?'

Jane turns away and begins to walk to the promenade.

'I'm cold. Let's go.'

* * *

'Are you sure you're alright?' Tommy asks.

Jane nods. She hadn't liked the way that Shelley had looked at her when she had talked about women fancying Yusef.

Had he told her they'd slept together?

Shelley is making no secret of the fact that they are obviously together. They're walking in front of her and Tommy. Shelley hanging on Yusef's arm and occasionally her hand reaches down to squeeze his bum.

She had called him Yus – not even Yusef.

'What do you think?' Tommy whispers and nods at the young couple in front. 'She asked us to go with them to the pub. That's a result, isn't it?'

'Yes, I'm really pleased for you, Tommy. Have a good time.'

The last thing Jane wants is to be sitting having a drink with them watching Shelley all over Yusef like a rash.

Fortunately, he pulls on his shirt but he is strutting like a peacock with a beautiful girl on his arm, throwing his head back and laughing loudly at everything she says. Jane wonders if they are laughing at her.

At the top end of her street, she stops. 'Thank you. I've had a lovely evening,' she says truthfully; but she can't look at him. 'I'm sorry, Tommy. I'm too cold. You go with the others and I'll see you tomorrow. I need a hot shower.'

What would he say if he knew? He might be disgusted that she would sleep with a boy young enough to be her son. She must never let him find out.

'Shall I walk you home?'

'No. I'm fine. You go.' She pushes him along the street while she ducks out of sight down a back alley without saying goodbye to the young couple. She's walking quickly, her heart thumping, while she silently curses herself.

What a bloody mess, you bloody stupid, old woman.

* * *

Jane spends the weekend in hiding — working. She's ashamed. She knows she was abrupt and rude to Tommy but she's caught in a quagmire of her own feelings. She'd been having such a wonderful time with him. It had been so perfect and then Shelley and Yusef had come along and ruined it all.

When Tommy phones her on Sunday she asks, 'Are you happy they're together?'

'Yusef's a nice lad.'

'I thought she was hanging around with Ricky and his girlfriend.'

'They're seventeen and still at school, whereas Yusef is that bit older.'

'Do they sleep together?'

'I suppose so,' Tommy sighs. 'I haven't thought about it.'

'Does Yusef stay at your house?'

'I don't know. Erm, I don't think so. I've never seen him.'

'Tommy!'

'What?'

'How can this go on?'

'Jane, I'm not sure I understand you, Shelley is twenty — not sixteen.'

'I know but she must have some sort of responsibility to you—'

'Why?'

'She's staying at your house.'

'I know, and she's stuck to her bargain of having dinner with me once a week and she texts me.'

'Oh, so she tells you if she's staying at Yusef's?'

'Yes, mostly. Now, I just guess—'

'What about her job?'

'She's happy in the pet shop but it finishes in a week. She's confident she'll find another one.'

'And what about...?'

'Yes?'

'What about... Almond Blossom? Who is looking after her?'

'Me, of course.' Tommy chuckles. 'I'm a bit of a sucker for the little thing. She's such a delight. I'd love you to meet her. You'll love her - the others did.'

'Others?'

'Ah yes, well, on Friday night we went to The Ship and bumped into Marion, you know it was her birthday, and some of her friends, a few of them, came back here.'

'To your house? What for?'

'For a drink. The pubs were closing and we were all having a good time.'

'So, Marion came back to your house?'

'Only for a drink.'

Jane is silent.

'Jane? Are you alright?'

'I'm fine.'

'Are you angry?'

'No.'

'You seem upset.'

'I'm not upset. I just can't believe—'

'What?'

'That you—'

'Jane, you said you were cold. If you'd come with us then we would all have been at the pub together and you'd have seen how the evening panned out. It was all very natural, fun and very jolly. We'd all had rather a lot to drink and Shelley seemed to think it was a good idea at the time.'

Jane has a vision of Marion leering over Tommy, who is so drunk that he's loving her groping him. Then there's Shelley, who is absolutely gorgeous, stunning and twenty-years-old with Yusef who'd been *her* lover. But Yusef isn't her lover now. He was a one-night stand and now he's obviously seeing Shelley — lots of her.

'Is it serious?'

'What?'

'Between Shelley and Yusef?'

'I shouldn't think so. She'll be leaving at the end of the summer.'

'Well, does she know what she's getting herself into? Yusef has a... reputation with women.'

Tommy laughs. 'I think he's all talk.'

'I don't.'

'He's been in love with a girl for years, but she's dumped him in favour of Ozan. He was devastated when he found out a few months ago but he loves his brother so much that he's letting them get on with it. He's a decent guy.'

'He told you this?'

'Yes.'

Jane sighs.

'I don't know what's wrong with you, Jane, but you seem particularly interested in Shelley and Yusef, and I don't know why.'

'I just don't want her to get hurt. I don't want her heart to be broken.'

'It won't. They'll be fine. Now, would you like to come over next week and meet Almond Blossom? I think you must be the only person from Harbour Street who hasn't met her.'

* * *

Jane spends Sunday evening staring at her phone wondering if she should call Yusef – but what if Shelley picks up his phone? Then she thinks she might text him. But if she does and Shelley reads it – what then?

She feels sick.

What if Yusef has already told Shelley? It could be too late.

Jane is about to go to bed when her phone rings just after ten o'clock.

'Jane?'

'Yusef?

'Listen—'

'No, you listen, Yusef. What the hell are you doing with Shelley?'

'She's a nice girl—'

'Out of all the girls that live here, and all the ones who are visiting as tourists, you have to choose Shelley?'

'Why not? She likes me.'

'You've done it deliberately.'

'No, I haven't.'

'How did you meet her?'

'I've seen her a few times in town. Then I met her in the pub a few times and we got chatting. She works in the pet shop.'

'I know that.'

'You sound angry.'

'I don't want you going out with her.'

'Why?'

'I don't want you hurting her.'

'Why would I do that?'

'Because, I know you.'

'No, you don't. You've never taken the time to get to know me. Just because we shagged—'

'Don't you dare!' Jane hisses into the phone. 'Don't you dare use that language.'

'Okay, just because we made love passionately one night, does not mean that you know me. You don't even know how upset I was that night. You were so wrapped up in yourself and that idiot in town who was trying to get you to have a threesome, you never even asked about me.'

'I did—'

'You were hammered, Jane. We both were. It suited us both very well and that's it. It's over.'

'Good.'

'So, I don't know why you're saying bad things about me.'

'I'm not.'

'You've told Tommy that I'm no good and you think I'll hurt Shelley. But I won't. You have no right to say these things.'

Jane scratches her head. 'You've told her, haven't you?'

There's a pause at the end of the phone.

'You have, haven't you?' Jane's voice is increasingly loud and she's gripping her mobile so hard her fingers are hurting. 'You promised me.'

'Look, she doesn't know it's you.'

'Who does she think it is?'

'We were all pretty hammered on Friday night, doing shots and everything back at Tommy's, and when she asked me who was the last person I was with, I said it was a mistake — I said I was with an older woman.'

'You told her?' Jane shouts.

'I didn't name names. I didn't say it was you.'

Jane sits down heavily at the kitchen table, her legs suddenly weak. 'Well, it won't take her long to work it out will it? There are not many women my age, who happen to have a shop across the road from your shop. And she'll have seen you popping over to me at every opportunity.'

'It's not like that, Jane.' Yusef's tone is pleading. 'I would never say anything bad about you and yet, you tell Tommy I'm no good. It hurts me, Jane. Don't do it.'

'Then don't breathe a word about me.'

'They will never know about us — not from me.'

'There is no us.'

'Goodnight, Jane. And remember, just say nice things about me, please.'

Jane sits and stares at the wall. The irony of it all is baffling. How did her life end up being such crap? And on top of everything, Marion has been around to Tommy's.

He's playing you for a fool. Tommy is stringing you along.

June

Tommy

This time last year Tommy was in hospital recovering from a heart attack and now he's spending most days in the harbour at the market stall with Noah. He's amazed at how much he's enjoying himself and how happy he is, only sometimes he feels guilty.

As they are closing the stall one evening, he talks to Noah.

'You see the thing is, Noah, after Sunita died, I was numb. I thought I'd never be able to do anything again. Nothing seemed worth it. What was it all for? Even the garden — it wasn't worth putting in bulbs or cutting things back, there was no one to sit in it with me. Anyway, I'd lost my mojo. I was very, very sad.'

They walk over to the bench overlooking the sea which has become their custom while they wait for Amber. Noah sits silently beside him. Tommy's phone pings.

Running a bit late. 30mins – sorry. A.

Tommy reads the message aloud then says, 'Not to worry, I have an idea.'

They walk under the clock tower and into Harbour Street

and, when they're inside *From The Heart*, gift shop, he asks Noah to choose a kite.

Noah face lights up as he studies all the different designs.

'You have to decide,' Tommy says, 'A dragon, a rainbow kite or a squid with long tentacles?'

Tommy laughs at his choice.

'That's the one I would have chosen.'

Back on the beach, Tommy tells Noah about the kite competitions all over the world and a big one he'd once seen on TV in Pakistan. He describes all the colours, shapes and sizes in detail and Noah nods and laughs.

Tommy hands Noah the reel and string. 'Start running,' he says.

Noah runs along the beach and Tommy lets go of the giant butterfly kite and, caught by the wind, it swoops up into the air. Noah turns around, running backwards as the kite soars into the sky. He continues running backwards and laughing, looking up at the sky, unravelling the string. His laughter is loud and excited.

This warms Tommy's heart. He remembers how his father had done the same thing with him. He laughs as Noah tugs the kite higher into the sky.

Amber arrives and stands watching them from the promenade. Noah hasn't tired of running on the beach and his legs are tanned, his cheeks glow and his eyes shine.

'You're doing really well with him, thank you,' she says, standing beside Tommy.

'I'm enjoying it, Amber.'

'You're looking much better, but I'm not sure if that's because of Noah or perhaps there's a lady who's taking up your time now.'

Tommy scratches his head, but he won't look at her.

'It's alright, I won't ask you twenty questions.' Amber slaps him on the shoulder. 'A man is entitled to his secrets.'

'There isn't a secret. I wish there was.'

'Really? I thought you and Jane went to the beach the other week.'

Tommy moves from one foot to the other. 'We did, but I haven't seen her since.'

'Why?'

'I don't know. One minute it's the two of us lying on the beach watching the sunset, talking about everything and nothing — things are going really well and then, the next thing I know, whoosh, she's running home and I'm left standing there in the middle of the street like an idiot, wondering what I did wrong.'

'Have you spoken to her?'

'Not really.'

'Why not?'

'Well, it's a bit awkward.' Tommy stares down the beach at Noah. 'You see, after she left, I went to the pub with Shelley and Yusef. We all had a bit to drink and then a few of them came back to the house and I don't think Jane is happy about it.'

Amber frowns.

Tommy continues, 'It was Marion's birthday. We did drink a lot and it seemed fun at the time. But I think that Jane is upset.'

'Do you like Marion?'

'She can be very funny. She likes a good time, that's for sure and she's an incredible dancer.'

Amber smiles. 'You're finally letting go and having fun.'

'We put a bit of music on. Everyone was dancing. It wasn't my fault.'

'What wasn't?'

'She was showing me how to samba.'

'Just samba?'

'Well, she did kiss me. Full on the lips.'

'Is that what you wanted?'

'Well, not really. I hadn't thought about it. I'd been with Jane all evening and it had been perfect on the beach; romantic, easy going, fun, and then suddenly it was like she just had to go — I felt abandoned.'

'And you didn't find out why she left?'

'She said she was cold.'

'Okay, so you then went to the pub, invited a few friends back to yours and ended up dancing the samba and snogging another woman.'

'It wasn't like that?'

Amber raises her eyebrows. 'I was a lawyer, Tommy. Those are the facts.'

Tommy rubs his cheek. 'I was hoping that Jane wouldn't find out.'

Amber shakes her head and focusses on the kite that begins to sink on the gentle thermal wind.

'Run, Noah,' she calls and they watch the boy run farther down the beach.

'Do you think she knows?' Tommy asks.

'If she's been avoiding you, she probably might.'

'What shall I do?'

'That depends on who you like. If it's Marion, then stick with Marion. If it's Jane, then stick with Jane. Don't string them both along.'

'I wouldn't do that.'

'I know you wouldn't do it deliberately. But sometimes things can happen and people might not believe you are naive and innocent — and you're probably a bit out of practice with dating etiquette.'

'You're right about that.'

They watch the kite fall and Noah bends over to pick it up.

'Amber,' Tommy says, after a few minutes. 'Do you have any idea why Jane doesn't like Yusef?'

'I think they get on, don't they?'

'Well, he used to take her coffee and they used to talk a lot. I often saw him in her shop and they get on really well, but she's not at all happy that he's seeing Shelley. Has she said anything to you?' he asks.

'No, but I think she would have told me if she had a problem with him.'

'That's alright then.' Tommy is relieved and in a louder voice he shouts, 'Come on, Noah. Time to go.'

Noah raises his hand and begins to run towards them, and Amber and Tommy are so pleased to see the transformation in him that their conversation is soon forgotten.

* * *

Marion insists, 'It will do you good, Tommy. You need a day out of Westbay. You spend all your time in that silly harbour looking after that boy who doesn't even speak to you and without being paid. You should have a day off. I'm sure Jane won't mind—'

'It's Amber that—'

'Well, never mind, you can't work every day. I'm taking a

half day on Wednesday and I insist. We're going on a picnic.'

They're sitting outside on the patio at the back of The Ship. It's cooler in the shade and out of the sun.

'What about the boutique?' he asks.

'Rachael is going to look after it for me.'

'I'll speak to Amber,' he says.

'There's no need. I've spoken to her already and she's arranged for Faisal to cover for you. We'll go to the dunes along the coast and find ourselves a snug place, just the two of us.'

Tommy frowns.

'We can stay late if we like. We won't be in a hurry. We haven't got anyone to rush back for and if there's no one around we can even do a bit of skinny dipping.' She grins at him and rests her hand on his. The pub door opens and Shelley walks outside, hand-in-hand with Yusef. 'Here come the happy couple. Now don't they look like they're in love?' Marion claps her hands together.

Tommy stares at them. Shelley looks radiant with a crop-top revealing a tanned tummy. Yusef, as immaculately groomed as always, is beaming happily. Shelley heads over to their table while Yusef orders at the bar.

'I didn't realise you were in here,' she says cheerfully, smiling at Tommy.

'We often pop in, don't we, Tommy?' Marion's hand is still covering his and Shelley stares at them before returning his gaze.

'Are we still on for Thursday night?' Shelley asks.

Tommy smiles. 'Of course.'

'Oh, what's happening?' Marion asks.

'Tommy and I always have a night each week on our own

together.'

'That sounds fun. Can anyone come?'

'No,' they both reply in unison and Shelley giggles.

Marion pouts in mock distress.

'Have you had a good day?' Tommy asks.

'I finished work.' She turns her mouth down at the corner. 'So, Yusef took me for a burger and now we've come in here.'

'So, what will you do for work now?' Marion's smile is a little smug, thinks Tommy, remembering how Shelley barely lasted a week in her boutique.

'I've got a few ideas.' She taps the side of her nose.

'Let's hope they're legal,' Marion laughs.

Shelley raises her eyes to the ceiling. 'Of course.'

'Well, we're planning a picnic tomorrow afternoon. We're heading off to the dunes.'

Shelley nods and glances over her shoulder to where Yusef is waiting for her at the bar. 'Well, if I don't see you, have fun.'

'We won't do anything, you wouldn't do,' quips Marion.

Tommy pulls his hand away and reaches into his pocket, he pulls out his wallet and takes out a twenty-pound note. 'Buy a drink for youself and Yusef.'

'Thanks, Tommy. You're the best uncle.'

Shelley leans over to give him a kiss on the cheek. He waves her away but she leans close to his ear and whispers, 'Mind yourself with that vixen.'

* * *

'I'm sorry, Amber, I don't like to leave Noah. I don't have to go.'

'Nonsense, Marion is right. You need time off. I'll take over or Jane will. Don't worry. One of us will be with him.'

'Erm, you won't tell Jane, will you?'

'About the picnic with Marion?'

He nods.

'It's none of my business, Tommy, but I won't lie. If she asks me where you've gone, I'll have to tell her, but I won't volunteer any information.'

'Thank you.'

She puts her hand on his arm. 'This outing might help you make up your mind.'

'I hope so, Amber, but it's not as simple as that. Jane is avoiding me and I just don't know what to do.'

'You will, when the time comes.'

'Will I?'

'You're in no hurry, Tommy. Just be cool with everything. In my experience things either work out — or they don't.' She grins.

He smiles back. 'They worked out for you and Ben.'

'Not in the beginning. Everything takes time, so be kind to yourself.'

'Do you think everyone needs to know the truth?'

'Do you mean about you kissing Marion?'

'She kissed me.'

'Well, I think you have to live with the truth, you also have to live with the guilt. Some people can lead double lives and for some people lies roll off the tongue with no effort, and other people don't even know when they're lying — it's their version of the truth.'

'That sounds very deep.'

'I believe, Tommy, that you must be able to look yourself in the mirror and like what you see.'

'And if you don't?'

'Then change.'

'I feel guilty going out this afternoon.'

'Don't. Everyone needs a day off and time for themselves. Sometimes love isn't this great big immediate thunderbolt from the sky; a massive collision of emotion, passion and sex. Sometimes love grows slowly. It takes time. Love must be nurtured. You love people in different ways and to be honest, I think you've been used to loving Sunita in a particular way, in a way that suited you — and her. But when you meet someone else — another woman — you will probably love her differently and that's okay. You have to find which sort of love suits you.'

'Phew! That's a lot to take on board for a fisherman.'

Amber laughs. 'You're not just a fisherman, Tommy, you're the biggest catch of the season.'

* * *

Marion lays out a pretty, soft blanket in the middle of the dunes, sheltered from the wind and away from anyone else. While she unpacks the contents of the picnic bag, Tommy stands up, stretches and looks out over the beach and the sea beyond. The tide is out and families are spread out along the sand, but there are dark clouds gathering. When he checked earlier, there was a suggestion of rain, perhaps even a storm after the mini early heatwave.

'Swim, first?' Marion asks.

Tommy shakes his head. He didn't like to tell her that he wasn't much of a swimmer. Most people might find that surprising as he'd spent most of his life at sea but the only time he liked the water was when he was in a boat or the bath.

'Do you miss fishing?' Marion asks as she pours a glass of wine for them both.

'Only half a glass for me.' He covers the top with his hand. 'I'm driving.'

'I bought a flask of coffee for after. Cheers!'

She raises her glass and smiles, and he wonders how her lips manage to stay so red. Sunita had always complained her lipstick came off so easily.

'I've got smoked salmon, crab, prawns and mackerel.' Marion busies herself unpacking plastic cutlery and plates.

'I do miss fishing, but more than that, I miss being at sea.'

'Have you thought of buying a boat?'

Tommy laughs. 'No, never.'

'Why? You could get a small one with an engine and we could motor down the coast in the good weather. If you get one with a cabin, we could sleep on it.'

She spills Marie-Rose sauce on her index finger and so she puts it in her mouth, sucking it slowly.

Tommy looks away. 'I don't know if it's what I want.'

'You're going to have to do something, you know that don't you? I mean once that boy leaves.'

'Noah?'

'Yes, him. You'll have nothing to do when the Artisan market closes.' She offers him a plate and begins spooning coleslaw onto hers. 'You don't want to disappear into yourself again in the winter. Shelley will probably be gone by then too, so you'll need company and we will need something to do. It could be a hobby for us both.'

Tommy eats slowly. 'I'm not sure.'

Marion pauses as she sips her wine. 'The thing is Tommy,

I saw a different side of you that night when I taught you to samba. You should come to Rachael's exercise class, I think you'd love it. You're a natural mover, you have great rhythm and when you move those hips...' She laughs. 'You're a bad boy.'

Tommy grins. He had enjoyed dancing.

Marion tells him about her foreign holidays, how she's always danced and all the places she's been to and the people she's met. Tommy is content to listen to her and after they've eaten and she's packed the food away, she insists on him lying on his back, so that she can rest her head on his shoulder. He feels her breath on his skin and her hand on his chest and, for a minute, he relaxes and closes his eyes. He hasn't felt this close to a woman for four years and although Marion isn't Sunita, she feels comfortable wedged under his arm. He thinks it might be pleasant to lie quietly, but then she slides her hand between the buttons of his shirt. He tenses.

Her fingers stroke his chest. It seems strange that this woman can initiate this closeness with him. She'd been like this the night she came back to his house and it had taken a great amount of persuasion for Yusef and Shelley to walk her home. Marion had been more than a little drunk and had protested. Tommy had picked up Almond Blossom and hugged her to his chest. 'You're stroking the wrong pussy!' she shouted as she stormed out.

Now, he feels her warm breath on his skin and he's not sure if that's the tip of her tongue near his ear. It tickles and he shifts a little, but she holds him firm with her hand on his chest and very slowly, she undoes the top button of his shirt and then the next.

'I'm pleased you're not hairy,' she whispers.

Tommy clears his throat and holds his shirt together but very gently Marion pulls his hand away and then to his surprise, she throws her leg over him and pushes against him with her hips.

'Marion.'

'What, baby?'

'We can't.'

'Can't what?' She's pushing her hand under his shirt and he feels her fingers inching towards the zip on his shorts.

'This.' He grabs her hand.

'Come on,' she whispers. 'No one can see us here. What have you got to lose?'

* * *

It's Shelley's turn to make dinner and she fries burgers in the pan, warms the buns and pushes the chips in the oven.

Tommy has laid two places in the kitchen.

'I thought the weather was going to hold,' Shelley says. 'Although it's quite nice to see the rain again. Did you get caught yesterday?'

'Caught?' Tommy's head shoots up.

'In the rain, when you went on your picnic? What's wrong?'

'Nothing's wrong. Yes, we'd eaten and then the rain came in very suddenly. We got drenched running back to the car.'

'Did you have a good time?'

'Yes.' Tommy folds two paper napkins and places them on the table.

Sunita liked a lovely laid table and he places the ketchup with the salt and vinegar in the centre. 'Beer or wine?'

'Beer, please.'

160

'How's Yusef?'

'He's good. He's gone to a cousin's birthday party in town. I've never known anyone to have so many cousins. Even he doesn't know who they are or how many he has.' Shelley laughs.

There's a ring on the front door and Tommy stands up. It's a delivery driver with a box for Shelley. Tommy needs two hands to carry it into the kitchen.

'Oh, great. I'll take it upstairs, after.'

'What is it?' he asks.

'My new venture, but don't ask me about it. It's a surprise.'

Having been woken up, Almond Blossom wanders into the kitchen, miaows and jumps up onto Tommy's lap.

Shelley puts their plates on the table and sits opposite.

'No phone or cats at the table.' She laughs.

Tommy places Almond Blossom on the floor and is rewarded by a loud vocal protest. They ignore her and Shelley asks, 'Have you seen Jane?'

Tommy shakes his head pleased that his mouth is full.

'I thought you two were getting really close that time when we saw you on the beach watching the sunset.'

Tommy shrugs. 'I think she's been really busy. She built up her online business during Covid, and then with the market stall — she's the one making all the jewellery.'

'I think she works too hard.'

Tommy nods wondering why Shelley is suddenly interested in Jane, but pleased she's not talking about Marion.

'I spoke to your mum this morning. She was asking me about you going back to uni. Have you given it any more thought?' he asks.

'Did she ask you to speak to me?'

Tommy smiles. 'How did you guess?'

Shelley eats her burger, her face thoughtful. 'Tell her that a lot will depend.'

'On what?'

Shelley shrugs. 'I can't say.'

'Yusef? Is it that serious?'

'He's sick.' Shelley smiles.

'Sick?' Tommy's eyes widen.

'Sick as in fit, as in gorgeous.' Shelley laughs and opens her eyes wide. 'I haven't told Mum about him. Please don't mention him to her.'

'Alright.'

They chat for a while about her mother, her health and her treatment, and then Shelley asks, 'Do you like him?'

'He's a good guy. He cuts hair really well.' Tommy rubs the back of his neck where Yusef had recently cut his. 'And Ozan is a good guy too.'

'They're very family oriented. I guess I'm a bit of a loner and it's good to have a night with you.'

Tommy smiles. 'I'm happy to oblige.'

'Great. Then you can carry that box upstairs for me after dinner — no questions and no peeking.'

'So long as there are no pets or animals, we're okay.'

'I promise.' Shelley finishes her burger. 'What are you going to do?'

'I'm going to watch TV.'

'No, I mean after the summer. I know you enjoy helping Noah but when the market stall closes you'll need something to do.'

'It's only June,' he says.

'Time will fly.'

Tommy's finishes his dinner and stands up quickly. 'Look, I'm sick of everyone asking me what I'm going to do. Why is everyone so concerned?'

'I didn't know they were,' Shelley replies quietly.

'Well, they are and everyone should mind their own bloody business.'

* * *

Tommy isn't sure why he doesn't see Shelley for a few days. He hopes it's not because of his outburst, but she texts him frequently and assures him she's fine. Tommy has taken full responsibility for Almond Blossom now and he puts a clean litter tray down for her each night, buys her tinned food and a grooming brush from the pet shop.

He likes having Almond Blossom in the house. He likes hearing her purr when he talks to her. 'It's like you're the only one who understand me,' he says.

Almond Blossom stretches and brushes against his hand. Tommy picks up his mobile and types.

If you're not busy tomorrow, can you look after Noah for a few hours on the stall?

Shelley types back almost immediately.

What time?

Tommy thinks.

2.30pm – I'll be back by 4pm.

Shelley writes.

No problem.

Tommy texts Amber.

Check-up tomorrow pm but Shelley will look after Noah.

Shelley has met Noah a few times and Tommy is happy that

she's agreed so readily. He's excited and also very nervous about his medical check-up.

* * *

Tommy is walking on air as he leaves the hospital. Driving back to Westbay he has time to reflect on his life and the conversation with the doctor. Just over a year ago, three of Tommy's four main arteries supplying blood to his heart were seventy percent blocked. He'd undergone coronary bypass surgery and he's spent months wondering why he's been saved. On the one hand he feels lucky to be alive but on the other he's bewildered.

Following surgery, he joined a two-month cardiac rehabilitation course where, in the group, he had pushed himself. He'd been determined to get better and with the help of a physiotherapist beside him he was confident and he felt safe — he knew he'd make a full recovery. After his heart attack, he was determined to get back to the life he loved. He missed night fishing most of all, looking up at the stars, with the swish of the water under the boat and the banter of his mates. He'd been determined, but when he got home from the hospital his resolve and confidence seemed to disappear. Just walking to the harbour gave him chest pains and he felt a failure. His body hadn't recovered. He was bitterly disappointed and angry and he would torture himself every day by going to the harbour and watching and waiting for the fishing fleet to come in. He had wanted to cry. Without Sunita he had never felt so alone. But, in the past few months with Shelley staying with him, his mind has been occupied with other things. More recently, helping Noah, has stopped him from thinking about his heart and his health.

Today, the doctor has said he is doing excellently and Tommy is thrilled. He needs the necessary paperwork for the insurance but he is determined to speak to Matt. He wants his old job back. He parks the car at home, knowing the harbour will still be busy and he walks briskly. He's been walking every day, everywhere he can, up and down Harbour Street and along the promenade and now he feels fit and healthy.

He dodges the tourists ambling though the marina. He gets closer to the stall but it's not Shelley who's there. It's Jane. She's hugging Noah. Tommy quickens his pace and as he gets closer he sees Jane bending down, speaking to him, drying his eyes with a tissue.

'What's happened?' he asks. 'Noah, are you alright?'

Noah won't look at him. He turns away and buries his head against Jane's shoulder. Tommy looks at Jane, but she's furious.

'He's been on his own,' she says.

'Shelley should have been here. She said she was coming.'

Jane rubs the back of Noah's curly hair. 'It's alright, Noah. You've managed really well on your own, well done.'

Tommy stands with his hands on his hips.

'Didn't Shelley come, Noah?' he asks.

'What do you think? Look at him?' Jane's eyes blaze.

Noah's shoulders are shaking. Jane moves towards the back of the stall and, as if they know there's a problem, people avoid coming to look at the crafted woodwork and jewellery.

Tommy pulls his phone from his pocket and calls Shelley, but she doesn't answer. Jane is trying to distract Noah with his handmade boats asking him which of his crafts he might sell next, but he still doesn't react.

Tommy feels helpless so he calls out, 'Come on, Noah, let's get you an ice cream. We'll get the one you like.' Noah looks up and Tommy smiles. 'You don't need any more tears. Let's call it a day. What do you think, Jane? Would you like an ice cream?'

Jane's face is screwed up in frustrated anger and Tommy can feel the heat of it directed at him. But to his relief, Noah leaves Jane's side and wiping the last of his tears away with the back of his hand, he stands beside Tommy looking eagerly at the ice cream van.

'Jane?' Tommy asks.

She shakes her head. 'I'll close up.'

'See you later?'

Jane turns her back and begins to pack away the stock and so Tommy, with his hand on Noah's shoulder, leads him through the throng of people to stand in the ice cream queue. When they are finally served, they walk aimlessly back to the stall, but like many of the others, it's now closed up for the day and Jane has gone.

'Come on, one look at the fishing boats then I'll walk home with you.'

Noah follows him, licking his ice cream and Tommy breathes a sigh of relief that no lasting damage has been done — well, not to Noah, but Jane is going to take some winning over.

* * *

The Ship is busy and Tommy buys a pint of real ale for himself and one for Matt. He nods his head to a quiet spot outside in the corner of the terrace where they won't be disturbed.

Matt has bushy hair, a short-trimmed beard and his hands are large. The gang call them his baseball gloves and the memory makes Tommy smile. He's one of the gang.

They drink their beer, watch the people on the terrace around them and talk pleasantries for a while. Tommy asks about Matt's wife and children who he's never met despite the years he's known him and then Matt says, 'You haven't asked me to the pub to ask about my family, Tommy. What's bothering you?'

'I got the all clear from the hospital today.' Tommy smiles.

Matt nods. 'I'm pleased for you. We all are.'

'Good, thanks.'

Matt is silent.

Tommy says, 'This means that I'm all sorted. I can come back to work.'

Matt takes a long draft of his beer and wipes his mouth with the back of his hand. 'It's not as easy as that.'

'Don't worry about the insurance. I spoke to the doctor and he said he can get me the paperwork. All you have to do is to send it off.'

Matt shakes his head. 'It's not about the insurance, Tommy.'

'Then what is it?'

'It's about the gang.'

'I know. I'm in the gang.'

'You were, Tommy but we've had to replace you with young Nigel.'

'Yes, but—'

'I can't just let Nigel go now—'

'Why not? Did you tell him it was only temporary?'

'His wife is about to have a baby and he needs—'

'It was temporary— didn't you tell him?'

'No, Tommy, I didn't because it wasn't — it isn't.'

'What do you mean? I thought we were mates?'

'We are, Tommy, but I have a duty, an obligation to the crew and they need to feel safe.'

Tommy raises his voice. 'What do you mean, safe?'

Matt holds up his hand. 'You know how hard it is at sea. Everyone has to pull their weight and you have to be fit.'

'I am fit.'

'I know you are but it's tough. You aren't as strong as you were and deep down you know that, Tommy. Just imagine if you were still fishing and I'd had a heart attack and wanted to come back, you wouldn't be happy, would you?'

'You're my friend.' Tommy's voice sounds lame.

'And you're mine and friends can be honest with each other without bullshit. We're all getting older. I've only got another couple of years myself, at the most, and then we have to hand over the reins to the younger generation and the likes of Nigel.'

'He's a boy.'

'He's a good, strong boy and he's a hard worker. He spends a lot of time in the gym.' Matt leans across the table. 'He's so fit, he's sick.'

Tommy sighs. That was a Shelley answer and he's suddenly reminded that he's got to speak to her to find out what happened this afternoon. All of a sudden Tommy feels his world closing in. Nothing is going right, nothing is working out, nothing is flowing.

'Look, Tommy. This heart attack was a warning. It's the universe's way of telling you to lighten up. Take it easy. Have some fun — meet someone. You only have one life, mate, and it's time you started enjoying yours. You've been though a rough time and it's been tough for you. I know you enjoy fishing and being part of the gang, but you're going to have to think about other hobbies, different challenges.'

'Like what?' Tommy drains his pint.

'Badminton, cycling, hiking. There's a lot of stuff you can do now. Think what it is you want out of life and how you want to spend your remaining years on this earth. It certainly shouldn't be fishing.' He leans across the table. 'I think you want to come back into the gang because you feel safe. You think it's where you belong and where you feel one of us, but this is a young man's game now. Fishing is getting tougher and not all the gang are happy. Some of them would love to trade places with you.'

'Then let them.'

Matt stands up. 'I'll get us another pint. Give it some thought, Tommy. What do you want out of life?'

* * *

When Tommy opens the front door, he knows he's had too much to drink. After a couple of pints in The Ship, Matt persuaded him to go for a game of snooker. They'd met up with some of the other harbour crew and before he knew it, Tommy was roped into a game of cards. For a short time, he felt like he belonged again. He'd felt like he was one of the boys. They'd downed a few whisky chasers and then Matt had said it was time to leave and insisted on walking Tommy home as if he was a geriatric.

Now, as Tommy fumbles for the light switch all he can hear is Almond Blossom's constant miaowing. He can't see his watch, but it's gone midnight and she must be hungry.

'Shh, ssh, little one.' He opens a can, tips the contents onto the saucer and some of it splashes on the floor. 'Never mind.' He refills the water bowl and then as he's half way up the stairs, he remembers his phone, so he plods back downstairs again. When he finds it, he screws up his eyes to focus on his messages and lumbers up the stairs. Just as he gets to the landing, the bedroom door is flung open and Shelley stands staring at him.

'You're drunk!'

'What are you doing here?'

'I live here, remember?'

'You didn't feed Almond B—'

'I forgot.'

'Where were you?' he slurs, holding on to the banister and swaying precariously.

'Me?'

'You were supposed to look out for Noah.'

'Go to bed, you're drunk.'

'Where've you been?'

She stares at him and he leans towards her, focusing on her face. 'Have you been crying?'

'It's none of your business.'

'What's happened?' He stands very still but everywhere seems to be moving. He can't concentrate on Shelley's face as it keeps going in and out of focus but she looks different. She's not wearing makeup and her hair is a mess. She's in her pyjamas but there's still something that's not right and he's trying to figure it out.

'What are you staring at?'

'You look different.'

Shelley stares at him.

'What is it?'

'I don't know what you're talking about.'

Tommy laughs and holds up one finger on his hand. 'I know. The glow has gone. You're not smiling.'

'That's because it's late and you're a mess.'

'I'm not a fisherman.'

'What?'

He shakes his head. 'I'm not fishing. They don't want me. Nigel's having a baby.'

'Who's Nigel?'

'He took my job and he won't give it back.'

'Come away from the stairs before you fall.' She pulls on his arm and he tumbles forward, crashing against the wall and Shelley makes the most of the momentum and she shoves him in his back propelling him towards his bedroom. He grips the frame of the door holding himself upright and pausing.

'My bed.' He stumbles forward, head first, and lies flat out on the mattress, fully clothed and face down. Shelley leans over to check he's still breathing then she closes the door and heads back to her bedroom.

* * *

When he wakes, Tommy's head is thumping. He staggers downstairs in his pyjamas, opens the fridge and drinks orange juice from the carton. He switches the kettle on and pops bread in the toaster while rummaging in the cupboard for pain killers.

Almond Blossom brushes around his leg and the smell of her litter tray makes him want to vomit. He can't face changing it now, so he opens the back door and puts it in the garden, leaving the air to flow inside.

He opens a can of food but can't find her bowl until he sees it under the stairs.

'How did this get here?' he asks.

Almond Blossom miaows.

'Shush, have some consideration, please. My head is thumping.'

The kitten ignores him and jumps on the table, nudging him, until he puts her food on the floor in the corner, her usual place. Perhaps Shelley had put the bowl there, she must have fed her.

He butters his toast, adds Marmite, drinks two cups of coffee and then makes another supply of toast. His head is clearing and Almond Blossom snuggles into his lap.

'Don't get too comfy, I have to go and see if Noah is okay and find out if Jane is talking to me.'

Bits of the night before are coming back to him — conversations with Matt, Nigel replacing him, feeling like one of the gang, whisky chasers, cards, playing snooker.

'I'm not a young man any more.' He rubs the kitten's ears. 'Life is for the young ones. Old? I'm not even sixty. You have it all ahead of you.'

He showers, dresses and as an afterthought, he knocks on Shelley's door.

'Shelley? Are you home?'

There's no answer but he thinks he can hear something or someone inside.

'Shelley?'

There's a small noise and he tries the door handle but it's locked.

'Are you okay?'

'Fine.'

'Look.' He leans with his back against her bedroom door. 'I'm sorry I was drunk last night. That wasn't nice for you to witness and I'm really sorry. See? I've said it twice. I know when I'm wrong and when I've made a mistake.'

'Go away.'

'I've apologised. Now, it's your turn. Where were you, yesterday?'

'Leave me alone.'

'This is called being a grown-up, an adult. It's about taking responsibility. I asked you to look after Noah and you agreed. You know he has issues. He finds talking difficult and that's why Amber doesn't want to leave him on his own. Now I have to go and explain to Jane and Amber why Noah was left on his own, so you'd better have some fantastic excuse that is going to redeem me in their eyes. I trusted you.'

Suddenly, Shelley pulls open the door and Tommy loses his balance. He regains it just in time not to fall into her room.

She's still wearing her pyjamas, only this morning her eyes are red-rimmed with dark circles underneath. Her hair is dirty and unkempt and she looks thinner, as if she hasn't eaten for weeks.

He holds onto the door frame and steadies himself while she looks at him with disdain.

'Why did you get so drunk?'

'I got the all clear from the doctor and I thought I could get my job back but they don't want me.'

Shelley stares at him. 'Well, that was a shitty day all-round then, wasn't it?'

'What do you mean?'

'Jane was right all along.'

'About what?'

Shelley's eyes narrow and tears fall down her cheeks. She says, in a tightly-controlled voice, 'You can tell her Yusef has dumped me.'

July

Jane

It's early when Tommy appears at Jane's shop holding two cups of coffee from Harbour Café.

'It's a peace offering,' he says, placing one on the counter by her elbow.

Jane doesn't want to look at him. Her emotions are so mixed: on the one hand she's furious with him, yet on the other, she's pleased he's made the effort to come and see her. It's been a month since she ran off and left him after they'd eaten fish and chips on the beach. She'd been so riddled with guilt and shock at seeing Yusef and Shelley holding hands and so clearly and obviously in love, that she'd pretended to be cold — and she'd run home.

It hadn't helped to hear, a few days later, that Tommy had happily gone to the pub without her and ended up taking Marion back to his house. She heard how they'd all drunk too much but then Jane had blocked off. She didn't want to know any more. Tommy wasn't the man she thought he was and she'd spent the past month thinking she'd had a very lucky escape.

So, by all accounts, when she'd popped down to the stall yesterday with some new stock, she had assumed he'd be there with Noah. She was prepared to see him but instead she'd found Noah crouched behind the stall with his hands covering his ears. He was alone. It had taken her a while to get him to talk and she found out that he'd been left to deal with customers. He'd found it overwhelming. He had started to cry and buried his head in her shoulder.

Annoyingly, Tommy arrived looking radiant and happy and with a ready smile on his lips but then she'd seen the smile disappear to be replaced by fear and horror as it dawned on him that Shelley hadn't turned up. Jane knew it wasn't his fault but it certainly didn't endear her towards Shelley.

Secretly, she'd wondered if Yusef had been the distraction.

Today Tommy was determined to talk to her. 'I've apologised to Amber and again to Noah,' he says. 'Now it's your turn.'

'Don't bother.'

Tommy sighs. 'Don't make this harder for me, Jane. I want to be able to talk to you. We were friends and I don't know what's happened.'

Jane looks at him. He clearly didn't understand that she wasn't going to compete with Marion for his attention. She'd seen them a couple of times and she'd heard rumours, but Jane wasn't going to be churlish. If he wanted Marion, then he was welcome and good luck to him.

'Let's start again, shall we?' He smiles and Jane feels her heart thawing.

She nods. 'Thanks for the coffee.'

'I had to go to the hospital yesterday afternoon and Shelley agreed to look after Noah.'

'What's wrong with you?'

He looks surprised. 'Everything's alright. It was a check-up and they gave me a clean bill of health.'

'That's good.' She smiles. 'You look well.'

'I was silly enough to think I might get my old job back but—' He rubs his head. 'It's not to be. I'm too old and they don't want to take the risk of having me onboard in case there's a problem with my heart again.'

'I'm sorry.'

'On a more positive note, Matt did suggest I take up ballet, cricket or tiddlywinks.'

Jane laughs and ignores Tommy smiling back at her. She wasn't falling for all that nonsense again.

'I haven't seen much of you,' he says softly.

'Tommy, I really have been busy. It's crazy and I know it's a cliché, but there aren't enough hours in the day. I don't know if I can continue to keep doing all this.' She waves her hand around the shop. 'Between the online business, the market stall and the shop, it's just been frantic and I can't make the jewellery fast enough.'

'Is that why I haven't seen you?'

'Yes,' she lies.

He nods. 'With all that going on, perhaps you'd like me to cook dinner for you one night? It might be a break?'

'Thank you, but to be honest, by the time I finish my online orders to send off, I'm exhausted and I'm probably not very good company.'

'I can take the chance.'

Jane sips her coffee wondering why he's pushing it. If he wasn't such a good looking, funny guy, she wouldn't care. She doesn't want to care. 'What about Marion?'

He has the grace to look away. 'Marion is… complicated.'

'I don't want to know, Tommy. I don't want to be involved in any of this.'

'It's not how you think.'

'I don't care. I'm too busy and too tired. How is Noah today?'

'He's solid. Amber is with him and I've said I'll pop down later this morning.'

'What happened with Shelley yesterday?'

Tommy sighs. 'Well, I'm a bit worried to be honest. She's split up with Yusef and she's not in a great place. She's locked herself in her room. She looks terrible and she's not eating.'

Jane thinks back to last month when she saw them walking hand in hand along the promenade. 'They seemed happy. What happened?'

'I don't know. She hasn't said but she's not interested in anything. She's not even feeding Almond Blossom.'

The shop door opens and a customer comes in and Tommy stands aside while Jane finds the repaired bracelet and rings up the till. After the customer has gone, Tommy continues, 'I'm worried about her.'

'Can you speak to Yusef?' she asks.

'It's nothing to do with me. She's a grown up.'

'Then you must get her out of her bedroom. The longer she's in there on her own the harder it will be.'

'I know.'

The shop door opens and a couple come in and ask to look at rings. Jane smiles apologetically at Tommy and he leaves discreetly. Jane places the tray of rings on the counter for the couple, but not before she watches Tommy walking down towards the harbour. That was a lucky escape, she thinks. He only invited you for dinner in the hope that you would sort out

Shelley for him. Well, that would have to be Marion's job now, wouldn't it? She had been polite and friendly but inside she was still furious. She had seen Shelley's vulnerability and she had warned Yusef not to hurt her. What is he playing at?

*   *   *

Later that evening, Jane has finished packing up four packets of earrings to send to a client in Northumberland, and three bracelets to a shop in Manchester. She pours a glass of white wine and ventures outside to her small garden. It's still warm and the sun is setting somewhere over the sea, but on the quiet patio of her back garden, Jane stretches and yawns contentedly.

She checks her phone messages and she's angry and disappointed that Yusef hasn't replied. Taking a chance that he's on his own, she calls his number determined to leave a message but he answers on the first ring.

'Hello.'

'Yusef?'

'Hi Jane.'

'You didn't answer my message.'

'There's a lot going on.'

'What's happening?'

'I don't know.'

'Don't mess with me.'

'I don't. I really don't.'

'Is it Shelley? I told you not to hurt her.'

'I haven't. It's the opposite, I really like her.'

'Then what is it?'

Yusef doesn't reply and Jane can hear him breathing. 'I think it's me. I think I'm a bit full-on. I can't help falling in love, Jane, I really can't —'

'Did you tell her?'

'Of course, I thought it was the right moment, you know — after you —'

'Enough!' Jane sighs loudly.

'Sorry.'

'So, why is she so upset?'

'I don't know. She sort of froze and then she mumbled something about she couldn't do this and she was going to uni and life was shit. Then she pulled on her clothes and left.'

'So, you didn't end it with her?'

'Well, I wasn't happy, and if she didn't love me, I said we should split up.'

'Have you spoken to her since?'

'I've left her messages but she won't take my calls.'

Jane looks out at the garden thinking she needs to weed and water the pots.

'Jane?'

'Yes.'

'Can you talk to her for me?'

'I'm not getting involved, Yusef. You're adults.'

'But you didn't want me to hurt her—'

'I didn't want you with her in the first place—'

'I know, but—'

'I knew this would happen.'

Yusef sighs. 'Don't get mad at me. I can't help who I am.'

'You fall in love too easily.'

'I can't help it if girls only want me for my body. You're not genuine. None of you are. You all take advantage of me. You'd soon complain if it was the other way around. She's the one who's hurt me — like you did.'

'We were never in a relationship.'

'But I wanted you as a friend.'

'I am here for you, Yusef. I want to help.'

'Then speak to Shelley for me?'

'No, you're a twenty-four year-old man. I suggest you either write her a letter and put it through her letter box explaining your feelings, or you go around there and try and speak to her.'

He asks softly, 'Do you think she loves me?'

'It certainly looked like it when I saw you both on the seafront, last month.'

* * *

It's Tuesday evening and Jane is walking back from the post office. The weather last weekend brought everyone to the coast, but now there's a chilly sea breeze and Jane pulls her pink jacket around her shoulders. She's thinking about what she might eat for dinner when she bumps straight into Tommy coming out of The Ship.

'What a lovely surprise,' he says, kissing her cheek spontaneously.

Jane looks around to see if he's on his own. 'How's Shelley?'

He slips his arm through hers and asks, 'Where are you going?'

'Home.'

'Can I kidnap you, and take you to meet Almond Blossom? I have to get back, she'll be hungry and lonely.'

Jane grins at his pouting smile.

'I can make you a chicken stir fry because I have a suspicion that Shelley will have gone out.'

Jane's tired yet she's in the mood for some company. Working so many hours makes her realise that she can take some time off so she allows him to lead her up the hill towards his house.

Tommy opens the front door and Jane's surprised at how comfortable his home is. There's a beach theme with paintings of boats, photographs of sunsets, lighthouses and on the table is a half-finished jigsaw of a farm.

'Mike Jupp? I love these.'

'You like jigsaws?' Tommy looks up from the kitchen counter where he's opening a tin of cat food.

'I find them relaxing. Where's Almond Blossom?'

'Probably outside.' He opens the back door but before he can call her name she darts inside, sleek and dainty.

'Goodness, she's beautiful.' Jane bends down and the kitten heads toward her outstretched hand. She rubs her ears against Jane's fingers, miaowing loudly.

'Hello, gorgeous.'

Almond Blossom purrs in appreciation until Tommy places her bowl on the floor then suddenly, Jane is ignored and she's eating hungrily.

Tommy takes a bottle from the fridge. 'Pinot?'

'Lovely. Is Shelley here?'

'I'll pop upstairs and call her but I don't think she is.'

When he comes downstairs he's smiling. 'She didn't answer so I assume she's gone out. Yusef came around this morning and asked me to give her a letter which I did and that's it.' He shrugs. 'I'll text her now to make sure she's alright.'

He types quickly.

'You're managing very well with her here.'

'She's a good kid but I'd like to see her doing something she enjoys.'

'What's that?'

He shrugs. 'I don't know. Tomorrow is supposed to be our weekly dinner together so I might get the chance to ask her a bit more. She's an intelligent girl. I wish you knew her better.'

'Why?'

'Well, I guess I feel inadequate sometimes. It's difficult for her I suppose, talking to an uncle she hardly knows. Women have more affinity with their emotions and you all tend to confide in each other, what is it — sisterhood?'

Jane laughs. 'I don't have any sisters.'

'Well, you speak to Amber and you're friends with Frances. I bet you could confide in them?'

'I suppose so, although we tend not to.'

'Really, why?' He begins chopping chicken and then along with the vegetables, noodles, garlic and soy sauce he tosses them all expertly into a large pan.

'Amber and Frances both have partners, so I guess they talk to them.'

'But if you had a problem or you were worried about something, you could talk to them.'

'I don't think there's a need to tell someone everything.'

'Don't you?' He looks surprised.

Jane blushes thinking about Yusef. 'Some things have to remain a secret or they're best not talked about.'

Tommy nods.

'This looks a very healthy dinner.' Jane stands beside him. She's conscious of her closeness. Apart from Yusef, it's been months since she's been this close to a man, and she takes comfort in his strong presence.

He tops up their glasses.

'I've cut down on saturated fat and I'm eating less cheese, cream and fatty meats. Although, when it's Shelley's turn to cook I often get a burger, but I don't complain.' He grins. 'I'm just pleased to have her company.'

They eat dinner sitting at the small bistro garden table. After dinner, Tommy wraps a warm blanket over Jane's shoulder. 'It's too lovely to sit inside. I try and stay out for as long as possible.'

'You should get an outdoor fire pit.'

'I would if I could share it with—' His phone pings and he leans forward to read the message.

He grins. 'Shelley, is fine — again.'

'Is she with Yusef?'

Tommy nods.

Jane smiles. She's relieved they've healed their rift. The jealousy she once felt has disappeared. She has no rights over him, no control and she can hardly expect him not to look at young girls. This is all for the best and she raises her glass. 'Cheers!'

Tommy smiles. 'Cheers. Here's to love.' That's when Almond Blossom jumps onto his lap and he laughs. 'In any way, shape or form.'

* * *

It's a cooler on Friday morning and rain is forecast later. Jane is in the harbour with Amber and Noah and they're unpacking the stall.

'We need more help,' Amber says. 'It's high season and I've never known it to be so busy. It's crazy in the café and in the

Bistro.'

Jane lays out Noah's carved boats.

Amber continues, 'We need someone who wants the work.'

'You'd think there'd be loads of students or young people looking for work.'

'I had thought Eva's twins were coming home for the holidays but their father's taken them on a road trip across Canada. I've been thinking about Shelley — she's not working. I saw her last night with Yusef. Perhaps she could help out?'

Jane's mind is thinking quickly. 'So long as she doesn't let us down.' She nods at Noah who is staring out at sea with meaning.

'I'll speak to her but I wanted to run it past you first.'

Jane is distracted. Tommy is with Matt and the other fishermen. It looks like they're preparing to go out because Tommy has on his fisherman's jacket and boots. She watches him clamber down the steps and onto the fishing boat. 'What the—?'

Amber turns around and Noah runs to the railing. Jane follows, leaning over the railing. 'Tommy?' she shouts out. 'What are you doing?'

He looks up and waves. 'Nigel's wife has gone into labour. They need me!' He shouts over the noise of the engine. 'I just texted Amber — sorry!'

Amber appears at Jane's side and pulls out her phone.

'I didn't hear the message— oh no, it came through half an hour ago.' She smiles and waves at Tommy. 'Have fun!' she shouts.

Tommy grins and waves back and then he's busy. Jane watches him as he falls into his work, knowing his job and responsibilities and it's as if he's never been away. Beside her,

Noah watches in silent fascination.

'This is exciting, isn't it?' Jane says to him feeling anything *but* excited. Hadn't Tommy said that Matt wouldn't take him on any more trips? What on earth is Tommy doing?

Noah grips the railing and, when the boat is untethered, he waves again. Tommy's arm moves back and forth waving until the boat leaves the safety of the harbour.

Amber looks at Jane. 'I'll see if I can get hold of Shelley this morning and have a chat with her.'

* * *

Jane returns to the shop and it turns out to be a busier morning than expected. She barely has time to look up and when she does it's lunchtime so she heads to the harbour. The weather has kept some people away. It's beginning to drizzle and Noah has pulled up his hoodie so she can hardly see his face.

Ben greets her with a smile. 'Faisal is covering our kiosk but I think we'll close up soon.'

'Thanks Ben, I can stay for an hour.'

'Amber is trying to get hold of Shelley. Noah's had pizza for lunch and he wants to come back to the studio with me as he's working on a boat for Tommy. Is that okay? Amber should be here in a while.'

'No problem.'

'Great, come on then, Noah. Let's go.'

Jane holds up her hand and Noah gives her a high five and a big smile.

Ben pauses. 'Have you lost a lot of weight, Jane?'

'I don't think so.'

'I know how hard you're working but make sure you eat.'

She places a hand on his shoulder. 'I will, Ben. Don't worry.'

After they've gone, the rain begins to fall harder and Jane is pleased she's remembered her coat. She chats with some of the other stall holders and then Faisal closes his kiosk. There's no-one around so she closes up the stall and walks over to the railings. Some of the fishing boats are back but not Matt's. She watches and waits. Rain falls heavily and she checks her watch. Jane knows that she must get back to the shop, but she can't move. Matt's fishing boat seems unusually late and she checks her watch again. Four-thirty. She's beginning to feel cold and damp. Jane checks all the social media pages for the local news, but there's nothing. She walks over to the RNLI launch site and is pleased the rescue boat is still in its shelter.

'That's a rotten afternoon,' Femi says, appearing beside her.

'I'm waiting for Matt's boat.' Jane digs her hands into her pockets. 'Are you on duty?'

'Just for a few hours.'

'How are the boys?'

'They're all busy; Ricky is doing shifts at the pub. Ahmed is at the refugee centre and Albert is helping Lawrence and Gladly with the wedding decorations.'

'Wedding?'

Femi smiles. 'We're keeping it low-key. Just a few people - family and close friends. My grandma, Gladly, wants to take charge but we're having to play it all down.'

'That's exciting.'

Femi nods. 'I'm very lucky.'

'You and Lawrence are a great match.'

'Thank you, Jane. I appreciate you saying that.'

Jane frowns and looks out across the sea. 'Do you think

they're alright?'

'It's an engine malfunction but they're getting it fixed.' Femi points at the radio in her hands. 'We've been in touch with them. They're not in trouble.'

Jane exhales.

'Are you worried about Tommy?' Femi asks.

'I'm not sure if he should have gone out with them.'

Femi nods. 'I understand your concern.'

'You saved his life the last time.'

'I stabilised him. The doctors saved him.' Her radio crackles to life and she lifts it to her ear. Jane holds her breath and then Femi smiles and turns to Jane. 'They're heading home.'

'Phew, what a relief.' Jane hunches her shoulders and then relaxes them.

'Does Tommy know how much you care?' Femi asks.

Jane shakes her head.

'I was the same with Lawrence. It's hard when you're older, isn't it?'

'I don't think it was easier when I was younger. I think some women find love very easily and very quickly, whereas I find it hard to speak about my feelings.'

Femi places her hand on Jane's arm. 'I have to go back inside.' She nods at the station. 'But perhaps you should tell Tommy. I think he might be pleased that you care so much.'

After Femi has gone, Jane walks over to the railing and waits in the rain. Although Tommy had cooked dinner for her and she had a lovely evening, she still isn't sure where he stands with Marion and that makes her very uncomfortable.

When the boat eventually chugs around the corner and into the harbour, Jane breathes a sigh of relief. She recognises Tommy on deck, and she knows he's alright so she turns quickly away, and without a backward glance, heads to her shop. She wouldn't want Tommy knowing she'd waited for him. It wouldn't be right.

* * *

Later that week, Jane walks down to the harbour one lunchtime. Amber has explained about the market stall and how to set up and how to write down and charge for sales and Shelley seems very much at home sitting in the camping chair, while beside her, Noah sits whittling a piece of wood.

'Hi,'

'Hello Jane.' Shelley looks up from her phone.

Noah high fives Jane.

'Is that a lighthouse?' she asks.

Noah nods and returns his attention to his wood. Shelley puts her phone in her pocket and stands behind the stall.

'We've been busy,' she says, showing Jane the sales ledger, a pocket book with a list of items sold.

'The earrings are really popular and well-priced.'

'Good.' Jane is unsure about Shelley's enthusiasm.

'I love the sea horses and the turtles and I was thinking maybe you could do matching necklaces and bracelets.'

'That's a good idea. It's just a time factor.'

'They're fiddly little things, aren't they?' Shelley agrees. She looks much better. She has colour in her cheeks and her eyes are vibrant and sparkling. She seems excited again — animated. Perhaps she's meeting Yusef.

'Do you want to take a break? I'll wait here until you come back. You can get something to eat.'

'If you don't mind, Jane?'

A family with two teenage girls comes to the stall and Shelley picks up her bag. 'I'll just grab some chips or something.'

Jane nods, already distracted by the clients. They ask her about a matching bracelet for the dolphin earrings and Jane hears Shelley say to Noah, 'Hey, come on, you need a break, I'll get us some lunch.'

From the corner of her eye, Jane watches them leave, wandering through the crowds side by side, and she's pleased. She'd never expected Shelley to look after Noah and her spirits lift. Tommy had said she was a kind girl and perhaps he was right.

* * *

It's late afternoon and Jane is working late in the shop when she happens to look up to see Shelley and Noah walking past. She checks her watch. She hadn't realised it was that late but then, to her surprise, Shelley opens the door and pops her head inside.

'We've finished for the day. Noah is going to the art gallery to see Ben. Do you need any help?'

Jane looks down at the orders she must send, weighing up if it would be easier to explain to Shelley or do it herself.

'I'm a fast learner.' Shelley smiles, stepping inside.

'I could do with a hand.' Jane explains about the padded envelopes, the return slip of paper and the small brochure she includes with every online purchase and Shelley gets to work at a table at the back of the shop. This leaves Jane free to serve a customer, work out the repairs to send off, and check her online orders for the morning. They work harmoniously and mostly in silence and then Jane looks at her design book and contemplates the next batch of orders.

'Did you draw these?' Shelley is looking over Jane's shoulder.

'Yes, I've been keeping this sketchbook for years, making notes of ideas, but there's never enough hours in the day to make all of them.'

'You need an assistant.'

'There aren't many people into this sort of thing.'

'You should have contacted the local uni, I'm sure they must have a design class or students who would be interested.'

'You're right. I've never thought of that.'

'You need a student who is keen to learn and works hard.'

'Yes.' Jane closes her notebook. 'Right, I need to take these parcels to the post.' As Jane packs up, she steals glances at Shelley, wondering if she's lingering in the hope of seeing Yusef in the grooming salon across the road but Shelley doesn't seem at all interested. Instead, she's looking inside the cabinets and taking an interest in the jewellery for sale.

Jane picks up the parcels and with them tucked under her arm, she accepts Shelley's help in locking the shop and lowering the shutters.

'See you tomorrow, Jane.'

'Bye, Shelley. Thanks for your help.' But for the first time Jane sees the angst of a young woman. Although Shelley is smiling there's worry behind her eyes that's deeply fragile and as she walks up the road, Jane is wondering if it's all to do with Yusef.

* * *

Jane couldn't say no to the annual summer church fete. In fact, people rarely said no to Frances, she was too kind, bubbly and popular. Jane has a stall in the church garden on a hot Sunday midsummer afternoon and the perspiration is trickling down the back of her white blouse. She gulps water from a bottle and wipes her forehead, careful to stay in the shade of the makeshift stand.

It's busy fete with music, laughter, families, ice cream and even burgers — once again the local community has pitched in to help. Ian the grocer, Derek the butcher, Mario and Lucas from the pet shop, Eva with some dried flower arrangements and Jane with costume jewellery. She'd worked hard every evening for the past fortnight and now she wants to sit down. Her legs ache and she's tired. She's mid yawn when a voice says, 'You need a holiday.'

She turns quickly. 'Hello, Tommy.'

'Actually, you probably need a swim.'

'That sounds a dream. I haven't been in yet this year.'

'I go most mornings or evenings depending on the tide. Tonight is perfect. High tide at eight fifteen, would you like to join me?'

'I don't think I know where my costume is.'

'I'll go and buy one for you.'

Jane laughs. 'That's not necessary. I'm sure I'll find it.'

'So, that's a yes then?'

'How was your fishing trip last week?'

'I loved it.' His eyes take on a dreamy, lost look but then he snaps back to look at her. 'But, it was a one-off.'

'Really?'

'Yes, they've replaced Nigel while he's on paternity leave with another young man.'

'I'm sorry.'

He shrugs. 'I'm lucky to have gone out one last time and to be honest, it made me realise that it's time for me to move on. You can't keep hankering after the past or what could have been, that's all a waste of time and emotion. I have to live my life with the cards that I've been given. But that doesn't mean I'm not going to push myself —hard.'

'So, you're aiming to be the tiddlywinks champion?'

Tommy throws back his head and laughs and, in that moment, Marion and Rachael walk past with Frances.

Marion stops suddenly. 'Tommy, how lovely to see you.'

'Ah, hello Marion, Rachael.'

'Have you recovered after the dance class on Monday?' Marion smiles.

Tommy looks quickly at Jane who is standing with a fixed smile on her face.

'I was a bit sore — out of practice.' He rubs his cheek.

'Me too,' says Frances. 'It's amazing how quickly you forget to move.'

'Well, you'll do better this week, I'm sure.' Rachael smiles at him, then she turns to Jane. 'You're still welcome, Jane. I know music probably isn't your thing but this is a four week course for the summer.'

'Thanks, but I'll have to give it a miss. I'm far too busy.'

'I've hardly seen you, Jane.' Frances looks over her shoulder at the jewellery on sale. 'You're always working. I don't know how you find time to make all this. Some of it is beautiful.' She picks up a pair of silver frog earrings and she laughs.

Marion links her arm possessively through Tommy's and pulls him aside.

Frances says, 'I'm going to buy these for my sister.'

'Take them — as a gift.' Jane is trying to focus on Frances

but she wonders what Marion is whispering in Tommy's ear. He seems to consider before nodding his consent.

Frances pulls a note from her pocket. 'I always pay my way.'

Jane takes the money and gives Frances her change just in time to hear Marion.

'See you later, baby,' she whispers loudly, purring, and she reaches up to kiss Tommy on the cheek. 'Bye, Jane. We'll be in the pub later if you want to join us?' But she doesn't wait for an answer and she strides off with Rachael in her wake.

Frances is distracted by Derek, serving slices of Spanish jamon and Jane is suddenly left alone again with Tommy.

'So, about that swim? I'll see you on the beach at eight? On the far side of the harbour where we watched the sunset.'

Jane nods and reaches for her bottled water. She didn't care about Marion. She wanted a swim and if Tommy was going in the sea then it would be great to have company.

Why shouldn't she go? Tommy was her friend.

* * *

It's a warm evening and the atmosphere is muggy. The water is refreshing and, at first, tingles her skin into goose-bumps. Jane swims well, stretching her arms and kicking, then because she hasn't been in the sea for a long time, she swims along the shore with neat rhythmic strokes. When she's had enough she stops and floats on her back, her arms outstretched and her legs wide like a starfish staring up at the blue sky. The sea laps at her ears and she hears the hissing and gurgling of the sea and the murmur of a voice.

'You're a good swimmer.' Tommy splashes up beside her. 'I'm a novice. It's something I've never really liked.'

'Then why are you doing it?' Jane begins to tread water, using her hands as stabilisers.

'It's on my list of new things I'm doing.'

'What else is on the list?'

'Walking — when it gets cooler. Dance classes on a Monday. Bridge classes in September.'

Jane closes her eyes and enjoys the warmth of the sun on her eyelids. She was sure she could sleep if she let go.

'I've got to have things to do. I have to find a purpose. It's time I sorted myself out.'

Jane flips on her back and kicks her legs and Tommy swims alongside her with careful breaststrokes.

'If you could go anywhere or do anything, what would you do?' he asks.

'I'd like a holiday. I have a cousin who lives in Scotland whom I haven't seen for years, so I'd like to visit her.'

'What about going abroad?'

'I like travelling but I've never been on holiday with anyone, well once. We went to Rome. It was beautiful and I loved it but the week after we got back, he told me he was married.'

'You didn't know?'

Jane shakes her head. 'Dad knew him. He owned the shop next door. We thought he was divorced. It just turns out that he and his wife had an open marriage and lived separate lives. It wasn't what I was looking for.'

'What are you looking for?' he asks.

'Someone kind, funny, sensitive, honest.... I often wonder if that's too much to ask.'

'I think that's reasonable.'

They stop swimming and tread water for a little longer, watching the sun sinking on the horizon.

Jane asks, 'What about you?'

'I'd like someone who has a zest for life, who has conversation, who wants to live. Someone attractive with a lovely smile.'

Jane swims away and he follows. The swim that she had hoped would be relaxing is now fraught with tension and she doesn't want to get upset. She has no wish to learn what he thinks of Marion.

'Shall we get some chips on the way home?' he asks, following her into the shallow water and climbing out of the sea.

'No thanks, Tommy. I need a shower and an early night.'

* * *

Jane is repairing a fiddly catch on a locket. It's dainty work and she peers through her magnifying glass and frowns. When the shop door opens, she curses under her breath. She thought she'd switched the sign to closed and locked the door. She puts down her small tool and when she stands up she's surprised to see Marion at the counter. She's wearing a short-sleeved navy dress that reveals a deep brown cleavage. There's a frilly, lacy bra that Marion isn't even trying to hide.

'Hello, Marion.'

'Hi, Jane. Look, I'm going to keep this short because I know how busy we both are but I just wanted to make you aware that Tommy and I are an item.' Marion pauses, 'I don't want you to make a fool of yourself. I know you've been chasing him and—'

'Chasing him?'

'Yes. I know you went swimming with him last week and I

know that you invited yourself to his house for dinner—'

'No, I didn't.'

'Well.' Marion holds up her hand. 'I just want you to understand that I really like Tommy and I know he likes me. And I think it would be such a shame if you mistook his kindness for anything more than it is. Tommy is an innocent man. He's been seriously depressed since his wife died and I'm making a huge difference to his life. He's taking an interest in everything — more than he has ever done — and I'm encouraging him to find fulfillment and... love.'

'That's fine.'

Marion shakes her head. 'I don't think you understand me at all. Tommy is falling in love with me. I know him. He's thoughtful and caring and—'

'Marion that's fine. If you think there's anything else between me and Tommy then you're wrong.'

Marion stares at her. 'Have you slept with him?'

'That doesn't even warrant an answer. Now, I must get on with my work. I have a lot to do.' Jane turns away.

'You don't fool me, you know. You come across as Saint Jane, all innocent and vulnerable, yet you're not are you? You're quite a girl, aren't you?'

Jane stares at Marion.

'I've seen your Tinder profile. I know you meet men on dates in town. I know that you won't meet anyone here in Westbay in case anyone finds out. But your secret is safe with me.' She smiles. Her lips are ruby red. 'But one step out of place and Tommy might not be too impressed. He doesn't like a woman who's been around. He needs to be protected and looked after.'

Jane laughs. 'Tommy can look after himself.'

'Oh, I don't think so.'

'He's managed very well without you since Sunita died.'

Marion taps her chest. 'I make a difference. I care about Tommy. I have his welfare at heart.'

'That's fine.'

'Then you'll back off?'

'I haven't backed on.' Jane smiles and with more bravado than she feels, she adds, 'If I was seriously after Tommy, you'd know all about it.'

'The thing is —' Marion stops.

The shop door opens and Yusef puts his head around the door. 'Have you seen Shelley?'

Jane shakes her head but it's as if Yusef can detect the tension between the two women and instead of backing away he walks confidently up to the counter.

'Can I wait for her?' He looks at Jane and then turns to Marion. 'I'm not interrupting you lovely ladies, am I?'

Marion shakes her head and turns on her heel. 'I've said everything I wanted to say. Jane, just remember, okay?'

She closes the door and Yusef turns to Jane. 'What's all that about?' he asks.

Jane shakes her head in exasperation. 'She's a desperate woman.'

'She's got her claws into Tommy.'

'How do you know?'

Yusef smiles. 'I've seen them in the pub and Shelley has told me.'

'So, you've patched it up with her?'

'I think so, yes, but I don't know where she is? She's being very secretive. Do you know what she's up to?'

'No.' Jane shrugs. 'She's been working on the market stall

today because Tommy had to go into town and then she came into the shop to help me again.'

'She's been avoiding me.'

'Take it slowly with her. She'll go off to uni next term or even go back to live with her mother.'

'She likes it here.'

'Even if that's true, she might not want to settle down right away. She's young. She wants to have fun.'

'I know, but I have to get up and work in the morning. She's a real party girl. She's been hooking up with a group who are here on holiday. They've got lots of money and they're real serious party people.'

'Where do they go?'

She wonders if Tommy knows that she has a new set of friends or if it's even important. One thing Jane does know, is that Shelley is an impressionable young girl.

He says, 'They hang out at one of those big houses on the cliffs just outside of town. They seem to have a party there most nights.'

'Well, she's turning up for work.'

'She won't let me in her bedroom,' he says, then laughs. 'Let me qualify that statement. She always comes to mine and now it's like she's hiding something.'

'Some girls just want a little privacy. Stop stressing and just enjoy her company and the summer.'

'She likes working with you.'

'I think she's enjoying it and she's really good with Noah.'

Yusef sits on the chair. 'He's a good boy. I cut his hair yesterday. I think they've found a family for him. He'll be leaving soon.'

'Tommy will be upset.'

'They hang around the harbour together. He's always talking to Noah. Have you thought about what Tommy will do after the summer when Shelley leaves and Noah is gone?'

Jane looks thoughtful. 'There are lots of people who care for him. I think he's making great progress in finding out what he wants in life.'

'Has he got a thing going with Marion?'

'She thinks so.'

He nods. 'She's a cougar, that one.'

'You haven't...?'

He laughs. 'No, not me. She's got a reputation though. One of our cousins last summer... but I won't say any more.'

'Good.'

'Poor Tommy,' says Yusef.

'Poor Tommy,' agrees Jane.

August

Tommy

'It was a stupid thing to do,' Shelley shouts. 'What were you thinking of?' They're standing in the kitchen. Tommy has fed Almond Blossom, changed the litter tray and Shelley has come home earlier than usual. She doesn't want dinner, but she doesn't seem to be eating much lately.

'I don't know why you're so upset, it's my job,' replies Tommy. This certainly wasn't the reaction he was expecting or needing.

'It *was* your job but it isn't any more. Why did you have to try and prove yourself. Are you turning all macho or have you got a death wish?'

He puts the kettle on and says slowly and emphatically. 'I went out on the boat, a few weeks ago, nothing happened.'

Shelley has bags and dark purple circles around her eyes.

He says softly, 'You need an early night. Tea?'

'Stop trying to change the subject, Tommy. Have you told Mum?'

'There's nothing to tell. It was a one-off. I'm not doing it again.'

'And how do I know that? How do I know that you're not suddenly going to get this stupid idea again and disappear?'

'I didn't disappear. I texted you. Besides, I didn't have time. Nigel got the call, so he had to dash home and take his wife to the hospital and I just happened to be there.'

'That's not good enough, Tommy. You risked your life.'

'I didn't,' he says calmly. 'It's a job.'

'A dangerous one, especially when you've already had a heart attack at sea. I'm surprised Matt would even think about it—'

'He was desperate.'

Shelley sits at the table and glances down at the jigsaw. 'You're supposed to be taking it easy.'

'I told you. I got the all clear.'

'Not to go back to fishing. Besides, what would have happened to me?

'What do you mean?' Tommy sits opposite her and watches her lift a piece of the puzzle and fit it into the correct spot.

'Well, if anything happened to you, and to Mum, then what about me?'

She looks scared and he sees the stark vulnerability etched in her eyes. She's upset and insecure. She needs him at the moment as much as she needs her mother. He puffs out his cheeks. 'I'm sorry. I didn't think.'

'Look, I know it's not all about me but what if something had happened? What would I do? Where would I go?'

Tommy thinks about this for a minute. 'Well, there's Frances or Jane, and of course Amber and Ben.'

'You don't get it, do you?' She shouts.

'I do, Shelley, and I'm sorry. It's been a few years since I had to be responsible for someone and I... I forgot.'

'Thanks.'

He grins. 'Not in a bad way. I didn't forget about you. I just forgot myself and my responsibility and my promise to your mum.'

Shelley nods. 'Right, I'm going for a shower and you can spend the rest of the month making it up to me. But only on one condition.'

'What's that?'

'You promise never to do it again.'

* * *

Shelley's barely speaking to him. He also knows she's not going out with Yusef every night. But she won't tell him what she's doing or who she's with. He tries not to care but he's worried.

'I'm not a child,' she says, as she sips orange juice before going to work in Jane's shop. 'I'm not doing anything wrong.' She strokes Almond Blossom's head absent-mindedly.

'Then tell me where you're going at night and I won't worry.'

'That's emotional blackmail.'

'Your mother worries.'

'She has nothing to worry about unless you tell her.'

'So long as you're still contacting her, I'm happy.'

Shelley finishes her juice.

Tommy says, 'You must eat something or you'll be ill. You need more than juice every day.'

She pokes her tongue out. 'It's too hot to eat.'

'Are you walking down with me?' Tommy grabs his keys and shoves his phone in his pocket. 'Your mum has asked me to look at university courses with you.'

'Later.'

'It's August. You can't leave it too late to apply.'

'I might not go.'

Tommy holds the door handle so she can't go anywhere. 'Why not?'

'I have other plans.'

'Like what?'

'It's a secret until I have something more concrete. Come on or I'll be late. Jane might fire me but you'll still be smelling of roses.'

Tommy laughs. 'Jane and I are just friends.'

'Yeah.'

They walk down the street towards town.

'How's Marion?' she asks.

'I suppose she's fine.'

'You're enjoying the dance classes?'

'Not really but they're preferable to yoga. Besides, I often see Frances and we chat about... things.'

'The purpose of life, I presume?' Shelley laughs.

'Normally it's some such topic: guilt, responsibility, death — all the cheery subjects.'

'You should have been an undertaker.'

'They're quite optimistically cheerful as it happens — most of them.'

Shelley asks, 'Do you think mum will be okay?'

'Yes, I do. Is that why you're having second thoughts about uni? Do you want to go home to be with her?'

'She doesn't want me there at the moment.' Shelley shakes her head. 'I'll tell you in due course about uni.'

They reach Harbour Street and Tommy insists on buying

three coffees. Karl serves them and he and Shelley banter and joke while Tommy takes a moment to look at his niece. How she's changed in just a few months. Elsie will be amazed at the strong woman she's becoming; independent, hard-working, funny and he feels a sudden pang of sadness for his sister. He hopes and prays that she will be alright but there's a small niggle of doubt that's nestled at the back of his throat like an irritating lump and although he can't say anything to Shelley — he's frightened.

'Coffee to go,' calls Karl, offering Tommy the card reader. 'One day Shelley might even pay for your coffee, Tommy.' He jokes and they all laugh. 'Mind how you go, and remember — behave yourselves. August is a wicked month.'

The town is busy and before they can join the flow of pedestrians heading to the harbour, Marion calls out from her boutique across the street.

Tommy waves and nudges Shelley to keep walking to the harbour, and she laughs.

'What's wrong with you, Lothario.'

'What?' Tommy stops in the street. 'What did you call me?'

Shelley giggles. 'Lothario.'

'Why?'

Shelley walks on and he lengthens his stride, catching up with her.

'Why do you say that?'

'Well, Marion thinks you're joined at the hip and Jane *was* interested in you, but you blew it.'

'No, I didn't.'

'You liked her earlier in the summer. You were watching the sunset together and you both looked so happy and perfect together - but then you didn't follow it through.'

'She left me. She went home.'

Shelley laughs. 'Yeah, and you went to the pub and got hammered and invited Marion back to the house.'

Tommy frowns in recollection. 'Um, when you put it like that — it doesn't sound good.'

'Jane will also know about your picnic with Marion—'

'But Jane's not interested in me.' They reach the shop and Tommy looks through the window but Jane's not looking outside, she is already serving a customer.

'Not any more, she's not. I told you, you blew it. But I will tell her that you bought the coffee.'

* * *

It's their night to have dinner together and Tommy is cooking chicken, peppers, mushrooms and tomatoes on the BBQ. It's a warm evening and Shelley's made a big salad and now she sits drinking white wine and scrolling through her phone.

'No phones, remember!' Tommy waves the fork at her before turning the chicken.

'I'm waiting for a call. I'm going out later.'

'With Yusef?'

'No.'

Tommy turns around. 'Who with?'

Shelley looks away but Tommy insists.

'Who are you meeting?'

'Just a couple of friends.'

Almond Blossom purrs around her ankles and Shelley picks her up and strokes her ears.

'Are they local?' he asks with his back to her.

'They've rented a house on the far side of the harbour.

They're business people.'

'How old?' He doesn't turn around but Tommy's body has tensed.

'Thirties.'

'A family of single people?'

'There's a gang of them, guys and girls.'

Tommy puts the chicken and vegetables on a plate and places it in the middle of the table. 'Bring them to the harbour sometime, I'd like to meet them.'

Shelley laughs. 'They're not Artisan market people. They're loaded. They have online businesses and stuff. Their businesses are doing really well.'

'What sort of businesses?'

'IT.' Shelley helps herself to salad. 'That's where the money is and they're all over social media too.'

'Is that why you keep looking at your phone?' He grins. 'You'll have to show me.'

Shelley ignores him and eats sparingly, feeding a piece of chicken to the kitten.

'That's bad training,' he says.

'So what? It's only tonight as a special treat.' Shelley's phone pings and she glances down at it. When she looks back up at him, he frowns, shakes his head but smiles. It must be hard to be young with all the modern technology. Time moves quickly and he must seem quite dull by comparison. He feels old. After going back out to sea he realised his limitations, and although he's resigned to a different type of future he's not quite sure what he will do.

'Is that alright?' Shelley asks.

Tommy wasn't listening.

'I'll be home by eleven. This is a business meeting.' She

stands up and carries her half empty plate into the kitchen. 'Thanks, Tommy. I'll make it up to you.'

'If it's a business meeting, don't give them any money,' he calls.

* * *

Tommy is reading in bed when he hears Shelley come home. It's past midnight but he's relieved. He puts his book down and listens to her footsteps on the stairs. She's sniffing. Does she have a cold? He turns out the light and listens to the sounds of her moving around, going into the bathroom, then switching on the water for a shower. He lies on his back and stares at the ceiling. She seems to be in there a long time. He feels tense and he wonders if he should get out of bed. The bathroom door opens and he calls out, 'Shelley? Are you alright?'

'Yeah.' Her voice is muffled.

She closes her bedroom door and he waits and listens but there's nothing. The house is silent apart from Almond Blossom, who Shelley must have let out of the kitchen and is now miaowing. He pulls on his dressing gown, opens the bedroom door and the kitten jumps in.

'Night. Shelley,' he calls, but there's no answer, then he sees the light go off from under her bedroom door.

Tommy can't be bothered to take Almond Blossom back downstairs. 'Come on then, just this once.'

She's purring loudly and before Tommy is back in bed she's curled up and fast asleep on top of the duvet.

* * *

Tommy and Noah are eating whippy ice creams when Amber arrives at the stall.

'There's pizza in the freezer for your dinner. Just pop it in the oven. It's only a short dress rehearsal for Femi and Lawrence's wedding next week in the church, so if you're bored after dinner you can always walk down to meet us.'

Noah nods.

'He can always come back to mine.' Tommy offers. 'We can watch a film and you can call in on your way home?'

Amber looks at Noah. 'Would you like to do that?'

Noah nods.

'Okay, well text me if that's what you decide to do, okay?'

Noah nods and smiles before licking ice cream off the cone.

'Where's the reception?' Tommy asks.

'It's a very small church wedding and then they've booked the Bistro for the evening. It's what they wanted, an intimate dinner outside on the patio, and there's a singer booked. It's all very low key.'

'They're a lovely couple and Femi saved my life,' he says.

Noah stops eating his ice cream and stares. Amber, who has already heard this story, makes her excuses. 'Don't get into any mischief, you guys.' She laughs and then she's gone.

That reminds Tommy and he checks his phone. There's no message from Shelley. He didn't see her this morning and she hasn't replied to him.

They close up the market stall. The crowds have thinned out and people have already changed into their evening clothes and are making their way to the restaurants or to the beach for fish and chips, but Tommy's in a hurry. He wants to get to Jane's Jewellers, before she closes. They dart under the clock tower, dodge a man driving an electric wheelchair like he's on a Formula 1 Grand Prix track and Tommy is relieved when he pushes the door. She's still open.

Jane is standing with her back to him, checking stock and placing jewellery into boxes. She greets them with a smile and a high five for Noah.

'Is Shelley here?' he asks.

'She left about half an hour ago.'

'Right.' Tommy scratches his head. 'Was she alright today?'

'I think so, we were pretty busy, so we didn't have much time to chat, why?'

'She didn't answer my text messages.'

'Did you try calling her?'

'No, they don't really do that do they? I did when she first arrived, but she never picked up so now I mainly text. Did she say she was going home?' he asks.

Jane shakes her head. 'No idea.'

Noah wanders around the shop. He appears intrigued with the wooden cuckoo clock when it suddenly strikes seven o'clock and he laughs.

They both turn to look at him. It's the first time he's laughed aloud. They swap glances and smile.

'I think she's upset with me that I went out on the boat and if anything had happened, she would have been left alone.'

Jane closes the boxes, locks a cabinet, and looks at him.

'So, Noah and I are getting a takeaway for dinner, want to join us?' Tommy smiles.

Jane smiles back. 'Is it too hot for a curry?'

'Never.'

'I wonder when Sanjay will be home. It's like he's been gone forever. Eva must miss him.'

'His food is still the best. I'll get enough for Shelley, in case she's at home.'

* * *

But Shelley isn't at home. Tommy calls out and goes upstairs to knock on her bedroom door but there's no answer. He's tempted to look inside but he can't do that. He wouldn't like her to look in his bedroom, not that he has anything to hide, but it's a matter of privacy — and trust.

'She's not here,' he says, coming back down onto the patio.

Jane is laying out plates and forks and spooning rice onto the plates.

Noah is crouched on the floor clicking his fingers, trying to make Almond Blossom come to him, but she's wary of new people and she shelters under a bush.

Tommy pulls out his phone. 'I'll text Amber and tell her we're all here.'

As they eat, they talk about Femi and Lawrence's wedding. Although they know them, they're not close friends and wouldn't expect an invitation but they're happy for them.

'It will be a special day.' Jane eats heartily and Tommy is pleased she's drinking wine with him in his garden.

'I wouldn't do it again,' Tommy says. 'Once was enough. Sunita had a big family and although I begged Elsie and Frank to come — they didn't. Dad had passed but Mum liked Sunita. It was in a registry office and then lunch in a hotel near where Sunita grew up in South London.'

'I'd like to see some photos sometime. I'm so sorry, I don't remember Sunita at all. I don't think our paths ever crossed.'

'You would have liked her. She would have liked you too. She was very easy company and now that I think about it, she wasn't demanding. You know like some women always want you to do this or that?'

Jane laughs. 'That sounds awful.'

'I've decided that relationships are all about caring, what do you think?' he asks.

'Most definitely.'

He toys with his fork before saying, 'I saw you in the harbour waiting for the fishing boat.'

Jane concentrates on her food and doesn't look up.

'Were you waiting for me?' he asks.

Jane shakes her head. 'I was out and I bumped into Femi. She was on duty.'

'Yes, I saw her too.'

Jane finishes the last of her curry and sits back in appreciation, hugging her stomach. 'I always eat too much.'

Tommy smiles. 'I was pretty sure you were waiting for the boat to come back. I could see you on the quayside.'

'We were talking about Femi's wedding.'

Tommy says, 'Shelley is furious with me. Do you think I was silly to go out?'

'You have to do what you think is right, but I think if you were to do it again, then that would be crazy.'

'Would you tell me, if you were waiting for me?'

Jane smiles. 'If I was, I would tell you — but I wasn't.'

Tommy pours them more wine and after they've finished eating, he texts Shelley again.

'She's met a new crowd,' he says.

Jane sits back in her chair toying with her wine glass. 'She mentioned some guys in a big house and that they're Internet millionaires or something. She seems quite taken with them.'

Tommy frowns. 'I'm not sure about any of it. You know

when you just get a feeling?'

Jane stares at him. 'Do you think she's alright?'

Tommy looks over to where Noah is sitting on the grass, playing and stroking Almond Blossom. He lowers his voice. 'It's very hard being an uncle. You have to get the balance right or it could seem a bit creepy. You know, a young girl staying here and me keep asking her where she's going and what she's doing. I want her to be as independent as possible but it's hard. I never thought parenting would be so challenging. Not that I'm her parent but it's that sense of responsibility — for Elsie.'

'She must miss Shelley.'

'Well, Shelley had gone to Bristol uni, but didn't like it. She dropped out after a few months, but Elsie didn't want her at home watching her going through all the treatment again so...'

There's a noise in the house and they both turn around.

'Shelley?' Tommy stands up. 'Thank goodness you're home.'

'Why?' Shelley calls out and then wanders outside.

'What have you been doing? You look terrible.'

'I'm tired.'

'There's Indian food here for you, I bought extra.'

'I'm not hungry.'

'Have you eaten anything?'

'I'm tired.'

He checks his watch. It's only just gone nine.'

'I'm going to bed.' Shelley turns on her heels and then she comes back to the terrace table and she stares at Tommy. 'You haven't been in my room, have you?'

'No.'

She glares at him and then looks at Jane and nods. 'Good.' Then she disappears upstairs.

Tommy looks meaningfully at Jane, blows his cheeks out then whispers, 'What do you think?'

'Is she seeing Yusef?'

'I don't know,' Tommy replies, whispering so Noah can't hear. 'But she's not behaving normally, is she? Do you think she's taking drugs?'

Jane turns down the corners of her mouth. 'She's not eating and she looks exhausted. I don't know.'

Tommy runs his hand through his hair. 'This isn't easy.'

'I'll try and speak to her tomorrow,' Jane says.

'Thanks, Jane. I'd appreciate that.'

* * *

Amber and Ben come round after the rehearsal in the church and they stay for a quick glass of wine before walking Jane home. After they leave, Tommy tidies up the kitchen and it's gone eleven by the time he's finished. He treads the staircase softly. He doesn't want to wake Shelley, but when he turns out the landing light, he notices her bedroom light is still showing from under the door.

'Goodnight, Shelley.'

He waits and when he hears no answer, he turns toward his own room.

'Night, Tommy.'

He pauses and nods. That sounds a little more hopeful. At his heel, Almond Blossom miaows and she follows him into the bedroom.

'Don't get too used to this life. When the right woman comes along, you'll be booted out.'

* * *

Although he's not invited, Femi and Lawrence's wedding day is hectic. He knows all the staff from the café and the Bistro are busy setting up for the evening wedding supper and Tommy is taking charge of Noah — they will be spending the day together. He collects Noah from the Bistro just as Eva arrives with flowers. Ben is sorting out the decorations and Amber is making sure the fresh food has arrived and the wedding cake is kept cool.

'Come on, Noah, we're not wanted.' Tommy laughs and pats Noah's shoulder and they head down the road. For some reason Tommy recalls his comment to Jane about not wanting to get married again but now, after feeling the atmosphere, seeing the effort that Amber has made and all the hard work, he thinks he might be mistaken.

'After all, if it's the right woman and she makes you happy, then why not get married again?'

Noah looks at him and shrugs and Tommy realises he's spoken aloud.

They open up the market stall with practiced ease, each of them working around the other. Noah lays out his carvings and the jewellery, while Tommy greets the other stall holders. It's only after that, that he ventures to the railing to look out at the fishing boats. Nigel's wife had a baby boy and they called him Arthur. Tommy wonders if he'll grow up to be a fisherman or go on to have a completely different life. He wanders back to the stall and waits while Noah serves a customer. He manages to get by with just a smile and by pointing to the price tag. The customer must assume that he's deaf, certainly dumb, and Tommy wonders what might have caused this behaviour. He's never been one for psychology or analysis, but he is interested in Noah and when there's a quiet moment just before lunch, he asks him.

'Why don't you speak? Is it because you're shy?'

Noah turns away.

'Sorry,' continues Tommy, 'I don't want to upset you. I would just like to know. I mean, it would be great to have a conversation because I never know what you're thinking. I just chat away, and you listen, but I don't know if you agree with me or if you think I'm just a stupid old man—'

He feels Noah's hand on his arm and Noah shakes his head, then he's distracted by a customer and he walks away.

It clouds over after lunch and Tommy is torn between sitting in the chair reading the news or going to Jane's Jewellers to see if Shelley is there. If she is, then the chances are Shelley won't speak to him about anything important. Anyway, he mustn't be impatient. He must bide his time and see if Jane has the opportunity to speak to her.

Noah is carving a seagull from a piece of driftwood they found on the beach. Tommy checks his watch and stands up. He heads toward the railing and that's when he almost crashes into Rachael.

'Tommy,' she gasps, holding her hand to her throat as if he was going to collide with her and send her over the railing and down into the sea below.

'Sorry, I didn't see you.'

'That's not very flattering.'

He bites his lip. 'Sorry.'

'You haven't been back to the class?'

'No, I hurt my foot,' he lies.

She looks at his feet and then back at his face. 'I'm pleased

I've bumped into you, literally...' She laughs. 'We haven't seen you for so long. Have you been avoiding us?'

Tommy shakes his head.

'Well, it looks like it. Poor Marion is beside herself. She's very upset, Tommy. Why have you done this?'

'Done what?'

'Upset Marion. Don't you like her?'

'Well, yes—'

'Well then do something about it. I told her you were shy and that you needed a little prodding in the right direction, but you two are made for each other.'

'We are?' He scratches his cheek.

'You know you are,' she whispers. 'She told me.'

Tommy stares at her and blinks.

'Why not pop along to the boutique and speak to her today?'

'I can't. I'm minding the stall and Noah.'

Rachael looks over to the stall. 'He must be old enough to look after himself.'

'He is but he's had a difficult time and he likes company.'

'Can't he find friends his own age?'

'He's friends with Femi's youngest boy Albert. They play computer games together I believe.'

Rachael stares at him, her eyes are piercing and Tommy feels uncomfortable. 'Ask her out again, Tommy. Marion's so miserable. She's depressed without you.'

Tommy stutters. 'I'm sorry to hear that.'

'I'll tell her that you'll take her out.'

'No.'

'No?'

'No, I can't do that—'

'Why not?' Rachael puts her hands on her hips.

'Well, I just… I'm not dating at the moment.'

'That's not what I've heard. You seem to be spending more time with Jane than anyone.'

'She's just a friend. Shelley is working with her now, so—'

'So that's it. You've just dropped Marion. I see. At the beginning of the season when you wanted her to employ Shelley — who was a mess — you were wining and dining Marion. Shelley was unreliable and couldn't hold down a job and so then you started seeing Jane so that Shelley would find work with her. That's a despicable thing to do. You can't lead women on.'

'But, I haven't.'

'Well, it looks to me like you have. You've already broken one heart in Harbour Street, don't make that mistake again, Tommy.'

He shakes his head, lost for words.

'They say the apple doesn't fall far from the tree.'

'What does that mean?'

'Shelley is just like you by the look of things. She's used Yusef and treated him appallingly and now she's hanging about with that rich set from the big house on the cliffs.'

'Do you know them?

'Know them? The whole town knows them. They're party people; lots of money, fast cars, drugs and all sorts of sex goes on up there. I'm surprised your niece hasn't told you. She's up there every night.'

* * *

Tommy texts Jane.

Did you speak to her?

It's half an hour before she texts back.

Not yet. Very busy.

Tommy and Noah close the market stall and walks back via the shop but Jane is with a customer and Shelley isn't to be seen. They wander up the road and buy fish and chips for supper, which they take home to eat in the garden. Noah eats as he plays with Almond Blossom and Tommy texts Jane.

Well? Any news?'

Half an hour later, Jane texts back

She doesn't want to talk. Will try again tomorrow.

Tommy throws his phone onto the table and Noah looks up. When it rings Tommy reaches for it immediately.

'Hello?'

'Hi, Tommy,' Marion purrs. 'Rachael told me she'd bumped into you and that you wanted to speak to me.'

'She did?' He eats a chip, thinking quickly.

'She said you were lonely and all by yourself again down in the harbour.'

'I was with Noah, working.'

'Yes, she said you're trying to keep busy but that you seemed very... low.'

'Low?'

'Yes, a bit like me probably, a bit depressed. That's what happens when soulmates don't see each other.'

Tommy sighs. 'Look Marion, I have to be honest—'

'Good, that's what I've been wanting to hear.'

'I think you're a very nice person but I can't see you any more, you know, as in dinner or a drink or anything.'

'Why are you talking such nonsense?'

'Because it's the truth.'

There's silence on the end of the phone and Tommy thinks

she might have gone but then she says, 'I saw Femi and Lawrence today. They walked past the shop on their way from the church to the Bistro for the reception and they looked beautiful. She was wearing a soft yellow dress that was lovely against her dark skin and Lawrence had a matching silk tie and grey suit. They looked like they should be together — forever. They were holding hands and it was as if they had lived their whole lives as one and I couldn't help but think about us and how we would look on our wedding day. I mean, I couldn't wear white, as you know...' She giggles. 'But I think we look right together. I think it's our destiny.'

'No, Marion. You're wrong. It's not our destiny at all.'

'How can you not see it? What can I do to make you change your mind?'

'Absolutely nothing, Marion, thank you. Enough is enough.' He hangs up and he glances over at Noah who gives him a thumbs up.

'Did I have that on loudspeaker?' he asks.

Noah grins.

Tommy smiles. 'Well, consider that part of your education Noah. That was a masterclass in how to fob off the wrong woman.'

* * *

After celebrating the birth of Nigel's baby at The Ship, Tommy wanders home with his hands in his pockets, feeling very happy with himself. He's managed to maintain the friendship and camaraderie with the gang from the fishing boat — working men and his mates.

He's humming softly to himself as he opens the front door

and he's surprised and disappointed that Almond Blossom doesn't come to greet him. He looks into the kitchen and although the light is off, there's enough moonlight to see that the litter tray has been cleaned and there's food in the kitten's bowl.

Nodding in satisfaction Tommy heads up the stairs. There's a light on in Shelley's bedroom and the door is open.

He pauses. 'Shelley?' he whispers.

There's a rustling of bed covers and a miaow.

'Hello?' He pushes the door wider. Shelley is lying on her bed, fully clothed, with tears streaming down her cheeks.

'Shelley?' He's hesitant and he waits with his hand on the door handle. 'What's happened?'

Almond Blossom jumps off the bed where she's been comforting Shelley and springs toward him.

Shelley swings her legs off the bed and pushes the heels of her hands into her eye sockets. 'Nothing.'

He looks around the bedroom. On the table and the bookshelf there's an assortment of costume jewellery; rings, bracelets earrings and necklaces.

'They're crap. Don't look at them,' she orders.

'They don't look crap to me.'

'Well, they are.'

'Who says? Did you make them?'

'Of course.'

'Have you shown them to Jane?'

'No, she docsn't like me.'

Tommy stares as she wipes her eyes and blows her nose with a tissue.

'I'm sure that's not true.'

'It is.'

'I'm going downstairs to put the kettle on. Come and have some tea with me and, as a trade-off, I'll cancel our dinner together this week.'

'There's no need. I'd prefer to have dinner with you more than anyone.'

'That's what I like to hear.'

Ten minutes later Tommy has made tea and they're sitting at the kitchen table. Shelley has dried her eyes but they're still red and bloodshot.

'Is this about Jane? Is this why you're upset?'

Shelley shakes her head. 'No. It's worse than that.'

'Yusef?'

Shelley still shakes her head. 'I've been so stupid.'

Her nails are torn and broken and she's lost a lot of weight. How did he not notice the difference in her?

'Have you been taking drugs?'

Her head shoots up. 'Nothing much. I don't take them regularly. A bit of weed sometimes.'

'Phew!' Tommy smiles dramatically. 'Well, that's good. Now the rest, I can probably help you with. Tell me what's going on.'

Shelley's voice is hesitant at first. 'I didn't like uni and after I left Brighton, I didn't know what I wanted to do. That is, I didn't know what I wanted to do until I saw the jewellery that Jane makes. It's so original and different so I sent off for some basic tools. That was the box you carried upstairs for me and I started making some designs.' She sips her tea and warms to the theme. 'When I started working with Jane, she helped me a lot and I talked to her about designs and stuff but mostly I serve the customers. I didn't want to make it too obvious that I've been making stuff. I didn't know if it was any good.

Then, a few weeks ago, a guy came into the shop. Jane wasn't there and he was really charming. He was on holiday but he said he was into Social Media and things and he could raise the profile of the business. He said that he could sell her stuff online and make a fortune. I pretended that I'd designed most of her stuff. I thought, if he could help her, then he could help me sell my designs. So, I told him Jane had a new range of jewellery not on show and we agreed that I'd visit the house they've rented for the summer....and I took my jewellery to show him.'

Tommy is bursting with questions but he waits, wrapping his hands around his mug, holding his tongue.

'Anyway, there were lots of people, you know the sort of thing, drinking, drugs, some sex upstairs and stuff but I really wanted to speak to Troy.'

'Is that his name?'

'Yes.' She smiles. 'But he was very elusive and he suggested I became more party-like, and, well you can imagine—'

Tommy tightens his grip on the mug. 'Did he hurt you?'

'No. But he wasn't kind. He looked at my designs and said they were crap and he dissed me in front of everyone. It was humiliating. I was really upset. Then last night, I agreed to meet him with his friend Charles. Troy said he might finance my online business. But Charles was really seedy. He's old, fat and bald and he obviously wasn't going to do it for nothing.' Shelley bows her head. 'It was like he was treating me like a prostitute, farming me out to this rich, ugly guy on a promise of an internet start-up business.'

Tommy is trying desperately to keep his rapidly beating heart calm. 'Did he do anything?'

'He said I was a prick-tease. I pushed him away...' She looks down at her wrists. Tommy leans across the table and lifts back the sleeve of her blouse. There's a bruise and swelling on her left wrist.

'Did he do this?'

Shelley nods and continues. 'He told me the new range of jewellery is cheap like me and that he was only interested in the classy stuff in the shop.' Shelley looks up through tear-filled eyes. 'I guess that was a lesson I had to learn. That will teach me to tell lies and pretend that Jane's business was mine.'

Tommy finishes his tea. 'Why haven't you told Jane any of this?'

'I can't. She's kind to me but she's not... friendly. It's not as if we can share gossip or intimacies. She holds her own counsel and she never speaks badly about anyone.'

'That's a good thing.'

'True, but it's harder to forge a friendship.'

'If it's friendship you want then you have to try harder. Perhaps if you share a little bit of you, she will understand you more. You can be a little cold—'

'Me?'

'Yes, you do your own thing. You've let her down on the stall. She's also friends with Yusef. She's given you a second chance so she must think something good about you.'

Shelley sighs. 'She's only done that to keep you happy.'

'She might have done in the beginning but the fact that you're still there speaks volumes. Jane doesn't suffer fools and she won't waste her time on silly things. I think you're in a very good position to speak to her. Ask her advice and see where you can take all this.'

'I can't—'

'You confided in this Troy — a complete stranger — and you trusted him to help you. I think you're better off working with people you know. Jane is a better business woman than you give her credit for, and remember, you don't have to go global. Just so long as you enjoy what you do and make a decent living from it.'

Shelley sighs. 'You're right.'

'Do you want to be one of these social media influencers who are making videos all day?'

'No! I want to design and make jewellery myself. I'd be good at selling too. I like finding new ideas.'

'Then you have your answer. Perhaps I could help you write a business plan and you could take that to Jane and she will see that you're taking it all seriously.'

'What do you know about writing a business plan?' she grins.

Tommy shrugs. 'Nothing but you can find everything on the internet. We just have to download some help and support - a template or something.'

'Thanks, Tommy.'

'It's time I took an interest in what you're doing. But, it's late now. This can all wait until tomorrow. You need a good rest, a decent meal and we need to get that smile back on your face.'

Shelley nods. 'I have to see Yusef. I haven't been kind to him. I texted him earlier and I hope he'll forgive me.'

'Did you tell him about Troy?'

She shakes her head. 'No, but I will.'

'Tomorrow. You need to sleep.'

'Goodnight, Tommy. I'm really pleased you're my uncle and I'm here with you.' Shelley kisses him on the cheek.

After she goes upstairs and Almond Blossom follows, Tommy sighs deeply. He'd never really understood the intricacies of family love until now, but that love, comes with worry and responsibilities.

September

Jane

It's early. The sun is rising and there are a few people already in the sea. Jane sits on the beach, sipping her coffee and staring out to the horizon. Since she went swimming with Tommy, she hasn't been back in the water. As she hugs her knees, she wonders how everything has gone so wrong.

It was all fine until last month when she saw Femi and Lawrence. They had just got married and were walking out of the church. Jane was on her way back from the post office and she'd stopped to watch them from a distance. They were a good-looking couple; Femi had that lovely Jamaican vibe with the elegant yellow dress and matching hat. She had looked radiant. Lawrence was tall and dignified, and he couldn't take his eyes off her. Jane recognised Ricky, Ahmed and Albert — Femi's three foster boys - who were well-groomed and looking grown-up and handsome. Femi has given them all a new life and Lawrence gets on well with them too and then Femi's grandmother, Gladly, who must be in her eighties, had looked resplendent in pink. It was a very special moment as they gathered together for a family photo. Ahmed set up his camera in the archway of the church and Frances had pressed the button.

It was idyllic.

Now, Jane stares out to sea. A large cruise ship moves slowly in the distance and Jane imagines the people onboard. She sighs, wondering how she is going to shake off her melancholy mood. It's been creeping up on her like the tide on the beach, gradually getting nearer and nearer, filling all the small holes, suffocating her optimism and sapping her energy.

I'm tired. It's been a busy summer, Jane reasons.

What did she *really* want?

She sips her coffee watching Femi who is walking along the promenade, toward the RNLI station. She's in her uniform and is on duty this morning. They must be back from their honeymoon already.

Jane turns away. She doesn't want to wave and she doesn't want to be sociable. She doesn't know what she wants. She checks her watch. Then she stands and smooths down the hem of her dress.

Noah and Ben are in London today and Faisal offered to look after Jane's market stall. One less thing to worry about.

If only she didn't feel so lethargic, tired and fed up.

What's it all for? What's the point of working all these hours? What's the point of living at all? Where is all the fun?

There's a glimmer of a memory and she pulls her phone from her pocket. Perhaps she'd give this online dating another go. It might be different, after the summer. She's going to have to do something positive or she will go mad. Besides, with the kids going back to school and the summer coming to an end, Jane wasn't prepared to sit at home alone in the cold and dark. She needed love, and she was determined to find it.

* * *

Shelley arrives in the shop a few minutes after Jane. As always, they greet each other breezily and then Shelley loads the stock in the window and dusts everywhere, while Jane goes in the back. Today she's fixing a gold bracelet.

When Shelley follows her, she looks up at the CCTV camera and the reinforced back door. 'I bet you feel safe in here?'

'I do, yes. Besides, it's necessary for the insurance policy.'

Shelley watches Jane work at her table. She says, 'I think Yusef had a fling with an older woman — a while ago — before me.'

Jane doesn't look up. She concentrates on the tool she's holding as her hand begins to shake very slightly.

'What if it's Marion?' Shelley asks.

Jane lets the silence fall between them, unable to speak. Eventually she replies, 'I wouldn't lose any sleep over it. It may not even be anyone in Westbay. Maybe he's just trying to make you a little jealous?' Jane suggests, admiring her handiwork.

'You're probably right,' Shelley agrees. 'He does like to tease me.'

When Yusef comes over at midday, Jane watches him kiss Shelley on the lips and she looks away. She's still mortified that she slept with him and still terrified that he may say something.

She keeps busy and ignores them whispering together, returning to the back of the shop. She'd look on Tinder tonight plus she'd also read about another 'select' site for mature people.

'Do you fancy a drink tonight?' Yusef pokes his head around

the door.

Jane can feel her face flush.

'Shelley and I are going for a drink. We're celebrating. Did Shelley tell you?'

'No.'

'She's got a place at Leeds uni.'

'Oh?'

'Come for a drink?'

'No thanks.'

'Why not?'

'I'm tired.'

'Just come for one?'

Jane shakes her head. 'No, you go and enjoy it.'

After Yusef leaves, Shelley goes for a lunch break and the afternoon drags on. Jane is tired and she needs some fresh air. When Shelley comes back, she looks like she's bursting with excitement but Jane doesn't want to know.

'I'm just popping out,' she says.

'Now?'

'I'll see you later, Shelley. I haven't seen Tommy for a while, is he okay?'

'He's working on a business project.'

'Oh?' Jane doesn't wait, she leaves the shop quickly, shoving her phone in her jacket pocket and heading toward the harbour. She'd forgotten how busy it was. The market is full of tourists having a late lunch and enjoying this final burst of summer weather. Jane walks quickly. She wants to be alone and she inhales deeply until she's on the beach, sitting on the pebbles gazing out to sea.

Everyone seems to be living their life but not Jane. She wipes her cheek, lifts her phone, signs in, and starts scrolling for a match. Surely her luck might change soon.

* * *

By the following morning Jane has four potential matches and she's excited. Her spirits have lifted. Revived and refreshed after a good night's sleep she hurries down to open the shop, only stopping to buy the Saturday newspaper.

She's working alone today as Shelley has the weekend off. She mentioned something about university so Jane can only assume she'll be leaving soon.

Tommy will miss her. She's surprised Shelley hasn't mentioned more about leaving but while she's here she's a great asset. It will give Jane more time to slope off early and get ready for her dates.

Jane keeps busy and she's surprised when Amber calls into the shop. Her eyes are pink and raw as if she's been up all night crying.

'What's happened?'

Amber sits at the counter. 'Noah is leaving us.'

'Oh, Amber.'

'It's for the best but we've got used to him being around.'

'Can't he stay with you?'

'He needs more than we can give him. He's enjoyed the summer but he has to go to school and meet other kids. He has to talk again.' Amber sighs. 'We're having a small party for him this evening in the café after it closes. Will you come?'

'Of course.'

'We might have to look after Tommy. I think he will miss him.'

Jane nods in understanding. 'He's a funny little chap and

although he doesn't speak, you always know when he's with you.'

'I hope you mean Noah and not Tommy.' Amber grins and not for the first time, Jane wishes she had Amber's positivity and sense of humour when faced with a crisis.

* * *

The café is busy when Jane arrives. There's Femi and Lawrence and the three boys, plus Ricky's girlfriend, Ashley, and Faisal, Karl and Molly, Frances and her husband, and Tommy and Shelley.

There's a cream tea with an assortment of finger sandwiches, scones, cream and jams, and a delicious chocolate cake all laid out. The guests sit in the middle of the room where the tables have been put together in a long line.

Tommy insists on sitting beside Jane.

'How have you been?' she asks.

'I'm helping a friend with a business project.'

Jane raises her eyebrows. 'I'm impressed.'

'You will be.' He smiles.

They're distracted by Ben making a quick speech about how Noah has become a very special part of this community. There's applause, compliments and Albert punches Noah on the shoulder and Jane can see they've become close. Noah smiles. Everyone drinks tea and there's talk of Femi and Lawrence's honeymoon, Ricky's shift work at The Ship, and then it's time for everyone to clean up and leave.

'I need a drink.' Tommy says. 'I'm dreading this next bit.'

'Me too,' Jane replies. 'Let's get it over with?'

Tommy hugs Noah. He keeps it short and brief and Jane

does the same. Afterwards, she's relieved to get out and into the street.

'Phew!' Tommy rubs his hand over his face. 'I hate goodbyes at the best of times.'

'That's probably why Amber and Ben did it that way, to dilute the emotion for everyone and leave straight away.'

'I told them we were going to the pub if they wanted to come later.'

Tommy opens the door for Jane and they step inside. He orders large gin and tonics, and they find a table outside on the patio.

'It's chilly out here,' Jane says, 'but I want to feel cold.'

Tommy nods. 'It's the heat of the emotion.'

They sit quietly for a while, each of them lost in thought and assessing the situation.

'He's only a young boy and I feel very sad for him.' Jane wipes her eyes.

'I saw you give him that envelope. Did you give him some money?' Tommy asks.

'It's only a bit of pocket money to thank him for his work in the summer. I checked it was alright with Amber first.'

Tommy smiles. 'I have a gift for him but I bottled out.'

He pulls a small package from his pocket and lays it on the table. 'It's only something silly, but I—'

'Tommy, you should have given it to him.'

He shakes his head and rubs his nose. 'Nah.'

'Do you want to go back and give it to him?'

Tommy shakes his head.

Jane is distracted. Standing in the doorway of the pub, Ben waves at them. Then Noah ducks under Ben's arm and runs toward them. He's carrying a parcel the size of a shoe box and he puts it on the table and smiles at Tommy.

'Hello Noah. Goodness, what's this?'

Ben joins them at the table. 'Noah wants to give you this, but he didn't want to do it in front of everyone.'

Tommy looks at Noah's smiling face and then at the package. 'Shall I open it?'

Noah nods but Tommy's fingers are already pulling the paper away. He unwraps a wooden boat that is carved to perfection. It's the fishing boat.

Tommy whistles. 'You've even painted it the same colours.' He reads the name of the boat. 'Morning Maiden,' he whispers, 'this is amazing. Noah.' He slaps him on the shoulder and after looking at it again he shows it to both Ben and Jane for them to admire. Then, he picks up the small package on the table.

'And, I have this for you. I didn't want to give it to you in front of everyone either.'

Noah unwraps it quickly with shaking fingers. He pulls out an exquisite ship in a bottle and Noah covers his mouth in surprise.

'Do you like it?'

Noah nods and holds it up for Ben to look at in more detail, then he turns to Tommy and flings his arms around his neck.

Tommy holds the young boy. His eyes are closed and when he opens them they are wet with tears and he wipes them away with the back of his hand. 'I'm a silly old man,' he says and Noah laughs.

Ben hands Noah the ship in a bottle and places his hand on his shoulder. 'Happy now? Can we go?'

Noah smiles and nods. They turn and walk away and then as they get to the door Noah suddenly turns and runs back to the table. He leans and whispers in Tommy's ear. Jane can't hear what he says but she sees the look of astonishment on Tommy's face.

* * *

After Noah and Ben have left and while Tommy wipes away his tears, Jane gets them another drink. The past few days have been challenging. She's felt so low, maybe it was because Noah was leaving. Now he's gone and they've said good-bye, perhaps she'll feel better. She would miss Noah and his cheeky grin. She would always remember the summer with Noah and Tommy at the Artisan market in the harbour and how they'd kept the coffee and ice cream kiosks in business. It had been an unusual time, but then Westbay wasn't an ordinary place at all. All of life happened here. There was always something going on.

Jane puts their drinks on the table and wraps herself in a pub blanket.

'I can't keep doing this,' Tommy says. 'I can't keep losing people.'

'Noah is going to a proper home.'

'I know but it's not Noah, I'm worried about. I just can't keep investing this emotion, time after time. Elsie and Shelley — it's too much. Sometimes, I'm even angry with Sunita.'

'Anger is a stage of bereavement, Tommy. You have to be kind to yourself.'

'But it's everything. There's been too much change. The heart attack, not being able to work, Elsie's cancer and the worry about if she's going to pull through and what about poor Shelley?'

'It's life, Tommy. You have to live and enjoy each moment

and learn to have fun, or what's the point in living?'

'Sometimes I'm scared, Jane. I'm scared I'll wake up and I'll be all alone again. I enjoy having Shelley at home, but I'm realistic enough to know that she's not going to stay forever. She gives me purpose but she'll go to uni in a few weeks. Move on, move away and then what?'

'Then you'll find something else to fill the gap.'

'There has to be a less painful way.'

'I guess you could block off all emotion, but then you'd be robotic.'

Tommy grins. 'Maybe a life with an artificial intelligence friend would suit me.'

'Tommy, you're a softie, you'd probably fall in love and get withdrawal symptoms with a robot.'

Tommy stares at Jane and appears to be considering his words carefully. 'Did you hear what Noah whispered?' he asks.

Jane shakes her head. 'I've never heard him speak. It must be very special and I don't need to know. Keep those words close to your heart.'

Tommy frowns. 'I'll tell you one day.'

Jane shakes her head and sips her drink. 'It's not necessary, Tommy, but I'm here if you want to—'

'Do you like Shelley?'

Tommy's question takes her by surprise and she frowns.

'Of course, why?'

He shrugs.

'Tell me, why do you ask? She's been working with me for a few months now—'

'Do you think you've got to know her?'

Jane frowns. 'We've been busy. But she's a hard worker and

she likes to party and have fun, sometimes she's a bit late but she's a good girl and very willing to help.'

'Even now?'

'She's been quieter the past few weeks. Why?'

'She thinks you don't like her.'

Jane frowns. 'I'm sorry if I've given her that impression.'

'No, it's fine, it's only because—'

Suddenly feeling very upset, Jane stands up. Her emotions are in turmoil. It's not like her but she can't believe that Shelley has told Tommy that she doesn't like her when she has done nothing to deserve it. She's always been kind to her.

'I'm sorry, Tommy. I'm going home. This has been an emotional afternoon for us both and to now suggest I don't like Shelley, is—'

'No, please, sit down, Jane. I don't mean anything by it—I—'

'I'll see you tomorrow. I wanted to have a relaxing evening and a quiet drink, not this.' She turns away.

'Jane—' Tommy calls but she's already disappeared across the patio and into the pub.

* * *

On Monday morning, Jane drags herself into the shop. She spent Sunday afternoon shopping in the city. She had to get away from Westbay and everyone in it. She thought a spot of retail therapy would help her but it hasn't. The feeling of sadness stays with her. She's tired and she needs a break.

Jane's unpacking a new stock of three very expensive watches when Shelley arrives late. She looks pale and tired and her eyes dart nervously around the shop.

'Sorry, Jane. I did text you.'

'That's okay. We're not busy.'

'I was sick.' Shelley slips out of her jacket.

'You should have stayed at home.'

'I didn't want to let you down.'

'It's quiet anyway. And, congratulations on your university place.'

Shelley smiles but she looks exhausted. After hanging up her jacket in the back, Shelley stands beside her. She's the picture of misery. She looks how Jane feels on the inside.

'These watches came today. What do you think?'

Shelley picks one up. 'They're cool, expensive and I'm sure they'll sell.'

'I'll only stock these few because I can always order more.'

Shelley moves around the shop working on autopilot, picking up the duster and flicking it at the shelves. Maybe Shelley hates her life as much as Jane hates hers at the moment.

Jane says brightly, 'I'm working on a new necklace design; would you like to see it?'

Shelley's face lights up. 'I would.'

They go to the back of the shop and Jane takes her sketchpad from the table and turns it to face them. She flicks through it and pauses at the last page.

Shelley gasps. 'When did you do this?' she asks.

'At the end of last week, why?'

Shelley shakes her head and she's suddenly looking much paler.

'Are you alright?' Jane asks.

Shelley moves quickly, pushing past Jane and into the small bathroom at the back of the shop. Jane can hear her retching into the bowl.

When she returns Jane says, 'Maybe you should go home.'

Shelley shakes her head.

'Is it something you've eaten?'

Shelley won't look at her.

'Have you any other symptoms?'

'I think — I've missed a period.'

'You think?'

'I think I missed one but that's because I wasn't eating much.'

'Have you done a pregnancy test?'

Shelley eyes fill with fear. 'I don't know—' She shakes her head. 'I feel so awful.' She slides onto a chair and puts her head in her hands. 'What a mess. I don't want a baby,' Shelley cries. 'I can barely look after myself. What will mum say? And Uncle Tommy? He will be furious. He won't believe me, especially after last week.'

'What happened last week?'

'He went to see Troy, the guy I've been hanging around with. Tommy wasn't pleased.'

'Is that the group of guys from the big house on the cliffs?'

'You know about them?'

'He came in here one day spoofing off about creating an online business and I told him I already had one.'

'You met him?'

'He was a jerk. I told him I didn't need him or his venture capital investors as he called them.'

'Oh, Jane. He came in here when I was alone and I was stupid. I pretended the shop was mine.'

'Well, you do work in it.'

'I know but I didn't have the right to pretend I owned it.'

Jane smiles. 'No harm done.'

'Only to my ego. He told me I had to lose weight and then there was this wealthy guy. He wanted me to sleep with—'

'Did you—'

'No!'

Jane nods. 'Good.'

'Do you believe me?'

'Of course.'

'Yusef doesn't know, I didn't tell him. I was hanging around with those guys and—'

'Why did you?'

'I wanted my own online business and they said they'd help me with social media and that I'd have millions of followers and become an influencer.'

'Is that what you want?'

Shelley lowers her head. 'I don't know any more.'

'You're going to uni?'

'Mum wants me to, but I don't think it's necessary. I'll end up with a massive student loan and it will take years to pay off. It really isn't worth it when I already know what I want to do.'

'You do? What's that?'

'This. I want to work with jewellery.'

Jane stares at her, wondering how she could have missed all the signs during the summer. Shelley was always interested in watching her work.

'Why didn't you say something?'

Shelley shrugs. 'I never had the confidence.'

'Well, you can't do anything or make any decisions until you know if you're having a baby. Stay here,' Jane says, grabbing her purse.

Shelley stands up and faces her. 'Would you be upset?'

'Me?'

'If I was having Yusef's baby.'

Jane stares at her and blinks slowly. 'This isn't about me.'

Jane marches quickly to the chemist in the square and fifteen minutes later she's back with the small package.

'Here. It tells you what to do. The instructions are inside. It's quick and simple.'

Shelley takes the box warily. 'What if I am?'

'Then we can deal with it but until then all your plans are fresh air. Let's deal with facts and what we know, and then you can make an informed decision.'

Shelley taps the box on the back of her hand. 'I'm frightened.'

Jane pulls her into her arms and Shelley relaxes against her shoulder. They stay like that for a few minutes until Jane pulls away. 'If you want to go home and do this, you can.'

Shelley shrugs. 'This is as good as home. What will I tell Tommy?'

'Let's see what happens.'

'This could be life changing,' Shelley says softly.

Jane smiles. 'Things happen for a reason and sometimes we never know why. What will be will be and nothing is ever insurmountable. If you're having a baby, it will be well loved and cared for... whatever happens.'

The door opens and Jane glances into the shop.

'Oh, gosh, it's the vicar,' she says. 'How appropriate.'

Shelley giggles nervously and then without looking back, she disappears into the bathroom leaving Jane staring at the closed door behind her.

* * *

Jane rearranges her face into a friendly smile. Frances is her friend and she feels sorry that she hasn't seen more of her over the summer.

'Hello, Frances. This is a lovely surprise,' Jane says, brightly. 'I've been meaning to ask you to have dinner with me. We've got a lot to catch up on.'

'Gosh, anytime Jane, but life's been manic and I don't know where the summer has gone, so now, I'm panicking. I'm looking for a birthday present for Graham. It's his big birthday next week.'

Jane takes out an array of watches while surreptitiously peering through the back door to see if Shelley will give her then thumbs up or the thumbs down.

'Have you seen Tommy recently?' Frances asks.

'Not for a while.'

'He's been very low since Noah left,' Frances says. 'I thought you might have seen him?' She glances at the tray of watches.

Jane shakes her head.

Frances sighs. 'He's going to need to do something, Jane. I keep wracking my brains but nothing's happening. I can't think what he can do.' Frances looks at the selection of watches, picking one up and placing it on her wrist, then putting it down again. 'I don't know how to help him and, when Shelley leaves, he'll be even worse.'

Feeling awkward, Jane glances over her shoulder wondering if she should tell Frances that Shelley is in the back of the shop. But there's no sign of her.

'He's been doing so well, you know under the circumstances. He's been going out more with Matt and the gang, and I've seen him out jogging. I think Shelley is good for him, but I'm worried that when she leaves he'll have some sort of setback. What do you think?'

Jane is silent and then she feels Frances watching her, so she replies, 'Well, we are all here to help him, Frances. It's a good community.'

'I'll take this one. This is the one Graham's had his eye on.' Frances smiles, as Jane wraps the gift. 'You can tell me to mind my own business but I thought you and Tommy might end up as more than friends. I saw you a few times together in the summer and you looked so happy, I thought—'

'Are you paying with cash or card?' Jane wonders if Shelley is in a terrible state in the back of the shop, listening to Frances's view of her uncle's love life.

But Frances won't be silenced.

'I'm only saying this because I thought you might perhaps look out for him. I know everyone will tell me to mind my own business but I have said it to Amber, and to Marion, we have to look out for each other, don't we?'

Jane nods while Frances inserts her card into the machine.

'Anyway, give it some thought. I think he's taking up golf. At least that will give him something to do. But he will need more than that, Jane, especially with winter coming and we all know how lonely those long winter nights can get.'

'Here you go, Frances. Please wish Graham a happy birthday.' Jane smiles.

Frances takes her gift-wrapped parcel. 'You know this is such a lovely shop, I should really pick something out, as Graham never knows what to buy me but I'm not one for jewellery.' She smiles. 'No offense, but I'd prefer a good book.'

'They're a lot cheaper.' Jane laughs.

After Frances has gone, Jane heads to the back of the shop.

Shelley is standing with her back to her in the small kitchen.

'Well?' Jane asks, looking at Shelley's back and hunched shoulders.

Shelley turns around and there are tears in her eyes. 'Negative.'

Jane sighs. 'Phew!'

'I would like a baby. Just not yet.' Shelley opens her arms and throws them around Jane's neck and pushes her nose into her cheek. 'Thank you, thank you, thank you. I've been worried sick and I haven't wanted to take the test. I had no one else to speak to, thank you, Jane.'

'You must look after yourself, if you've missed a period and you've been sick.'

'I know, but I'll be more sensible now and I'll eat more.'

'And, no more drugs or smoking weed?

'How do you know?'

'I was young once.'

'No more drugs,' says Shelley. 'Troy told me I had to lose weight to have an internet presence but I don't care about any of that any more. He wasn't kind or nice to me.'

'Then stay away from unkind people. You're young and you have all the time in the world to meet nice people.'

'Yusef is lovely.'

Jane nods. 'He's a good guy.' She returns Shelley's hug. 'I'm here for you Shelley. I'm sorry, I should have told you that when you arrived. I never thought. You must have been going through so much, worrying about your mum and everything.'

Shelley nods. 'In some ways, I'll be pleased when her treatment is over and in other ways I don't want it to end — just in case it hasn't worked this time.'

'It's such a worry for you.'

'She's living on borrowed time.'

'Yes, but then you could argue, we all are.'

Shelley nods. 'That's why I feel so sad for Tommy. Sunita never even got a chance to say goodbye. She never had time to say anything that would make things better. It was all over.' She clicks her fingers. 'Like that.'

'That's why we have to make the most of everything,' Jane says.

* * *

That afternoon, after she closes the shop, Jane goes home determined to change her life. The advice she gave to Shelley, she decides, she can apply to herself. She pours a glass of wine and spends the evening updating her profile on a new dating site, and then spends a few hours scrolling through potential dates. She hadn't had time to pursue the previous four matches but she now messages them and is pleased when one replies back immediately. But by ten o'clock she's exhausted. Her energy is dwindling and her enthusiasm for dating is waning, so she heads to bed for an early night. She's just brushed her teeth when her phone pings with a message.

Haven't seen you for ages. Sorry if I upset you. Thanks for being kind to Shelley. Tx

Jane pulls back the duvet and climbs on the bed. She frowns. Surely, Shelley didn't tell him about her pregnancy scare. She texts back:

I'm fine. I was over tired and sensitive. Sorry. Shelley is a good person.

A few minutes later he texts:

Coffee tomorrow?

She replies:

Yes please, night, night.

She turns off the light and gazes up at the ceiling, remembering Frances's words. She had enjoyed Tommy's company in
the summer and she had been upset when he'd so flippantly
replaced her with Marion.

But Tommy is only a friend. She enjoys his company and
they get on well and that's that. She blocked off any other
emotional connection months ago. She could be Tommy's
friend now without getting hurt. It wouldn't bother her if she
saw him with Marion – or if he went on a dating site. In fact,
Jane sits up, that's a great idea. She could help him. She could
help him find a partner so that when Shelley leaves he won't
be lonely.

Jane smiles in the dark. Maybe that's what Frances was
hinting at. Frances knew that Jane had a bit of experience
with dating sites so maybe that's what she wanted Jane to do.
She could get him spruced up, smart, take a few pictures and
upload his profile and — it would be great fun. She lies down
in bed again. Wouldn't it be funny to see them both on the
same dating website?

Jane's phone pings.

She reaches out and squints at the small screen.

Night, night, sleep tight, Tx

* * *

The next morning, Jane opens the shop and Tommy arrives with coffee. Jane refuses to tell him why she's smiling so mischievously.

'It looks like you've been up to something.' He laughs.

'I haven't. Not yet.'

'Are you going to tell me?'

'I'll tell you later.'

Shelley breezes into the shop a few minutes later. 'Sorry, I was on litter-tray duty.' She grins at Tommy.

'You're just in time,' he says. 'Jane is acting weird and maybe you can tell me why?'

Shelley looks at Jane and then back at Tommy. 'I have no idea.' She hangs up her jacket and joins them in the shop.

Jane takes a deep breath. 'I've been thinking, and I've come up with a good idea for Tommy.'

Shelley's eyes widen and Tommy sits up.

Jane continues, 'He's going to miss you when you leave for university and rather than him be on his own, I think it would be a good idea, Shelley, if we find him a girlfriend.'

Shelley gasps and Tommy blinks rapidly.

Jane says, 'The thing is, this is a small town and there isn't a lot of choice and so I think that we should sign Tommy up to a dating website. That way he can have fun meeting and dating which will help his confidence and it will hopefully help him find the right woman.' Jane claps her hands excitedly.

Tommy stares at her.

Shelley looks from Jane to Tommy.

'Well, what do you think? 'Jane asks. 'There's a new site, for older people, it's a little more expensive to join but it's worth it.'

'How do you know?' asks Shelley slowly.

'Because I've joined.'

'You have?' Tommy clears his throat.

'Life's too short. And, after chatting to Shelley about life, I've decided I need to do something about my life. I was on a site before, but this time I feel different.'

'Why?' Tommy's voice is a croak.

'Because I feel more positive and optimistic. I'm not old and I have a lot to offer. Shelley, don't you think it's a good idea?'

'Well, if it's something Tommy would like.' She turns to him. 'Would you?'

Tommy shrugs and looks at the floor.

Jane grins at Shelley and winks.

Shelley replies, 'Well, let's give it a go. Jane, come round tonight for dinner. It's our night to eat in together. I'll get the computer and we'll sign Tommy up.'

'Great idea, thanks Shelley. Now, Tommy, wear something nice and I'll take a good photo of you. It's amazing how many people put up fake ones and I don't think it does anyone any good. You need to be you.'

Tommy focuses on a spot on the carpet.

The door opens and a young couple walk in.

'Have you got any engagement rings?' the boy asks nervously.

* * *

'Are you sure this is a good idea?' Tommy is sitting at the

kitchen table and Jane is pointing her phone camera at him.

'Smile.'

Tommy smiles.

'That's not a proper smile. Smile like you've just seen Marilyn Monroe lift her skirt.'

He laughs loudly.

Click.

'That's better. I'll airdrop it to you Shelley.'

'Okay.' Shelley sits at the kitchen table. She's tapping keys and staring at the screen. 'What other hobbies have you got?'

'Fishing. Snooker.' Tommy stands behind her and looks over her shoulder.

'Hardly romantic material, are you?' Shelley laughs.

'What about your dance classes. Didn't you do yoga?' Jane prompts.

'I hated them both,' he replies.

'What about sport?' Shelley asks.

'Tiddlywinks.' He grins. 'Does that count?'

'Tommy, you'll never meet a woman like this.' Shelley complains.

'I don't just want any type of woman. She has to be special. She has to have other qualities than liking dancing or knitting...' Shelley giggles and he nudges her. 'None of your smutty nonsense.' He grins.

'Put down that you like the cinema and nice restaurants. You like both of those.' Jane taps the screen with her finger. 'You also like the beach and swimming.'

Shelley taps quickly. 'Right, now what are you looking for?'

'Someone who's kind,' he replies immediately.

'Apart from that.' Shelley raises her eyes to the ceiling. 'Who do you imagine yourself with?'

Tommy shakes his head in exasperation. 'I didn't know there was so much choice. It's like a supermarket.'

'No, it's more refined than that.'

'This seems like an awful lot of effort just to—'

'No, it's not, Tommy.' Jane places her hand on his arm. 'It may seem daunting but it's not. Think of it as a pub, a big pub where there are lots of single people and you're a bit shy, and although you like the look of a person, you haven't got the courage to walk up and speak to them. This way, you get to look at them, send them a message, chat for a bit and then if you still like them, you can meet up and see where it goes.'

'You make it sound interesting but it's hard work. I don't want to text a stranger.'

'But you'd want to chat to a pretty woman in a bar, wouldn't you?'

Tommy shrugs. 'I suppose so.'

'Good.' Shelley leans back and stretches. 'That's you all set up and running, Tiger Tommy.' She giggles.

Tommy picks up Almond Blossom and strokes her absent-mindedly. 'Did you tell them I like cats?'

Shelley giggles. 'Let's have a look at some profiles, shall we?' Shelley leans forward. 'I can help you message them if you like?'

'What will I say?' He pulls his chair closer.

'Let's start with looking at them first.'

'Looks aren't everything,' Tommy replies seriously.

'Well, you don't want to date someone ugly.' Shelley laughs.

Tommy looks at Jane. 'This is a nightmare and Shelley is—'

'Not taking it seriously enough for you?' Jane finishes.

Tommy nods. 'Shall we go to the pub instead?'

Jane grins. 'I found it a bit daunting the first time too.'

'Let's have a look at Jane's profile.' Shelley taps the keys and then Jane's photograph appears.

'That's not a good photo,' says Tommy. 'You're much prettier in real life.'

Jane blushes.

'It says here you like eating out, cosy nights in and walks on the beach.' Shelley reads aloud. 'Jigsaws?'

Jane nods.

'Did you write that I like jigsaws?' asks Tommy.

Shelley yawns.

Tommy looks at the screen and seems to be reading quickly. Jane wishes they hadn't looked at her profile. It makes her feel uncomfortable.

'It says here that you like making costume jewellery,' Tommy says. 'But you're so talented. You've done yourself down. You haven't said you run a thriving business or how hard you work.'

'You can't say everything.' Jane looks around for her jacket. Signing Tommy up hadn't been as much fun as she thought it was going to be and she feels a bit in the spotlight now that they're analysing her profile.

'I'm surprised you haven't been snapped up,' Tommy says, still reading.

'Well, I'm not in a hurry to meet anyone, it's just a bit of fun. And with the cold, dark winter evenings on their way, it's something to do.'

'I wonder if Elsic has thought of this,' Tommy says.

'Tommy! I think mum has more than enough on her plate.'

Tommy sits thinking and then in a dry slow voice he says, 'Well, if it works this well, then why are there still so many single people?'

'Lots of young people meet online now.'

'Perhaps it won't take any time at all to meet someone.' His voice takes on an excited tone. 'In fact, I'm really coming round to this idea. I could find the perfect partner. It would be great to know I'm not going to be on my own any more.'

Jane pulls on her jacket. She doesn't know what she expected. A gloominess invades her heart as she fumbles for her car keys.

'Thanks for dinner. I'll see you guys tomorrow.'

Tommy kisses her cheek briefly before sitting back down in front of the computer. Jane is half way out of the house when he shouts, 'I think I could become addicted to this!'

* * *

It's Friday afternoon and Shelley is just leaving the shop.

'Yusef is taking me to the new fish bar in the square tonight.'

Jane looks up from her desk. She's fixing a tricky locket, but her eyes are tired and she wants to go home. 'Have a great weekend.'

'Are you sure you don't need me tomorrow?'

'No, enjoy your day in London with Tommy.'

'He's very kind to take me there for my birthday. We're doing a city tour and everything.'

'Just have fun.'

'It's my last weekend before I go to uni.'

'I know. Make it special.'

'Oh, I nearly forgot.' Shelley opens her bag and pulls out a sketchpad. 'Do you remember I said I designed some jewellery in the summer. Will you take a look and let me know what you think?'

'Sure. Leave it there and I'll look at it over the weekend.'

Shelley nods and then suddenly she's gone and the shop is quiet. Jane notices the silence more now. It must have always been like this before. Just her and the clocks ticking time away. And to think she'd never noticed. It really is very quiet.

Tommy wouldn't be the only one who misses Shelley.

Jane suddenly notices that she's forgotten to place an order so she picks up the phone and is placed on hold. While she's waiting she turns the pages of Shelley's sketch pad.

Each page is titled and dated. Each page holds the most exquisite drawing. Jane is surprised. Shelley is an incredibly talented artist but when Jane looks closer she realises that her designs are all original, imaginative and extremely detailed. She's fascinated.

The voice on the end of the phone takes her order and Jane hangs up. She takes her time looking at Shelley's ideas, and then she turns a page. There, to her complete surprise, is Jane's own necklace design. Jane gasps. The colours are different, but in essence it's the same piece of jewellery she had created, only Shelley's work is dated two weeks earlier than Jane's designed piece.

Jane stands up and checks her notebook.

Her sketches are also dated and she lays the drawings side by side. It's incredible. Jane has spent years learning this craft. Jane's father was a great designer and now Shelley has done all of this on her own, without going to university. Without any help.

Completely mesmerised, Jane continues looking through the sketches of rings, ankle bracelets and piercings. These are things Jane has never designed but she understands Shelley's theme and begins to realise her undeniable talent.

Jane picks up her phone, but then changes her mind. She decides she will think about it over the weekend and work out what to do for the best.

October

Tommy

'The house is empty without them.' Tommy leans on the harbour railings and glances out to sea. 'I didn't think she'd take Almond Blossom, but she did.'

Jane stands beside him hugging the cup of coffee they'd bought in Harbour Street.

Tommy swallows hard and holds back his tears. 'But on a positive note, Elsie is doing well, and she might come and visit later in the year.'

'That's fantastic. Have you heard from Shelley?'

Tommy doesn't want Jane to think he feels sorry for himself all the time. He doesn't want to be a wet weekend, but he feels so miserable that he doesn't know what to do. 'It was all different in the summer,' he says, rambling, 'Noah was here then and Shelley was in and out of the house. I had a purpose. Life was somehow different, wasn't it?'

'You had Shelley living in your home, and the cat, so you're bound to miss them. We knew this would happen, didn't we?'

Tommy doesn't reply. 'I've thought about getting a job. They were looking for someone to work in the supermarket and I thought it would be a good place to chat to people.' He grins. 'I think I became more sociable in the summer.'

'Or is it all those dates you've been on?'

Tommy laughs. He likes it when Jane teases him and he likes the way she spends time with him. They often meet at lunch time in the harbour and sometimes they share a sandwich in the café. The Artisan market is closed now until next year. 'I loved the summer, but you don't realise how much you enjoy something until it's over. I didn't give it much thought. Do you remember the day we sat on the beach looking at the sunset? That was one of the most magical times.'

Jane smiles. 'Until I ran off.'

'You never said why.'

'I've forgotten,' she replies.

He nods. 'It's often best to forget some things. Like the fact that I asked Marion back to my house.'

Jane laughs. 'Yes, best to forget it.'

'What about the time we went swimming?' he says.

'I loved that. We should do more of that.' Jane finishes her coffee. 'Do you need to work, Tommy? You know, financially?'

He shakes his head. 'I'm not a millionaire, but the house is paid for, and I have some savings. I'm very lucky.'

'Then I have a great idea. Come on.' Jane tucks her arm in his. 'I've just seen someone we know.'

'Where are we going?'

'If I tell you, it will ruin the surprise.'

They walk around the harbour to the RNLI station where Femi is climbing out of her car.

Jane waves and Femi calls out, 'I thought I recognised you two.'

'We're getting some fresh air before I go back to the shop.'

Tommy smiles at Femi. He's always been so grateful to her, but she never expects recognition for saving his life. 'How are the boys?' he asks.

'Ricky is excited. He wants to go off to uni next year. Albert has gone up a year at school and loves his new teacher. He's getting on so much better. And Ahmed went to Turkey in the summer to meet his mother, so that was a big step for him.'

'Will he go back to Syria?'

'He'll stay here for now. His mother has remarried and although he was pleased to see her, he considers this his home now.'

'Faisal is happy too?' Jane asks.

'Amber and Ben have given him a brilliant training. I think he'd like to work in London but he knows how lucky he is here. Time will tell.' Femi checks the sky. 'That's a fierce wind, Tommy, I hope Matt and the gang will be okay.'

Tommy smiles. 'Matt got the boat fixed so they'll be good.'

Jane says, 'Femi, how does one volunteer here?'

'They just turn up and they chat to me or the boss, and then we train them and show them around and things. Why?' Femi looks at Tommy. 'You?'

Tommy looks at Jane. 'Me?'

'Absolutely you. This would be perfect. You'd be down at the harbour, looking out to sea at all the boats every day *and* you'd have company.'

'I'm sure you know most of the team here, Tommy. You're like one of us already.'

Tommy blinks quickly. He'd never thought of volunteering here. It had never entered his head but now he thinks about it, it would be absolutely perfect.

'You'd have to do shift work Tommy and sometimes you'd

be on call at night. But you wouldn't be going out to sea.'

'Don't put him off now, Femi. Wait until he's all signed up and then tell him the down side.'

They all laugh.

'Right, well are you coming in, Tommy? The boss is upstairs and you can chat to him.'

'I'm going back to the shop, see you both later.' Jane waves and walks off smiling.

Femi heads inside the station and Tommy stands still.

Why has he been blessed to have these lovely women in his life? They really are special friends and for the life of him, Tommy can't work out what he's done to deserve such kindness.

'Coming?' Femi calls.

He follows her into the station but not before he glances out to sea and whispers, 'Thanks Sunita. Thanks for looking out for me.'

* * *

Tommy loves his new life volunteering at the RNLI. He's spent a few weeks training and he's keeping busy. One evening, after he's finished work and heading to The Ship for a drink, he pauses at the pet shop.

He knows Mario and Lucas and he was always grateful that they employed Shelley for a few weeks in the summer. He often stops to chat, but today, something catches his eye. Sitting in the doorway is the sweetest little puppy with big brown eyes. Mario is feeding him a treat.

'Who's this little fella?' Tommy asks, leaning down to stroke him.

'It's a her and we're not sure. Someone tied her to the lamppost outside the shop this morning, but they haven't come back.'

'Is she chipped?'

'I'm about to close up the shop, so I'll take her to the vet now and find out.'

'She's a pretty little thing. What is she?'

Mario rubs her ears. 'A little mixed breed.'

'Let me know how you get on,' says Tommy.

When he's in the pub, chatting to Paul, he wonders why he said that. But she was the cutest little thing he'd seen since Almond Blossom. The next morning, he finds himself telling Jane about the puppy over coffee.

'Go and find out,' she urges him. 'Go now, the pet shop will be open.'

'Well, I'm not sure.'

'A dog might be just the thing you need.'

'I had dogs growing up, but they're a bit of a tie.'

'You'll find a way to manage.'

Tommy heads back up the street to the pet shop. 'How's the puppy? Where is she?' he asks.

Mario replies, 'She's not chipped and Lucas is at home with her now. He'll take her to the rescue centre later today.'

Tommy scratches his head. 'That's not right, is it? Poor thing.'

Mario laughs. 'Do you want to adopt her?'

'I'm not sure.'

'I'll ask Lucas to bring her down after lunch, if you like? I'd prefer you to have her. I know how much you miss Almond Blossom. I was surprised Shelley took her with her.'

'Well, she found a flat-share and they said she could have a cat.'

Tommy wishes Shelley hadn't taken her, but the idea of a puppy that he can take for walks on the beach would be something very special. This little puppy might be just perfect.

* * *

'It was love at first sight.' Tommy tells Jane. They're in the jewellers and he's so excited he can barely contain himself.

'What is she?'

'No idea. A bit of a mix but she's so affectionate.' Tommy gently pats the puppy's ears, and she rolls over to have her tummy tickled.

Jane sits on the chair and lets the puppy gnaw her fingers.

'What's her name?' she asks.

'Morning Maiden? Haven't decided yet — Titanic?' Tommy grins.

Jane smiles. 'Definitely not. She needs a pretty name.'

'Marie.'

'Marie? Are you joking?'

'Marie Celeste?'

'No.'

'Aphrodite?'

Jane laughs. 'No, Tommy. Nothing related to the sea or a boat. She's a puppy not a ship.'

Tommy laughs when the puppy chases her own tail around the shop floor. 'She likes it in here,' he says.

Jane laughs.

'You could do with some company,' he says.

'What's that supposed to mean?' she asks.

'Well, I thought on the days I'm at the RNLI, you could have her in here with you.'

Jane stares at him with a look of incredulity spreading over her face that makes him laugh. 'That's impossible,' she says.

'Look at her. Look at those brown eyes. How can you turn her down?'

'I'm not. I'm turning you down.'

The puppy squats on the floor.

'Oh no!' Jane exclaims.

'I'll clean it up.' Tommy shouts. 'Where's the stuff?'

'In the kitchen under the sink.'

'I wish Shelley was here,' he says.

'She wouldn't want to clean up after a puppy.' Jane laughs. 'She's your responsibility.'

'Please help me.'

'I can't.'

'You can. Just for a couple of weeks, Jane. Just until she gets settled. I can't leave her when I do my shifts at the station. She's too small and she'd be so lonely. I could buy her a bed and she could sit in the back with you and sleep while you're working—'

'Tommy.'

'Please?'

'No.'

He sighs. 'Don't you find the shop quiet without Shelley?'

Jane replies quietly, 'Of course, I do.'

'You don't have to live a life of misery, you know. You don't have to be alone. You can time share her.' He points at the puppy now chewing the chair leg. 'We can time share her together.'

* * *

Tommy isn't sure what he's doing but after he's been to the pet shop and bought a bed, collar, lead, bowls and food, he makes his way home smiling happily.

He thinks about calling into the pub for a quick pint, but he's not sure the puppy won't wee over the floor and that would be far too embarrassing. Once at home, he's actually relieved that Almond Blossom isn't purring and rubbing around his ankles.

He unpacks the goods. 'Are you hungry?'

The puppy is excited. She's sniffing everywhere and running around and Tommy sighs happily.

'You'll soon settle down. This is your home now.' He opens a can of soft food, recommended by Lucas. He spoons it into the bowl and places it on the floor.

'Come on, little one,' he calls. He sits at the kitchen table and reaches for his phone. He scrolls through names: Bella, Lucy, Daisy, Molly, Maggie, Lola, Sophie, Chloe. He sighs as the puppy heads to the bowl, sniffs and then walks away.

Tommy pretends he's not looking. He ignores her and she lies in the corner, under the radiator by the wall, staring at him.

He phones Jane and says, 'She's not eating.'

'What do you want me to do? Come over and cook her steak and chips?'

'She's lying on the floor. She's staring at me.'

'She's probably tired. Where's her bed?'

'Under the stairs.'

'Put it by the radiator.'

'Hold on.' Tommy shifts the bed and cajoles the puppy who isn't impressed. 'I think she's tired.'

'Then she'll fit in nicely with you.'

'Don't be sarkie!'

Tommy watches the puppy close her eyes. 'Do you think she needs a wee?'

'She did enough in my shop.'

He laughs. 'Your face was a picture.'

'Yours was funnier. You had to clean it up.' Jane chuckles down the phone.

'I'll walk her tomorrow and then I'll drop her in to you after lunch.'

'Let's hope she's fully house trained by then.'

'She's tiny. She'll soon get the hang of it all. Oops, she's woken up already. Stop! Stop! Stop jumping.' There's a pause and then Tommy says, 'She's chewing the skirting board.'

'Did you get her any toys?'

'Er no, I forgot.'

'Then you'll have to improvise. You'll have to tire her out and then she'll sleep.'

Tommy sighs. 'That's fine. I can do that.' Although Tommy is exhausted and wants to go to bed, he knows what he has to do. He yawns. 'What are you doing?'

'I've eaten a jacket potato and now I'm having a glass of wine.'

'That sounds nice.'

'You've a puppy to train. I suggest you get on the internet and find out how to train your dog.'

The puppy barks at the back door.

Tommy scratches his head. 'She might need to go out.'

'Let her sniff everywhere and that will tire her out.'

'You think so?' Tommy hops off the chair. That sounds like it's something he can do. 'Night, night, Jane.'

'Night, night.'

'TMC says good night.'
'Who is TMC?'
'Titanic, Mary Celeste.'
'No! Definitely not.'

* * *

Tommy is woken at three, at four and at five in the morning by little doggy yelps, so he pads downstairs in his pyjamas and bare feet. He rubs her ears and settles her with a biscuit before heading back upstairs again.

By the morning, he's exhausted.

His phone rings at nine.

'Hello, Uncle Tommy.'

'This is early for you!' He laughs.

The puppy has eaten breakfast and been outside fifteen times and Tommy's trying to eat his cereal at the kitchen table while finding the missing blue piece of the jigsaw that makes up the sky.

'I wanted to make sure you haven't forgotten me.'

'Take my word for it, Shelley, no one could forget you.'

'How are you managing without me?'

'I've got a new puppy.'

'No!'

'She was abandoned outside the pet shop, so I've brought her home.'

'Send me a photo?'

Tommy laughs and aims the camera at the puppy who is playing with an old tennis ball Tommy found in the garden.

'She's so cute,' Shelley exclaims a few minutes later.

'I know.'

'How will you manage when you're at work?'

'Jane is going to help. We have a time-share dog.'

'Please tell me she isn't sleeping on your bed. Because that's very bad training and you'll never get a girlfriend.'

'No, her bed is in the kitchen,' Tommy says firmly, trying not to remember the moment of weakness when he almost picked her up and took her upstairs.

Shelley laughs. 'Almond Blossom will love her.'

'How is she?'

Shelley is quiet and Tommy waits frowning. He's about to ask if she's alright but Shelley says, 'I think she misses you. And, all this uni malarkey is a pile of pap. I honestly don't know what I'm doing here.'

Tommy sighs. 'Give it a chance.'

'It's a waste of money.'

'It's early days yet.'

'They're not telling me anything I don't already know.'

'You can't have every creative idea. You will learn something. You have to give it a chance.'

'That's what Jane says.'

'Jane? Have you spoken to her?'

'Yes, a few times. I've run some ideas past her. Did you finish the business plan?'

'It's taking longer than I thought but I will finish it. It will be done by the time you leave uni.'

'That's three years away,' she groans.

Tommy looks at the puppy. He's happy the puppy is here but he's much happier that Shelley is in touch with Jane. 'Well, give it time. Have you spoken to your Mum?'

'I went to see her last weekend. She's tired and it'll take a few months until they know anything for sure.'

'But it looks positive?' Tommy watches the puppy open her legs to squat and he jumps up, runs over and catches her under her belly, and lifts her outside the back door.

'She loves hearing from you, Tommy.'

'I've asked her to come and visit and get some sea air, but she says she's got lots of hospital appointments.'

'Look, I've got to go.' Shelley is suddenly in a hurry. 'Have you met anyone on the dating app?'

'I haven't looked. I've been too busy.'

'Okay, well that's a good sign.'

What does that mean?' he sounds indignant.

'Well, you sound happy, so take a look at those around you.'

* * *

Jane walks with Tommy down to the harbour where he's starting his shift in ten minutes at the RNLI station. Jane holds the lead and laughs when the puppy chases her tail and falls over herself.

'This won't do, Tommy. You've had her for over a week and she still hasn't got a name.'

'She's a sailor,' he says, watching the puppy sniff the lobster pots and the fishing ropes. 'She loves the harbour. She's a sea-dog.'

'I think you have a fanciful imagination. She's much more refined.'

'She's hardly a jewellery designer,' he scoffs.

'She's gentle and petite.' Jane is defensive and she bends down to tickle the puppy's ears.

'I don't finish until seven,' Tommy says. 'Will you be alright?'

Jane shakes her head. 'This is temporary, Tommy. Just until you get her trained but, I'll tell you what, I'll make supper for you when you collect her.'

'Can you cook?' he teases.

'I can always get us a takeaway.'

'I like home cooking.'

'Any requests?'

'Roast chicken?'

'It's my speciality.'

* * *

Tommy is tired when he arrives at Jane's home that evening. It's homely and warm and the smell of dinner is welcoming. He shakes off his jacket and accepts a glass of Merlot with a happy smile.

'This is what I need. Hello!' He laughs as the puppy jumps up onto his lap and nibbles his fingers.

'She's been fed,' Jane calls from the kitchen. 'She just needs attention.'

Tommy leans down and tickles the puppy's ears.

'Just a typical female,' he says. 'Needs constant attention.'

'The puppy barks playfully and Tommy picks up a rope lying on the floor. 'Did you buy her this toy?'

'I popped into the pet shop,' she calls back.

Tommy smiles and pulls the rope gently from the puppy's mouth. 'I knew she'd fall in love with you.'

'What's that?' Jane appears in the doorway smiling.

'Nothing.' Tommy sits up straighter and sips his wine.

Jane nods. 'Dinner is ready.'

Tommy likes the kitchen-diner extension in Jane's house

and he particularly likes the windows in the roof. As the rain begins to pound against the glass, he feels relaxed and happy. He accepts another glass of wine and tucks into the succulent chicken and jacket potatoes, declining butter but enjoying the courgettes and leeks.

'This is a healthy dinner,' he says. 'Thank you, Jane.'

The tired puppy is tottering about on her little legs and they both watch her finally topple with unsteady feet onto her bed.

'Did you buy the bed too?' Tommy asks.

'It was in the sale.' She grins and he looks at her wondering if she's wearing make-up or if her hair is different. She looks younger and she's smiling. She seems happy and for a quick moment he has a pang of fear.

'What's wrong?' she asks.

He shakes his head. 'I supposed you're used to younger company. I must seem a bit old for you.'

Jane's face freezes. 'Why do you say that?'

'Well, I must be seven or eight years older than you—'

'It's not age, Tommy. It's what you have in common and how well you feel with a person.'

'I guess I'm just thinking about the dating site and meeting people my own age.'

She leans across the table. 'Have you been in contact with anyone?'

He laughs nervously, sips his wine and eats slowly. 'It's a complicated process, don't you think? I mean, what are you supposed to be looking for? There are all sorts of women out there — as there are men — but gosh, it's a nightmare. It's so complicated. And all for what?'

'Don't you want to meet someone?'

'Of course, but I don't think it will be on a website.'

Jane stares down at her plate.

'What's your story, Jane? You must have been in love once?'

Jane pushes the serving dish toward Tommy so he can help himself.

'My love life has been a disaster; the wrong men, married, selfish, arrogant but, more recently, I've been thinking it's not about the men, it's about me. I've let people treat me badly and I'm not doing it again. I have my pride.'

Tommy hears the defiance in her tone and sees the way she holds her head in a challenge. He admires her. 'I wish I were younger,' he says.

Jane blushes and then she looks away.

'Have I said something wrong?' he asks.

'You know, don't you?'

'Know about what?'

'Don't torture me, Tommy. Tell me the truth.'

Tommy is flustered. 'I only wished I was younger, figuratively speaking, and that you might consider...' His voice trails off and he's suddenly uncomfortable that Jane is staring intently at him.

She takes a deep breath, tops up their glasses and then says, 'I'm going to tell you something that I've never told anyone else.'

Tommy takes a gulp of his wine, unsure if he's ready for any confessions.

'I,' she pauses. 'I had a one-night stand with a very young man.'

There is silence in the room and Tommy wonders if the music has stopped or maybe there wasn't any on earlier. He places his knife and fork together and sits back to digest Jane's revelation.

'Right.'

She sips her wine quickly. 'It's not something I'm proud of but... well, it happened.' She looks at him, her eyes blazing defiantly.

Tommy sips his wine. Never has he felt so inadequate, unless he remembers that awful afternoon in the sand dunes with Marion.

'I'm sorry, have I upset you?' Jane asks.

Tommy looks at the floor and focuses on the sleeping puppy. Then he looks at Jane who is now clearing the table.

He focuses on his hands. Sunita always said he was a kind and caring lover but how would he know?

Jane places her hand on his shoulder. 'Are you alright, Tommy?'

'Yes.' He drains his glass.

'Would you like another?'

'I'd best be going.' He stands up, feeling like an old man. An old man who's had a heart attack, a man who lost his wife and all his confidence.

'Come on, little one,' he calls. 'Time to go home.'

By the time he pops the lead on and gathers the puppy's things and thanks Jane for the meal, he's flustered. He can't wait to get outside and into the fresh air and walk the puppy home. He's better off on his own. This is worse than a date.

'Night, night,' he says at the door and he kisses Jane on the cheek without looking at her and once he's out in the cold air he wishes he hadn't kissed her. Her cheek had been warm and soft. She'd smelt lovely and he'd had such a wonderful evening but now, he walks up the road, cursing himself and his life — and his age.

* * *

It's a bright early morning and Tommy is on his way to drop
the puppy off with Jane when he bumps into Marion in Harbour
Street.

'What's that you've got Tommy?'

'She's an abandoned puppy.'

Marion stares at her and then looks back at him. 'I haven't
seen you around,' she says.

He shrugs.

'I thought you were different to all the other fellas, Tommy
but then do you know what?'

He shakes his head.

'I realised you weren't. And, I've met someone else. That's
why you haven't seen me around in Westbay. He's got a big
house in the country and he plays golf, and I'm getting lessons
now. You know, at the club, and I'm very happy.'

'I'm pleased for you, Marion.'

'I don't know what's wrong with you?'

He shrugs and watches the puppy sniff at Marion's shoes.

'I mean, we could have been a great couple but I really don't
know what you want. Do you know what you want? Have you
worked it out yet?'

Tommy shakes his head.

'The thing is, you're too preoccupied with everyone else.
Look at you. If it's not Shelley, it's the cat or it's this puppy.
You never put anyone first and I'll be honest with you, Tommy.
No woman will put up with that. No woman wants half a man.'

Tommy squares his shoulders and looks her in the eye. 'I'm
pleased, you've met someone special, Marion. You deserve
the best.' He hopes she won't notice his cheeks twitching.

But she turns her heel and steps toward her boutique and calls over her shoulder.

'I only ever wanted love, Tommy but you couldn't give me that. Always remember that when you're lying in your lonely little bed. I could have been yours.'

* * *

'You're smiling, Tommy. What's made you so happy?' Jane greets him in the shop and bends down to loosen the lead from the puppy's collar.

Tommy watches her. He notices her dungarees with yellow sunflowers and her blue neck-tie and he smiles as she calls the puppy into the kitchen.

'Come on, sweetie. Pup with no name. There's water here for you.'

He places the coffees he bought from the Harbour Café on the counter and yawns. His encounter with Marion has finally released him completely. He'd felt nervous about bumping into her and he'd managed to avoid her, but as luck would have it, she has very easily transferred her emotions and affection to another lucky man. He sits on the chair in the shop and listens to Jane in the kitchen.

'Don't eat your bed, soppy socks,' Jane scolds.

Tommy has a vision of the summer. He remembers how Marion had tried to lie on top of him in the dunes. He'd felt embarrassed and exposed. He hadn't wanted to make out like teenagers. He wasn't a novice and he didn't like sand on his skin. Nor did he like the growling sounds she made in his ear and when she'd become more demonstrative he'd finally pushed her away. 'This isn't working for me,' he'd said.

'So, it's all about you, is it?'

Tommy had taken the barbed comments she'd made all the way home and put up with her sarcasm. She'd hinted he'd never be able to satisfy her and then she'd suggested he needed counselling.

'Your wife died four years ago,' she'd complained.

Tommy had resisted the urge to tell her that he'd made love with several women after Sunita. He'd gone to London a few times. He knew bars where he didn't have to be lonely and although he'd had sex, it wasn't what he was looking for. He wanted a relationship.

'Tommy?'

He looks up startled.

'Are you alright?' Jane looks concerned. She points at the puppy, on her hind legs at the door, pawing to get out. 'I think she needs a walk.'

'She's had one.' Tommy stands up. 'Perhaps I should have got a ten-year-old dog and not a puppy.'

'Nonsense.' Jane laughs. 'This one will keep you young.'

* * *

Tommy is leaning over the harbour railings with the puppy beside him sniffing the quayside when he hears a familiar voice.

'Yo, Tommy, my main-man, how you doin'?'

'Yusef? Hi.'

Yusef slaps him on the shoulder and they fist-bump. 'Who's this baby?' he asks.

'She hasn't got a name yet.'

Yusef laughs. 'How can she not have a name, bro? How long

have you had her?'

'A few weeks.'

Yusef kneels down and the puppy jumps on his lap and licks his ears. Yusef laughs. 'She's so cute. You have to give her a name, man.'

'We can't agree on one.'

'We?'

'Jane and I. We're time-sharing her as I'm volunteering at the RNLI station.'

Yusef stands up holding the puppy in his arms. 'Sharing her, eh? Who's a lucky girl?' He kisses her head. 'But you need a name.'

'Jane doesn't like my seafaring names.'

Yusef laughs. 'It's your dog, bro.'

Tommy smiles. 'You know women.'

Yusef smiles. 'I know Jane. She's a strong woman.'

Tommy nods uncertainly.

'The bitch knows what she wants.'

'Pardon?'

'This puppy, look, see how the bitch bites? She knows what she wants.'

Tommy swallows.

'You okay, man? I told Shelley I'd look out for you but it's been crazy in the salon, and—'

'I'm fine.'

'Sure?'

'Yes.'

'She said she'd hooked you up with a dating site. How's that going?'

'Slowly.'

Yusef nods in understanding. 'Some of these relationships

are more agro than they deserve, bro. These women, they hang us out to dry.'

'Can I ask you something?' Tommy stares at Yusef. He'd always liked him and admired his casual attitude toward life, and he knows that he was good for Shelley. He gave her space to grow and develop and she'd enjoyed being with him. He trusted this guy and for some reason it feels easier to speak to him than to Matt or one of the gang in the pub.

'What's wrong, bro?'

'What would you do, if you liked someone, but they were probably into younger men?'

Yusef laughs. 'Much younger than me and they'd be in jail.'

Tommy shifts from one foot to the other and wishes he'd never mentioned anything.

'Look, a woman is a woman. You turn the lights out man and you show her your talents. You know what I mean?'

Tommy glances at his watch. 'I better go, I've got my shift and—'

Yusef pats his shoulder. 'You've nothing to worry about man, she likes you.'

'Who?'

'Jane.'

'Why do you say that.'

Yusef laughs. 'You'd hardly timeshare a dog if you didn't like someone.' Yusef puts the puppy on the floor. 'Once you agree a name then it'll be plain sailing, man. Hang on in there.' He slaps his shoulder and walks away whistling.

'Have you heard from Shelley?' Tommy calls.

Yusef waves over his shoulder and shouts, 'A gentleman never tells.'

* * *

It's late and he's thinking of going upstairs to bed when Elsie phones.

'How are you?' he asks. 'I've been meaning to call you.'

'I'm doing well but I'm worried about Shelley.'

Tommy's heart sinks. 'I spoke to her last weekend and she seemed fine.'

'She's not happy. She wants to leave.'

'But she has to give it a go, doesn't she?'

'That's what Frank wants, but if it's not what she wants to do then it's not helping her. I think she's lonely. I even think she misses you.'

Tommy laughs and pulls the puppy into his lap and glances back at the jigsaw. He'd wanted to finish it tonight but his eyes were tired and he yawns.

'Are you looking after yourself?' she asks.

'I'm trying to think of a name for the puppy.'

'Thanks for sending me the pictures. She looks lovely.'

'I hope you'll meet her in person. Are you coming to visit?'

'Once I get the all clear.'

'Good.'

'Tommy, I want to make sure you're okay. You've been too long on your own and it's not healthy.'

'I have a puppy.'

'That's not the same and you know it. I know I didn't know Sunita but I do know what she meant to you. But it's been four years, Tommy. I know that time isn't relevant but you must let the past go. You have to live in the present and I've learnt that the hard way. Now I live for each day, not knowing if I will see Shelley or you, but that's not right either. I want to live.' She laughs. 'I'm dying to live, and if I could do things differently then I would.'

Tommy sighs.

'Tell me something,' she says. 'It wasn't all perfect with Sunita, was it? Relationships are never without problems, so don't put her on a pedestal that no one can reach. Don't think she was so perfect that she can't be replaced, because love is different. You will love the next person in a different way and that won't be perfect either. You'll have problems, arguments, disagreements, but you'll learn to get over them and at least you'll be sharing your life again, Tommy. It's not healthy to be on your own.'

Tommy laughs. 'Thanks for the lecture, but what about you?'

'I've actually met someone but I haven't told Shelley.'

Tommy stops petting the puppy. 'You have?'

'I'm not dead yet, Tommy and I'm going to live until my last dying breath. So, lead your life.'

'I am.'

'You're lacking in confidence.'

'You don't know that!'

'Shelley told me.'

'What does she know?' he replies dismissively.

'What about Jane?'

'Jane?' He's shocked. 'How do you know Jane?'

'Shelley told me. She told me last weekend how she signed you up on the same dating site and you still didn't get the hint that Jane is the one.'

'Jane isn't—'

'Have you asked her out?'

'I see her all the time.'

'On a date?'

'We're time-sharing the puppy.'

Elsie laughs. 'That's the first time I've heard it called that.'

Tommy laughs. 'It's not how it sounds.'

'Then it should be, Tommy. Sort yourself out. Time is running out.'

* * *

Tommy showers, shaves and dresses with care. He's wearing jeans and a fisherman's crew cut navy jumper and duffel coat. Yusef cut his hair earlier in the week and he checks his appearance quickly in the mirror before putting the puppy on a lead and walking her down the hill and into Harbour Street.

He stops at the art gallery and Ben is pleased to see him. He picks up the puppy and lets her lick his ears.

'So, has this little floozie got a name yet?'

Tommy shakes his head. 'Jane and I can't agree. I call her Neptune and Jane says it's too fishy like fish fingers, so she calls her Duchess and I tell her that sounds like a potato.'

Ben laughs. 'Well, I won't confuse you with any more names.'

'How's Noah?' Tommy asks.

'I think he's doing well. We have no way of knowing but you did a great job with him. He liked you a lot.'

Tommy rubs his cheek. He's secretly pleased. 'He's a good lad. I know you help a lot of these boys, Ben - but don't you ever get upset, you know, when they move on and leave you?'

Ben smiles. 'They never leave me, Tommy.' He holds the puppy in one hand and taps his heart with the other. They're always here and they were never mine to begin with. I only help them on their journey like a stepping stone in the stream of life.'

Tommy nods. 'I think I've got to get that balance sorted out. You know, which ones to keep and which ones to let go.'

Ben looks at him and frowns. 'When I met Amber, I was in a terrible state. I'd been in prison, framed by a liar who ran the The Ship before Paul. I wasn't welcome here but after travelling the world I wanted a home. So, I came back and I was determined to stay. My parents had died and they'd left me the house. But it was Amber who just got me. She understood me and she knew what I'd been through. Some relationships are like that, but others are different. Sometimes you can be friends and love grows. But you just have to look a little further or dig a little deeper and more importantly have the confidence to follow your heart. Perhaps that's where you're struggling?'

Tommy sighs.

Ben continues, 'It's alright to love more than once. I often think monogamy was invented when everyone died at thirty. Now people live until they're a hundred. Girls tell me they want different men for different things: one as a lover, one as a father to their children, and a different man again after parenting is over. Perhaps that's normal?' Ben shrugs. 'What do I know? But would Sunita want you to mourn her forever when you have so much love to give?' Ben puts the puppy on the floor and takes Tommy's arm and looks him in the eye. 'There's a very special woman out there for you, and you know exactly who she is.'

* * *

With Ben's endorsement, Tommy heads confidently down Harbour Street preparing his words carefully. Perhaps he should have booked a table in the Bistro, but could Neptune be left on her own for a few hours? Maybe he could organise a takeaway tonight. The Indian is good and Sanjay's cousins are keeping it up to standard.

Tommy pauses outside Eva's flower shop. Perhaps he should buy flowers or a plant. He's deliberating over the choice when Rachael appears beside him.

'Hi Tommy. Oh goodness, what a beautiful pup.'

Tommy explains how he found her, kept her and how he's time-sharing her with Jane. Rachael scowls.

'Well, that might keep her on the straight and narrow, I suppose.'

'What do you mean?'

'I think she's punching above her weight with Yusef.'

'Yusef?'

'They were in the pub last night. Huddled in the corner, no one could get near them. They're as thick as thieves, laughing and canoodling without a care in the world. Everyone could see them. She's old enough to be his mother.' She spits.

'But they're just friends.' Tommy protests.

Rachael holds up the palm of her hands. 'Gullible, Tommy. She's not interested in you. You're far too old and decrepit. She likes them young and he was bathing in all her attention. Anyway, have you seen Marion?'

Tommy doesn't reply. He gathers Neptune closer to him on the lead.

'Did you know she's getting married?'

Tommy's head jerks up. 'That didn't take her long.'

'Look, Tommy, when you get to your time of life, you take

what you can get. You really missed out with her.'

'Well, I'm fine.' Tommy bristles.

'Well, none of it has anything to do with me. I'm happily married - I'm one of the lucky ones. But you'll probably be on your own forever now.'

* * *

Tommy continues walking to Jane's shop but he's dazed and he can't shake the image from his head. Jane was with Yusef in the pub last night. She'd told him she was busy. She said she was going out but she didn't say it was with him — Yusef.

'She likes younger men,' he mumbles to himself, pausing again to look in the art gallery. 'But he's Shelley's boyfriend — or he was.'

He ambles on down Harbour Street, taking his time, reluctant now to see Jane. 'That's ridiculous,' he says loudly and heads with determination to her shop. He's just about to open the door when he looks through the window. Jane is leaning on the counter. Yusef is beside her and they're looking at something, turning pages and smiling. Their heads are close together and there's an intimacy to them that he finds bewildering. Suddenly they laugh and he feels an electric shock from the door handle. He lets it go and turns away, pulling the puppy with him. He walks quickly to the harbour, not turning around and not looking up. His eyes are downcast, kept firmly on his feet and the puppy until he smells the salty sea water and the fishy smells of the harbour.

This is his place of safety and refuge. He takes a deep breath. 'This is where we always come,' he says to the puppy who is busy sniffing at the lobster pots. 'This is where everything makes sense.'

Only today, it doesn't.

He leans on the railings and looks out to sea. There's no sign of any of the fishing boats. It's still too early for them to come back so he walks along the promenade and past the beach huts. He doesn't notice the rain at first, he's lost in his own world. It falls as a light mist onto his face and he's momentarily brought back to reality. He rubs his cheeks and then he feels his phone vibrating in his pocket. It's Jane's number but he doesn't answer it. He pushes it firmly back in his pocket. He heads home, but he knows he has to see Jane. He wants the truth. It will be simple. He'll know if she's interested in someone else. He will tell by the way her face lights up and the way her eyes crease at the corners, and the way her nose wrinkles up when she giggles.

He pushes open the jewellery shop door and is overcome by warmth and the smell of Jane's soft, sweet perfume.

'Thank goodness, you're here!' she exclaims. 'Gosh, you're soaking, Tommy. Where have you been? Let's get that coat off you. Come in the back and get dry. I'll put the kettle on.'

In the kitchen, and before he can struggle out of his coat, he can tell that Jane is nervous. Her cheeks are flushed and she's bursting with excitement.

'I've got something to tell you,' she says, suddenly facing him.

His heart sinks.

She tilts her head and frowns at him, but then she's distracted by the puppy jumping up. She tries to hop onto Jane's lap which sends her flying backwards against the kitchen units and she sits with the dog licking her face and her shoulders shaking.

'Are you alright? Are you hurt?' Tommy is alarmed.

There are tears rolling down her cheeks. 'I've got the perfect name for our pup.'

She says to the puppy, 'Hello, Coral.'

'Coral?'

'What do you think? Do you like it?'

'Coral?' Tommy gazes at her. He watches how she wipes her eyes and her laughter is infectious. How could he refuse her anything? He nods slowly, thinking quickly. He could always call her Neptune when no one else was around.

November

Jane

'I never signed up for this, you know that, don't you? It was never part of my future plan. I was supposed to go online, find a handsome man, fall in love and live happily ever after. It didn't include sharing a spoilt little cross-breed. And — don't look at me like that, Coral —don't whine at the hand that feeds you.'

Coral sits on the kitchen floor staring up at her.

'You're doing very well, little one. You're not too worried about those fireworks, are you? You're a brave little girl.'

Coral stands and waggles her tail, while Jane spoons the dog food on top of the kibble and places it on the floor. 'How come you are always so hungry? You sleep, run, walk and you're into everything. I don't know how you're still going. It's eight o'clock, but don't get too comfy as you're going home soon. Daddy is coming to collect you.'

Jane kicks off her shoes, pours a glass of wine and heads into the lounge, where she flicks on the TV and lies on the sofa.

A few minutes later Coral trots into the room, wiggling her bottom and licking her lips.

'Don't even think about jumping up on me,' she says. 'Your basket is in the corner. Go on, off you go.'

The little dog sits by her feet and Jane flicks the channels until she finds the Dog House programme.

'You'll enjoy this,' she says. 'It's about dogs who find their forever home.' She giggles. 'Just like you did with Tommy.'

The puppy jumps up on the sofa and lies beside her. She glances at Jane, then at the wine glass before laying her head on her paw and watching the TV.

Outside there's the bang of a rocket and whoosh of a firework going up into the night sky but Coral doesn't flinch.

'Don't get too comfy, little one. You don't live here.'

Coral snorts and Jane laughs.

Tommy arrives a few minutes later. 'How's she getting on with the fireworks?'

'She's barely noticed them.' Jane laughs. 'She's been far too comfy watching TV and having a cuddle.'

Tommy laughs and rubs the puppy's ears. 'It was a quiet shift today, thank goodness. It's a wet and windy night.'

'I thought the fireworks might be cancelled.'

'It's stopped raining now.'

'Wine?'

'Thank you.'

'Hello, Coral, aren't you the best girl?' he says, easing into a comfortable chair and stretching out his legs in front of the log burner.

'Hungry?' Jane calls from the kitchen.

'I ate earlier, thanks.'

Jane comes in with a glass of wine and she watches him cuddle the puppy. He looks at her, and when she looks at him he smiles and looks quickly away. They sit in companionable silence for a while with the TV on mute while Tommy pays attention to the puppy.

She watches him. This is so easy and relaxing. This is how life should be — comfortable with no problems. Is it wrong to ask for this sort of contentment? She doesn't need to be giddy and deliriously happy and in love. Besides, she's too old for that. She'd settle for good company and someone dependable to share a bottle of wine with in the evenings. Jane likes watching Tommy. His hands are big and strong and Coral looks tiny beside him. 'I suppose she'll grow.'

'She will, but she won't be too big.' He smiles and after a short pause he says, 'I've been meaning to ask you about Yusef.'

Jane's body stiffens and her stomach somersaults.

If he asks, she will have to tell him the truth but she knows she will lie. She has to.

'He spends a lot of time with you. I mean, he's often popping into your shop...'

Jane regards him carefully, trying to work out why he's worried now. Perhaps he's heard something. She's trying to weigh up what to tell him. She's sworn Yusef to secrecy about their one-night stand and he's promised he's told no one.

'We're good friends.' Jane sits opposite him, and then gets up to throw another log on the burner. It's a minor distraction but a necessary one.

Tommy sighs. 'There's quite an age gap.'

Jane shrugs. 'Maybe he sees me as a mother figure?'

Tommy stares at the fire.

'How's Elsie?' Jane changes the subject.

'She's doing well, I want her to come and visit but she says she's still not strong enough to make the journey.'

'Could you collect her?'

'It is a long way. I dare say I could but she needs to feel well enough, and I guess Shelley will go home for Christmas.'

Jane isn't ready to talk about the one time of the year that makes her depressed. Halloween was bad enough and tonight with the November the 5th firework celebrations and the shops already filled with Christmas decorations, she can feel her spirits sinking.

'I miss her, don't you?' Tommy asks. 'We got on really well in the end. It's amazing how young people bring a different energy into the room. They have a different way of looking at things and I think she changed me in a funny sort of way. Bringing Almond Blossom home made me realise how lovely it is to have a pet in the house. She was company for me and I guess that's why I found it so easy to adopt Coral—'

Jane's mobile buzzes and she checks the caller ID.

It's Shelley, but she doesn't pick up.

'Get it if you want to,' Tommy says.

Jane shakes her head. 'It's not important.'

Tommy stands up. 'I won't keep you. I don't want to be a burden.'

'You're not—'

'I'll go.' Tommy looks around for Coral's lead and Jane wonders what she can do to stop him from leaving but it's too late. Tommy has already pulled on his coat. 'I'll leave you to phone your friend back, I'm sure he's more important than me.'

She places her hand on the sleeve of his coat. 'That's not true.'

'Say goodnight, Coral. Thanks, Jane,' he says breezily.

'Enjoy the rest of your evening.'

* * *

After Tommy leaves, Jane pours a glass of wine and reaches for her mobile.

'Shelley?'

'Hi, Jane. Thanks for calling me back. Did you get a chance to look at the designs I sent you?'

'I looked at them earlier and I like them.'

'It's more than my lecturer does. She's not into commercial stuff. She wants me to explore my inner creative side and when I tell her that I am, she won't believe me.'

'Look, you're doing well, you just have to stick with it.'

'I've told mum I'm only staying until Christmas. I hate it here—'

'You can't hate it—'

'I can and I do.'

'I think your tutor is just trying to get the most out of you. The important thing is to develop a variety of ideas, use different materials and learn processes and techniques.'

'I learnt more with you in the summer than I'm learning here. It's a waste of time. You saw my latest set of drawings, didn't you? And if I develope these, Jane, then we could expand.'

'Expand what?'

'Your business. You said yourself that you're struggling and that you have too much work, online and stuff and there are never enough hours in the day. I could work with you—'

'I'm not taking you out of uni. Perhaps when you finish your course we can think about it—'

'What? When I'm almost forty grand in debt that I'll have to pay back to the government? If I start working with you in the new year then I can start earning money. Please, Jane. Tell me you'll think about it.'

'I'll think about it.'

'Tell me you'll think about it more than you did the last time, because you haven't changed your mind since we spoke two weeks ago.'

'I can't be responsible for your future.'

'You're not. It's my choice and my decision. I can leave—'

'I haven't offered you anything, so you'll have to stay at uni.'

'Maybe I'll leave anyway and get a job in the pub—'

'Don't be silly.'

'Why not?'

'It would be a waste of your talents.'

'Well then, you know I'm talented and you also know that we get on well together at work.'

'That's not the point. You're there to learn. Uni will teach you so much that I can't—'

'I'm not interested in uni and besides...' There's a catch in her voice. 'I'm lonely.'

Jane stares at the dying embers of the fire and thinks carefully before she replies.

'You have this amazing opportunity to go out with people of your own age and people that like the same things as you,' she says softly. 'I couldn't go to uni, Shelley. I had to care for my dad. I didn't have this opportunity. It's the one time in your life where you have no responsibility and you can go out and have fun. Go and party with your friends, Shelley. Enjoy life.'

Shelley is quiet. 'I think I'm too old to be here. You know, I suppose with mum being ill, I've had to grow up and face things — and staying with Tommy this year made me grow up too. And then meeting Yus—'

Jane holds her breath.

'I'm in love with him, Jane. I miss him more than you can imagine.'

Jane exhales slowly.

Shelley is crying.

'Are you okay?' she asks.

'I just miss home. But then I feel guilty because home isn't with my mum any more. Home is down in Westbay with you, and Tommy and Yus.'

Jane drains her wine glass. 'Give yourself another few weeks until the end of this term and try your best to really give it a good shot. Really try hard to enjoy it. Meet people and have fun and learn as much as you can.'

'And if I still hate it at Christmas?'

'Then we can talk about it.'

'Great.' Jane can hear the smile in Shelley's voice. 'Besides, Almond Blossom misses Tommy.'

Jane laughs. 'Tommy is obsessed with Coral.'

'He sent me pictures and she looks adorable. I'm sure they'll get on. Jane, please don't tell Tommy that I speak to you. I do contact him, but I'd hate him to think I didn't confide in him. It's different talking to you—'

'Yes, it's called emotional blackmail.'

Shelley laughs. 'You know it's for the best, but please don't tell Tommy until it's — definite.'

'I will not make a decision without Tommy being involved.'

'Have you seen him?'

'He came by earlier to pick up Coral.'

'He's not seeing anyone, is he?'

Although Jane is on the phone, she shrugs. 'I don't know.'

'Not that awful Marion-woman he was seeing in the summer?'

Jane sighs. 'I don't know.'

'Gosh, I just wish you two would stop messing around and get on with it.'

'With what?'

'You know. You're made for each other. You hang out together every day and you even time-share the dog. Doesn't that tell you anything?'

Jane shakes her head. 'We're just good friends.'

* * *

The pub is busy and Jane makes her way to a small table in the corner.

'I got you a large gin and tonic.' Yusef stands up and helps her off with her coat and hangs it over the chair beside them.

'Gosh, I need this.' She takes a deep gulp.

Yusef grins at her. 'You look knackered.'

'I am. How come you never look tired? You work hard too.'

'I'm a young buck, baby or had you forgotten?' He grins.

'No, I haven't forgotten and thanks for reminding me. You can be quite nice when you're not so cocky.'

Yusef thinks this is hilarious. They're both still laughing when Yusef looks over her shoulder.

'Your mate Tommy has just arrived.' He nods to Tommy standing at the bar with his back to them. 'Do you mind if we don't invite him over? I'd like to keep this a secret for a bit longer?'

Jane turns her back. 'Okay. Don't look and let's pretend we haven't seen him.'

They lean closer over the small table.

'What do you think?' Yusef asks. 'Do you think it will work?'

Jane pulls out a piece of paper from the pocket of her coat and reaches for a pencil from the other pocket. 'It might work. I've given some thought to your idea but the clasps will have to be different. It's an original bracelet and the entwined fingers might not hold it securely in place.' She draws with precision and neat strokes, explaining how the interlocking fingers would work.

Yusef watches intently. 'Do you think Shelley will like it?'

Jane smiles. 'If she knows you've designed it, then yes, I think she will love it.'

'Do you think she misses me?' he asks. 'It's a long time until Christmas but I promised I wouldn't contact her. I want her to come back to me because she loves me, not just as an excuse to live here.'

'It's not much longer to wait.'

Yusef shifts in his seat.

Jane continues, 'But, if she likes the course, then you'll have to wait four years.'

Yusef looks at her intently. 'You know me, Jane. You know what I've been through.' He waves his arms wide. 'I've had so many girlfriends but it's not who I am. I messed up with the first girl I ever loved and now she'll probably marry Ozan. But I'm over her now. Shelley is the girl for me and I'm prepared to wait for her.'

Jane nods.

Yusef places his hand over Jane's 'You're my lifeline to her.

I don't know what I would do without you. This bracelet will be the perfect present for her — and for all your help and the love and friendship you give me. I love you— Oh, hello.' Yusef stares over Jane's shoulder and then suddenly he let's go of her hand. 'Hi, Tommy. Do you want to join us?'

* * *

Jane turns, embarrassed that Tommy caught Yusef holding her hand, but she smiles bravely while Yusef grabs the drawing of the bracelet, his idea for Shelley's Christmas present, and shoves it quickly into his pocket.

Tommy stares at them both.

'Hello Tommy,' Jane smiles.

'No Coral, tonight?' Yusef grins.

Jane pulls her coat off the chair for Tommy to sit with them.

'Was I interrupting?' he asks.

Yusef shakes his head and turns his mouth downwards. 'No, man. It's always good to see you, my friend.'

Tommy sips his pint and turns to look at Jane. 'Everything okay?' he asks.

'Fine.' Jane is uncomfortable under Tommy's heavy scrutiny.

'Have you heard from Shelley?' asks Yusef.

'Are you still interested in her?' Tommy sounds angry and Jane frowns.

Yusef's eyes open wide and he glances quickly at Jane for reassurance, but Tommy says, 'I'd have thought a young man like you would have found someone else by now.'

'No.' Yusef seems visibly bewildered. 'Shelley is very special to me.'

'It looks like it.' Tommy wipes froth from his mouth with the back of his hand.

'I don't understand,' Yusef replies.

Jane realises that Yusef can't tell Tommy about his feelings for Shelley, probably for the same reason she can't tell Tommy that Shelley speaks to her.

Neither of them wants to be responsible if Shelley leaves uni.

Jane places her hand on Tommy's. 'It's not what it looks like.'

Tommy stares at her and there's hurt in his eyes.

Yusef stands up. 'I'd better go.'

'Don't let me stop your romantic evening,' Tommy's voice rises. 'It's none of my business if you two are—'

'Tommy!' Jane says sternly.

Yusef pulls on his bomber jacket. 'I'll see you tomorrow, Jane.'

'I'll see you tomorrow, Jane,' mimics Tommy.

Yusef looks unsure and with a quick flick of his eyebrows to the ceiling, he leaves.

'That was unnecessary,' Jane says.

'I don't want you to make a fool of yourself.'

'I'm not.'

'You know how people talk.'

'I'm not interested in what people say.'

Tommy stares at her. 'Is he that important to you?'

'He's my friend and I don't think anyone has a problem with that.'

'He's young enough to be your son.'

'I know. Thank you. I don't need reminding.' Jane blushes suddenly remembering her physical relationship with Yusef earlier in the year.

Tommy straightens his shoulders. 'It's no wonder you've been on the dating websites,' he says. 'Be careful, Jane. You saw what he was like in the summer with Shelley. He was all over her and as soon as she's gone he's sniffing around your shop. Don't let him make a fool of you, Jane. You're worth more than that. You're worth *much* more than that.'

* * *

The dreaded Christmas decorations are going up around her and Jane's spirits sink as she observes Tommy from a distance. She watches him every day walking Coral to the harbour. He doesn't come in for coffee and he doesn't stop outside the shop or wave as he passes. He keeps his head bent down and his eyes on some distant object. He's avoiding her.

Jane is ashamed. He must know about her fling with Yusef and she feels sick. He must have found out somehow and now she spends her time hiding. If she's leaving the shop and if he's in the distance heading in her direction, she darts back inside.

She's in the Harbour Café one morning and Amber asks, 'Are you coming to the meeting tonight about the Christmas parade? We're meeting at Frances's house at seven.'

'I'd forgotten,' Jane replies. 'But I'll be there.'

'We need all the support we can get this year. Everyone's on a tight budget and some shopkeepers are complaining about the cost of having Christmas lights. Then there are the doom-sayers who are convinced we're affecting global warming. I'm fed up with them all.'

'They can be a touchy lot.' Jane says, picking up her coffee.

'But I'll see you later.'

Amber leans across the counter. 'I'll get Ben to see if Tommy's okay. It's great he has Coral now, but it's not the same as having Shelley in the house. I think he needs company — female company.' Amber looks at her and Jane looks away. 'Can you speak to him too?' Amber asks.

Jane looks up. 'If I see him I'll mention it, but we're not close.'

'I thought you were time-sharing the puppy.'

'We were, but we both have different lives.'

Jane leaves the café but not without feeling Amber's hot and heavy stare on her back.

* * *

The Christmas committee meeting is well attended in the vicarage. Graham, Frances's husband, pours her a glass of red wine and she sits on the sofa beside Mario and Lucas from the pet shop. She takes in her surroundings in the comfortable room and recognises the other shopkeepers in Harbour Street. She's dismayed to see Marion on the far sofa, smiling, preening and positively glowing.

'How's Coral?' Lucas asks, leaning toward her. 'Isn't she growing?'

Jane smiles. She hasn't seen the puppy for a few weeks and she's upset with Tommy. He'd wanted to time-share the puppy and now she wonders who is looking after her.

'Hi, everyone,' Frances says, tapping her glass with her nail. 'Thank you for coming. I know we've all had a busy day and that we're all tired, but I'm going to hand you over to Amber, our Christmas Committee Chair. And, I believe the first thing we have to do, is re-elect Amber this Christmas.'

There's a smattering of applause but Amber is looking at her phone.

'Amber?' Frances prompts.

Amber is reading a message and then suddenly she jumps up. 'I'm really sorry,' she says. 'There's been an emergency. I must go.'

There a murmur of concern as Amber rushes to the front door with Frances in her wake. 'Amber, is everything alright? What's happened?'

Jane hears a murmur of voices, then the front door slams and Frances returns looking shocked. 'Amber wants us to continue without her,' she says.

'What's wrong?' asks Jane.

Frances shakes her head. 'I don't know, but she mumbled something about having to go to London with Ben.'

'Can we get on with the meeting?' asks Rachael. 'I have a dance class in half an hour.'

'I'm in a hurry too,' adds Marion.

Frances blinks at the sea of faces staring at her. 'Well, I guess it will just be a formality to reinstate Amber as the Christmas Committee Chair. Shall we take a vote?'

Rachael lifts her hand. 'I wasn't here at the last meeting and I didn't vote for Amber.'

'I think we need a change this year. I think we need to rotate every couple of years,' Marion says.

'Amber has done a brilliant job over the past two years,' Jane says.

'That maybe true, but she's a busy woman and I don't think she has the time to dedicate to it this year. I think her running out tonight is a prime example.'

'It was an emergency,' says Frances. 'I'm sure she wants to be Chair.'

'Well, what Amber wants, Amber doesn't always get,' says Marion. 'I'm all for a change and I think that the people here, who have bothered to turn up, have the ultimate vote.'

Derek and Ian nod.

'Who else can we vote for?' asks Lucas.

Kit looks at his watch. 'I need to get back to the kids, but I'm happy either way.'

'I'll put myself forward.' Marion raises her hand and smiles. 'You all know how experienced I am—'

Jane interrupts. 'Yes, but—'

'I have the time, the inclination and the energy, and besides, my fiancé is happy to pay for the lights in Harbour Street this year.'

There are cries of disbelief and joy and a smattering of applause. Marion smiles.

'I nominate Marion,' says Rachael.

Jane looks at Frances and they both shake their heads in silent bewilderment.

'I nominate Amber,' says Frances.

'Her time is over.' Marion smiles. 'Time to move on and pass the baton on to someone who is actually here and interested in working for the community.'

'Rachael? I know you work for Marion sometimes but you need to be a shop owner to vote.' Jane attempts to keep her voice calm, but there's an edge to it.

'I am a shop owner.' Rachael smiles.

In her mind, Jane goes through Harbour Street, the butchers, the grocers, Eva - although not here - is an owner, as is Ben and Amber - also not here. She's furious that Yusef and Ozan haven't turned up. Sanjay isn't back and his cousins aren't here and with an overwhelming sense of disbelief, she can see Marion's early but victorious smile.

'I have the beauty salon beside Harbour café.' Rachael smiles.

'Tracey's beauty salon?'

'She rents it from me, so she doesn't have a vote this year. I'm using it.' Rachael smiles. 'Is it unanimous, then? Is everyone voting for Marion?'

'I'm voting for Amber,' says Frances.

'Me too,' says Jane.

Derek and Ian nod in unison and Jane can see that they have been easily persuaded. The less they pay for the lights or anything else, the better for them.

Marion stands up. 'Really, I think it's best if I tell you my ideas for this year. We will have the best lights and the biggest Christmas tree beside the clock tower. My boyfriend knows FreakPak, the biggest techno DJ in the UK. He's going to switch on the lights and — I suggest—' Marion smiles. 'We have the best street par-tay, ev-er.'

Rachael shrieks with laughter and the other shop owners look impressed.

'I love FreakPak!' Lucas claps his hands excitedly.

Marion nods demurely. 'Will you take the minutes then, Frances? I think we need to formally register that I'm the new Chair.'

* * *

'How did that happen?' Frances asks.

The last shop owners have just left and she's returned to the living room where Jane is still sitting on the couch, nursing her glass of wine and reeling from shock.

Frances reaches for the bottle and tops up their wine. 'I can't believe it.' Frances collapses on the sofa and exhales a deep, frustrated breath.

Jane shakes her head. 'It's unbelievable. They've outmanoeuvred us.'

'What will I say to Amber?'

'You'll have to tell her what happened. That Marion bamboozled them with her boyfriend's money and connections, and that they all fell for it.'

'But if this top DJ comes here, it will be more than a street party. This isn't for children.'

'I know, and when Marion said it was time for the adults to have fun, I really thought they might change their minds.'

'Oh goodness.' Frances puts her head in her hands. 'It's going to be awful.'

'She had it all arranged.' Jane sips her wine. 'Even with Amber here, they would have all still voted for Marion. We were complacent. Yusef and Ozan aren't here. Eva didn't turn up and Sanjay is still away. Ben would also have had a vote. If Amber had been here we might have won.'

'Paul voted for Marion,' Frances says.

'Marion is always in the pub. She's a good customer and besides, he'll make far more money with young people drinking than he will with families.'

'But this is a family street – a family town – or it should be. Marion doesn't even want a Santa this year. It's just going to be a big party.' Jane finishes her drink.

'What happened with Amber? I hope she's okay. I'll call her tomorrow.'

'I will too. I'll have to tell her the news. She won't believe it.'

Jane stands up. 'Do you ever have the feeling that some things will just never work? I mean, everything you do suddenly gets twisted or doesn't ever work out? I haven't time for this, Frances. I don't know what to expect with my life now. I do my best but nothing ever seems to work. Time after time after time, I think I'm going in one direction and then suddenly God throws me a curve ball and I wonder how the hell I'm going to cope.'

'If you believe God throws you a curve ball, then believe he will help you find a way out of it.'

Jane shakes her head. 'I wish I could believe you, Frances, but with what's just happened and everything else in my life at the moment, I can't help but feel there's a terrible disaster looming and I'm powerless to stop it.'

Frances places her hand on Jane's arm and pulls her into a hug. 'It will all work out — everything does with time.'

'But what happens when time runs out and it's all over? It's all too late by then. Everything is too late and you wonder if it was all worth it.'

Frances looks at her. 'If all what was worth it?'

Jane shakes her head. 'I don't know. I'm tired. Too much work on at the moment leading up to Christmas. I'll be better in the morning.'

Frances walks her to the front door. 'It's cold outside and there's a sea mist. Take care.'

As Jane walks across the square and down Harbour Street, she whispers, 'Whatever you're planning, up there, I just hope that you keep Tommy safe.'

* * *

Amber isn't in the café when she buys coffee the next morning and Karl doesn't know where she is, so when Amber doesn't pick up her phone, Jane spends a few minutes texting her.

It's mid-morning when Ozan darts across the road.

'I heard the news,' he says. 'Marion was in the shop before eight thirty. We can't believe it. Yusef is furious, you know how much he likes riding the bike beside Santa.'

'He's just a big child. You should have been there to vote.'

'We should be able to vote by proxy.'

'It's all based on the assumption that if you care about Harbour Street then you'll turn up at the meeting. Then we wouldn't be having this DJ, rapper-person, taking over. It sounds more like a rave than a Christmas event for a family.'

Ozan shakes his head. 'Well, maybe it's not such a bad idea for a change. FreakPak is brilliant and I love his music.'

Jane stares at him. 'If you've come over just to tell me that, you can go.'

'No, not at all, Jane. I came to look at engagement rings.' He grins.

'For you?'

'For Naomi.'

Jane smiles. 'You're going to propose?'

'I have to do it properly with a ring.'

Jane pulls out a tray of rings and lays it on the counter. 'Take a look at these. Where will you get married?'

'Naomi's from London, so probably in Ealing.'

'And Yusef?'

Ozan smiles. 'I have spoken to him. He is a gentlemen.'

Jane nods remembering the beginning of the year. Yusef

was in a state when she met him and they were both drunk.

'Do you think I'm wrong to marry her?' Ozan asks.

'Is it not very soon?'

'I have known her for as long as Yusef. They dated for almost five years, but he was never faithful to her. I used to say to him, Yusef, she's a diamond, why are you unfaithful? But he could never answer me. I think he had his chance. Fortunately, we are all happy now. It's time to move on. If you don't grasp the moment then you can't blame someone else for taking it from you. It's called opportunity.' He glances down at the tray of rings. 'And timing.'

* * *

After work, Jane closes the shop and heads to the Bistro but Amber isn't there. The waiter tells her she's next door in the art gallery with Ben.

Jane is pleasantly surprised when she walks into the art gallery. It's serene and calming with soft music and lighting, and she feels herself breathing more slowly. She hadn't realised how tense she felt.

They are in the back of the shop, but Ben hears her. He looks around the door and his face lights up.

'Jane? What a lovely surprise.'

She kisses him on the cheek. 'I was worried about Amber. She left in such a hurry last night. Are you okay?'

Ben looks exhausted. There are dark circles around his eyes and he hasn't shaved. 'Noah ran away from his foster home, but we managed to find him.'

'Is he alright?'

'He's with us and we're hoping that he might be able to stay, so fingers crossed.'

'That would be amazing, Ben.'

He grins. 'Wouldn't it? We got quite used to having the little fella around and it wasn't the same after he left.'

'Do you know about Marion and what she did last night?'

Ben nods. 'Frances told us—'

'I'm so sorry—'

Ben takes her arm. 'Don't be, there are more important things in life, Jane.'

'But it's the Christmas parade and Amber always does it so well. She's a brilliant organiser and everyone loves it, and now we're going to have some DJ who will draw everyone here from the big towns. It won't be the festive family fun we've come to love. It will be more like a rave.'

Ben smiles in weary understanding.

'You're tired,' Jane says, 'Sorry, Ben. I'll go.'

'But you must wait. They'll be here in a minute. She only popped up the road to see Tommy at the station.'

'Tommy? Is he alright?'

'I think so, why?'

Jane shakes her head, feeling very confused and that's when the art gallery door opens and there's a rush of cold air around her legs. She turns around and Amber walks in. Beside her, Noah is smiling.

'Oh, my goodness,' she gasps.

Then to her complete surprise and delight, Noah throws his arms around her waist and she's kissing the top of his head. 'What a lovely surprise, Noah. Welcome home.'

* * *

Ben takes Noah home while Amber walks back to Jane's house with her.

'It was a shock when they said Noah had run away,' she tells Jane, kicking off her shoes and accepting a glass of Prosecco. 'Just one glass. The restaurant is full tonight - the Christmas party season starts happening in November now and we have a big group later.'

'Why did Noah run away?'

'We don't know yet, but Ben was beside himself. He knew where Noah's old haunts were, so he phoned around all yesterday morning trying to find him.'

Jane listens as she lights the log burner, then she sits opposite Amber, sipping bubbles, enjoying them popping on her tongue.

Jane continues, 'When I arrived at the vicarage, Ben texted me. He was worried that Noah had gone back to one of the drug houses and would get hooked into that scene. That's why he insisted on going up there. I wasn't going to let Ben go alone.'

'You're pure muscle.' Jane laughs.

Amber grins. 'Well, I was a lawyer and I do have contacts. And, just in case there was a problem I could pull in a few favours. Luckily we found Noah in time. Ben spoke to him and persuaded him to come back with us while we contacted social services.'

'So, what happens now?'

'He will stay with us for a few days, but he was desperate to see Tommy — and you were next on his list.'

Jane smiles happily. 'Tommy really misses him. Is Noah speaking?'

'Not much, but he does seem different, that's why I'm happy

to be here with you. I'm hoping he will open up, and if he talks to anyone, it will be to Ben.'

'What do you think of Marion taking over as Chair of the Christmas committee?'

'I can't do anything now. I guess if everyone voted for her and that's what they want, then....' Amber shrugs.

'Is it really what people want though? It's going to be more of a massive party.'

Amber laughs.

Jane continues, 'I mean it, families don't want that sort of thing. What about the children and Santa?'

Amber shrugs. 'I guess Marion and her wealthy new boyfriend will cover all bases. I think she told Frances this morning that Santa can have a stall on the square and give out toys, away from Harbour Street and where the DJ will be.'

'You don't seem upset, Amber.'

'What can I do? It's all decided and I wasn't there. So, let her have her moment and let's see what happens. If she makes a success of it and does well, then that's good for all of us in Harbour Street. And if not, then we can take over again next year.'

'Next year seems a long way away.'

'Jane, relax. You seem very tense. Have you seen Tommy recently?'

'What's Tommy got to do with anything?'

'Well, you guys seemed really close and I thought there might be something between you, and now it seems you never see each other.'

'Who told you that!' Jane is indignant.

'Tommy.'

'What? What did he say?'

'He seemed upset. To be honest, he seems to think you have someone else in your life.'

'Me?'

'Do you?'

'No. No, not at all.'

'Do you like Tommy?'

'I would if he didn't stop sending me mixed messages.'

Amber laughs. 'I think there's two of you in it, each of you giving out mixed signals. You're not even time-sharing Coral now, are you?'

Jane sips her drink and looks at the fire. 'No.'

'You must miss them both.'

'I do, but it's all so complicated.'

'Right,' Amber says, 'Well, it's time we made sense of it all. Tommy thinks you're having an affair with Yusef. Are you?'

'No.'

'Right, good. If Tommy were to ask you out, would you be interested?'

'Well, of course.'

Amber smiles. 'Great, see how easy that was?'

* * *

Just before Jane goes to sleep that night, her phone pings.

Come for Sunday lunch? A&B and Noah xx

Jane looks up at the ceiling thinking it's been such a long time since she's shared a meal with anyone and, more than anything, it would be lovely to see Noah again.

She replies.

Fantastic! Thank you for thinking of me.x

* * *

Jane dresses carefully for Sunday lunch at Amber and Ben's house. She's bought a new pair of mustard dungarees and a pretty blue and beige blouse. She adds mascara and pink lipstick and then looks at her reflection in the mirror.

'That's as good as you're going to get,' she says, picking up a special bottle of Spanish sherry and a plant she bought from Eva's.

'Come in.' Ben greets her with enthusiasm and exclaims delightedly over the sherry. 'I'll open it now.'

Their house has been modernised. It's contemporary and open plan. Before Jane has removed her coat, she sees Tommy standing at the bifold doors overlooking the garden with Noah is at his side.

'That's the robin with the red breast, and over there, look! That's a blue tit.'

Coral comes running up to her and pushes her paws against Jane's knees. Jane squeals in delight. 'Coral, my lovely.'

Noah and Tommy turn from the window and Jane moves toward them with Coral still jumping up at her. Noah runs to Jane and squeezes her tightly.

'Hello Jane.' Tommy smiles. His shoulders are broad and he looks slimmer. His hair is shorter and he's grown a neat beard. He leans to kiss her lightly on the cheek. 'It's been a long time.' He smells of spicy aftershave.

'You look well, Tommy.'

'You look amazing,' he replies.

Amber breezes into the room behind them, followed by Ben carrying glasses. 'Dinner won't be long and we have plenty of time to catch up.'

For the next thirty minutes Amber and Ben waft in and out of the room, while Noah sits on the floor and plays with Coral.

'Do you like dogs?' Jane asks him.

Noah nods.

'I think she's grown,' Jane says.

'She's always hungry.'

'How have you lost weight?'

'I bought a bicycle. I've been cycling every day and running.'

'It suits you.'

'Have you been busy?'

'Always.'

'Shelley misses it,' he says, looking at her over the rim of his sherry glass. 'I don't think she's happy at uni.'

'She should give it a go.'

'That's what her mum's told her.'

Jane nods. 'I'd have loved the opportunity.'

'It's not for everyone, but she dropped out of the last course, so she'll have to stick with it now, I suppose.'

'How is Elsie?'

'She seems fine. They've asked me to go up there for Christmas.'

'Oh?'

'It's very kind of them and Elsie wants to meet Coral.'

Jane nods. The thought of Christmas makes her feel depressed.

'Will you be here for the Christmas lights switch on?' Amber asks, coming into the room and hearing only half of the conversation. She places two large serving dishes on the table. 'Please sit down, Ben's just carving the chicken.'

'It's on Saturday, isn't it?' Tommy gets up and walks with Jane to the table. He sits opposite her and beside Noah, leaving

Ben and Amber at the head of the table.

'It's going to be a disaster,' Jane says.

Ben comes in with white and red wine. 'It might be fun. Noah likes FreakPak, don't you?'

Noah nods.

Jane looks at the food on the table; crispy roast potatoes, asparagus, carrots, honey-glazed parsnips and roast chicken. 'Delicious,' she says.

'It's lovely to share a meal with friends,' adds Tommy.

Jane looks up sharply and he looks back at her with a sad smile.

'So much time goes past and you're sitting there on your own with no one to share it with,' he adds.

'At least you have Coral,' she replies.

Tommy nods. 'I couldn't imagine my life without her. I was far too lonely and I hadn't realised how it was all affecting me.'

'So, you're not lonely now?' Amber asks, sitting at the table.

Noah helps himself to potatoes and Ben passes the gravy dish around.

'I love having Coral and taking her for walks, and I'm doing more shifts at the RNLI but it's not what I want to do at the weekends. I'd much prefer to be going out, you know, to the cinema, the theatre or out for dinner.'

'And what about you, Jane?' asks Amber.

Jane stares at her. Amber's match making is so blatant that she feels very exposed, but it's Ben who bursts out laughing. 'Amber, stop it. This is Sunday lunch, not a match making dating service.'

Amber pokes her tongue out at him. 'Well, I didn't like you when I first met you.'

'Time to eat,' Ben says, pointedly.

Jane pushes some chicken onto her fork and savours it slowly. It's been so long since she's had a meal with other people. In fact, it was probably with Shelley and Tommy in the summer.

'Has everyone got what they need?' Amber smiles.

Tommy looks at her and smiles. 'This is more than I could possibly have asked for; I have my puppy, and I have —' He stares at Jane. 'I have my best friend back.' He turns to Noah and rubs the top of his head. 'My mate, Noah is back, and that makes me the happiest man.'

When Jane looks up Amber gives her a huge wink.

'We'll have to take some photos,' says Tommy. 'We can send them to Shelley. She would love to be here.'

'How is she getting on?' asks Ben.

'She finishes next week for Christmas.'

Noah looks up. 'Here?' he whispers.

Tommy shakes his head. 'No, she's not coming back here. She's going home to be with her mum.' Tommy wipes his mouth with his napkin and Jane is sure that she can see tears in his eyes. He clears his throat and says, 'How about we fly that kite after lunch together?'

Noah smiles.

* * *

It's Saturday afternoon and the Christmas concert is in full swing. DJ FreakPak's voice comes over the speakers drowning out the sounds of the beat and thump of the constant music. Harbour Street is packed. There are people everywhere. It's a massive crowd, lurching and turning together like a wave of bodies on the surf. Occasionally, there are shouts from the crowd and singing en masse, arms waving and chanting. It's tribal and Jane finds it intimidating.

It's been going on since two o'clock, just after lunch, and now it's almost five. She's tired and she hasn't eaten all day. She hasn't ventured out of the shop and now she's hungry. Business was busy this morning, but she felt too intimidated by the crowds to open the shop after lunch. She's spent the afternoon finishing off some jewellery orders before Christmas, trying, unsuccessfully, to block out the noise from the street.

She'd seen Marion and her boyfriend earlier, riding through the street in a convertible Mustang with DJ FreakPak waving frantically at everyone. He had a buzz cut, he was overweight and he wore bling around his neck and on his thick fingers. The stage had been set up right under the clock tower, which seemed ridiculous because that's where everyone passes though on their way to the harbour — especially children and families. Jane thought it blocked the flow of people from the harbour to the town.

It's dark now and it seems later than it is. Jane is about to close the blinds, when there's a face at the window.

Startled she gasps and Yusef bangs on the glass. 'Let me in!'

She opens the door and he falls through in a flurry of excited energy.

'You frightened me. I didn't recognise you,' she says.

'It's mad out there, baby. Why are you still open? We closed at one o'clock. It's crazy — so many people. I mean, crazy people going wild with the music and drink and stuff—'

'Anyone you know?'

'Nah, these people are all from out of town.'

'And Santa?'

Yusef shrugs.

'What about the families?'

'I don't know, Jane. I didn't see no families. Maybe they're in the harbour or something?'

Jane shakes her head and closes the blinds of the shop. 'I'll go out the back.'

'Good idea. I'll come with you.'

Jane didn't always use the back door that leads into a small patio with a wired fence on top of the wall, but today it would come in useful.

'I'll get my bag.'

'Tommy is finishing his shift at the station but he's worried about Noah who's at his house with Coral. There are some dodgy people around. I can walk you home or back to Tommy's house, Jane.'

'I'll be fine.' Jane pulls on her coat and scarf and opens the back door with the security locks. The patio is in darkness but she switches on a light. 'It will go off automatically,' she says.

BANG!

Instinctively, Jane cowers.

BANG!

A body hurtles towards Yusef. In the small space of the patio he's knocked to the ground. He shouts, but suddenly there are arms and feet, and legs and bodies, of at least three men. Jane crouches low, her key still in the half open door. The inside light is on. Suddenly her arm is wrenched behind her back. She kicks out and screams. Yusef scrambles to his feet, and in an attempt to stop one of the men from pushing Jane, he lashes out with his fist.

A man in a hoodie smacks Jane against the wall. Her head

bounces off the brickwork and she screams and falls to the ground. He clambers over her and into the shop, but Jane lunges for his leg and he stumbles. Another man grabs Jane from behind and holds her by the throat. Suddenly, she's choking. She's shoved up against the wall while a hooded figure is barking orders in her face that she can't understand. His voice is muffled behind his black scarf.

Instinctively, she jerks her right knee up between his legs — hard. He doubles over grabbing his crotch but then his fist connects with her face and the pain on her cheek ricochets through her head. Enraged, she fights, her arms spinning wildly as another man enters her shop. She pulls free, but has only taken two steps when someone grabs her legs. She's dragged to the floor and her cheek hits the patio. She turns, kicking, shouting and swearing. Beside her, Yusef is lying on the floor. He's covered in blood and a man is repeatedly kicking his ribs.

'NOOOOOO!' Jane lashes out angrily with her Doc Martens, connecting with everyone and everything. Overcome by a primeval anger that's so deep and fierce, all her pent-up frustrations come to a head as she thumps, hits out and kicks. She doesn't see the glistening steel blade at first, she's so consumed with anger.

Yusef rolls on his side. 'JANE! NO—'

The knife pierces her skin, entering her body. It's a surreal moment of disbelief. She covers the wound with her hand but blood flows through her fingers, bright red and glistening. She sinks slowly to the floor, on her knees. She no longer has any strength. She's dizzy and her head is foggy. She has run out of time. It's all over. She collapses to the ground.

December

Tommy

Jane was triaged quickly to the operating theatre. Now, outside in the corridor, Tommy sits gripping his hands together and staring at the hospital floor. He can't work out where it's all gone wrong. He's been through a massive change: Sunita, Shelley, Almond Blossom, Coral, Jane and yes, even Marion. There had been times during the year when he and Jane had been close, but then they had drifted apart.

Why?

Tommy had loved Sunita and he always would. But it was time for him to live. He was still a young man. Not yet sixty. There was still time.

After Sunday lunch at Amber and Ben's house, although he would have preferred to go home with Jane, he'd gone with Noah to fly the kite.

He'd missed Jane and so had Coral, so during the past week Tommy had started taking morning coffee into Jane's shop again. They would chat until it was time for Tommy's shift or take Coral for a walk.

This morning, the day of the Harbour Street Christmas

Celebration, as it had been christened by Marion, had started frantically. Vans, lorries and trucks carrying massive equipment and giant speakers had filled the street. There were cables everywhere and Tommy could only think it was a safety hazard. Harbour Street owners were complaining; Eva was furious and Ben appeared frustrated.

From his position in the RNLI station, Tommy had heard the music thumping through the harbour all day. For some bizarre reason, the stage had been set up under the clock tower, which is exactly the point where the people walked into the harbour.

Kit, as usual, had dressed up as Santa, but he sat in the square. By four o'clock, he was bored, and Santa's helpers had gone to the pub.

Tommy had kept an eye on everything because he'd had a terrible premonition that things weren't right. He'd worked a long shift and he'd been increasingly worried by the number of people surging into the harbour. At one point, some of the volunteer staff warned the crowd to get away from the harbour railings, but they'd been ignored. The crowd were fuelled by alcohol, excitement and the music by the legendary FreakPak.

Thump, thump, thump.

The crowd began jumping up and down, shaking the very foundations of Harbour Street.

Amber appears beside him, jolting his memory, and hands him a coffee. 'Are you alright, Tommy?'

They're sitting near the operating theatre.

'Thank you,' he says, sipping the hot drink, listening to the soft footfall of the hospital staff, the bleeps of the life support machines and hushed voices. Tommy hangs his head in tiredness and rubs the tension in the back of his neck.

A surgeon still wearing scrubs appears. 'Are you relatives?'

Tommy looks up sharply. 'Good friends.'

'Has she got family?'

Tommy shakes his head.

It's Amber who answers. 'The police are looking into it. They have her phone. We looked through the numbers but....' She shrugs. 'We are her best friends.'

The surgeon looks tired. He has an Indian accent and his eyes are red-rimmed, but caring. Tommy glances at his watch. It's past midnight.

'Is there anything we should know?' Amber asks.

'We've done what we can and she's stable. There's nothing more you can do tonight. You should go home and call tomorrow.' The surgeon's voice is a whisper.

'Thank you,' Amber whispers. 'Come on, Tommy.'

'Can I see her?' Tommy asks the surgeon.

'It's best she rests now.'

'Will she be alright?' he asks.

The surgeon replies, 'She's a fighter.'

Amber takes Tommy's arm and leads him down the silent corridors, normally filled with families and friends, past the walls that echo their hollow footsteps.

'What shall we do?' asks Tommy.

'Get in the car and we'll go home. Ben and Yusef have left A&E. They're at home now. Yusef's had ten stitches in his forehead, and he's got a few broken ribs, but he'll be okay.' Amber drives carefully and calmly through the quiet streets.

'I don't know what I'd have done without you and Ben tonight,' Tommy says. 'The whole episode was a nightmare.'

'It was a good job that you went to the shop to check on Jane.'

'I had a bad feeling about it, Amber. It was crazy, and some of the kids had jumped into the water in the harbour. Nothing seemed right.'

'Did you tell all this to the police?' she asks, navigating the traffic lights and roundabouts.

'I told them I went home via the jewellers. The shop was closed, but I was surprised to see a light on behind the gate, in the patio behind. I could hear shouting and scuffling. The door was on its hinges so I ran as fast as I could. Then I saw Yusef on the floor and Jane lying in a pool of blood…. there was so much blood — the people who'd done it had gone.' He rubs a hand over his head. 'I called 999 and then Femi — she was nearer. She'd just finish her shift and she came running. How she got through that crowd I'll never know, but she saved Jane's life, I'm convinced of that.'

'It was lucky there were some police on hand,' Amber says, indicating, turning the car into his street.

'The ambulance took forever,' Tommy replies angrily.

Amber places a hand on his knee. 'You were there for her, Tommy. If you hadn't been looking out for her, no one would have known. She's lucky to have you.'

'I'm just pleased you and Ben came so quickly.'

'We're family. We're not blood relatives but sometimes you can be closer than that. We're the chosen family. We're her logical family and so are you.' She pulls up outside his front door.

'Thanks, Amber.'

'Noah went home a few hours ago. He might not say much, but he's very good at texting. Coral is fed and watered and hasn't been alone for long. Get a good night's rest and I'll see you tomorrow.'

He leans over and kisses her on the cheek. 'Do you think

Jane will be alright?'

'I do.'

'But the shop is a wreck. I think they stole everything.'

'She should have insurance and we will help her. Hopefully, the police will find them and, anyway, she still has the one thing they couldn't steal.'

'What's that?'

'You.'

* * *

Tommy can't sleep. He pours a whisky and sits at the kitchen table. The jigsaw still isn't finished and Coral is curled up asleep in her bed by the radiator. He checks his phone. Three messages from Shelley and he can see that she's online.

He dials her number.

'Shelley?'

'I've been texting you.'

He takes a deep breath. 'There was a robbery today in the jewellers—'

'What?'

He tells Shelley what happened and he reassures her that Jane and Yusef will be alright.

Shelley says, 'I've been worried about Jane recently.'

'Why?'

'She's seemed very low. Depressed.'

'You've spoken to her?'

'I asked her to look at some of my designs. She mumbled something about hating Christmas.'

'Really?'

'I guess not everyone enjoys it.'

Coral stretches and comes over to lean against his legs and Tommy rubs her ears.

'I want to come and see her — you — Yusef, all of you. Will you look after Jane?'

'Yes.'

'Promise?'

'Yes.'

'Thank you, Tommy. Night night.'

'Talk soon.'

'I love you,' she whispers and a lump forms at the base of Tommy's throat. But before he can reply, she hangs up.

* * *

'Take it easy. Slowly. Easy. Easy. Slowly.'

'Stop it, Tommy.' Jane laughs. 'You make it sound like I'm ninety.'

'You've just come out of hospital.'

'I know, but I'm going to be fine.'

Tommy unlocks her front door and follows her inside her cottage. She'd agreed to give him the key in the hospital so that he could get in some shopping for her - milk, cheese and fruit. Now he looks around checking everything was where he'd arranged it.

'The flowers are lovely.' She smiles at the baskets of red and pink cyclamen. 'Thank you.'

Tommy almost bought red roses, but then he'd bottled out at the last minute. Jane sits wearily on the chair beside the fire. 'It's Baltic outside, Tommy.'

'I'll light the fire and warm us up,' he says.

Tommy has laid the log burner with new wood and it only

takes a minute before flames are licking the inside of the fire and warming the room. He feels at home pottering in her kitchen, putting on the kettle and fussing over her. He'd considered bringing Coral with him but Amber insisted he went on his own to pick Jane up from the hospital, leaving Noah on puppy duty at Tommy's house.

'I was going to cheer the place up a bit, but I couldn't find any Christmas decorations.'

'I'm not bothering this year.' Jane stares at the flames.

Perhaps Christmas is not a conversation for tonight. 'Hungry?' he asks.

'I'd murder a whisky.' She grins. Her right eye is bruised and her cheeks is swollen. There's a jagged cut on her forehead where glass has been removed and five stitches.

'With tablets?'

'I'm only taking a couple of pain killers. Come on, Tommy what's the worst that can happen after what I've been through? There's a bottle on the shelf above the microwave.'

Tommy finds a bottle of Chivas Regal and two glasses.

'Have you seen Yusef?' she asks.

Tommy straightens his back. 'No.' He hands her a glass and pours in the liquid.

She cradles the plaster cast on her left wrist.

'It's a good job you're right handed.' He smiles.

'Will you go and see how he is tomorrow? Please, Tommy. He saved me.'

'He didn't save you. Look at you.'

Jane places a hand on his arm. 'Please don't be angry with him. I don't know what would have happened if he hadn't been there.'

Tommy sighs heavily. 'I didn't know who to contact,' he

says. 'There's no one in the contacts in your phone with the same name.'

Jane sips the whisky, leans back and closes her eyes. She ignores him. He knows she's bandaged around her waist and he imagines she's in a lot of pain from the knife wound and is suffering silently. She lost a lot of blood and it was only a few millimetres from rupturing her kidney.

'I must thank Femi, too,' Jane says.

'It will take time to build your strength back up,' he says. 'It might be a while.'

Jane's eyes are closed and silent tears fall down her cheeks.

Surprised and alarmed, Tommy moves quickly to kneel beside her. 'Jane, please,' he whispers.

Her tears flow freely and Tommy places his arm over her shoulder and she leans against him. He feels her wetness on his shirt and her silent sobs. He holds her and smooths a strand of hair from her face.

'It's alright,' he whispers. 'It's shock. Everything's alright. You're home. You're safe.'

Jane's tears turn into wracking sobs and he holds her for what seems like a very long time before she falls silent. Her body feels like a dead weight against him.

'Jane?' he whispers. 'Jane?'

She stirs.

'Come on, let me get you upstairs.'

She leans heavily against him. She's exhausted and without a word, hanging onto the banister, he helps her upstairs to her bedroom. She lies wearily on the bed.

'Stay with me, Tommy, please?'

Tommy removes his shoes and lies beside her. He strokes her hair, caresses her shoulder and holds her close. He is overwhelmed with a feeling of tenderness that he never knew possible. He'd felt protective toward Noah but he'd never felt this way toward a woman. He'd never seen Sunita injured or sick or ill. Her accident had been tragic and immediate. It had been a quick death for her and for that he was eternally grateful. She hadn't suffered. One short, quick blow to the temple and she was gone.

Frances had been there for him. Their monthly chats had helped him and he'd written their appointments religiously in his diary. She had healed him and so had Noah. Tommy had invested his emotions in the boy and talked to him but it was Jane and her friendship that really made him want to change. He wanted more than friendship though. He was ready for a relationship. He was ready for the future and he wanted to enjoy whatever time he had left with Jane

Now, as he lies in the darkness of her bedroom, he has countless questions running through his mind.

Why does Jane have no family?

Why is she all on her own?

Why have they never talked about it?

Jane's phone pings in the darkness and Tommy opens his eyes immediately. Leaning slowly so that he doesn't disturb her, he removes his arm from the back of her head and picks up her phone.

The screen is lit up with a message.

Hope you're okay? I love you xx

It's from Yusef.

* * *

After Tommy's made breakfast for them both, he settles Jane

on the sofa in front of the fire, cuddling Coral. He's promised to look in on the shop and he's pleased to be outside in the cold air. It clears his head, giving him determination and resolution. He strides purposefully from the cottages behind Harbour Street - from Jane's house - imagining her walking this route every day.

Harbour Street looks innocent in the early December light. It's Wednesday morning. The dust carts have cleared the debris, and although the stage is still in place under the clock tower, it's a ghost of the town it had been at the weekend. Shops are opening. Tommy waves to Derek the butcher and Ian the grocer, but he doesn't stop.

Karl is opening up Harbour café.

'You're up early, Tommy. Is Jane alright?'

'She will be.'

'It was crazy here in the café. We closed early. Molly was frightened. Where are you going?'

'Stuff to sort out.'

'I'll be five minutes getting the machine heated. Come and have a coffee?'

Tommy slaps Karl on the shoulder. 'I will. Thank you.'

He stops at Jane's jewellers and looks through the window, but the blinds are still drawn. In the alleyway the back gate has been cordoned off with police tape. He ducks under it. The lock on the gate is busted. The robbers must have kicked it in but the backdoor is secured. There are still traces of Jane's blood on the concrete.

'Thank goodness Femi came in time or it might well have been a different story,' he mumbles.

There's a noise behind him and he spins quickly, his hands clenched into fists.

'Tommy? I wasn't sure it was you, my man.'

Yusef backs away and Tommy lowers his guard and stares at the younger man. He's bruised and beaten and he's clutching his ribs.

'Are you alright?'

'A few cracked ribs.' Yusef pulls himself upright. 'I was in the shop and I saw someone come down the alleyway.'

'You can't work, can you?'

'I can't sleep either. I might as well be working. How's Jane?'

'She's sleeping,' he lies.

'Good.'

Tommy is pleased that he's in charge and that Yusef is asking him about Jane. But Yusef looks at the blood on the ground and Tommy's heart softens.

'Jane will be alright,' he says.

Yusef gives a weak smile and that's when Tommy sees he's missing a tooth at the front.

'Did they do that?'

Yusef nods and closes his mouth quickly.

'I'll contact the police later,' Tommy says. 'Jane will want to know what's happening with the shop and insurance and everything.'

'They got away.' Yusef leans against the wall and holds his ribs, obviously in pain.

'The most important thing is that you and Jane are alright. That's all she cares about.'

Yusef nods but doesn't appear convinced. He shakes his head. 'I don't know what they took.'

'Jane will have to do an inventory for the police and the insurance company. I'm trying to get her to rest, but she'll probably be here tomorrow, knowing her.'

Yusef nods and suddenly aware they're close in the confines of the patio, he moves, limping heavily.

'You'll have to rest up, Yusef. Take some time out. Is there anything you need?' Tommy asks.

Yusef turns down the alleyway to Harbour Street but then he turns around. 'You need to know one thing, Tommy. It was never my intention, but—'

Tommy rests his hand on Yusef's shoulder. 'It's alright. I know. I was with her last night. I held her because I didn't think she had anyone else, but I know she's yours.'

'What?'

'I understand.' Tommy's shoulders slump, and suddenly he needs a coffee. He'd take Karl up on his offer.

'You slept with her?' Yusef shakes his head.

'I stayed with her for a while. Don't be upset. She came out of hospital, and she was upset. She has no one and I can't get her to talk about her family.'

Yusef closes his eyes and Tommy can see tears flowing down his cheek. Then Yusef begins to laugh uncontrollably. 'Oh, man! This is seriously weird, dude. This isn't happening. I think we've lost the plot. This is like some stupid film.'

'Yusef, stop! Calm. Please. I give up. You can't beg someone to love you if they're not interested and their heart belongs to someone else.'

Yusef is clutching his stomach and he laughs harder. Tommy frowns, his anger growing. Yusef is probably high on pain killers. He tries to push past him; his humiliation is too much.

'Tommy, mate. My friend, Tommy. My man, I love you, man, but you are seriously delusional. There's nothing between me and Jane, man.'

'I saw your text last night.'

Yusef slaps Tommy on the shoulder. 'I love Jane. She's my best mate. She's my go-between.'

'Your what?'

'She's my only link with Shelley. I promised I wouldn't contact Shelley as I want her to make a go of this uni course. It's what's best for her.' Yusef stares at him and then, as if he's about to make a final confession, he takes a deep breath. 'Tommy, my man, don't you get it? I love Shelley, I always have and I always will.'

* * *

The next morning Tommy insists on going with Jane to the shop.

'You might need me to lift things for you,' he says. 'Noah is walking Coral this morning and I'm free until my shift this afternoon.'

He's pleased that Jane doesn't object. They go in through the back gate and Jane glances at the patio floor. Tommy is pleased that he came down earlier and scrubbed off her blood.

'It's a good job it's a security door,' Tommy says standing behind her.

'You have to - for insurance. I'm just annoyed that I hadn't locked up by the time they kicked in the gate.'

'Well, I'm not. Goodness knows what might have happened to you if they'd tried to take the key. You wouldn't have let it go easily.'

Jane gives him a wry smile and he pushes open the door.

'What a mess,' she whispers.

Tommy walks in behind her. The kitchen looks like someone has swept the entire contents from the cupboards and shelves onto the floor, and in the shop there are boxes and trays overturned everywhere. He picks up a necklace slung aside that the robbers missed and upturns the chair he normally sits on, placing it beside the smashed glass counter. Jane's table, where she normally repairs jewellery, has been over turned. He lifts the lamp and finds her special magnifying glass is smashed. Jane reaches out to help.

'Don't lift anything. I'll do it.' Tommy rights the furniture. 'The police have definitely finished here?'

'They said they have. They gave me the keys back.'

Tommy feels a sense of despair. All Jane's hard work and diligence to create this business has been shattered and all her stock stolen.

'Where do we start?' he asks.

'The insurance company will have to know what's missing,' she explains. 'Then I'll have to assess what jewellery came in for repair, and... I don't know.... Just go through everything, I guess. A stocktake will show what's missing.'

'For the insurance or the police?'

'Both — in case they can find any of it, I suppose. And, for the customers who ordered presents.'

Tommy moves around, tidying and picking up small pieces of jewellery, discarded and dropped in the mayhem - rings, earrings, necklaces. He opens the blinds and looks out at the quiet street. He can see Ozan in the barber's shop opposite, but not Yusef.

'I think I put quite a bit of stock in the safe,' Jane says. 'I don't always bother, but the crowd had worried me and that constant beat of music was driving me mad.'

Tommy works quietly and meticulously, cleaning up and arranging jewellery on Jane's desk to help.

'At least the thieves didn't get everything,' Jane says, opening the safe and groaning in pain as she lifts out several boxes. 'The more expensive jewellery is here.'

'They could have forced you to open it.' Tommy wishes he'd been here earlier on Saturday. It breaks his heart to see Jane with a broken wrist and a bruised face. She looks defeated and exhausted and he knows that she moves awkwardly with the dressing on her wound. She's lucky to be alive.

She sits at the table and spends, what Tommy thinks is an extraordinary long time going through receipts, documents and other paperwork, comparing them with the jewellery that's left.

Tommy says, 'The police will probably never catch them.'

'It must have all been recorded.' She nods at the small device in the corner of the ceiling.

'I didn't know you had CCTV,' Tommy says.

'It's not the sort of thing I advertise. It's an insurance requirement.'

'You're quite sensible then.'

She laughs. 'Tommy, I've had to be. I've had to do everything. There's only been me since dad died.'

'That upsets me, Jane. Someone should be looking after you and I'm worried. When I looked through your list of phone contacts in the hospital, there was no one that I could see who was family.'

Jane turns away and flicks through more receipts.

'You can ignore me or I can ask you this again over a glass of wine later?' Tommy smiles when she looks up. 'But I'll be honest, Jane. I'm not messing around any more. I'm just going to be upfront and tell it like I see it. I feel as though we've been misunderstanding and misinterpreting everything for months and it hasn't got us very far.'

She looks amused. 'Why do you say that?'

'I saw Yusef yesterday and he told me the truth.'

Her eyes widen. 'He did?'

'Yes, it's not a secret any more. He told me he loves Shelley and that he promised not to contact her at uni to give her a chance to settle in. He said he didn't want to ruin her life and that he only wanted the best for her. And that, you — you, Jane - are in touch with her. The go-between. Is that true?'

Jane smiles. 'I'm trying to sort out these receipts, Tommy.'

'You never told me.'

'Told you what?'

'Anything!'

Jane looks at him. 'What do you want to know?'

Tommy shakes his head. The colour has drained from Jane's face and he can see that the exertion is taking its toll on her body.

There's a tap on the glass window and in the street Amber raises two coffee cups in the air. Tommy opens the front door.

'Gosh, this place is a mess. Do you want a hand?'she says.

'Tommy is helping me, Amber, thank you.' Jane sounds remarkably calm and relaxed, but by contrast Tommy's agitation is growing.

He says, 'I'm worried, Amber. I've just said to Jane that we didn't know who to call. We couldn't find any family contacts for Jane, could we?'

Amber looks at Jane and raises her eyebrows. 'Is there anyone, just in case there's a next time.'

Tommy explodes. 'There won't be a next time. I won't let

this happen again.'

Jane rests her hand on his arm while taking a sip of coffee. 'I don't have any family,' she says simply. 'Well, I probably have lots, but I'm not in touch with any of them. You see, my father and my mother were cousins and it turns out that the family were all against them being together. They thought it was unnatural and not right, so they blanked them and I grew up not knowing any of my relatives.'

'But it's legal,' says Amber. 'There's nothing wrong with that.'

Jane shrugs. 'Some families can be judgemental.'

'Bigoted,' mumbles Amber.

'No contact at all?' says Tommy. 'In all these years - ever. How can that be?'

'I suppose one generation poisons the next generation with their bias. Then, I guess, after a while they forget all about you. You're not important. You don't exist and you become this weird product, or the off-spring of a couple who have been cancelled by their relatives. And life moves on. Time has no meaning, then it's one generation after the next—'

'So, you have uncles and aunts?'

'Of course.'

'Nieces and nephews?'

'Tommy, those are blood relatives. My family is here in Westbay. You guys; you and Amber and Ben. Femi who rescued me, Yusef of course ...'

'And Shelley.'

Jane smiles. 'Of course, Shelley.'

Tommy frowns. 'And Noah, and Coral.'

Jane puts a hand on his chest and he feels the heat of her hand through his shirt. 'It's alright, Tommy. This is enough for me.'

Tommy shakes his head.

Jane heads to the kitchen and Amber follows, looking at the mess on the floor and the security door, while Tommy stays in the shop.

He hadn't realised until this moment how similar they were.

When he had his heart attack he'd been reluctant to contact Elsie but after Sunita had gone, there was no one else. He knew that Matt and the gang were his mates but they had families and their own lives. Tommy needed someone for himself. He's shocked to realise that Jane is, and always has been, in the same predicament.

Tommy stares out of the jewellery shop window. Across the road he can see into the Grooming Esquires where Ozan is cutting the hair of a young man. All this time, Tommy has believed that Yusef and Jane were lovers but it's evident to him now that their friendship is more important.

Tommy had spent the summer trying to decide if Jane liked him, plucking up the confidence to ask her out and the year has passed; each week, each day, each hour and each minute trickling past while he was losing out.

He shakes his head in exasperation. How stupid.

If only he'd relied on Coral.

Coral loved Jane and was never happier than when she was here in the shop, time-shared by two loving parents.

Tommy rests his head against his arm and leans on the glass shop door, remembering snatched images of the summer like a picture book, a film trailer: his heart attack, Elsie's cancer, Shelley arriving, Almond Blossom, swimming with Jane, Noah going away, Shelley leaving for uni, Jane in hospital.

What else was going to happen before he realised he didn't

want to lose everyone?

It's about time he sorted himself out. There's no time for excuses.

Behind him, Amber and Jane are laughing.

He turns around from the window.

Jane says, 'Don't move, Tommy. You're striking the perfect pose in the window. Maybe I'll close the jewellers and open a strip joint.'

* * *

Tommy takes Jane home for lunch. Noah walks down with Coral and they all sit in the kitchen while Tommy makes toasted ham and cheese sandwiches. Jane makes a fuss of the dog and Noah watches silently. He's never been in her home and Tommy notices how he takes in the detail of her kitchen. He leaps up to get kitchen roll as napkins and he makes the tea.

'Noah's the best tea maker,' Tommy says proudly.

'You sound like you've taught him.' Jane laughs.

'He's also the best dog trainer.'

'Ah, another one of your skills that you've passed on.'

Tommy grins. He loves Jane's attention. She seems more upbeat than he'd imagined. She had concentrated and worked diligently all morning, often in silence, but when he'd spoken, she'd looked up, never irritated, but always listening and paying attention.

After they've finished lunch, Tommy's phone rings.

'Shelley,' he cries with delight. 'This is a lovely surprise.'

'I tried getting hold of Jane. Is she alright?'

'She's sitting here with me now.'

'I saw on the news about the shop.'

'It was on the news?'

'The local news online.'

'You bother with that?' Tommy is surprised but then he thinks of Yusef and her connection to Westbay and it begins to make sense. He still hadn't quite worked out all the details of their relationship, but one thing was clear; they had allowed Shelley to disengage from them so she could make friends and start a new life at uni. They all, in their own way, had wanted her to have the best opportunity and the best crack at making a go of her new life.

'Can I speak to her?'

Tommy holds out the phone to Jane. 'She's not interested in speaking to me. Only to you.' He grins.

Jane takes the phone with her right hand and there are pauses as she listens and responds to the questions. Tommy can only imagine what Shelley is asking.

'Hi, there. Yes. Fine. Fine. Yes. No. The insurance should cover it all. It may take some time. Don't worry.' Jane laughs. 'No. Maybe. Christmas? I don't know. Stop worrying. Bye. You too. Bye.' Jane hands the phone back to Tommy.

'Hello,' he says.

'I'm coming to stay, is that alright?'

'What about uni?'

'It finishes on Friday.'

Tommy pauses. 'Well, you'll have to go home for Christmas.'

'I know. Mum wants you there too.'

Tommy looks at Jane, but she's already moved into the lounge and is lying on the sofa.

'Tommy? Did you hear me? We can travel up to mum's

together for Christmas.'

* * *

It takes the rest of the week for Jane to sort out the shop.

'You're not up to opening it on your own,' Tommy argues.

'I'll be fine. It's only a broken wrist.'

'You look like you've done three rounds with Mohamed Ali.'

Jane laughs. 'You're such a worrier.'

'Shelley arrives tonight. She'll insist on helping you tomorrow.'

'It's all fine. Stop fussing over me. I'm not used to it and it will be awful when it stops.'

'It doesn't have to stop.'

'I'm not an invalid.'

The shop door opens and Eva walks in. Jane hasn't seen her for ages and she's surprised at how young she looks. Her eyes are dancing and she's carrying a large bouquet of flowers in her arms.

'These are not from me,' she says in her Polish accent. 'Marion came to my shop and she bought them for you, so I thought I would deliver them myself and tell you how sorry I am, for what happened to you.'

'Thank you.' Jane takes the flowers. 'They are beautiful.'

'I don't think flowers will make up for the robbery or that you were almost killed. Marion is disingenuous and I am angry with her for her silly, stupid idea of having this concert here. She disguised it as a Christmas festival, but her boyfriend is a music promoter and I think she did it for him. She's a very silly woman.'

'And dangerous,' adds Tommy. 'It was a very poorly

executed event.'

'Amber is getting the police to investigate it. Everything was wrong about it. Luckily, I didn't open my shop that day, but the gangs were terrible and I think Kit's shop was also robbed.'

'You did the right thing not opening, Eva.'

'Well, it was fate. Did you know that Sanjay came back?'

'No.' Tommy and Jane say in unison.

Eva smiles. 'He's home at last.'

Jane laughs. 'It's no wonder that you look so radiant.'

'A woman in love,' agrees Tommy.

Eva smiles. 'I'm a very lucky woman. He left almost a year ago and I thought I may never see him again.'

Jane places the flowers on the counter and with one arm she reaches out and embraces Eva. 'I'm so happy for you — for both of you.'

'We'll call in and get a takeaway later. It will be great to see Sanjay again,' Tommy adds.

Eva leaves the shop and Tommy picks up the flowers. He goes into the street and spies an elderly woman wheeling a trolley. She has on a thick coat and a woollen cap pulled over her head.

'Hello,' he says. 'These pretty flowers are for you.'

The woman looks surprised. 'For me?'

Tommy places them on her trolley. 'Can you manage them?'

'They're beautiful. How very kind of you.'

'It's a pleasure.'

The woman giggles. 'My husband, Arthur, will wonder who gave them to me.'

'It's never too late to make your husband a little bit jealous.'

'Nonsense, he's not the type, but he does like flowers.'

Jane watches him as he comes back into the shop.

'You didn't want them, did you?'

Jane shakes her head. 'No. I want absolutely nothing from that woman.'

'That's what I thought and I didn't want them going to waste.'

* * *

Tommy leaves Jane in the shop and he's just reached the art gallery when he turns to look over his shoulder. Yusef is crossing the street, about to go into the jewellers. He sighs heavily. Feeling curious and still a little jealous, he turns back. He's cautious at first. He peaks through the shop window where Yusef is waiting at the counter and Jane is pushing a small gift bag towards him.

Tommy feels like a spy and he turns away, shaking his head, angry with himself and wondering what they are doing. But he can't be late. He waits at the train station thinking, worrying and wondering, until Shelley's train arrives. He climbs out of the car to help her with her suitcases.

'I thought you were only coming for a few days. Oh, hello Almond Blossom.' He puts his finger inside the crate and she miaows.

'At least you've brought the car this time.' Shelley grins. 'You made me walk the first time I came here.'

Tommy laughs at the memory. At his house, he helps carry her bags inside. He's tidied her bedroom, cleaned the house and Noah has taken Coral to the beach for a walk.

'Wow! The tree looks amazing. It touches the ceiling.'

'I thought you might like to decorate it later.'

She kisses his cheek. 'Thank you, Tommy.'

Shelley takes a while to settle in and eventually Tommy ventures upstairs to check that she's alright - but mainly because he's excited to have her home. He glances around her bedroom.

'You've settled back in, it looks like you never left.'

'I'm not going back to uni.' Shelley folds her arms and stares challengingly at him.

'What? Have your told you mum?'

'Not yet.'

'What will you do?'

'Work with Jane.'

'I don't know if that's even a possibility at the moment.'

'How is she?'

'In a lot of pain, but I also think she's in shock. Sometimes it takes a while for it all to come out.'

'I'll talk to her tomorrow.'

'She'll tell you to go back to uni.'

'That's only because she never got the chance. She was a carer for her father and she never had the opportunity to go to uni, but she can't lead her life through me. I am not her.'

'A carer? How did you know about her father?'

'She told me back in the summer.'

Tommy feels disgruntled. Why did he not know these details?

'Look, Tommy. You have to stop messing around. You either want to be with Jane or you don't — but if you do, then you have to be open and honest. You have to tell her.'

Tommy nods.

'Have you definitely lost interest in Marion?'

'Marion wasn't my type. She just flattered me.'

'Thank goodness. Jane is lovely, and I think you guys will be great together.'

'I've already made my decision and I'm going to talk to her about it.' He looks at his watch. 'I suppose you're going to meet Yusef?'

Shelley looks surprised and grins. 'I thought you'd want me to eat here with you, but if that's okay, I'd love to surprise him.'

'Good. Oh, and by the way. I'm not going to your mum's for Christmas, you'll have to go on your own. I'm not leaving Jane.'

Tommy's phone pings.

Sorry for the short notice – we're having a party tonight. Sanjay is home. Harbour Café – 7pm – Hope you can make it. A&B xx

*　*　*

Tommy insists on walking Jane from her cottage to the café. As they walk up Harbour Street, arm in arm, they pause to look at the Christmas lights hanging outside shops and along the street, illuminating their pathway.

'The lights are beautiful,' Jane says.

'They're the ones Amber bought last year for Harbour Street. They're like the ones Sanjay lent us the first year from the Diwali celebrations. Do you remember?'

Jane smiles, she remembered it very well.

'Only one more week to go. I love Christmas, don't you?' Tommy tucks his arm closer to her wondering when he might get a chance to speak to her privately.

'Who doesn't?' she replies.

Her voice is flat, so he replies in a jolly tone, 'You'll have to put your tree up, Jane. Let's get in the festive mood. Have you got decorations? I couldn't find any.'

'Somewhere.'

'I can help you find them.'

'There's plenty of time.'

'Shelley was pleased I'd bought the tree. She's going to decorate it tomorrow. She wanted to see Yusef tonight. Maybe you'll come and have supper with us and we could all do it together?'

'Maybe.'

They arrive at the café and Tommy opens the door and ushers her inside and out of the cold. The Christmas decorations are perfect. A beautiful tall tree in the corner near the window with pretty wooden decorations. The sound of Christmas music floats down from the rafters. Tommy feels his heart lifting, but when he looks at Jane he's concerned and he's not sure why.

The café is busy. Tommy greets Frances and Graham, Amber and Ben, and then Femi and Lawrence. Albert, Femi's younger son, and Noah are playing with Coral who is enjoying the attention.

Amber pulls Jane to one side and Tommy gets separated from her. He greets Sanjay with a hug.

'It's good to have you back,' Tommy says. 'We've missed you. It's been a long time. It smells good in here — I could murder a curry.'

Sanjay laughs and Tommy can't help but think he would look well in a Bollywood movie.

'I'm so pleased everyone supported my cousins while I was away. I wanted to invite you all to some Indian food. I am very thankful.' He dips his head.

'It's been a strange year.' Tommy rubs his hands together. 'And, it's great you're home.'

'You won't believe how happy I am to be here.' Sanjay looks over to where Eva is laughing with Amber. Jane is beside them, but she's not smiling. She looks tired and withdrawn. She appears to say and do the right things, yet it's as if she's robotic, aloof, as if she's watching the scene in the café from afar.

'This is home,' Tommy says. 'You were gone too long. We all missed you, especially Eva.'

Sanjay scowls. 'Poor Jane, I'm sorry for what happened to her. I called into the shop yesterday with Frances and I hate that she's suffered so much. It was a stupid idea of Marion's to have that concert.'

Amber overhears their conversation. 'Marion won't be having a concert like that ever again. I've already lodged a complaint with the police and they're looking into the whole event. It appears that they didn't have the correct permissions or licenses. There were so many safety hazards — and I think there will be a big inquiry, especially into Marion's boyfriend's credentials.'

'I hope they're looking into the robbery too.'

'They are, Tommy. They've already taken the CCTV footage from Jane's shop and I think they're optimistic about catching them. They weren't aware they were being filmed.'

'You're the best lawyer,' Sanjay says, patting her arm. 'You are so diligent, Amber.'

'I care what happens, Sanjay. It's in my nature, I guess.'

Frances joins them. 'I've spoken to the other shop owners and they're bitterly disappointed. They regret voting for Marion - so I think it will be a long time until she has anything to do with our Christmas plans — if ever.'

'She's a disgrace,' adds Eva.

Jane turns away. She seems to be taking in the Christmas decorations and the pretty decorated table. Tommy wants to be beside her, but Noah is suddenly pulling on his arm and showing him that Coral will lie down for a treat. Tommy is distracted and Ben and Amber get everyone seated. There's excited chatter and laughter and Eva pulls Tommy's arm to sit beside Sanjay.

At the other end of the table, Jane is seated beside Karl and opposite Amber. She doesn't look at him. She barely looks up at all and Tommy feels a pang of regret. This wasn't the evening he'd planned. He wants to speak to her, explain his feelings and tell her that he needs to be with her.

Ben stands up. 'I'd like to say a few words to this wonderful group of warm and loving friends. Some of you may not have relatives but friendship for Amber and I, is a bond as strong as family. We call you our logical family. The people we choose to be with and the ones we help and love — our very special friends who we share our lives with. Each time we meet up, our family grows and we are lucky that we have this abundance of love and support in our community. Let's raise a glass and toast to us - our logical family.'

Glasses are raised and then one by one as the curry, rice, poppadums, onion bhajis, sags and dahls are passed around, the conversation gathers excited momentum. Tommy is surprised that Jane drinks her wine quickly. Karl refills her glass and then another time Faisal reaches over to top up her glass. She appears not to speak much but she smiles and nods, listening attentively, not meeting Tommy's gaze. The evening races past and suddenly Jane is putting on her coat and Tommy is at her side.

'I'll walk you home.'

'No need, Tommy. I'll be fine. It's only around the corner.'

'I want to speak to you—'

She places her hand lightly on his arm. 'I'm really tired. Can it wait?'

'Of course.'

She leans forward and kisses him lightly on the cheek. 'Goodbye, Tommy.' Then suddenly she's gone. He watches her through the café window, walking with her head bent, her coat wrapped around her like a protective shield while the wind pushes against her battered body.

'Tommy, are you having a top up?' Ben points to his wine glass.

'How did you find Jane, tonight?' he asks.

'Tired. Very, very tired,' Ben replies.

'That's what I thought.' Tommy turns away, finds his coat on the peg and calls out. 'Rain check, Ben?'

'No problem.' Ben waves.

Tommy hurries down the street. That's the problem. There *is* a problem. Tommy lengthens his stride with a feeling of utter horror creeping down his spine.

* * *

Jane's house is in darkness. No lights are on inside. He bangs on the front door but there's no answer. He hurries back to Harbour Street and peers through the window of the jewellery shop, but the blinds are drawn. He checks the back gate, but there's no sign of a light. He turns quickly and suddenly he catches sight of a familiar figure walking under the clock tower, toward the harbour.

He runs but he loses sight of her. His heart is racing and he's panting heavily. By the time he reaches the fishing boats, lined up along the quay, his heart is thumping manically.

He negotiates the lobster pots and fishing lines with ease. This is his territory. The harbour is in darkness apart from one light at the far end, near the marina where the pleasure boats and yachts are moored. Tommy is confident that he could find his way blind-folded if he had to; but he can't find Jane. His frustration grows. He knows each crack in the pavement. His panting is laboured and his breath is heavy. He stops suddenly. There! She has one leg over the railing, straddling, ready to drop into the water.

'No, Jane, please no,' he whispers, running.

The water is high in the marina and it's also extremely cold. If anyone falls in hypothermia would set in quickly. They may not survive.

She's looking down into the deep, swirling sea.

'Jane.' Tommy moves but his legs are heavy and his movements slow. He runs, reaching out, knowing he can't possibly get there in time. 'Jane,' he calls.

Suddenly, Jane places her leg back on the ground and Tommy grabs her around the waist. 'Jane, I won't let you do this.'

'Tommy?'

He holds her tightly, wrapping her in his arms. Her face is pressed against his neck. 'I knew something wasn't right.' He's relieved she isn't struggling and he holds her firmly, their heads close together. He feels her wet, silent tears on his cheek. Her body is shaking, convulsed in silent sobs.

'I —I couldn't even—'

'Shush, it's alright,' he whispers. He cradles the back of her head with his hand. 'I won't let you go.'

Her ragged breathing subsides and she pulls away, wiping her nose and her eyes on her hand.

'What are you doing here—'

'I followed you. You're upset.'

Jane shakes her head. 'I'm fine.'

'You're clearly not fine. It looks like you were—'

She places her hand on his chest. 'I couldn't, Tommy. I couldn't even throw myself in.'

Tommy grins but he doesn't let her go. 'Thank goodness for that.'

Jane shakes her head. 'I'm sorry.'

'I'm pleased I was here.' He shifts his feet so that he can be better placed if she suddenly lunges and throws herself in the sea.

'I'm alright now,' she whispers.

He steps back to give her space, but pulls her away from the railing. 'I can't lose you, Jane. I need you.' He wraps her in his arms again and she buries her head in his shoulder.

'I need you too.' Her voice is muffled.

'Thank goodness for that.' Tommy smiles. 'Phew! So let's go home and talk this through, Jane, because I was on my way to have a conversation with you when Ben texted this afternoon.'

Jane leans against him. 'I feel so helpless — so bloody useless.'

'You're used to being in charge. You've looked after your father and his business, then you came to Westbay and built up your business without any support from your family. You've had a shock with the break-in and had to face everything alone

— but no more.'

'No?'

'No,' Tommy says firmly. 'Life is short. Life is precious and we have time on our side to enjoy it — together.' He puts his arm firmly around her shoulder and leads her home. 'So, what's all this about?'

Jane sighs. 'I haven't got any more energy, Tommy. You're right. I can't keep doing everything on my own. I... I... I thought if I just get it all over with, then I won't have to face it all...'

They walk under the clock tower. 'Well, let's break it down slowly. What are you dreading most?'

'Christmas. I hate it. It's never been much fun. After mum died, I was on my own with dad. He had MS and I was his carer for years. I've been on my own ever since he died.'

'Well, that's what I was coming to tell you. I've already decided that I'm staying in Westbay and I'm spending Christmas with you. I don't want to be with anyone else, Jane. I have to be with you.'

Jane hugs him closer as they turn into her street.

'Key?' he asks.

She reaches into her pocket and Tommy opens the door.

'Where's that bottle of Chivers Regal? We've got lots to celebrate tonight. Life is for the living and we're going to start living, Jane.'

They take off their coats and Tommy pours two generous helpings of whisky. 'I've been a silly, jealous old fool, worrying myself sick that you're with Yusef. I know you're not. You're a good friend and I also know he loves Shelley.' He frowns and takes a deep breath. 'But there's something I must tell you, about the summer, about Marion—'

Jane holds up her hand. 'No, Tommy, we've both had a past and until this minute, until right now, there was nothing binding us together. We were both finding ourselves. Nothing matters until this moment. We don't need to make confessions.'

'I think I've loved you for a long time, Jane,' he says.

She leans against Tommy and he kisses her forehead.

She replies quietly, 'I couldn't actually have done it, you know. I've never felt so relieved to have your arms around me. I was just so low thinking about another awful Christmas alone.'

'Well, I've been thinking, we're not just going to be together for Christmas. Let's spend our time wisely and make a bucket list.'

Jane laughs. 'I suppose it's better than kicking one.'

* * *

It's Christmas Eve, mid-afternoon, and Tommy's preparing salt-baked sea bass for supper with boiled potatoes and vegetables. He's insisting on spoiling Jane in his home, and he's slicing the vegetables with precision.

Jane is finishing the last of the jigsaw while sitting at the kitchen table. Coral wanders into the kitchen, sniffing for leftovers on the floor but walks away in disgust when there's nothing. The Christmas tree, decorated by Shelley, looks beautiful and there's an air of anticipation and excitement.

'So, the police think they've found the thieves and some of the jewellery?' Tommy says.

'They recognised some of the gang members from the CCTV and tracked them down in London.'

'That's great news. So, I guess the court case will be next year?' Tommy sweeps the sliced beans and carrots into a pan. 'We'll all be here to support you.' He cleans up the work counter and then puts the kettle on and pulls out teacups.

Shelley wanders in and throws herself into a chair opposite Jane.

'Why are you so fed up?' Tommy asks.

'Yusef's been really strange. I just hope he hasn't changed his mind about me.'

'I'm sure he hasn't. He's coming to have dinner with us.'

'Ever since Mum said she was going away and I said I wanted to stay here for Christmas, I've got a horrible feeling that he's planned on spending it with someone else. And now that I've quit uni — maybe he's frightened. Commitment phobia—'

Jane laughs. 'I shouldn't think so.'

Shelley shrugs. 'I bet it's a commitment thing. I haven't spoken to him since yesterday.'

Tommy looks up. 'Then you must ask him. No misunder-standings - be open and honest.'

Shelley laughs. 'Well, well, well, you've come a long way this year, *Agony Uncle* Tommy. Listen to your advice.'

He smiles and winks at Jane and she grins back at him.

'It did take me some time. But I got there in the end and I'm just relieved that it's all worked out.'

Tommy squeezes the tea bags. Since he found Jane in the harbour a few days ago, they've grown closer. They've even talked about moving in together so that Coral has proper parents and not time-share ones. They are a couple now and Tommy can't believe how happy he feels and how much better Jane is looking. All he needs is her and all she needs is him.

Jane's phone pings and she looks up from her message.

'Amber just texted about the robbery.' Jane wanders out of the kitchen with her phone and into the lounge.

'I don't know what you've done to Jane but I've never seen her so happy.' Shelley grins.

Tommy smiles. 'It's called love.'

'Ooooohhhh, I thought that was why you haven't been coming home at night.'

'Coral likes it at Jane's.'

'I'd say Coral isn't the only one.' Shelley giggles.

Jane calls out, 'Come in here, Shelley, I want to show you something.'

Shelley raises her eyebrows to Tommy and he shrugs.

'No idea,' he says.

When Tommy carries the tea into the lounge, Jane is sitting on the floor leaning back on the sofa with her legs stretched out in front of the fire. Almond Blossom is curled up asleep in her lap. She has a sketch pad beside her and another thinner note pad with text and drawings.

'What's this?' Shelley asks, kneeling beside her.

Coral stretches out in front of the fire.

'Well, as you kept phoning me all term, I thought, hypothetically, if you were to quit uni, how we could work together. So, I studied your business plan—'

'Tommy? You finished it?'

'I said I would.'

'You needed to give uni a go and you did but it didn't work out, so it's all in here for you both to read. This is my business proposal.' Jane taps the papers with the hand that's still in plaster. 'There's only one condition and I'm sorry to say this, but it all depends on the bank. If I can get the loan, then we can expand and that will give me the finances to grow the business.

I'd like you to go to conferences and trade fairs, Shelley, and build up our business abroad and online. This will help us with new ideas and we can design the jewellery accordingly.'

'Really?' Shelley's face lights up. 'Commercial jewellery—brilliant! Jewellery that is actually aimed at a buyer rather than some silly, fanciful university tutor with no idea of what will sell!'

Jane laughs and holds up her good hand. 'There's room in here for a healthy salary for you, plus commission and in five years, if things go well, a stake in the business.'

Shelley's mouth drops open. 'Why would you do this?'

'Because you're smart and talented.'

'And family.' Tommy grins.

Jane laughs. 'I'd planned all this weeks ago — before you made a move on me, Tommy.'

'I can't believe it, Jane.' Shelley flings her arm over Jane's shoulder. 'You're amazing. I really don't know what to say.'

Tommy shakes his head. 'This is all news to me.'

'Happy Christmas, Shelley,' Jane says.

Tommy picks up the notepad and skims through the pages and his eyes rest on the finances. The front doorbell rings and, distracted, he passes it back to Jane. But Shelley is too quick for him. She stands up quickly and hurls herself past him and down the hallway to the front door.

'Yusef,' she cries.

In the lounge, Tommy and Jane smile at each other.

'That's a relief,' he says. 'I don't know what that boy is playing at!'

Jane laughs. 'They'll work it out. We did.'

Tommy sits beside her and kisses her fingers. 'I can't wait for you to get this cast off.'

'Me neither.'

'Do you remember in the summer, the day Noah left? Do you know what he whispered to me in the pub?'

Jane shakes her head.

'He said, Jane's the one.'

Jane kisses him.

'We need a holiday,' Tommy announces.

Jane replies, 'I've put money aside to pay for a new tooth for Yusef but perhaps we might get away in the new year.'

'Especially now Shelley is back. This is an amazing business opportunity — thank you. She's a happy girl.'

Jane smiles. 'Fingers crossed.'

'Oh, and don't worry about the bank loan because I took a quick look at the figures and I can cover it.'

'You can?'

'Well, that's what husbands do, isn't it? I think Beckham does that for Victoria?'

'Ha, you'll be wanting me to sing next.'

'Well, I'm not sure if a career on stage would suit you.' He laughs.

'I want to make you happy, Tommy.'

'You do, Jane. Every day I'm with you.'

'Thank you for saving me.'

'You rescued me.'

'I know you've given up being with your sister this Christmas to be with me and I can't tell you what it means. This is the best Christmas, ever.' Jane kisses him tenderly.

There are footsteps in the hallway and they break quickly apart. Standing in the doorway is an older version of Shelley. She is more lined, more gaunt and more tired than he could imagine but she has the same massive smile.

'Elsie?' he cries and leaps to his feet. 'Is it really you?'

'Tommy?'

'I can't believe it!'

He stands up and rushes to his sister and holds her close. There are tears rolling down his cheeks but then he realises they are her tears too.

'Is it really you?' he whispers.

Young Shelley appears in the doorway, holding Yusef's hand. She says proudly, 'Yusef drove all the way up there to get mum. He phoned her and persuaded her to come and spend Christmas with us. He wanted to surprise us all.'

Tommy wipes his eyes and then can't stop laughing.

Although Jane's wound is healing, she's still sore and she grimaces as he helps her up off the floor.

'Elsie, this is Jane - my future wife.'

Shelley claps with delight. 'And my business partner.'

'Business partner?' asks Yusef.

Jane reaches forward and gingerly, she hugs Elsie. They hold each other carefully, both happy and smiling.

'Look what Yusef's given me.' Shelley shows off a beauti-ful hand-crafted bracelet of entwined fingers. 'He says he designed it and you made it in secret, Jane.'

Jane smiles.

'*That* was the secret,' he whispers.

Jane says, 'It was lucky I put it in the safe the night of the robbery.'

'And I gave him my necklace. Look.'

Yusef steps forward and smiles with a gap in his teeth. He puts his half of the necklace with the half that Shelley is wearing.

'When the two halves are together it says, *Together, forever, never to be separated.'*

'How beautiful.' Jane smiles.

Elsie grins. 'I feel as though I know you already, Jane. Yusef told me all about you on the drive down here. We had lots of time to get to know each other.'

'Yusef's a good guy. And you being here, Elsie, makes it the perfect Christmas.'

'We have lots to catch up on.' Tommy reaches for a bottle of champagne while Yusef gets the glasses. 'This is a true celebration and a happy Christmas for us all.'

Elsie beams at him. 'I can't tell you how happy I am to be here.'

'Oh, you can.' Jane smiles. 'You truly, truly can.'

THE END.

Janet Pywell's Books

The Westbay Romance Series:
Someone Else's Dream
Someone Else's Child
Someone Else's Truth

Ronda George Thrillers:
The Concealers
The Influencers
The Manipulators
The Ronda George Thriller Boxset - books 1-3

Mikky dos Santos Thrillers:
Golden Icon – *The Prequel*
Masterpiece
Book of Hours
Stolen Script
Faking Game
Truthful Lies
Broken Windows

Boxsets:
Volume 1 – Masterpiece, Book of Hours & Stolen Script
Volume 2 – Faking Game, Truthful Lies & Broken Windows

Other Books by Janet Pywell:

Red Shoes and Other Short Stories

Bedtime Reads

Ellie Bravo

For more information visit:

website: www. janetpywellauthor.wordpress.com

All books are available online and can be ordered through major book stores.

If you enjoy my books then **please do leave a review** from wherever you purchased the book. Your opinion is important to me. I read them all. It also helps other readers to find my work.

Thank you.

About the Author

Janet Pywell writes gripping international mystery and crime thriller novels that will keep you quickly turning the pages.

After the Covid pandemic Janet published the first book in the **Westbay Romance Series** — *Someone Else's Dream* — a feel-good novel about courage, integrity and friendship. The other novels in the series will also leave you tingling with emotion.

Janet has a background in travel and tourism and she currently lives on the Kent coast.

In April 2022, Janet Pywell published her first non-fiction book: **Ten Simple Steps for Writing Your Book**.

You can connect with me on:

- https://janetpywellauthor.wordpress.com
- https://twitter.com/JanPywellAuthorTwitter
- https://www.facebook.com/janet.pywell
- https://www.instagram.com/janetpywellauthor
- https://janetpywellauthor.wordpress.com

Subscribe to my newsletter:

✉ https://www.subscribepage.com/the-westbay-romance-series